The Twisted Yarn

Rosemary Milne

ABOUT THE AUTHOR

Rosemary Milne began her working life as a lexicographer and ended it as a childcare worker. She now spends part of each year in Paris and part in the south-west of Scotland. She has three children and eight grandchildren scattered about the globe.
This is her first novel.

Typeset in Crimson Text and MrsEaves

Editing, design and publishing by UK Book Publishing

www.ukbookpublishing.com

ISBN: 978-0-9926433-9-3

In memory of *Kate* and *Sidney Hill*

Acknowledgements

They say it takes a village to raise a child. It certainly takes more than one writer alone in a room to write a book. Among those who helped me I want especially to mention *Anna Pook, Isabelle Llasera, Martin Raim, Min Ku Alverson, Pamela Shandel, John McLaren,* and *Ruth Lunn* and *Jason (Jay) Thompson* at *Consilience Media,* and for their unfailing support and encouragement, *Anna-Louise Milne, Richard Milne* and *Madeleine Milne.*

'Imagination grows by exercise and, contrary to popular belief, is more powerful in the mature than in the young.'

W Somerset Maugham

Part I

Chapter 1

At the age of sixty-two, after forty-three years of living and working in London, Helena Otterley decided to move to the north of England. It was of no consequence that she'd barely set foot there since she was a child, she'd been born a northerner and she'd always intended to go back to her roots. She went about choosing where to live with her usual energy and resolve, finally opting for the market town of Clitheroe on the edge of the Pennines. It was about the right size, had the kind of shops she liked and was only a short bus-ride away from open country. She was looking forward to the joys of a quiet retirement after the noise and turbulence of London. Helena had no desire for adventures and no expectation of any.

She found a flat to rent on the High Street. It was the upstairs part of the newsagent's shop, owned and run by Mr Ernest Frank, a Clitheroe man born and bred. His shop was like a magnet for the whole street. Some might have found living there a shade too busy and noisy but not Helena. She had had decades of looking out on the hanging baskets and empty cobbles of a London mews. The ebb and flow of customers downstairs was as novel as all the rest. And Mr Frank was so considerate and kind. It was he who had told her about the wool shop, further along the street and he who had said she might put a washing line up in the back garden if she cared to, and let the clean north wind blow her clothes dry.

On the second Thursday of her new life Helena was following Mr Frank's directions on both counts. She came out of Parker's hardware shop with her new washing line, marvelling as usual at how everyone seemed to know everyone else, how complete strangers said good day to you and looked you in the eye as they did so. With her washing line tucked under her arm, she walked further down the street in search of the wool shop.

It was easy to miss. Only the sign overhead called attention to itself. The words, *The Twisted Yarn* , stood out against a pale grey board, the letters done in the same dark red paint as the door. The final hook of the 'n' on *Yarn* made a thread that curled into a ball of wool that had two needles stuck through the heart of it, gleaming as if the silver paint they were done in was still wet. A metal strip tacked above the lintel had the words 'A. PURSELAIN, PROPRIETOR' printed on it in capitals and an OPEN sign hung lopsided on the frosted glass of the door. A few knitted jerseys and trousers in faded pinks and blues were suspended on a string across the only window, blocking any view into the interior.

She pushed the handle down. There was a flat plink of a bell and she stepped inside, letting the door swing shut behind her. The buzz of the street vanished, leaving a thick, soft hush in its place, like the stillness of a church or a quiet museum. What met her eyes was a welter of colour and texture, a veritable cornucopia of yarn: stacks of it on shelves from floor to ceiling, loose balls and plastic-wrapped bundles piled on the floor and hanks hanging, thick as moss, over an ancient hat-stand positioned sentinel-like near the door. She skirted that and the overflowing wicker baskets – 'Sale – 30% off price on label' – and walked into the centre of the room. Now she was beyond the hat-stand she could see there was a massive oak counter on her right, the far end of it bristling with pots of needles, as if someone had skinned a giant porcupine and pegged it out flat to dry. The rest of the surface was empty and in the subdued light from the window the wood seemed to give off a warm glow. The only other large piece of furniture was a lectern with an open folder of knitting patterns on it. Other folders were lined up on a shelf below the window and in capitals down the spine of each, 'DOUBLE KNITTING, 'MENS', 'WOMENS', 'ARANS', 'BABIES AND CHILDREN', 'CROCHET', 'MISCELLANEOUS', 'HATS, SCARVES AND GLOVES', 'SHAWLS AND THROWS'. Sample squares of knitted wool poked out at intervals along the shelves, bright pennants of colour that struck a vaguely festive note in the dim light.

She walked back to the hat-stand and sank her hand deep in the soft mass of wool draped over it. As she did so she heard a faint rustle. An elderly woman had appeared at the counter and was watching her intently. The rustling noise came from a bead curtain which was swinging back into place behind this small apparition. The woman was wearing a fawn overall over a cherry-red jersey and there was a stub of pencil lodged behind her left ear, poking out through the grey-brown curls. She held her head cocked to one side, like a friendly, bright-eyed robin.

"Good morning. Can I help you?" Helena was surprised by her voice. It was much deeper and stronger than she expected from her build and height.

"Good morning." She came up to the counter. "I heard about your shop, from my new landlord. I'm really just in for a look round but I'm wondering, now I'm here... Have you got some odd balls of double-knitting?"

"You mean not matching?"

"Yes. I promised ages ago that I'd knit some jackets for the Battery Hen Protection Society, for their rescue hens to wear. The hens get badly pecked while they're confined you know. They end up bald. The jackets keep them warm while they grow their own feathers back in. You'd think it wouldn't work, dressing hens up in jackets, but the hens don't seem to mind at all."

"Just a moment." The woman pushed back through the curtain behind her. A moment later the beads chattered and danced once more and she came out holding a bag which she turned upside down on the counter. Ten balls of different coloured wool fell out.

"Here you are. There's plenty of different shades so they can tell one hen from another. They can kit them out as peacocks and parrots. It's double-knitting." She pushed them across the counter and shook her head as Helena got her purse out. "I want nothing from you. You're the first person I've served that's making hens' jackets. I've no use for those balls. There's not enough in of any of them for big jerseys and most knitters don't like double wool for babes. Take them as a contribution to the welfare of our feathered friends!" She chuckled and tucked her hands away inside her overall pockets as if to underline her wish to be rid of the said balls of wool.

"Are you sure? That's so kind of you," Helena said and pushed the balls back inside the bag. She couldn't help feeling that something more was required of her in return for this unexpected generosity but the usual small talk about the weather and the general state of the world seemed out of place in this setting and with this diminutive, bright-eyed person.

"Is it your shop?" she asked.

"It is."

"It's incredible. You hardly notice it from the outside, but once you come in... I've been knitting for decades but I've never seen so many different kinds of wool in one place. I'll definitely be back. I've only just arrived and I'm still settling in but I want to do lots of knitting – maybe try weaving as well. I've brought my hand loom. It used to belong to my mother. I haven't set it up yet but I will. Knitting the jackets will be a good way to get started. You know when you live in London, it's so easy to say you'll do something like that and then never do it. You just forget. It gets lost." Helena stopped short, realising that she'd said more to this stranger in two minutes than she'd said to anyone since she arrived. But the little woman didn't seem to find it strange at all. She smiled at her customer and the warmth of the smile sent an unexpected pulse of happiness shooting through Helena that formed itself into a smile on her own face and brought a sparkle to her eyes.

"You've come to the right part of the country. I've plenty more through the back, cones as well as hanks and balls. Every kind of yarn you could want – mohair and angora and bamboo and sugar cane and Lord knows what. Every time the reps come round they've got another kind of yarn they want me to stock. I'll be selling balls of seaweed to make into guernseys before I'm done. Have you seen this?" The woman came out from behind the counter and went over to the hat-stand. She lifted one of the hanks off a hook and held it out. "Feel it. It's silk: wonderful to knit and as light as thistledown to wear." Helena ran the strands through her fingers.

"It's lovely. I don't know who I could knit it for, except me of course, or friends. I've no family, only me." Helena was rewarded with another radiant smile.

"You'll be surprised what happens once you get started. A good knitter can always find customers."

Helena thrust out her hand. "I should introduce myself. I'm Helena Otterley, recently arrived but planning to stay. I'm really pleased to meet you."

The woman took the outstretched hand in both of hers, as if shaking hands with a new customer was something she did every day. She held it for a moment.

"I'm pleased too, very pleased indeed. Amelia Purselain at your service," she said. "Enjoy knitting the jackets and I'll be glad to help you again, when the time is right."

(see appendix for pattern for hens' jackets)

Chapter 2

It was another warm day when Helena made her next visit to The Twisted Yarn. Someone had propped the door half-open with one of the big baskets of wool. A bar of bright sunlight lay across the worn planks of the floor. That dash of brightness apart, the shop looked nothing like as enticing as she remembered from her first visit. The hanks of wool looked tangled and messy on the hat-stand and the knitted pennants seemed to be drooping from their pigeon-holes. Once again there were no other customers. The shop wasn't empty, however. A very tall, gaunt-looking man was stationed in the shadows at the counter-end. Despite the warm day he was wearing a lumpy tweed jacket with a yellowish woollen scarf knotted round his neck.

When Helena walked in he was leaning forward slightly so his hands rested flat on the counter and his bony wrists poked out of the sleeves of the jacket. The hands were long, narrow and unusually pale, almost translucent, the thin fingers splayed out like needles on the dark grain of the wood. He turned his head in Helena's direction as she crossed the sunny patch on the floor but the rest of him remained motionless. There wasn't a hint of a smile and no 'good morning'.

"Is Mrs Purselain on her day off?" she enquired, going over to the counter. The man shook his head.

"Not a bit of it. Mrs Purselain is not in the habit of taking days off. She's gone to a trade fair and won't be back till late on Friday. She said you'd likely be by though. It's Miss Otterley, isn't it?" He looked her up and down, wrinkled his beaky nose as if to stave off a sneeze and brought out a large handkerchief which he blew into noisily. Thrusting the handkerchief back in his pocket he launched into speech, a torrent of words pouring from his mouth, as if he feared he'd be stopped in mid-sentence. Helena could only stare in blank amazement.

"I know what you're thinking. How's he know my name? Has herself been snooping round, making enquiries? And how did she know to expect you? There's nowt clever about it. This bit of the High Street's not got much to talk about. Don't know the last time we'd anyone new in that flat you're renting. Then you were seen at the post office with a package. Purselain said that'd be the hens' jackets going off. Purselain said you'd be wanting other wool. She says you've moved here for the wool and the weaving. You're from London aren't you? I expect they have wool shops there but not like this one, I doubt. There isn't another like this in the whole country, not as well-stocked either."

"Of course they have wool shops in London,' Helena cut in at last, irked despite herself, at the idea that people were gossiping about her in the queue at the butcher's.

"Saying that," he went on as if he hadn't heard, but more slowly this time, "isn't to say it's all straightforward in here." He stopped and clapped one of those frail hands over his mouth like a guilty child.

Helena seized her chance. She drew herself up to her full five feet eight inches and mustered her chilliest tone.

"I'm not interested in what the local gossips have to say, Mr Purselain. I am here for wool. Judging by what's on the shelves I've come to the right place," she said, swinging her arm round and noticing, for the first time, another door at the far end of the room.

"Steady on," he said. "First off, the name's not Purselain. The name's Hogarth, Cornelius Hogarth. Second off, this here's a wool shop, you're right about that, and we'll have just what you're looking for I'm sure. But it isn't only a wool shop, for the lucky ones…"
and to Helena's astonishment he gave her a knowing wink. "You been through the back yet? Through that door there?" He pointed along the wall. "She said I was to let you, if you wanted to. She mostly doesn't let the public through but she says you can, and if it's patterns you want to look at there's a great stack of them on the shelf in there and a nice, comfy chair too."

"I don't need a pattern thank you. All I want is wool and there's more than enough to choose from right here."

"There is too," he said. "She warned me you mightn't want to go, said you'd lived a quiet life so it'd be unlikely you'd take a look right away. It's a big step, going off into the unknown. You've made a start, leaving London. It's a good beginning, but it's only a beginning."

When he paused for breath this time Helena was standing at the open door.

"I was hoping to see Mrs Purselain," she said. "I'll call in again when she's back." It was on the tip of her tongue to add something about his unfortunate manner with customers but she thought better of it, seeing the crestfallen look on his face.

"I hope I've not put you off, with my big mouth," he said. "Once I get going there's no stopping me. You sure I can't help you?"

"No thank you. Not today," said Helena firmly.

"Come back at the weekend. She'll be here then. Leave the door open," he added, seeing Helena pulling on the handle as if to shut him in. "I like a bit of sunshine when I'm stuck in here."

Chapter 3

Saturday arrived. There was no sun, just the steady drip of rain from the cracked gutter above Helena's sitting room window. For the first time since leaving London she felt drained and listless.

"Whatever was I thinking of? Who said leaving London was a good idea?" she muttered, surveying the street. Apart from a few shoppers, huddled in their anoraks the High Street was deserted. Clots of wet litter hung round the lamp posts, cigarette butts and crisp packets were floating along the gutter. She sighed and went to get her raincoat. There was no point planning a walk in this sort of weather. Better to go along for the wool she'd not bought the other day. She pulled on her boots and picked up the umbrella.

The weather was even worse than it looked from inside. There was a brisk wind driving the rain down the street in cold sheets. The umbrella tugged and pulled in her hand like a kite. She began to run, head-down behind it, and she didn't stop until she arrived breathless but warm, in the wool shop doorway. She shook out her umbrella, smoothed her hair and pushed on the handle.

This time Mrs Purselain was there behind the counter and there was someone with her – not the man Hogarth, but a woman in a fawn anorak and a brown knitted bonnet, sitting on a high stool with her back to the door. As Helena closed the door the woman twisted round and looked her up and down in silence. Something about that look made Helena feel sure they'd been talking about her. Her hackles rose. Being quizzed by that mad scarecrow Hogarth was bad enough but being given the once-over by this brown bundle on the stool as well...

Mrs Purselain seemed to sense her unease.

"The rescue hens lady! How nice to see you again," she said, "and on such a dirty day. I was just saying to Bridie here, that I didn't expect much business. How can I help? Have you finished the jackets?" There was the same warmth about her that Helena remembered. She felt her irritation melt away.

"Thank you, they've all been sent off. I've got wool left over so I'll make some more eventually. I'm in for something else. I came by earlier in the week when you were at the trade fair. Your assistant told me."

"You met Bert did you?"

"A very tall man. He didn't call himself Bert. He said his name was Cornelius Hogarth."

"Yes, that's Bert."

"No, he definitely didn't say Bert," Helena insisted. "I know he said Cornelius."

"I'm sure you're right," Mrs Purselain said soothingly, "but that's Bert all over. Some days he is plain Bert – you know, the name he was given when he was a child – the next he's something else altogether. He was calling himself Lancelot for a while. It really depends where he's been, who he's been seeing. Wasn't Cornelius some kind of an astronomer? No I'm thinking of Copernicus of course."

The woman sitting on the high stool gave a 'hrrmph!', leant across and landed a sharp tap on Mrs Purselain's hand.

"The lady's in for wool, Amelia," she said. "She's not interested in what that old fool Bert's been up to, with his silly names and tall tales." Then, turning to Helena, "That's right, isn't it dear? It's wool you're after, not Bert's folderols and riddles."

Mrs Purselain looked flustered. The pink of her cheeks had deepened to red.

"Of course. What am I thinking of? Well, here's a lucky thing – I've brought some wonderful new shades back with me from the fair. Wool and silk mix, in all the colours of the ocean. I'll show you."

And once again, before Helena could say either yes or no, she disappeared behind the bead curtain, leaving Helena with the woman called Bridie. Not wanting to get drawn into conversation, she began working her way along the shelves, examining the knitted squares. Bridie was not to be deterred, however.

"Bert's all right really," she said from her position on the stool.

Helena walked back to the counter. "Is he? I didn't take to him. He said Mrs Purselain had told him to expect me. He knew exactly who I was and what I've been doing. I felt as if the whole street has been watching my every move."

"Did he now? Amelia will be cross, upsetting you like that."

"He kept on and on about how much there was to choose from."

"He's right about that," said Bridie. "Amelia stocks the biggest selection of wool in the county."

"I can believe it. There's another room through the back apparently. That man said Mrs Purselain told him he was to let me through there if I wanted – to look at patterns. He said something else that was odd." Helena paused.

"What was that?" Bridie said.

"He said Mrs Purselain told him I'd lived a quiet life so I might not go through there straightaway. I haven't a clue what he meant. He knows nothing about me, and neither does she." Helena was going to add more but stopped, noticing Bridie's expression.

"Well that takes the biscuit." There was no mistaking Bridie's tone. "Amelia *will* be cross. You think you can trust people and then you find they've gone about stirring up trouble."

Before Helena could ask her what she meant the beads swished apart and Mrs Purselain reappeared with two packs of yarn, one a moss-green and the other a deep-ocean purply-blue. She pulled open the packaging and took out a ball of each.

"It's a tiny company makes it. These are from what they call their 'sea shades'. They use only natural dyes; that's the one difficulty. You get more variation in the tones than with the chemicals. The way I see it though, the ocean's not a solid shade either. It's changing all the time. How many balls do you need? Is it for you? There's some lovely greys through the back as well. Shall I get them?"

"No, there's no need," Helena said, wondering what it was about the shop that made the people working in it talk so much. "It was a dark blue I was thinking of but this is beautiful too," and she pulled out a ball of the green yarn. It had the texture of rough silk. She lifted it to her nose and smelled in its depths a faint whiff of the moor, wet peat and heather. "This is the one," she said. "I'll take ten balls. That should be plenty."

She had put the wool in her bag and was about to leave when Bridie spoke again.

"Don't go without telling Amelia what Bert said, will you dear? She needs to know."

"What's Bert been up to?" said Mrs Purselain.

"He's been meddling," said Bridie quickly. Helena gave her a look and turned to Mrs Purselain.

"I mentioned to your friend..." she began, and she proceeded to recount her meeting with Hogarth for the second time. By the end Mrs Purselain's cheeks had turned a vivid pink again.

"I'm vexed," she said. "Bridie's right. He ought not to have troubled you like that. He's overstepped the mark. I'll have a word with him."

"It doesn't matter. Honestly, let's just leave it," said Helena, going over to get her umbrella from where she'd left it by the door. And then it came, a tingling warmth and excitement running through her, from the tips of her toes to the hairs on her head. She looked round. Mrs Purselain was smiling at her. Bridie was smiling too, as if she could also feel the electricity in the air. She sprang down from her stool and came to stand in Helena's way at the door.

"It's funny how you turned up this morning just when we were talking about the hens' jackets. Can you write the pattern out for me? I'd like to make some too." Helena heard the rain rattling against the shop window and saw the grey light through the panes. She was in no hurry to get back to her empty flat.

"No problem," she said. "I can do it now if you want. It'll only take me five minutes."

"Come on then," said Bridie. "We can do it through in the back shop. There's a chair and we'll be out of Mrs Purselain's way." A piece of paper and a pen had appeared on the counter top in front of Mrs Purselain. Bridie handed them to Helena and, with a flourish of her arm and a mock bow, said, "After you, madam!" Helena hesitated, but curiosity won over suspicion. She folded the paper, pushed it in her pocket with the pen and marched over to the door leading through to the back of the shop, Bridie jostling at her heels like a little collie dog herding a reluctant sheep into the fold.

Chapter 4

Beyond the door was a narrow passageway no more than ten feet long and, at the far end, another door with a notice on it: NO ENTRY – STAFF ONLY. There was no handle on that one, just one old-fashioned bolt halfway down. The bolt was pushed home but it slid back easily under Helena's fingers and the door creaked back, revealing a square room shelved all round, except for the far wall which had a low window midway along it. Unlike the front shop there were no piles of wool, no boxes or baskets lying about the floor. The only furniture was a shabby armchair with a square of matting in front of it and a standard lamp with a fringed shade. The lamp was not switched on, nor was the single bulb in the centre of the room.

Helena blinked and took a step back. Why was the room so bright? And what was happening on the shelves? Either her eyes were playing tricks on her or the balls of wool were shifting about in their pigeon-holes, like weed swaying gently in the current of a river. She grasped the door to steady herself and stared harder. As she did so the room grew brighter still and undulating strands, of yellow, green, turquoise, orange, scarlet, lilac, purple, began twisting off the balls and weaving themselves together into a single multi-coloured stream that cascaded from the shelves and down onto the floor.

The spectacle was so utterly improbable and beautiful that for a moment all Helena could do was stand and watch. The river of coloured light began to spread in a pool across the floor. Seeing this she let go of the door and took a few tentative steps into the room so that the colours lapped softly at her boots, like water but without substance. At first the rainbow pool was no more than ankle deep but, in what felt like seconds, it had reached the top of her boots, then the hem of her raincoat. Still it poured down off the shelves like a mountain stream after rain. Now it was waist-high and she could swish her fingers through the iridescent layers of it, cup her hands together and try to scoop up the colours as they twisted and turned as if playing with her. The light poured on, over her chest, round her throat, her mouth, her nose, her eyes, until she was immersed from head to toe in it. She was filled with a wild euphoria, and she twirled round, so the colours flared out from her fingertips and burst like firework flowers high above her head. As they drifted down Helena heard, very faintly, strange noises: the echoing call of a bird, the growl of thunder, wind whispering through grass, shouts of children and the hiss of a snake.

She felt something like a gust of wind at her back. It carried her across the room towards the armchair. Bridie appeared, a squat, dark shape breaking through the coloured strands. Without saying a word she gestured to Helena to sit down. Helena looked at the armchair. It too was bathed in a cloud of coloured light and seemed to be bobbing gently, like a moored boat on a choppy lake. She lowered herself into it gingerly. As her bottom made contact with the cushion the chair lurched sharply to one side. She let out a panicky arrgh! and clutched the arm. From deep within the chair there came a noise, halfway between a sigh and a groan, and everything went dark as if someone had thrown a heavy cloth over her head.

The heat was intense, pumping up through the soles of her boots. Every breath she took seared the inside of her nostrils. She felt around for the chair but there was no chair nor was there a lamp or shelves full of dancing, light-emitting wool. The smothering blackness had gone too, replaced by a sun so bright she was forced to screw up her eyes and shield her face from the glare. She saw that Bridie was standing a few yards off, still in her anorak but without her brown bonnet. There was a bulging black plastic bag beside her, tied at the neck with a blue ribbon.

"Lordy, you forget what real heat can be like. We should have brought your umbrella for shade. Let's get moving before we're burnt to a cinder."

Helena might have taken some comfort from Bridie's businesslike tone if she'd heard what she said but at that moment she was deaf to everything except the ringing in her ears. She began turning slowly round, looking for a road or a sign of habitation. Whichever way she looked the view was the same. There was nothing but sand and rocks – on and on into the hazy distance. Meanwhile Bridie had hitched the bag over her shoulder like a sack of coals and was setting off purposefully to climb the slope ahead of them.

"Hey, stop!" Helena yelled, finding her voice all of a sudden. "Come back! Where are we? What the heck is going on? You can't walk off and leave me. Where are we? Who are you?" This outburst had some effect. Bridie dropped the bag and shouted back. She sounded quite different from the kindly woman Helena had met in the shop.

"My name is Bridget Sullivan but most people call me Bridie. You're Helena Otterley. What I've been told is you live on your own and you're a knitter. Don't tell me you've come out in the wrong clothes. I can't help that. I'm the same. Anyway, you'll see soon enough, underneath the heat there's cold. Now, if you don't mind, I've got a job to do and I haven't got all day." She slung the bag back on her shoulder and stumped off up the hill again. Not knowing what else she could do, Helena followed her.

It was a long, slow climb and she had to watch every step she took on the loose stones and rocks. The sun soaked into the dark fabric of her coat and trousers. Sweat pricked at her skin, trickled into her eyes and down her nose. It wasn't long before her legs were aching, her mouth was dry and her breath was coming in short, painful gasps. She had to stop. She bent down and picked up a stone. It glittered white and sharp-edged in the sun.

"Quartz," she said, turning it over and over, "and it's definitely a real stone. The heat's real enough too." She loosened her coat and with a single quick movement, shook it off, pulled her high-necked jersey over her head and put her coat back on.

She began the ascent once more, her mind racing. There was no rational explanation for what had happened but there was no denying something had. Something ...impossible... a kind of out-of-body experience? But weren't you supposed to float around and see yourself from above with one of those? If so it couldn't be that. She was definitely right inside her body and very uncomfortable it was too. Maybe she'd had a stroke and this was what it felt like when you lost consciousness. No, that was plain silly. She was walking and thinking normally. So this thing that had happened was coming from somewhere else, or someone else. Bridie? Possible but unlikely. Still, Bridie was the only person in this rock-strewn wilderness who could give her some answers and she was getting further and further ahead. Any minute now she'd be out of sight and the situation would become desperate. Helena began climbing again, faster than ever.

The collar of her coat had rubbed a sore place on her neck and her cord trousers felt as if they were glued to her skin by the time they reached the top. The country stretched away below them in wave after wave of rock and rubble, dotted here and there with scrubby patches of grey vegetation. Everything was flattened out under the merciless sun. There was no sign of life at all.

"We'll die in this place," Helena said, jerked into speech by the immensity of what faced them. "There's nothing here. I'm dying of thirst. We haven't a drop of water between us. I don't know why you've made us climb up here. It's all just rocks and dirt. It's a death-trap." She swallowed hard and ran her tongue over dry lips.

"Nonsense!" Bridie's voice was sharp. "We're going the quickest way. There's no more climbing and we'll get water soon enough. We're nearly there." She made as if to set off again.

"Nearly where?" Helena said. "Now look here. You say you've got a job to do but I didn't ask to get dragged along. You give me some answers. I'm sitting down here until you do and I don't care if we both die of the heat." To show she meant business she sat down and started to pull off her left boot.

"What do you think you're doing?" Helena heard the alarm in Bridie's voice. She kept on tugging. "You take those boots off and you'll never get them on again, not while your feet are so hot."

"I've got a stone in it," said Helena. "I'll wear it without a sock if I have to but I've got to get the stone out." The boot came off all of a sudden, leaving the sock inside. She fell back laughing in spite of herself.

"Hey, that feels good," she said, wiggling her toes. "You should try it." She shook her boot out, put the sock back on and shoved her foot back in the boot. "So," she said, shading her eyes and looking up at her companion, "tell me. What's the job, who's the customer? If there is one. What's in the bag?"

"Customer? I wouldn't call her that. Charity case more like," said Bridie. "We're going down there. See, over there. That's where she is." She pointed into the middle distance.

"Where who is? Bridie, for heaven's sake, stop talking in riddles."

"There's no riddles," said Bridie huffily. "You're here with me and we're going to deliver the covers in this bag to Mrs Hubbard. She looks after kids – kids that've been abandoned, orphaned, kids no-one else wants."

"But what country are we in?"

"What country? Now there's a silly question. It's nowhere on any map you've got but does it matter? We're not staying long and we're not here to visit the tombs of kings or ride on camels, are we?" She laughed but Helena didn't join in.

"OK then. It doesn't matter *where* we are but why?'"

"Because someone's got to. I told you there's cold under the heat. It's freezing here at night. The kids wake up and cry and she gets mad at them and she goes round with her stick and knocks the spots off them. So they cry louder than ever and that keeps Mrs Purselain awake at night and she needs her sleep as much as Mrs Hubbard. So we came up with this for an idea. We've been knitting for months and we've made these blankets."

"And where exactly do I fit in?" asked Helena, still hoping Bridie would clear up the mystery in one simple sentence.

"You tell me! I was all ready to go when Mrs Purselain heard about you. Then she met you and next thing I know she's decided it would be good if you came too. I tried telling her it was a bad idea but she wouldn't hear it. So now, as well as delivering this lot," she gestured towards the bag, "I've got to make sure I get you there and back again in one piece. You want answers to your questions? You ask Amelia Purselain. She brought you across, not me. I just do what I'm told. While you're with me you'll do the same, if you don't mind." Bridie shook her head as if to say that life was very hard and people were most unreasonable.

"So where is she – the woman we're taking the blankets to?" said Helena, deciding that now was not the time to enquire further into Mrs Purselain's motives but determined to wring more information out of the other woman. "I can't see a house or tents or anything like a place to live in."

"You can't see it? Something wrong with your eyes? Over there."

Helena screwed up her eyes against the dazzle. This time she did think she saw something, a vague outline, a misshapen structure of some sort, like a broken-down barracks floating far away in the distance. Suddenly she knew what that faint outline was. It was a boot. Not a boot a man might wear. This would be a boot for a foot as big as a barge, with toes like railway sleepers. Then out of nowhere, a few lines came into her head:

> 'There was an old woman who lived in a shoe,
> She had so many children she didn't know what to do.
> She gave them all gruel without any bread
> Then whipped them all soundly and sent them to bed.'

Helena bent her head to hide her smile. What was it her mother used to say when they went outside in the dark to look at the stars? "Just imagine all the other worlds up there. Millions of them we can't see, let alone ever visit." She repressed a sudden urge to leap up and hug Bridie.

"Do you want me to carry the bag for a bit?" she asked, thinking it was better not to mention the nursery rhyme at this point.

"No, you're all right. You didn't bargain for this I know. Just you keep up with me. She's a ratty old soul but she'll have some water for us and there'll be shade once we get there."

They started scrambling down the hill. A lizard darted from under their feet. The rocks on this side were a glittering, greyish black and down below the valley bottom was scarred with the deep channels of a dried-out river bed, the plaited loops of hardened mud stencilled on the pale greys of the surrounding land. The slopes behind them shimmered and danced like water. Finally they landed on the flat ground. Bridie shifted the bag to the other shoulder.

"So, this bad-tempered Mrs Hubbard," Helena said, falling into step beside her and finding the walking easier now the ground was sandy and soft under their feet. "I thought she was the one with a dog that wanted a bone? She had a cupboard that was bare and the dog didn't get one. There's no nursery rhyme about her having any children."

"Hubbard's got a dog all right, two in fact, and I don't suppose they get many bones either. Maybe they get to gnaw on the bones of the kids that die."

"The kids that die?" Helena stopped and looked at her. "Why do they die?"

"Usual reasons. Nothing to eat, dirty water, worms eating them from the inside out, wild beasts, cuts that go bad, broken bones. There's more ways to die than live, if you're stuck in a place like this."

They walked on in silence, the only moving things on the face of the earth. The boot was out of sight for the moment but Helena didn't need to see it to be reminded of how enormous it was. She let the thought that was hovering on the brink of her mind come right up to the surface. It was crazy but it was obvious all the same. A boot that big could only have belonged to a giant. And it hadn't landed in the desert by chance. It had been dropped or discarded. So the terrifyingly enormous creature that had thrown it away or lost it was probably somewhere nearby. She felt the rock faces on either side bearing down on her, squeezing her in an ogreish iron grip.

"I know what you're thinking." Bridie spoke quietly but her voice rang out loud in the emptiness. "You're thinking where's the giant that wore that boot?"

"Ssh!" said Helena.

"There's no need to whisper," said Bridie. "He's miles and miles away. There's no giants hereabouts any more. They need bigger hiding places than these hills." She looked at Helena for a moment then added, "Mind you, you do get dragons but they're not a problem. It's all nonsense about dragons. They wouldn't hurt a flea."

Chapter 5

Close up the boot was a scabby old thing, an unsightly lump of cracked and scuffed brown leather. It towered over them as high as a two-storey building. The shoelace hanging down one side was as thick as a ship's hawser. There were dozens of kids swinging about on it. The two ladders propped up against the side also had children on them and there were more running in and out of a hole in the toe as big as the mouth of a cave. How many children altogether? Helena estimated there were fifty at least, clambering about and playing in the dust. Mrs Hubbard was nowhere to be seen.

Bridie's face was a fierce shade of puce. She put the bag down and wiped away the sweat dripping off her nose. A little girl came and stood a few yards off. She was barefoot, a scraggy specimen with a scrap of rag round her waist to serve as a skirt. She fixed two dark, hostile eyes on the strangers but said nothing. Bridie stepped forward two paces. The child retreated.

"Don't you run away, little miss. We're looking for Mrs Hubbard. You go and find Mrs Hubbard for us, there's a good girl. Tell her Mrs Sullivan's arrived and she's got some good things in her bag."

The child scampered off. Other children began to wander over and form a circle round about them, keeping a safe distance all the same. They were all as emaciated as the girl.

Bridie sank down on her hunkers, overcome with the heat and the load she'd insisted on carrying all the way. Seeing this Helena said nothing for a minute or two but her need to know more was too urgent.

"Where on earth have all these kids come from?" she asked. "There's nothing here, no roads, no shops, no schools or clinics."

"You'd have to ask them yourself," Bridie said. "Every one of them will have a story as would make you weep. Hubbard is a whacker – much too quick with her stick – but I'll guarantee not one of these kids would speak bad of her. It's rough and ready but it's a haven

compared to what they'd get anywhere else. They'd be taken off
for soldiers, sold to factories, dressed up like monkeys to entertain
nasty men, made into potted meat and jelly beans." She gave Helena
a nudge, "Here, she's coming now. Let me do the talking. You're my
apprentice if she asks. You're learning the ropes. You are too; it's not
a word of a lie!"

The woman who was making her way towards them looked as
if she was more than one hundred years old. She was very bent and
leant heavily on a big umbrella she grasped in her right hand. Her
dress – if you could call the ancient robe she was wrapped in a dress
– came right down to her feet. They weren't bare like the children's.
She looked to have on brogues of some kind and she had a straw hat
with a big brim, pulled down low over thin grey locks. The little
girl who'd gone to fetch her was walking beside her carrying a jug
very carefully. Another two children, both boys, completed the
procession. One had a stool in his hand, the other three cups on a
tray.

She stopped ten or more yards away from them and motioned
to the boy carrying the stool. He set it down in the full sun and she
lowered herself onto it. The girl put the jug down and the other boy
set the tray of cups beside it. She pulled the umbrella in front of her,
sprung the catch and unfurled it so it threw a small patch of shade
over her head and round about the stool. Having done this she sat
for a moment looking at the pair of them, as if at creatures in a zoo
enclosure.

"You've taken yer time, Sullivan." Those were her first words –
not a hint of a greeting. "It's months since you was last here. Let's
hope you've brought sommat more useful than last time. Who's
the stooky that's with you? Never seen her before and you know
fine well I don't like strangers comin round unannounced and
uninvited."

Something told Helena this wasn't as bad as it sounded. Bridie
did not return the greeting. There was silence on both sides for a
minute. Then Bridie spoke, "Are you going to keep us standing out
here in the baking sun all day, Mavis? What's in the jug? If it's water

we'd be better drinking it than letting it fly off in the heat."

"I'm not stoppin you gettin out the heat. I don't bite. I use my stick but I don't bite – couldn't anyway, no teeth left these many years past." And the old woman opened her mouth to reveal bare gums inside. "What's she called – the one you've brought with you? I need a name to call her by."

"She's Helena Otterley, the new apprentice."

"Otter'll do fine for me. It suits her – she looks wet behind the ears, and I don't mind guessin she's 'otter 'n she was when she set off!" And she gave a great cackle at her own joke.

"We'll be fine now," Bridie whispered to reassure Helena, "now she's got a name for you."

Mrs Hubbard leant forward and waved a finger at Bridie.

"Stop that mutterin Sullivan. I don't like mutterers. If you've got sommat to say come over here and say it." Which, as Helena realised immediately, was exactly the reaction Bridie was looking for. She seemed to know how to handle this toothless, crabbed old crone.

Helena moved closer to the umbrella, propelled forward by the pressure of Bridie's hand on her back. The woman reached out and grabbed her coat. "Nice bit of stuff she's wearin. Wool inside. Not much use in this heat but she'll be glad of it later." Mrs Hubbard pulled on the coat. "Turn round, you silly animal. Let's have a look at you." Helena looked helplessly at Bridie who nodded. She swung slowly round.

"A bit long in the tooth isn't she? Don't look much like an apprentice to me."

"She's not in her first youth, I'll grant you that, but she's good for what we need. She's a knitter with a conscience. Mrs Purselain found her for me." Bridie's tone was crisp.

"Huh! What's that old mischief-maker doin now? She still moanin about the kids and their noise? I can't help the noise. Sixty-three little rats when I counted them up this morning, that's what I've got in that boot and not a pick on one of them. No use to me and no use to anyone. Can't sell them, can't breed from them. Can't even get a day's work out of them for myself. Noise and dirt and disobedience, that's what they are."

Bridie was squatting down again. She shook her head.

"I don't like hearing you talk like that Mavis. You're only trying to scare Helena but she's not scared. She's a good woman and she knows you mean no harm."

"Give her a drink, will you?" said the crone, ignoring the comment. "She's been eyein up that jug ever since I brought it." Bridie needed no further invitation. She leant over and poured some of the precious liquid into a cup and handed it to Helena.

"Drink it slow," the woman said. "Water's more precious than gold out here."

Helena did as was she was told and felt it sluice down her throat, as delicious and reviving as ambrosia. Bridie gave some to Mrs Hubbard and helped herself.

"So, what you brought this time? None of they papers and pens you came botherin me with the last time I hope. I can't read or write and neither can they and that's how it is and always will be. Book-learnin when we aint got food on the plate nor clothes on our backs, never heard the likes of it!"

"No, no books or pens this time. I've brought you what you said you wanted." Bridie began to undo the ribbon on the plastic bag. Hubbard leant closer and Helena smelled the sweetish smell of old age and unwashed clothes. The old woman was excited now. Her hands were trembling as she stretched them out ready to seize whatever Bridie pulled out.

What came out of the bag were acres and acres, so it seemed, of hand-knitted blankets. They just kept coming, in all the colours of the rainbow until they lay in a huge glowing heap on the sand. As the pile grew, that face that had been creased in a petulant frown began to bend and stretch in a smile of sorts. A little dribble of spittle trickled from the corner of her mouth. She pulled over one of the blankets and wiped her chin with it.

"Don't do that," said Bridie sharply. "I've not spent months knitting these for you to use them like a rag. Here have this," and she pulled her handkerchief out of her pocket.

"You'd better come in," the woman said handing the hanky back to Bridie. "I'll get some of the kids to bring these in." She pushed herself up from the stool, furled the umbrella again and without another word turned and hobbled back towards the boot.

Chapter 6

Bridie and Helena followed Mrs Hubbard in through the toe hole. It took them a moment or two before their eyes adjusted to the darkness after the brilliance of outside. Gradually Helena made out long tables and benches higgledy-piggledy up and down the room. The floor was bumpy and dented where the giant's foot had moulded the sole to fit his toes. There was some light from the toe hole but most came from a long, narrow crack in the leather along one side. No light filtered down from the top of the boot because there were curtains of cloth suspended overhead like a canopy. Mrs Hubbard had disappeared behind another curtain hanging vertically from a huge beam that had been jammed across the width of the boot about halfway along its length. The air was full of a high-pitched squeaking.

"What's making that noise?" Helena asked Bridie.

"Bats," she said. "They're up there, most of them on the other side of the curtains. They go out at night but daytimes they're in here. Ma Hubbard wages war on them but they come back. They've nowhere else to go, just like the kids. They make a terrible mess with their droppings; the curtain only stops some of it. Now you listen to me. You're nearly done here so I'd better give you your instructions for going back. I'm not coming yet. I've things to see to with her but you're to go. You've done enough for your first time."

"What do you mean I've done enough? I've only just got here and I haven't done anything." Helena was dismayed. "I want to stay. I'm just beginning to get the hang of it."

"It's what I told you. I'm following instructions. Amelia said not to keep you here too long. Hubbard's a tricky old soul. If she thinks she can use you there's no knowing what she might do. This was by way of an introduction. You see what's needed. These kids haven't a stitch to wear. You go back and get started, at whatever takes your fancy." Helena stared at her.

"What do you mean 'get started'?"

"Knitting, silly woman," said Bridie with more than a touch of irritation. "That's what you've been recruited for, isn't it? It wasn't for the light in your pretty brown eyes if that's what you were thinking. Now, get that paper out again – the one you were writing the pattern on when we left. You better still have the pen too. I can't be asking her for a pen. You heard what she said about writing. She doesn't like it." Helena felt in her pocket. The pen was there, and the piece of paper.

"Here's what you have to do. When we sit down together you get them out. I tell her you're taking notes for Mrs Purselain because it's part of your training. But you write out where you want to go – but you have to be exact. No use writing 'home'. Home's not specific enough. You write your address, with the post code as well, if you know it. You don't let her see it. She says she can't read but we think she's not telling the whole truth about that. You got it?"

"Yes. Of course I get it," said Helena impatiently, "but I don't see why I have to go so soon."

Bridie ignored this and Helena was prevented from saying more because at that moment Mrs Hubbard pushed the curtain aside and came slowly across to where they were sitting. She sat down facing Helena across the table. One glance at the expression on that face and Helena knew Bridie and Mrs Purselain were right about the old lady's intentions. She meant this newcomer no ill but she meant to keep her if she could. Bridie began to speak and Helena did as she'd been told and took out the pen and paper.

"What's she doing with that?" The tone wasn't friendly.

"She's doing as she's been told. She's taking notes for Mrs Purselain. She's new, Mavis. She's not done this kind of thing before. She'll be getting a tutorial when we go back."

"A tutorial? She don't need no tutorials." The old woman reached across the table as if to snatch the paper.

"Don't be messing with her, Mavis. She'll not come again if you take her paper off her. Mrs Purselain won't let her." The woman drew back her hand. "Now what else do you want? Helena's to make the list for us." Helena picked up the pen, waiting.

"Scarves, gloves, socks, coats, jerseys... What d'you expect me to say?" Hubbard's tone was plaintive now.

"I need numbers," said Bridie and nodded to Helena. She picked up the pen and wrote out her home address, right down to the postcode. As the last letter went onto the page, Old Ma Hubbard, her boot, Bridie and the bats all vanished as if sucked up and spun off in a wind.

Chapter 7

Long before night settled over Clitheroe Helena was sound asleep in the safety of her own bed. There had been no reliving of the day, no pacing of the floor trying to make sense of what had happened. It was as if someone had dropped a powerful sleeping pill in her tea. She had scarcely been able to keep her eyes open long enough to wash the worst of the grime and dust off her face and hands. Twelve dreamless hours later she came awake with a start. Someone was pressing on the door bell in short, sharp bursts. She pulled on her dressing gown and staggered out to answer it. There at the door was Mr Hogarth.

"Good morning," he said, as if he thought he was expected. "Better day than yesterday. I've brought your wool."

"That's very kind of you. And my umbrella too I see." Helena held out her hand.

"You just up?" he said, not handing either umbrella or bag over. "You usually sleep this late?"

"I don't know what time it is and no I don't," she said crossly. "I went to bed late and I didn't sleep well. Here." She went to take the umbrella and the bag from him. Then she drew back. Of course, he was the man she needed, the ideal person to pump for information, far easier to get talking than the inscrutable Mrs Purselain. She smiled at him.

"I'm about to put the kettle on. Are you in a hurry or would you like a cup of tea while I have my breakfast?" she asked. He grinned back.

"Never say no to a cuppa – that's my motto. There's nothing like a glass of clean water when you're parched. Know what I mean?" and he gave her a wink like he had in the shop. Helena resisted the urge to shut the door in his face. She swallowed hard and forced herself to sound more friendly than she felt.

"Come in then. It may be a better day than yesterday but it's not

warm enough to hang about at the front door in a dressing gown."
He followed her through to the sitting room and plonked the bag
down on the table. Helena opened it and looked inside. The wool
she'd bought was in there, but there was much more besides: a pile
of twisted hanks that would have to be wound into balls before
knitting.

"There's a mistake," she said, holding up one of the hanks.
"There's wool in here that isn't for me."

Hogarth shook his head. "There's no mistake," he said. "Purselain
don't make mistakes. She gave it to me. She says you'll be needing
what's in there, for your other knitting. You know – for the kiddies."

She dropped the hank back in the bag as if it was a snake. What
a fool she was letting this peculiar man into her house. Supposing
Mrs Purselain had sent him to whisk her away again. This time
she'd land in that desert wearing nothing but her dressing gown and
slippers! She rushed out of the room without a word of explanation,
leaving Hogarth standing by the sofa. When she came through
again, fully dressed and carrying the mugs of tea, he'd taken off his
coat and sat down. With his long legs stretched out in front of him
and his arms hooked behind his head, he looked the picture of placid
composure.

"You've got it nice," he said, waving his hand at the room. "You
like nice things, eh? What's your line of work? Something arty if I'm
not mistaken."

"I don't have a line of work any more," she answered. "I was a
book-dealer – old books, rare manuscripts, things like that. I moved
here when I retired."

"Retired are you? You look good on it. I heard Hubbard took a
shine to you. She's always sniffing around to see what she can get.
Sharp old bird. She sounds worse than she is mostly. What did you
make of her yourself?" He glanced up at her, waiting for answers,
then leapt to his feet, his hands out as if to catch her. Helena's eyes
were fixed on the wall behind him and she was swaying slightly
as if she was about to faint. She ignored his outstretched hand and
went over to the window. A bus was pulling away from the lights, a

dog was peeing against the lamp-post by the post office. Only yards from her sitting room Clitheroe was going about its business as usual. She could send this man away. She could go down and walk about among all those ordinary people: post a letter, call in for her dry-cleaning, buy a bunch of flowers.

"Mr Hogarth," she said, with her back to him, "I am really grateful to you for bringing me my wool. I must have forgotten it when I left the shop."

She got no further. Hogarth shot forward like a jack-in-the-box, and yanked her round. There was nothing solicitous in his manner now. His face only inches from hers, he growled at her, "Stop mucking around will you. You did not forget your wool, you silly, stubborn woman. You left it at the counter when you went through the back. And I know where you went. I've been there myself. And I know it was Bridie that took you. Now what are you going to say?"

She stared at him, wide-eyed. "Let go of my arm please." He stepped back. "I'm not sure what I can say, Mr Hogarth."

"Bert, call me Bert," he said, looking less fierce.

"Not Cornelius? Why did you say you were Cornelius? And why did Mrs Purselain say you've got a whole lot of other names too? If I'm going to talk to you, you've got some explaining to do first."

Hogarth looked embarrassed. "I was wondering if you'd bring that up. I oughtn't to have said all I did but we haven't had one like you in years. I got a bit ahead of myself. I was thinking you'd be more in the know, but I was wrong. You don't know much at all."

"Rubbish," said Helena sharply. "I know all sorts of things, but if you mean I don't know what goes on in that madhouse of a wool shop you're absolutely right. Maybe you're here to tell me what does? Has Mrs Purselain said you can? If you're doing this without telling her you'd be as well finishing your tea and leaving now. She was cross when I told her how you'd spoken to me."

Hogarth looked unruffled by this outburst.

"Mrs Purselain knows I'm here. It was her who sent me round. What she says to me was, 'Tell her it's all right. Reassure her'. So here I am. Can we stop messing about and get on with it."

"OK then." Helena sat down in the armchair. "You're right. I did have a funny experience. It was like I was swept off to a very hot desert. Bridie was there with a bag. We took some blankets to an old woman who looks after lost children. One moment I was in the shop and the next I was in that place, and the same when I came back, except I came back here not to the shop. So you're right. I didn't forget the wool."

"That's more like it," he said. "So what's bothering you? No offence, but you do look bothered. What d'you want to know?"

"Of course I'm bothered. I'd be as mad as the rest of you seem to be if I wasn't bothered," Helena said impatiently. "People don't go flying off to strange parts of the world just like that, Mr Hogarth. Bert, I mean. I know it can't really have happened, but I also know it did. I definitely bought that wool. When I got back here I was covered in dust. It was raining when I went to the shop so my boots should have been muddy not dusty. And I've got blisters on both heels and a sore place on my neck from where my collar was rubbing. How did I get those if I had a funny turn, or it was a dream?"

"Exactly," said Bert. "And then I land on your doorstep with a big bag of wool, telling you it's for the kiddies' scarves and hats. You've a right to be bothered, I can see that. If you don't know nothing about it all."

"Well I don't, so tell me. What's going on?"

"Where do you want to start?"

"What I want to know first is why has Mrs Purselain sent you and not Bridie? You weren't there. I've no proof you've ever been. Who are you anyway? How do you know Mrs Purselain?"

"Who am I? You're thinking old Bert's not the full shilling aren't you? I can see it in your face. Let me tell you, I've known Mrs Purselain a lot longer than Bridie Sullivan has. As for who I am – I'm a carpenter by trade. That's what takes me over there to the boot. But horses is really what I'm best at."

"A carpenter? Horses?" Helena looked at Bert's delicate hands and raised an eyebrow. He looked hurt.

"You think I'm fibbing? I've worked with horses since I was a boy of twelve. I've ridden some fancy beasts in my time, in different places, when I go travelling."

"And where do you go travelling if it's not to that desert I was in?" asked Helena.

"I mostly stay round here, in England. I've been out with some of the knights, when they go hunting or on a quest."

"What do you mean 'knights'?"

"Like I say – knights in armour, like Lancelot and Bedivere, and some others that you don't read about so much."

"Is that how you met Mrs Purselain?" said Helena, deciding it might be better to leave the subject of Bert's adventures with the knights to one side.

"No, all the King Arthur stuff came long after Amelia rescued me. I was working abroad and when I came back I had a spot of bother. I belonged here but I couldn't prove it. So they nabbed me and slung me in one of those places where they put folk they don't know what to do with, all barbed wire and high fences. I was going to be shipped out again but Amelia got wind of it. She stepped in and told them I was a relation, a long-lost nephew or something."

"So how old were you then?" said Helena.

"I'd have been twenty I guess. I'm not rightly sure. I don't know my birthday. They found me, you see, when I was a kid."

"Who found you?"

"A priest. I was in the bus shelter. They took me to the orphanage and they put up notices about me round the town, you know like they do with cats and dogs that get lost. 'Anyone wishing to claim this child, please contact...' kind of thing. I dunno. It's that far back I can't remember. Look, I haven't got long and Purselain didn't send me to tell you about me. What else do you want to know about what happened to you, like?"

Helena rubbed the sore spot on her neck, remembering the way the chair had bobbed about like a boat and the plunge into darkness. "You know how light flows out of the wool? Is that what does it?" she said after a moment.

"Does what?"

"Sends you flying off to that place. When I went through to that storeroom at the back of the shop, there was an amazing light display. The colours were streaming out of the wool on the shelves. They wrapped themselves round me and over me, as if they were alive. I heard noises too and I felt... happy – and light. I'd gone into the room supposedly to write out a knitting pattern for Bridie but that never happened. I sat down in the chair and the next thing I knew I'd been pitched out into that desert."

"It doesn't work like that for me," he said. "When I go it's like a trap-door opens up in the floor, like one of those chutes they used to chuck the coal down."

"You fall down a hole? You don't see the colours come out of the wool?"

"No, but it works different for each person. One time I seen Amelia fly right out the window at the back – just like a little bird she was. The window was tight shut as well. The hole I go down will be somewhere in that room but it doesn't concern you and it never will. If it was the colours that took you, that's how you'll go the next time."

"Next time? Am I going back? Can she make me?"

"You'll only go if you want to. Amelia won't force you and – I'm saying it again so as you're clear – you won't go shooting down a hole like me. How you get there has something to do with what your life was like when you were a kid. That's what Amelia told me once. What kind of a kid was you anyway?"

"Happy enough. Nothing out of the ordinary. They were lovely people, my parents. I was an only child but I don't ever remember feeling lonely or wishing I had a brother or sister. It was comfortable, you know, predictable. We didn't have much money but it never seemed to matter." She shrugged her shoulders.

Bert's face darkened. "Don't do that!"

"What?"

"Hunch your shoulders, like you're saying growing up safe and happy isn't much to shout about. There isn't anything in the world more important for a child than having a mum and a dad that love them and keep them safe."

"I know that," she said. "I didn't live in a bubble. I had friends. I saw how it was for some of them." There was an awkward pause. Bert got up.

"I've got to go. What'll I tell Amelia? Will you help or won't you? Am I leaving that wool or not?"

"You can leave it. I still don't understand any of it but I don't mind helping."

"The way I see it," he said, and he was smiling again, "you have to work your way into it. New things is like that. I'd say you're making the right decision though, and you'll be fine. Amelia Purselain's never wrong about the ones that's ready for a new adventure. Trust me, she won't let you get in any bother."

Bert had carried out Mrs Purselain's instructions to the letter. Helena was more than reassured; she was even a little excited. She wasn't going mad or senile. There was an explanation of a sort for what had happened to her, if she was to believe what Bert had told her. It was ridiculous, far-fetched, improbable in the extreme and she'd never dare tell anyone about it, but it was also true that right from the beginning she'd felt something odd about the shop and its owner. She didn't give a second thought to Bert's questions about her childhood or the significance it might have for her desert adventure.

When he left she came straight back into the sitting room and tipped the wool out onto the floor. The balls for her sweater lay among the hanks of brown, fawn, red and blue, like giant green eggs in a nest. They looked tempting but they'd have to wait a day or two. She got out her knitting patterns. "Hats first," she thought. "Start small and work up." She pulled over a chair and began winding the hanks into balls.

Chapter 8

By Wednesday of the week following Bert's visit there were four
finished hats in a pile on the table. Wednesday was the day Helena
and Mr Frank had taken to having their morning coffee together.
This time when she went downstairs to join him, she took her
knitting with her. They took their cups outside and Mr Frank lifted
out the chairs from his back office. The sun was just beginning to
touch the flagstones at the far end of the path.

"What are you making?" Mr Frank pointed at the knitting.

"A hat," she said, running the thread through her fingers.
"It's another thing I've taken on, not for hens this time, for some
children in a refugee camp. I could do with help – there's so much to
do."

Mr Frank lifted the lid off the coffee pot and looked inside.
"More coffee?" he said. "Why don't you ask that woman who runs
the wool shop if she knows anyone who could help?"

"I don't think so." Helena held out her mug. "It was she who asked
me to do this. If she knew other people surely she'd have asked
them?"

"You'd think so," he said. A robin flew down onto the path,
pecked up a biscuit crumb and fixed them both with its bright eye.

"What a pair of dafties we are," Mr Frank said all of a sudden.
"It's obvious. Put a notice on the pinboard in the front shop. It's only
two quid for five days. I'll bet you get more than you can handle."
He went into his office and came back with a blank card. Helena
finished her coffee and took it upstairs. At the top of the card she
drew a large, fluffy sheep sitting upright, wielding a pair of needles
and some knitting in its front feet and underneath she printed the
following:

'CAN EWE KNIT?

WE NEED COMPETENT KNITTERS TO MAKE JERSEYS,
HATS AND SCARVES FOR SMALL CHILDREN. WOOL,

NEEDLES AND PATTERNS SUPPLIED. PLEASE CALL HELENA ON 07856720501 TO FIND OUT MORE.'

Before the week was out seven people had rung her and she'd taken details from five of them. Mr Frank got quite excited.

"What did I tell you?" he said. "Bring them round here. I probably know some of them. I can tell you a bit about them." This was good advice and she fixed the meeting for the end of the following week.

It was a nervous beginning. First to arrive were Wendy Plackett and Sheila Rowbotham who knew each other because they helped at the mother and toddler group in the church hall. Next to puff up the stairs was Gloria Mountjoy, an over-weight lady in a low-necked black dress and a bright orange cardigan. Everyone recognised the fourth person, Phyllis Green, a regular helper in one of the larger charity shops on the street. The last to arrive, carrying a holdall, was a woman called Pat Meredith whom no-one knew. Pat had no sooner been introduced by Helena than she began pulling jerseys, gloves and scarves out of the holdall, like rabbits out of a conjuror's hat. An uncomfortable silence settled on the group. Wendy picked up a fair-isle cardigan in six different colours and held it up in front of her.

"If you need them to be as good as this, I can't help you," she said to Helena. "I don't mind doing a bit of a pattern but I like to knit while I'm reading or watching the TV. Mind, I said that to you."

"Same for me," said Phyllis, examining a batwing jersey, knitted in what looked like two-ply. "How did you do this? It looks as though you knitted it sideways on."

Helena stepped in, realising she was on the verge of losing half her volunteers.

"These are fabulous pieces of knitting," she said firmly, "but, like I said on the phone, what's needed are plain, hard-wearing sweaters, cardigans, tank tops, scarves, mittens – anything like that. There's nothing stopping you making them fancy if you want to but there is absolutely no need. Now, let me tell you a bit about the background –" and, while Pat took the hint and tucked her productions back in her bag, Helena sketched out the story she'd prepared, which sounded, even to her own ears, perfectly believable.

Mr Frank was waiting for her when they left.

"I saw who came," he said gleefully. "That Gloria Mountjoy's a bit of a gossip but she's got a good heart. Phyllis Green is a hard worker. How many of them are going to help you?"

"All of them. They all took wool away and they've all promised to make one thing to start off with."

"Did you give them a deadline?"

"I did. Finished garments to be returned to me in one month's time. Not bad for a couple of hours' work. Thank you for your help."

Part 2

Chapter 1

Mrs Hubbard was furious when the newcomer sitting opposite her vanished without so much as a wave of her hand.

"I knew you were up to sommat, Sullivan. I knew it as soon as I seen that paper. That's you and Purselain all over – give with one hand and take with the other. I aint as fit as I was and a big, strong woman like that Otter, she's just what I need round here. It aint right at all, you comin and showin her off then whiskin her back to the other place like that. How am I supposed to keep goin with no-one to help me with the little perishers? There's more by the day. I aint got nowhere to put them. They're no better than flies on a dung heap and they die as fast."

Bridie sighed.

"We know it's no picnic, Mavis," she said, "but Helena Otterley's not the answer. You said it yourself: she's wet behind the ears. She'd be as much trouble as ten kids together. Believe me, you're better off without her. She's a good knitter and I told you she's got a conscience. Conscience is fine if it's kept in check but how would you like it if she started bothering you with her ideas for the kids? I know what she was thinking when you were rattling on about the pens. She never said a word but I know she was thinking you'd do better to get the kids learning, keep them busy and give them a bit of hope."

"A bit of hope. Is that you puttin words in her mouth?" Mrs Hubbard fell silent, head in her hands. There was a noise from the toe and a cluster of children came straggling in, carrying the blankets between them. They seemed to light the gloom up and she sat up straight again, a half-smile on her face.

"They's lovely. I didn't say it before but I will now. You done us proud. There's not anything like enough but we can stretch them out and share them round."

"You'll get more if we let Helena get on with her work," said Bridie, mollified by the change of tone. "She'll be efficient and reliable, that's what Mrs P says, and she's had a good life. She hasn't got any children though and she doesn't know much about kids because she's never had little ones to care for. You know what our Bert says, 'horses for courses'. We'll use her for what she's good at and we'll try and find someone else to give you a hand."

"I wis thinkin," said Mrs Hubbard, "I wis thinkin… maybe I could get more out of the older ones, if I got the right person to bring them on. I use them as scouts where I can but there's only some of the big girls is any use with the little 'uns. They're cryin and fightin like crabs in a pail and I'm moppin up mess the livelong day."

She slumped down again as if overcome with the enormity of her task. And well she might be: the children who'd brought in the blankets had stayed inside and were leaping over the tables, racing up and down the bumps in the floor and rolling about like a litter of yapping puppies. She raised herself from the bench and yelled loud enough to send the ceiling of bats twittering frantically in the space above their heads. "Get out, you little blighters! Scram! Out now before you feel the weight of my stick on your backs."

The children needed no second telling. As fast as they'd come they disappeared again.

"What are you wanting scouts for?" said Bridie when they were alone once more. "You've never sent scouts about before."

"You don't know nothin," said Mrs Hubbard irritably. "I've always had my scouts. There's all sorts hidin out in those hills, waitin to hook a fish on their line. There's money in kids, not for me there aint, but for them that's willin to sell them on. But it aint that. We've always had the poachers and the brigands. It's new things that's botherin me."

"What new things?" said Bridie sharply.

"Bleedin giants is what."

"Giants? There's not been giants round here for as long as I've been coming."

"Well there's giants now, though sayin that, they aint like the giants we had when I was a girl: a quarter the size and ten times as greedy. Makes me wonder what their grandpas would be sayin if they saw them. The old 'uns liked their gold but they didn't make trouble. When they weren't tottin it up in piles they was eatin and drinkin, or fast asleep. But the young uns aint like that. Giants aint clever, you know that as well as me: bunch of big thickos if the truth be told, but they's cunnin like thickos often are. I heard it said they've been watchin what goes on in the other place, seein how folks over there gets rich and powerful. There's new words flyin about, nasty words, long uns I don't rightly know the meanin of."

"What kind of words? Can you remember any of them?" Bridie leant forward.

"Natrel reesauces wis one I wis told, exploitatin the natrel reesauces. Sommat like that, and sommat about a creatin a market though I don't rightly know who'd be buyin from a market hereabouts, except me, and I've not got a bean to my name."

"Natural resources? That's things like diamonds and oil and copper and the like," Bridie said.

"And water and wind as well, is what I've been told, but out here there aint none of the one and the other aint reliable either. There's two things botherin me, beside all the rest that never stops botherin me. First is the boys over to the west, them six sons of old Bogolan. They've decided this here bit of the desert is theirs and they're minded to come and dig it up and see what's under the rocks. They'll do it an all, and when they start we're done for. How many years have I been here? And how many kids have I kept out of the sand and the sewers? More than you'll ever know. But it's not goin on like it's been. It's all going to change and we're goin to be swept away like leaves in a wind." She sniffed and wiped away a tear.

"You said there were two things?" prompted Bridie, handing her the hanky again.

"Aye there is. Troubles never come in ones do they?" She gave

Bridie a weak grin.

"Threes is what they say."

"Two's more than enough to be goin on with. The second's much worse than the first. They've taken to fightin."

"Who's taken to fighting – the Bogolan boys?"

"No, no. They're fightin the other lot, the hairy ones from way up in the north. Bogolans is sayin round here's theirs and t'other lot's sayin it aint. It aint either of theirs. If it's anyone's its mine but I aint layin claim to nowt. I don't know much about the other lot, but they've a reputation and it aint a nice one. Word is they can throw a boulder further than anyone's seen in a long time. There's eleven of them we know about. 'The Wolves', that's what they call themselves, but I wis told their real name's Svalbad. They're as nasty in their own way as the Bogolans. Ol Bogolan weren't bad, he was a tight ol bugger, but his sons is a different matter."

"This is bad news. Funny, Amelia didn't mention it," said Bridie.

Mrs Hubbard tossed her head scornfully.

"Purselain don't know everythin. She'll know soon enough though, when whichever one of them starts puttin fire under they rocks to get at the gold. And worse, when they get to flingin their rocks at each other and we're sittin slap in the middle of their firin range. She'll not need tellin then but it'll be too late."

Another tear slipped down the wrinkled old cheek but she hadn't finished yet. "So now what's happenin is folks is havin to say which side they're on. There's banners flyin about. Bogolans are red with a jiggy-jaggy thing like a thunder bolt on it and the others are yaller – black flags with a big yaller wolf with its mouth open, like it's going to bite your head off. Some of my little uns are havin bad dreams and it's not even got goin proper yet. I've told the kids I'm not havin any red or yaller in my house but it don't make no odds. The kids are takin sides anyway."

"You're quite sure about this? I don't want to be alarming Amelia needlessly," Bridie said.

Mrs Hubbard dabbed her damp cheeks.

"Course I'm sure. You goin straight off, now? If you aint I can show you sommat. You can tell Purselain what you seen with your own eyes. One of my boys'll take you up the hill behind the house. There's lines of camels and asses backwards and forward all day long, and there's men with ropes and measurin rods and others with shovels and picks."

She got to her feet and yelled once more. "Bobby, come here!" A boy hopped out from behind the curtain and came over to the table. "See what you was watchin yesterday, up behind?" He nodded. "Well, be a good boy and take Mrs Sullivan up and show her. Mind and let no-one catch sight of you now. We don't want them comin here askin awkward questions."

She turned to Bridie. 'I'll be waitin for you here when you come back. Don't you go doin like that Otter, just fadin out when it suits you. You come back here and tell me what you saw. Here, I'll give you a hat. It'll be hot up there." She went behind the curtain and returned with a wide-brimmed, pointed hat in a shiny black material. Bridie took it nervously. Mrs Hubbard saw her hesitation.

"I see what you're thinkin but there aint no need to worry. Ding-Dong Belle went in the well long before you was born. She won't be reachin out to get it."

"You sure?" Bridie ran her hand round the inside and pulled it on.

The sun was low in the sky when she stepped outside. Heat was still rising up from the ground but the air was already cooler. The boy was barefoot but he skipped easily over the stones, looking back every so often to make sure she was following. They climbed a narrow track up the hill. Near the top he stopped and waited.

"Best let me take a look first," he said. "Sometimes they're right close up." He ran in and out of the rocks, ducking down from time to time, listening. When he waved to her to come on up she did the same, only more slowly. She took off the hat at the top and fanned herself, crouching down beside him.

They were looking down on another valley, narrower and even rockier than the one she and Helena had come along. Immediately below them at a distance of roughly two hundred yards was a flat area that had been cleared of scrub and marked out with stakes. In the middle of it there were fifteen ordinary-sized men, naked to the waist, all wielding pick-axes and shovels as if their lives depended on it. Ten men of similar height, with red bandanas tied round their heads, were positioned around the perimeter. At first sight it looked as though they were guards protecting the men from attack. But when one of the labourers stopped for a rest, leaning on his shovel, a guard nearby stepped quickly inside the stakes. They heard the crack of a whip. The man who was resting fell in the dust and gave a loud cry of pain.

"Oh you wicked man!" Bridie hissed. The boy shushed her with his hand.

"Noise travels bad from up here," he whispered. They watched for a few more minutes. The dust rose in clouds round the men as they loosened the rocks and prised them out of the ground. The man who had fallen struggled back to his feet and began thumping the ground with his pick again. She nudged the boy and nodded her head in the direction of the boot.

"That'll do," she whispered. "Let's get back."

They didn't stop until they were by the boot. The sun had slipped away leaving only a pink glow in the west. The bats were flying out through the crack in the side of the boot, wave after wave of them, like puffs of black smoke.

"How long's this been going on?" she asked him.

"Weeks," he said. "They're there from first light till the stars are out."

"What d'you think they're up to, digging like that?"

"I dunno. Can I go now?" He made as if to run off but Bridie caught hold of him by the arm.

"No, stay here and talk to me. Mrs Hubbard said you had to."

"Those ones are working for the Bogolans," he said. "They're putting down their markers first, so as no-one can come and take it off them."

"Take what off them?"

"The ground and what's in it."

"And who would want to take it off them?"

He scuffed the sand with his bare feet and didn't answer. Bridie insisted. "Who?"

"Wolves. The other lot," he muttered at last.

"Have you seen that other lot? Have they been nosying around?"

"No. But they come round at night, least we think they do. There's crashes. One time when I came up in the morning that place was littered with rocks and some of the stakes were broken in pieces. It looked like they'd been having a fight or someone'd been messing the place up on purpose."

"And when they've dug the hole, what then?" Bridie said.

"They'll bring out the gold, I s'ppose, make weapons, or maybe buy them from somewhere else."

"And where are those men with the shovels and picks from? Have you spoken to any of them?"

"I dunno. They say Bogolans pay well. I haven't spoken to any of them. Archy has."

"Who's Archy?" Bridie asked.

"One of the lads. He was thinking he'd go down and see if they'd take him on. He's a good worker, strong like. But the man said he didn't ought to risk it. He said it's not work for a young boy. They'd lock him up and keep him for going down the hole once they open it up, and he'd never see the light of day again." He shivered.

"Come on in," said Bridie, taking pity on him in his torn shirt and thin trousers. "Let's find Mrs Hubbard. You're a good boy."

Mrs Hubbard was sitting where they'd left her.

"Well?" she said. "You seen it? You got what you need to tell Purselain now?"

"I saw," said Bridie. "No camels or donkeys and not a sign of a giant. But there was a bunch of poor fellows heaving the rocks out of the earth. Being watched by a gang of thugs with red scarves wrapped round their heads and carrying whips – not for show either. Nasty lot, I'd say."

"Nasty aint the word. They're as dangerous as rattlesnakes and quick as them too. And that's not the Bogolans. Them's just the hired hands. Bogolans have got plenty gold to pay with. Their old man was a hoarder and they're not scared to raid the coffers if it means they don't have to do the hard work."

"Bobby said one of your boys was going to join them..."

"Aye, that's our Archy. I won't be keepin him much longer but I'm not havin him buried alive down there in the dark like one of they dwarves." Mrs Hubbard paused then went on, as if to herself, "You can't blame the boy. There's nowt for him here. No work, no food, no prospects. He's a clever boy but it's not clever that'll keep him alive with that lot."

"I'm leaving now," said Bridie abruptly, thinking of the gathering dark outside, the hordes of children to be washed and fed and put to bed. "I need to get back and talk to Amelia. I wasn't going to be back for a while but I can see I'll have to." Before Mrs Hubbard could open her mouth to protest she gabbled out, "The Twisted Yarn, 134 the High Street, BB6 8QF please," and she was gone.

Chapter 2

Mrs Purselain had her glasses on and was busy pushing new patterns into the BABIES folder when Helena walked in. She peered over the top of them at her visitor. "Hello," she said. "I was wondering where you'd got to. How are you? Goodness, you do look tired. I hope you're not doing too much."

Helena pushed the bag towards her.

"Here," she said. "What we've made so far. I am tired. I'm exhausted. I need to talk to you. It's driving me crazy."

"What is?" said Mrs Purselain.

"The noise, the crying. Every night this past week. You've got to do something about it. I'm not going on with the knitting if this is what it means. It's like they're right there in the house with me."

"Have you got neighbours with small children?" said Mrs Purselain.

"You know perfectly well I haven't. The noises I'm hearing aren't from ordinary children. They're coming from that boot but it's like they've got over the divide, or whatever it is, and they're in the room with me. Every night, for hours on end, there's this chorus of wailing and whimpering."

"They are not in your room," said Mrs Purselain. "They're nowhere near here. Well, they are but not so as they can get to you, if you see what I mean."

"No, I don't!" Helena shouted at her. "I'm completely in the dark. I feel used and abused if you want to know. I've had enough." She sat down hard on the window ledge, so the pattern folders clattered onto the floor.

"There, there, dear," said Mrs Purselain. "You mustn't be getting yourself all upset. Now, tell me again slowly, what you think you've been hearing."

"Don't talk to me as if I'm the village idiot. I don't *think* I'm hearing things. I am hearing them!" said Helena. "I hear children crying. Bridie said you hear them too – that's why you made the blankets, because they were cold. But there were loads of blankets in that bag and it's not like children would cry if they were just cold. It sounds like they're frightened. Also there's other noises, loud bangs. What's making those?"

Mrs Purselain frowned. "That's strange," she said. "I've not been hearing anything myself." She looked at the dark rings round Helena's eyes, the tense set of her mouth. "Well, well," she said thoughtfully, "who'd have thought it?"

"Stop this now," Helena snapped, "or this is the last time I'll be in with anything for that old creature and her kids. I'm sick to death of being treated like a... like a child!" She was close to tears. Mrs Purselain held out a hand as if to pull Helena to her feet.

"I tell you what," she said. "Why don't I shut the shop up? It's only half an hour to closing time. I can close early for once. We can go through to the back and have a proper talk."

"Through there?" Helena pointed towards the door to the storeroom. Mrs Purselain nodded, "We can sit in my office if you'd rather. Nothing funny's going to happen, but I can see you might be nervous after last time."

Helena got up. "No, let's do it," she said. "I've been wanting to see that room again–" and, without waiting for Mrs Purselain's permission, she flicked the sign on the shop door round to CLOSED and led the way through to the storeroom.

She stopped on the threshold, taking it all in: the high shelves, the grimy window, the pile of magazines on the shelf in front of it, and a tapestry pinned on the far wall. The armchair was there too, and the standard lamp. The wools were packed into their pigeon-holes and plastic wrappers, no different from the ones on display in the main shop. Nothing moved. There was no coloured light and the only noise was of a key being turned by Mrs Purselain who was opening a cupboard and lifting out a folding chair which she carried across and set up beside the armchair. She sat down on it and gestured to Helena to sit in the armchair.

"See," she said, "nothing funny is there? It's just like out at the front."

"Not exactly," said Helena. "Was that tapestry there last time?" She got up and looked at it more closely: an angel in a garden, hand outstretched to a peacock.

"It's one of mine," said Mrs Purselain. "One I did a long time ago. Now, where do you want to start?"

"I don't know," said Helena more calmly, seeing how normal everything looked. "Maybe you can explain how it is that I hear the children crying. Honestly, Mrs Purselain, it's unbearable."

"You must call me Amelia. I know we haven't known each other long but I do know you a little and you do know a little about over there. I know you were tempted to shut Bert out when he came round with the yarn but you didn't. I won't say I *knew* you wouldn't but I had a good idea you'd help."

"But how did you know? I'd never met you until that day you gave me the wool for the hens' jackets – was that what made you decide you could pull me in on this business?"

"It's not every day I come across a person in your situation, with such a strong background. I'd probably have sensed something, even if you'd not been knitting for hens."

"What do you mean?"

"Handling old books, rare books, full of marvellous happenings and strange characters. I'm obviously right too, otherwise you wouldn't be being bothered now like you are. I'm sorry about that. I'll do what I can to shut it off, I promise you, but you've got a strong link through there. That's nothing I've done. That's coming from you."

"I don't see how," said Helena. "I'm completely ordinary. I love books but I don't live inside them like some people do. I bought and sold them. I've never done anything unusual in my life, until I went gadding off with Bridie to heaven knows where. Where is it by the way, that place I went to?"

"I suppose the short answer is it's not really 'over there' at all. It's what's inside you, except as you've discovered, what's inside you can be outside you too. People often refer to the place you went to as 'the world of make-believe' – a most misleading phrase in my view, although you can see why they do. Far too many people never find it at all, or only ever visit it in dreams, which is strange, when you think how thin the membrane is between what we think of as the 'real world' and that other one."

Helena broke in.

"You know what they call people who can't tell the difference between their fantasies and the real world?"

"Mad?"

"Yes – lunatics, psychotics, fantasists."

"And you're none of those, are you? You're quite the opposite: feet on the ground, calm and orderly."

"I always thought so, until now."

"Try and see beyond yourself, Helena. What I'm talking about is much bigger than any one person's day-dreams or fantasies. It's where all the stories and poems and songs and plays that have ever been written are banked up. There's wickedness there and great goodness and everything in between, just like in story books and folk tales. And the folk there, well, they can't get through this side but they can make a din if they're not happy. Everyone could hear them if they listened properly but most people don't. Some are more attuned than others – like you as it turns out, maybe because of your work. The books have had a long time to wheedle their way right inside you. You can muffle the noise they make and I'll do my best to shut it off for you, but now you've heard it you won't forget it."

"It still sounds like low-grade science fiction to me," said Helena, "and it's all very well you saying 'get past the ego' bit. The fact is it's me it's happening to. It's like I've been taken over by malign forces that are able to manipulate me and take me to places that don't really exist, except in my mind or in other people's minds, and I can't do a damn thing about it."

"There's nothing malign about it at all," Mrs Purselain said firmly. "And it's not science fiction either. You're better off thinking of it as another dimension or as if you've woken up after a long sleep. The desert was always there. It may be make-believe but you haven't created it."

"That's another thing – the reality of it. When I got back I had dust on my boots and blisters on my feet. The blisters took days to heal. And I picked up a piece of quartz when I was climbing that hill. That was in my coat pocket."

"Ah, well that's another question," said Mrs Purselain. "The intensity of it, how real it feels, depends on the person. Some people never get a single blister however far they walk because it doesn't get that real for them."

Helena gave a great sigh and leaned back in the chair as if she'd just let go of a heavy weight.

"It's is a relief in a way," she said. "I don't mean being told I can't do anything about it. I don't like that side of it but it is a help to hear I'm not going mad. I really thought I was. It's alarming to think this was inside me all the time and I never knew. It's like a great big skeleton's fallen out of a cupboard."

"A skeleton makes it sound as though it's a dark secret and it's not. It is a little like a cupboard though, one you've finally found the key to. It's most unusual to meet someone with hearing as acute as yours who's remained so unaware of your own powers. Quite extraordinary."

"There's one other thing I need to ask." Helena stopped. "I don't know if I can though. It's too ridiculous."

"It takes a lot to shock me."

"OK then. Are you a witch?" She gave an apologetic laugh.

"Certainly not! And let me tell you witches are nothing to laugh about."

"Sorry," said Helena, "but I had to ask. You have to see it from my point of view."

"And I do. I really do," said Mrs Purselain. "And because you do deserve a full explanation I'm going to tell you what Bridie learnt after you came back home. I think that will help you understand what you are hearing at night."

Chapter 3

When Helena left Amelia Purselain's shop she was carrying another bag of loose wool. Mrs Purselain had promised her she would do everything in her power to block the children's noise. She would send Bert Hogarth round in a couple of days' time, to find out whether this had been successful or not.

"Why Bert? Why not Bridie?" Helena asked. "Bridie was my guide over there, not Bert."

"No, not Bridie, Bert."

"Why? I don't feel comfortable with him. It feels like he's holding something back all the time," Helena said, pitting her own stubbornness against the quiet authority of the woman opposite her.

"Maybe he's not comfortable with you either. It wouldn't surprise me if he finds you rather imposing. It makes no difference. Bert will be your guide. You'll have to find ways of getting on together."

"Imposing?"

"Bert's a simple soul. He's probably never met a sophisticated Londoner like you. The women Bert knows are like the ones in your knitting group, quite content with their lot, growing old happily. Think about it, Helena. How many women do you know confident enough to uproot themselves and make a new life in a strange town?"

"I'm not a Londoner though. I'm a northerner, like him. Doesn't he realise that?"

"Forgive me, but to us you don't seem like one. You bring a whiff of the south and the big city with you. I don't mean that badly," Mrs Purselain added quickly. "It's exciting to have an incomer like you but it takes some getting used to, especially for someone like Bert. By the way, has he told you what he likes best?"

"Horses," said Helena. "I felt bad after he said it. He must have seen my face. I couldn't see him managing horses."

"That just goes to show doesn't it? I've known Bert since he was a little boy. He's not changed much. He's a genius with animals, horses in particular and he's a good man. He will be an excellent guide for you. You couldn't wish for better."

Whatever Mrs Purselain did to block the noise of the children and the bangs of the fighting giants was only partly successful but, like when you live beside a busy road or underneath a flight path, after a while Helena got used to it and she began to think about the other place in a different way. She knew she had to get back to the boot but Amelia had counselled her against trying to do so for some weeks to come.

"You can't force an opening. You try and get through when the time's not right and all you'll do is make a lot of trouble for you and a lot for us as well. So be sensible. I'm saying this to you because I won't be able to stop you if you do try on your own, seeing the powers you've got."

Helena took her warning seriously. She had seen the acquisitive gleam in Mrs Hubbard's eye across that table. Supposing she went and couldn't get back? What if she got shut up in a tower like one of those princesses she read about as a child, commanded on pain of death to turn hay into gold thread or knit straw into coats of mail for the giants?

Bert came round to ask her whether the noise had lessened and was surprised by the warmth of his welcome. The following week he was back again, looking odder than ever, in a wide-brimmed Stetson with a feather tucked in the band and carrying a paper bag. He held it up. "I've brought us a cake, to make it like a proper tea party."

He brought something else as well. Just as he was leaving he pulled out a bent black and white photo, a picture of him as a very young man, grinning at the camera and clutching the halter of a cart-horse in his long, thin hands. The horse was standing beside him, towering over his shoulder as big as a small lorry and with feathered hooves the size of dinner plates.

"I know you think I was making it up about the horses. I thought I'd show you Charlie, so as you can see one of them. He was my first. I looked after him for two years. He won all the prizes. See his back. Broad as a table, mouth soft as a shammy. They don't breed them like that no more." He tucked the picture back in his pocket and buttoned up his coat. "Same time next week eh?" he said. "I'm enjoying our chats."

The next time he called by Phyllis Green and Wendy Plackett were already installed on the sitting room sofa, delivering more finished work. When he heard their voices Bert didn't want to come in but Helena insisted. He shook hands and sat down at the table. His unease filled the room and Phyllis and Wendy fell silent. Helena laid a pair of child-sized cotton trousers on the table in front of him.

"What do you think? Ten pairs. Wendy's not just a whizz with the knitting needles."

"Very nice," said Bert.

"And Phyllis has done some great pullovers. Show him."

Phyllis passed over three pullovers in bright green, red and blue.

"That wool came into the shop I volunteer in last week," she explained. "They know I'm knitting for refugee children. They said I could have it. I've got enough for three more."

"Very nice," said Bert again and got to his feet.

"You going already? Aren't you staying for a cup of tea?" asked Helena.

"No, I'll be off and I'll see you next week maybe. Nice meeting you," he said, half-bowing to the two women.

"Who's that?" said Wendy when she heard the door click shut. "You sly thing. You never told us you had an admirer."

Helena pulled a face.

"Bert my admirer? Not a chance! He works for Mrs Purselain, the woman who owns the wool shop. He's a kind of odd-job man. He brought the first lot of wool round and now he pops by to see how we're getting on." She piled the garments up. This was the opportunity she'd been waiting for, to let some of the group test the shop, see if someone else felt anything unusual about it or its owner.

"I've got to go along there now. I need other wool. Do either of you want to come?" Phyllis looked at her watch.

"I can't. I'm due at the shop. I've got enough to be going on with anyway."

"I'll come," said Wendy. "I'm out of wool. I'm looking after the kids next door later but I've got time."

It was Bridie not Mrs Purselain who was behind the counter. Helena explained that Wendy was one of her knitters and needed more wool to carry on with the work. Bridie disappeared into the office and brought out one pack of brown wool.

"That's all there is. Mrs Purselain's off at the doctor's and she won't be back this afternoon. She didn't leave instructions about giving out more. She wasn't expecting you," she said, fixing Helena with an accusing stare.

"That'll do for me," said Wendy taking it off her. "It'll be good for socks." Helena was roaming round the shelves, pulling out wools and taking them across to the window.

"What are you after?" said Bridie. "Is it wool for yourself you want?"

"No, not for me," said Helena. "I want to knit a shawl, for an old lady I know. It's got to be the right colour though." She grabbed a pack of mohair, pale grey with a silver thread through it. "Now that's lovely wool," she said. "I'll take four balls. That'll be enough for a shawl."

"I never knew there were so many different kinds of wool," said Wendy once they were out on the pavement again. "What an incredible place. It must be the High Street's best kept secret."

"What did you make of the shop assistant?" said Helena.

"She seemed OK," said Wendy. "Why?"

"No particular reason," said Helena. "I just wondered."

Helena hadn't talked to anyone about her plan. She was going to knit a shawl for Mrs Hubbard. She wasn't sure why she felt she had to do this. In the end she decided it was partly because she felt better disposed towards the old woman now she was out of sight. Her faults faded and her merits came to the fore. Her merits were by any standards considerable. Despite her age and her obvious frailty she was keeping at least sixty-three wild children out of the hands of brigands and slave-traders. Mrs Hubbard deserved to get something made especially for her.

The shawl was a complicated lacy network of fern leaves, with a scalloped edge. It started with a single stitch and ended with four hundred on a circular pin. It took hours and hours of knitting but Helena was well-satisfied with the result. Pinned out, it was as soft as morning mist over a dewy field. Later that day she went along to the wool shop. She found Mrs Purselain talking to a sales rep.

"I'm sorry I missed you the other week." Mrs Purselain said once he'd gone. "You were in with one of your friends, weren't you? And you bought other wool, Bridie said, for a shawl?"

"That's right," said Helena, choosing not to notice the question. She went on quickly, "Amelia, I've waited a long time. Do you think I can try and get back to the boot this week?"

"I've been wondering when you'd ask. Have you noticed Bert's not about? He went a couple of days ago with a sack of clothes for the children, the things you left here with your friend. I'll be glad if you'll go. You'll need to be very careful. If there's anything in the slightest bit worrying, you either write or say your full home address as quick as you can. That'll bring you out. The only time it won't is if you're around witches and that's not going to happen. I'm not hearing as well as I used to but I'd still know if there were witches mixed up in any of this."

"And if there are witches? I'd better know the drill, hadn't I?" Helena felt a shiver run down her back.

"There's no drill if you want to call it that, or none that you can use. Remember *not* to speak your address out loud if you're anywhere near them because they can change it as you say it. You could end up somewhere really awful, and I don't mean in this world. I mean somewhere else altogether. It would be next to impossible to track you down. So keep that in mind. It's the best advice I can give."

"There's another thing I've been meaning to ask you," said Helena. "What I want to know is, could I ever take someone over there, you know, like Bridie took me?"

"You couldn't *take* anyone," said Mrs Purselain. "It may have felt as if Bridie took you but the proper way to think of it is that you *went with* her. If the conditions were right you might go there with someone else. Having said that, it's really very unlikely. One must be extremely careful about mixing one's stories up with other people's. Everyone has a world of their own they can go to if they choose, if they are open to the power of their own imagination. They don't need yours. And you must treat *your* world with the seriousness it deserves. The desert isn't some kind of amusement park with a ticket booth at the entrance and people paid to dress up as giant mice and dogs. You've seen for yourself, there are real lives at risk and real children going hungry. Do you see what I mean?"

Helena gave a nod.

"Good. Now to practicalities. To make sure you land near where you want to be you must say the nursery rhyme to yourself, the one about the children and the shoe. You don't need to say it out loud – in your head will do – but you must concentrate. The wool will do the rest."

"I didn't say a rhyme the last time I went," said Helena.

"No, but Bridie did," said Mrs Purselain.

"I didn't hear it."

"Not out loud I know, but you did hear it. How do you think you knew it was a boot you could see through that heat haze?"

"I see," said Helena slowly.

"Good," said Mrs Purselain again. "Come back tomorrow, not too late. You should be able to go straightaway."

Helena went home and packed a small bag with the mohair shawl, five little jerseys she had made and – remembering her thirst and the blisters – a bottle of water and a pack of plasters. She was in such a state of excitement she quite forgot her compass. Mr Frank came out on the street as she was setting off.

"You look as though you're off for a hike," he said. "Going up on the moors are you?"

"Something like that."

"I hope you've packed a flask and an anorak in that bag," he said.

"The forecast's not good and it gets cold up there."

"I know what you mean," Helena said. "You get hot walking but underneath the heat there's cold. I've got what I need. See you later, Mr Frank."

The door to the shop was open when she got there. Mrs Purselain was standing looking out down the street.

"I was wondering when you were coming," she said, shutting the door behind Helena. "Are you sure you remember what I told you yesterday? I can't come through to the back shop with you. I'd have to go too and I can't do that because there's only me to mind the shop. Listen carefully to everything Mrs Hubbard tells you but keep it in your head. Don't write it down."

The store room looked very different from the first time. The colours had already seeped out of the wool when she walked in. They had gathered in a soft ball high over her head, a mass of pale blues and violets drifting about as if looking for a way out. The room felt chilly. She sat down in the armchair with a sense of foreboding, took a deep breath and began to recite the rhyme in a whisper. The effect was instantaneous. The room darkened. The chair lurched underneath her. A blast of cold air. A thump. Darkness.

"Hells teeth!" she swore. "Why didn't Amelia warn me it'd be night-time?" She pulled open her bag and tugged the scarf out, then groped around and found a rock to sit on.

"This is where I need my astronomer father," she said tying the scarf round her neck. "We went south-west I think, towards the sun, that day I came with Bridie. If I've landed at the same starting point I ought to be able to work out the way by the stars. But I don't know if I have, and anyway I can't. Damnation!" And she threw her bag down in dismay. There was a noise some distance off. She peered towards it, suddenly terrified by the idea of wild beasts and warring giants lurking behind the rocks. What hove into view however was no giant. It was indeed an animal but not one to fear: a bony horse, led by a very tall man. Bert pulled the beast up beside her and grinned.

"You got a shock, eh? Wasn't expecting me was you. I says to myself she'll be here any time now and she'll be in a pickle, seeing as she's landing in the dark. Amelia usually sends folk over in the daylight but maybe it was you that decided not to wait?"

Helena jumped up and flung her arms round his neck.

"Gently does it, there's no cause for getting excited like that," he said untangling himself from her embrace. "I knew to expect you. I just didn't know the time exactly. Now you're here we can get inside and get warm. Melodie needs her oats too."

"Melodie? Is that what your horse is called?" Helena stroked the animal's flank.

"She isn't a horse, she's a mule." He turned the mule so that it was facing back the way he'd come. "Here, hop on. It's not that far but you'll not be seeing well in the dark and Melodie's a steady beast." So saying, he gave Helena an expert shove with his free hand and she soared onto the mule's bony back. Luckily the animal seemed quiet enough. It shifted slightly but didn't seem to mind the extra weight. She felt high and exposed but the animal warmth under her was a comfort. It was definitely better than trying to keep up with Bert on foot.

At first the only sounds were the crunch of sand and stone under feet and hooves and the occasional quiet word from Bert to his animal. She began to get used to the slow rocking pace.

"Where are we going, Bert?" she said.

"Spratt's place. I've been holed up there two days now. I was at Ma Hubbard's but she was chasing me about the place all the time and I'd had enough. Never a minute of peace with that one."

"Who's Spratt?" asked Helena.

"He was in the army. He's retired now but he keeps his ear to the ground. More reliable than those scouts Hubbard's got. They're just a bunch of kids and don't know what's important and what's not. He's got a nice wife too. I thought you'd like that – a woman to talk to."

"I know who you mean," she said, pleased at how quickly she'd worked it out this time.

"'*Jack Spratt could eat no fat*
His wife could eat no lean...' Is it them?"

"That's the ones," said Bert.

"Another nursery rhyme, eh? ... interesting." She ran her hand absentmindedly along the bristles on the mule's neck. "It's weird being up here. I haven't been on a horse since I was a kid. I was friends with a girl called Josephine. They lived in a big house, up a gravel drive. There was a paddock. I remember asking my dad what a paddock was and him saying it was just a posh word for a field. She had a Shetland pony. Truckle he was called. She used to let me ride him sometimes."

"Shetland ponies can be stubborn little beasts," said Bert.

"Truckle was headstrong but I loved him. I rode him far more than she did. It was something she *had* to do, like playing tennis and learning the piano. I'd have given my eye-teeth to have a pony or learn a musical instrument but we never had the money. Does Melodie ever bite? Truckle used to."

"This one don't. I had one that did, a while back."

"This isn't your first then? What did you call the others?"

"Melodie. They're all called the same. Melodie the First, the Second and so on. This one's number six, aren't you girl?" He rubbed the mule's nose. They plodded on slowly and Helena fell silent, thinking how odd it was that Bert gave all his mules the same name but kept changing his own. Mrs Purselain had told her to ask him about his name and it crossed her mind that maybe this was the opportunity. "No, leave it," she thought. It would sound as though she was poking him again and he'd been so kind, coming out to find her in the dark.

"Naming things is a funny business," Bert said suddenly, as if he could tell what she was thinking. "I've never cared much for my name, Albert Hogarth. It's not my real name, the one my mum and dad must've given me. I never knew what that was. Matron called me Albert because it was her boy's name. He died in the war. It was like I got it second-hand."

"Most people get their names second-hand, or even third or fourth hand," Helena objected. "I'm Helena after my mum's mum. My mum was Jane because Granny loved Jane Austen and my dad was George, after the king."

"George, eh? What'd he do for a living?"

"He was an engineer with the waterworks, and an astronomer in his spare time. That's what he'd have liked to have been really." She looked up at the sky. "He'd have been in his element here. It's so clear and bright up there."

"Not long now," said Bert after a while. "You warm enough?"

"My hands are cold," said Helena, "but I'm warm otherwise, thank you."

"Here, have these." Bert took some woollen mittens out of his pocket and pulled the mule to a halt while she put them on.

"Oh, that's good." She flexed her fingers inside the gloves. "Mrs Purselain would be laughing if she could see us now."

"What makes you think she can't?"

"Could she? Go on, tell me: she's got a crystal ball. I'll believe you. I'll believe anything these days."

"Mrs P's a pro. Crystal balls are for amateurs." He patted the beast. "Ten more minutes and we'll be there. You're hungry, aren't you, girl? Your oats are all ready in the bucket." The mule evidently understood because it snorted, shook its head and began to speed up.

Chapter 4

Helena smelled the wood smoke minutes before the chimney pot of the Spratts' house came into view. As they got closer she could make out windows upstairs and down, a front door with a porch and a path leading up to it from a wooden gate.

"It's so strange finding this here, in the middle of nowhere," she whispered to Bert. "It's like the kind of house a five year-old might draw."

"Don't you say that to Mr Spratt," said Bert. "He's proud of his house. He built it himself, every stone of it." He pushed on the gate and led them up the path. Before his knuckles struck the wood, the front door flew open and a lantern sent a flickering light over the group. Melodie skittered to one side, nearly unseating Helena.

"Steady lass." Bert pulled her up. "You want a hand to get down?" He tossed the reins over the mule's neck and reached up to Helena.

"No, I can manage." Helena swung her leg over and slid off. As soon as the mule felt the weight off its back, it set off round the side of the house. Bert made no effort to stop it. The man holding the lantern held out his free hand to Helena.

"How d'you do, how d'you do. Miss Otterley I believe, a friend of Bert's, isn't that right? Jack Spratt at your service. Come away in and get warm."

"I'll be in once I've stabled her," Bert called and disappeared after his mule.

"This way, this way. Follow me please." Mr Spratt ushered Helena into the house and along a low passageway lined with framed certificates and rosettes and portraits of military men. All this happened so suddenly after the quiet ride in the dark that Helena was a little bewildered. It wasn't until she was standing in the kitchen that she saw her host properly: a man of medium height with a gleaming bald pate. He was, Helena thought, exactly as she wanted him to be: lean and hungry-looking with the upright bearing of the professional soldier.

As they entered the kitchen Mrs Spratt was down on her knees, working up a roaring blaze in the fireplace with a large pair of bellows. She was a big lady, a head taller than her husband and as round as he was thin. She clasped Helena briefly to her massive bosom and then drew up a chair for her by the fire and went back to the pots bubbling on the stove. Helena leaned forward into the heat, feeling a pleasant ache in her thighs from being astride the mule. It was so comforting and safe: the copper pans on their hooks glowing gently in the light of the lamp, the good smell of whatever Mrs Spratt was making, the neat dresser with its plates.

"Something smells good. I could eat a horse – but don't tell Melodie I said it." Bert shut the back door behind him.

"Sit yourselves down," said Mrs Spratt. "It's ready when you are. Warm food for a cold night. Stew and dumplings."

Once the meal was over Mr Spratt stationed himself at the end of the table, to give what he called 'his overview of developments in the theatre of operations'. Helena would happily have swapped the military briefing for a warm bed but, remembering why she'd come and her instructions from Mrs Purselain, she made herself sit up straight and tried her best to concentrate.

According to Spratt the Bogolan giants had turned the rock-strewn, pot-holed area that Bridie had seen into a vast flat surface. Benches had been built on three sides and on the fourth, the one facing the hill behind the boot, there was now a covered structure. Evidently the giants had decided to fight their battles the traditional way: armed combat between two or more warriors, with an audience looking on and judges adjudicating.

"Is this development good or bad?" asked Spratt. Helena stifled a yawn. "Let us consider the location." Spratt took a gravy jug and a plate off the dresser, and a folded cloth from the back of a chair. "The boot," he said, pointing to the gravy jug. "The arena," pointing to the plate. "And the hill separating them." He screwed up the cloth and jammed it between the plate and the jug. "I estimate there is less than five hundred yards between the combat area and the boot. If there are missiles – boulders, arrows, slingshot and the like – there is a high probability of collateral damage. Giants are notorious for their poor aim."

Helena raised her hand. Spratt looked along the table at her. "You've a question, Miss Otterley?"

"I have. I take it you mean children getting hurt or killed when you say collateral damage – well, is it any use petitioning the giants directly? It can't be in their interests to have a lot of civilian casualties on their hands?"

"It isn't like that," Bert butted in before Spratt could answer. "There's no chance of appealing to them. The only reason they haven't come and taken the kids away already is because they don't need them yet. They don't care if a few get whacked while they're sorting out who's getting at the gold. They know there's always more behind them."

There was a discreet cough from the far end of the table. Bert took the hint and let Spratt take over.

"I use the term collateral damage advisedly. We may find ways to protect the children. The boot itself is another matter and, were the boot to be damaged or destroyed…" The words hung in the air.

Helena thought of the shawl in her bag. It seemed such an irrelevant present in the face of what was happening. Still, now she'd made it she must give it to Mrs Hubbard. She raised her hand again.

"Miss Otterley?"

"Given the circumstances is it safe for someone like me to visit the boot?"

"On condition that you understand the risks and that you are ready at any time to evacuate the premises. We will all, children included, have to move at the double if it gets lively."

Helena thought she'd lie awake all night after what she'd heard but when she blew out her candle she fell asleep in minutes, waking in the bright light of day to the scent of frying bacon. Breakfast was on the table when she came down. Mrs Spratt was busy at the sink but neither her husband nor Bert was anywhere to be seen.

"Good morning to you," said Mrs Spratt. "Did you sleep all right?"

"Like a lamb," said Helena. "I didn't expect to. I thought I'd have too much on my mind but it was so peaceful. It's difficult to believe everything your husband said when it's so quiet."

"The desert's like that," said Mrs Spratt. "There's really a lot of noise but you've got to get used to the silence before you hear it – rustles and scrapings, little creatures running about. They keep out of sight in the day but they have to come out at night for food, whatever the risks." Helena sat down since there seemed to be nothing she could do to help. "Bert's off with Spratt," said Mrs Spratt. "They've gone to take another look at the site and see what's doing."

"Is it far?' asked Helena. 'Have they taken the mule?"

"No, they've gone on foot. It's too risky with the animal. Bert would be scared they'd take it off him, and they would too."

"Bridie said they've got whips."

"Whips is the least of what they've got. It's going to get nasty soon, like Spratt said."

Bert and Mr Spratt arrived back for breakfast but sat down without offering any information and Helena took her cue from Mrs Spratt who didn't enquire about what they'd seen.

"We'd best be off then," said Bert when he'd downed the last of his tea. "It's already baking out there so no point hanging around. You ready?" He looked over to Helena. She nodded.

The boot looked much as it had the first time. There were the same hordes of dirty children climbing on it, scrapping in the dust and running in and out of the toe. There was no hanging back and waiting for the old woman to come out. This time they walked right up to the toe hole.

"No need to warn her," said Bert. "The old woman's expecting me. She doesn't know about you but she'll not be bothered." They pushed past a group of small children at the entrance and made their way inside. A choking stench of ammonia filled the air. Helena coughed and put her scarf up round her nose. Her eyes were beginning to water. Mrs Hubbard appeared from behind the curtain. She looked exactly as Helena remembered: the same thin mat of hair over her shoulders, the same filthy old gown, even, as Helena was quick to see, the same disgruntled expression on her face.

"Well, well," she said looking Helena up and down. "So you've come back, eh? Not brought yer pal with you this time I see. Purselain sent you I guess. You come to see the mess we're in, eh? It don't smell nice in here, does it?'"

"Mrs Purselain knows I'm here," said Helena, "but she didn't send me. I came of my own accord."

"It's got a tongue in its head after all," said Mrs Hubbard. "Fancy. I thought she'd struck her dumb."

Helena didn't rise to this. She held out the jerseys she'd brought.

"Here's some more of our knitting for the children," she said. The old woman took them off her but her expression didn't change.

"It's more than knitted jerseys we're needin here," she said. "It's somewhere safe to live and none of they nasty men snoopin round and pinchin what we aint got enough of already. They took another of they sacks of barley you got us," she said turning to Bert. "They come before dawn quiet as mice and went the same. Didn't even waken the dogs. So quiet I was wonderin you know..." She looked meaningfully at Bert.

"No," said Bert. "There's no witches round here. Melodie would know if there was. She's a nose for a witch that one – it's why I bought her." Mrs Hubbard shrugged her shoulders as if not entirely convinced. She shouted at the curtain, "Bobby what's keepin you? We've got visitors and they need a drink and where's the boys that's doin the cleanin. Place smells like a sewer. Otter's eyes are waterin with it. Get a move on." The boy who'd taken Bridie up the hill appeared with a jug of water and cups.

"Best take it straight outside," said Mrs Hubbard, "round the back in the shade. It gets bad in here when there's cleanin goin on. I'm sendin the bats flyin," she said to Bert. "You says the muck they makes is useful but the kids are gettin sick with it again. Get my broom when you get the boys in." This was directed at Bobby who was still standing by waiting for his orders.

"What you going to do with that?" Bert asked.

She chuckled. "The kids will pull me up in the basket. They silly flittermouses is goin to feel the tickle of my bristles on their backs."

"Old woman, old woman, old woman, quoth I
Where are you going up so high?
To sweep the bats from out of the sky
And I'll be with you by and by.'" Helena said the lines out loud. "Do the children know the nursery rhyme, Mrs Hubbard?"

"No, and why should they? It's not comin from here. It's comin from you lot, over there. All the troubles we get come from you lot. They giants wouldn't be botherin us if they'd not been gettin ideas from your lot. Now get along with you – outside where you can breathe some clean air."

Helena and Bert sat down on the bench on the shady side of the boot. A few children came and stared at them as before, but since they seemed to have nothing to give them, they soon ran off again. Until Mrs Hubbard got busy with her broom the only noise was the shouts of the children from the far side of the boot and the occasional harsh cry of a bird. They knew when she started her sweeping, however: the air filled with the high-pitched screams of the bats. They streamed out in their hundreds, circled round the boot like flocks of starlings looking for a roosting place and sped off in looping clusters in the direction of the rocks. Some minutes later Mrs Hubbard appeared, her robe splattered with bat droppings.

"That's them away. Good riddance," she said. "It'll have to be done again but we'll have peace for a while."

"Where do they go when they leave the boot?" asked Helena.

"There's cracks and crevices in the rocks. It aint as comfy as what they've got in here but there's plenty places they can go." She sat down next to them. Helena decided the moment had come to hand over the shawl.

"This is for you," she said, taking it out and shaking it so that the silver threads glistened softly in the light.

"What d'you mean it's for me?" Mrs Hubbard pulled away as

if the thing might bite her. "I aint ordered nowt from you. I aint ordered anythin like that." Helena let the shawl lie in her lap.

"No. I know you didn't. It's a present. In our world, the real world..." Mrs Hubbard gave a snort.

"Aint no more real than here. You don't know nothin about real."

"No, I'm sure you're right," said Helena evenly. "Let me put it this way. Where I come from, when I give my friends a present I don't tell them what I'm giving them beforehand. It's nicer if it's a surprise."

"Who says we're friends?" Mrs Hubbard clearly wasn't to be brought round easily. "I aint got no friends. Friends don't go flyin off as soon as they come visitin, not to my way of thinkin." She folded her arms and looked off into the middle distance, her mouth screwed up in a childish pout. Helena tried not to smile.

"Mrs Hubbard, I can't believe you're still angry because I left like I did. I was doing as I was told. Whether here's just as real as where I come from doesn't make any odds. I had to get back there, on Mrs Purselain's instructions. But I'm here now. I've knitted quite a lot for your children, I've made you this, and I came of my own accord. That's maybe not much proof of friendship but it's a start."

Mrs Hubbard looked at her.

"Give it here," she said. "Let's see what you've done." Helena handed her the shawl and she ran it through her bony old fingers. "I aint ever had owt like this," she said after a while. "But I can't take it. It aint right, puttin sommat as beautiful as this over this." She pointed to her gown. "I'm grateful for your kindness," she went on, "but you're better givin it to someone as can wear it proper. It's too good for the likes of me."

"Nonsense," said Helena. "It was made for you. I can't give it to anyone else. It's got you knitted into it. If you don't believe me just wrap it round your shoulders and you'll see." And without waiting for permission from the old woman she draped the shawl round Mrs Hubbard's shoulders. Mrs Hubbard looked at Bert who'd been watching this scene in silence all the while.

"What d'you think?" she said. "I look daft as a brush, eh? She don't know nothin this one. She's mebbe a good heart but she aint wise in our ways."

Bert smiled.

"I'm not so sure you're right, Mavis," he said. "It looks grand on you and it'll keep you warm at night. There's a lot of work in that shawl, anyone can see that. And there's a caring shining out of it too."

Mrs Hubbard snatched the shawl off and looked at it.

"You sayin this thing's got a life of its own?" she said.

"Not a life exactly," said Bert, "but there's a magic in it, from how it's been made. The way I see it, even if you give her it back it'll not go. It's yours so you'd better get used to it." He picked up his tools. "I'm making a start on those shelves," he said. "You'd better come and make sure I'm putting them where you want them."

Helena wandered back round the boot into the sunshine. She found two of the older girls, sitting disconsolately by the toe hole, with a heap of crumpled clothes in front of them.

"Hello," she said, grateful to find someone to talk to while everyone else was busy. "Who are you? I'm Helena."

"I'm Marigold and this is Alice," said the taller of the two, getting up and dusting off her hands.

"What's this?" Helena pointed at the pile.

"It's mending," said Alice, who hadn't got up. "It's our turn. But there's loads and I hate it."

"We don't mind buttons," said Marigold. "It's patches we don't like, and it's mostly patches."

"It's not fair." Alice held up a pair of trousers with holes in both knees. "The boys make the holes but no-one makes them mend them. It's always the girls. Mum says it's girls' work."

"Mum? You mean Mrs Hubbard?" said Helena squatting down in the dust beside them.

"That's what we call her," said Marigold. "She's not our proper mum but she looks after us like a mum."

Helena lifted a ripped shirt off the top of the pile and held it up.

"I can help, if you like," she said. "Everyone else is busy and I've got nothing to do." The girls looked at each other.

"Come on," said Helena, taking the initiative. She scooped up the clothes. "You don't mind if I help, do you?" Marigold shook her head and grinned. "Great. Let's go round the back where it's cooler." Marigold beckoned to two little boys who'd been watching this exchange.

"You have to come too. We're supposed to be keeping them with us," she explained to Helena. "They were fighting at dinnertime and they're not allowed to play with the others. This is Dominic and this is John." She gave the boys a little push. "Say hello to the lady."

Dominic, a sturdy little boy with red hair and lots of freckles, jabbed his friend in the ribs. Both boys looked down at their feet and giggled.

They made themselves comfortable in the shade and the girls chattered on happily. Marigold said she'd been living in the boot seven years, Alice five.

"So you'd have been – what? – about four years old, Marigold, when you arrived and the same for you, Alice?"

"I suppose so," Marigold said. "I don't know my age exactly though, so I could have been three."

"You don't know when your birthday is?"

"My real birthday? Course not. Hardly anyone does."

"I do," said Helena. "I've got a piece of paper called a birth certificate that tells who my mum and dad were, where I was born, the exact time of day and the day of the month."

"Really?" Both girls looked at her as if she'd grown horns.

Dominic and John put a box they'd brought with them on a rock and set about scraping out a track in the sand.

"It's going to be a race track." Dominic saw Helena was watching him. "Bring the box here and show her," he said to the other boy. John carried it over carefully and opened the lid a fraction. Inside were two shiny black beetles.

"We're going to race them," he said and shut the lid again, "soon as we've made the track. You want to see something else?"

"No she doesn't!" Marigold tried to grab him but he twisted out of her reach. He hitched his shirt up and turned his back to show a jagged, purplish scar across the smooth brown skin. Helena winced.

"That must have hurt very much," she said, as calmly as she could. "How did it happen?"

"Troll," he said, tucking his shirt back in.

"Liar!" said Alice. "You never seen a troll in your life."

"I have so." He aimed a kick which caught her on the shin.

"Ow! I'll get you for that. I'll tell Mum." She leapt to her feet. Helena hesitated, unsure of what to do but Marigold stepped in immediately.

"Leave him alone," she said to Alice. "No-one's telling Mum anything." She grabbed John by the arm and shook him. "You say sorry to Alice and to the lady. It's not nice showing that off. It's nothing to boast about."

"I wasn't boasting," John said. "She asked me. That's why I showed it."

"Liar!" muttered Alice again.

By the end of the afternoon both beetles had escaped, Helena had made four new friends and the mending was done.

Helena sat back watching how the hills were reclaiming their shapes as the sun went lower. Pockets of shadow, no deeper than shoreline pools at first, began to fill the hollows. It made her think of the light in the back shop, alive and vibrant with energy but there was already a chill in the air and by the time Bert reappeared with a second bowl of the gruel she had been given earlier in the day she was glad to hold her hands round the warmth of it. The gruel itself was little better than hot water.

"I should have brought food, not those jerseys," she said. "I've got a cupboard full of biscuits, tins of soup, flour and sugar. I could have cooked them something nice for a change."

"Hubbard wouldn't have it." said Bert. "I get in the kitchen but only because she needs me for mending stuff. She doesn't like folk to see how bad it is."

"Is it really bad?" asked Helena.

"It isn't dirty if that's what you mean. She keeps a tidy kitchen. It's just poor like. Nowt much in there and she's sensitive about that."

"I would be too," said Helena. "But maybe she would let me in... If I stayed she'd have to."

"Nope," said Bert, "she doesn't want you for cooking. She wants you for knocking some sense into the kids."

"It didn't sound like that, the way she was talking last time," said Helena. "She said book learning's a waste of time. I don't think I could help like that anyway. I know nothing about children. I've never been around them."

"You was a kid yourself once," said Bert. "There isn't much to it. Get them on your side and they'll follow you like sheep. They're bored. They're hungry for more than gruel and rolling about in the dust."

"The thing is," said Helena after a moment, "I feel I'm the one that's here to learn. I'm not here to teach at all. It's all new to me. The people I know would laugh their heads off if they knew I'd spent the afternoon mending clothes with a bunch of kids. I don't mend anything at home. If something goes into holes I throw it out."

"That's what I mean," said Bert. "See what you've done already." He pointed at the neat pile by her side. "There isn't much to that either, once you put your mind to it."

"It's nice being here with you, Bert," she said. "You look after the Otter very well. I've learnt masses today. It's been good." She pointed to the golden glow spreading across the western sky. "It'll be dark before long though, and I've still not seen where they're going to fight. I've got to, before I go back."

"It's a bad idea going up there. It's a steep climb and it's risky once you're up at the top. You're out in the open with nowhere to hide."

"We don't need to hang around. It's just so I can tell Mrs Purselain. Come on, Bert, please. There's only you can take me." She got up. Bert stayed where he was on the bench. "Please, Bert. I promise I'll be sensible."

"All right. One quick look over the top and straight back down. That's all we're doing."

Helena pulled him to his feet.

The site was as Spratt had described. The rocks had been cleared and the holes had been filled in. The space was now relatively flat and sandy. There were rough looking benches on all four sides. The bench directly across from where Bert and Helena were standing was set slightly higher than the others – about ten feet off the ground. A canopy in some kind of dark material was stretched above it, held up by four tree trunks which had been dug in like stakes. There were no labourers in sight, only a handful of red-scarfed men, leaning on their sticks and chatting idly. Suddenly she felt the ground shake and she saw the men down below jump to attention. Bert grabbed her arm.

"Holy smoke!" he said. "There's one of them coming now. Get down. They've not got good eyesight but they can smell human a mile off. Lucky for us there's no wind."

"Can't we just run for it?" she whispered.

"No, the less we stir the air up the better. If he smells us it won't matter how fast we run."

The ground shook harder and harder and the noise of the footsteps got louder, a dull booming like thunder. Whoever was coming towards them was battering his way across the landscape at a great pace. Then she saw his shadow stretching ahead of him, like a mountain on the move and the giant came into view, about half a mile off, striding over the boulders as if they were pebbles. As he got closer she could see he was wearing the same red bandana as the guards, although his was the size of a tablecloth. It was wrapped around a huge head of dark hair. His black beard grew high up over his cheeks and cascaded down his front in a mass of shaggy curls. His arms were bare but he had a reddish-brown waistcoat tied roughly round his chest and leggings pushed into boots, very big boots but nothing like the size of the one Mrs Hubbard was living in. Mrs Hubbard was evidently right: if he was a typical giant, they were a lot smaller than they used to be. Not that small though. It was true his head didn't disappear in the clouds but he was thirty feet at least in height and his hands were as big and broad as cartwheels. The left one was gripping what looked like the trunk of a tree which he swung from side to side. The head of it was carved into a club and studded all over with nails as big as field mushrooms that flashed when they caught the sun's rays. He stopped a few yards from the site. The guards were lined up as if on parade.

"Where's the gaffer?" His voice was deep and sonorous out of that barrel chest. "Where's the lazy good for nothing gone to?" One of the men sprang forward and bowed.

"He'll be back shortly, sir," Helena heard him say. "We had spot of bother earlier and he's gone to deal with it."

"We ready then?" said the giant. "We'd better be. First round's tomorrow." He went round the square, pushing the benches to check they were solid. Then he sat down heavily on one of them and looked round. "No-one else been about? You've not seen any of those nippers the old woman in the boot's been sending out?"

"Not a sign," said the man.

"That's funny," said the giant and raised his head and sniffed loudly. "There's a queer smell about. I'd have said it was them… whiffy… human smell. Coming from up there." He pointed up the hill.

Bert put a hand round Helena's head and pulled her ear close to his mouth.

"Better move after all. He'll be on us in a minute. Follow me. No noise." He began to squirm back down the slope. Helena tried to imitate him but, in her haste to get away, she sent a small stone scuttering down the slope ahead of her. They both felt the ground shudder again. The giant had leapt to his feet. In two bounds he was at the top of the hill. Bert had managed to slide like a lizard into a crack in a rock but Helena was not so fast or so agile.

"Ha!" the giant roared, and the sound split the sky like thunder. "I knew there was something wrong! Pesky humans spying on us." He bent down and squinted at the curled-up shape at his feet. "It looks like a woman too. What's a woman doing up here I'd like to know. We'd better ask her hadn't we?" And in an instant he swooped his great hand down and grabbed Helena. She was lifted twenty feet off the ground between a giant finger and thumb. The shock of it was so complete she had no time to feel afraid. He brought her up close to his face and peered at her, short-sightedly. "What you doing up here, eh? She sent you to spy on us? We don't like spies and we have ways of dealing with them. Not nice ways."

"Put me down!" said Helena, kicking and wriggling in his fingers. "How dare you grab me like this! Put me down at once! I am not spying on you. I'm a visitor. Where I come from people don't treat visitors like this." The giant gave a huge laugh at that, a genuine Ho! Ho! Ho! kind of laugh that made Helena think of Jack and the Beanstalk and the grinding of human bones into bread. She struggled frantically but he only gripped her tighter.

"No point wriggling," he said, "I've got you and I'm not putting you down yet."

"You will when I tell you who I am and who I know," said Helena looking up at him defiantly. "You'd better watch how you treat me."

"And who d'you know, you little bit of nonsense? Who's going to scare the living daylights out of Walter Bogolan? Come on give us a treat!" And the rocks shuddered as he sat himself down, holding on tight to Helena so that she was still dangling above the earth.

"Have you heard of the Inferno by any chance?" Helena said. "Do you know the name Dante? Does Dante Alighieri mean anything to you? If it doesn't you'd better listen hard, because if my friend Dante gets to hear of this, you'll be wishing you'd been born a field mouse not Walter Bogolan."

The giant looked puzzled.

"Dante? Never heard of him. Where's he come from? He sounds like one of those forrin types with a name like that. Come on then," he said, swinging her gently between those huge fingers. "Tell me what your Dante's going to do to me. I'm listening."

And that was how, hanging between his fingers like a flag on a still day, Helena told Walter Bogolan as much as she could remember of Dante's Inferno, adding her own extra bits and generally painting a most terrifying a picture of the circles of hell, the demons and serpents, the swamps, the fires and the ice, the terrifying punishments inflicted eternally on giants who abused their power and failed to respect the ordinary laws of hospitality to strangers. If Dante got wind of her plight and came to her rescue there would be no hope for Walter Bogolan. Neither club nor shield would save him from the fate that awaited him. When she'd said all she could, the giant sat quiet for a moment. Then he put her down on the ground. She straightened her clothes and looked way up at him.

"Thank you," she said. "Now if you don't mind. I'm going on my way. I hope the next time we meet it isn't in such unhappy circumstances." She turned and started down the hill. The giant watched her for a moment. Then, as if he'd changed his mind, he reached out and grabbed her again but this time he held her more gently so her feet stayed on the ground.

"You're one cheeky madam, you know that? I'm letting you go this time but I'm not promising I'll be so kind the next. I like a good story and that was a cracker, even if I don't believe a word of it. Or your friend Mr Dante. You were lucky it was me found you. You'd be pulp by now if my big brothers Liam and Seamus were here. Mind that. Don't mess with us or there isn't a thing your pal Dante will be able to do to keep you out of the pie."

"I'll take heed of your advice," said Helena. "Thank you for letting me go. I appreciate it." She bowed to him. To her surprise he did the same to her, then with one earth-shattering stride he went out of sight over the ridge.

She was right down at the bottom of the slope before Bert caught up with her. He grabbed hold of her arm and pulled her round to face him.'

"You all right?" he said.

"Yes, I'm all right," Helena said and burst into tears. Bert put his arm awkwardly round her.

"I never saw anything like it. It's the first time I've ever seen anyone get round young Walter. Mind, he's the best of them but that's not saying much." Helena leant against him and Bert gave her little pats on the back as if she was a child that had fallen and scraped its knees. Gradually her sobs lessened.

"I'm OK now," she said. "I'm sorry I've made your jacket all wet. It was such a shock, hanging up there like that, face to face with a wild man – well, not a man exactly." She hiccupped.

"I shouldn't have took you. I'd an inkling something bad would happen," he said. "The old woman will go mad at me."

"It's nothing to do with her," said Helena. "I'm perfectly capable of deciding what I do and you were in as much danger as me only you were better at managing it. Imagine if I'd tried to go on my own? I might be going through the mincer now." She giggled then hiccupped again.

"Don't laugh. It isn't funny," said Bert. "They don't all eat human flesh but that pig Liam and his fat brother Seamus do. Walter's right – they make pies. Mrs H has lost kids that way."

"You mean they carry children off to *eat*? I thought it was for slave labour." She sank down on a rock, overwhelmed with the horror of it.

"Aye, that as well. Mind, I'm not saying it's happening every week but now and then it does. There's still a lot of ogre in that Bogolan lot. Now," he said, changing the subject because he could see the effect it was having on Helena, "tell me this, how d'you think up that story? Are you going to tell me you knew all along that stories like that are what giants like best? Anything with plenty of suffering and gore – it's like meat and drink to them."

"It's the queerest thing," said Helena slowly. "It came into my head from nowhere. I've sold hundreds of copies of Dante's Inferno over the years but haven't read a word of it since I was at school. How did it come to me like that? I had no idea what I was going to say but once I opened my mouth the words just started pouring out."

"Well it did the trick with Walter. Come on," said Bert. "You've had more than enough for one day. Let's get you home." He hauled her to her feet.

"Home?" said Helena standing stock still. "Bert I'm not going home, if you mean back to my house – not yet anyway. You heard what he said to the guards. They're having their first fight tomorrow. I can't go back. I may be needed. Take me to the Spratts but don't send me home." By now they were outside the boot. There wasn't a child to be seen and the place was eerily silent.

"Where've the kids gone?" she said.

"Inside I expect. Hubbard will have called them all in when she heard the steps." He looked gloomy. "You wait and see how she is. She'll go through me like a dose of salts."

"I won't let her," said Helena, taking his arm. "Come on, let's go and face the old baggage," and she led the way into the boot.

It was as Bert had said. The children were inside but there was no leaping over tables or rolling around this time. Some of the littlest ones were being comforted by the bigger children. Mrs Hubbard was sitting on a high chair at the far end, like a hawk waiting to dive. Deciding that attack was the best form of defence, Bert marched straight up to her.

"He's away. She sent him packing," he said, pointing at Helena.

"So that makes it all fine does it?" said Mrs Hubbard, leaning over him from her perch. "If you were one of mine you'd be feelin the weight of my stick on your back now. Takin her up there without as much as a word to me. There's rules Hogarth and you broke them. And she's in your care. You're a wicked, silly man and you deserve a good leatherin. I'll be tellin Purselain about this." She would have kept going but Helena broke in.

"Excuse me but you won't need to tell Mrs Purselain anything because I'll be telling her myself. Now let *me* tell *you* something Mrs Hubbard – if we hadn't gone up there no-one would know what's going to happen, not next week or in a month's time, but tomorrow!"

"What's happenin tomorrow?" said Mrs Hubbard.

"They're having their first fight. He was up to check the place was ready. He wasn't looking for us but he caught the scent of us. That's all that went wrong."

Mrs Hubbard snorted.

"He caught your smell and that's all that went wrong. Bert was playin with fire and he knew it. You aint got no idea where that giant could have taken you if he'd found you."

"Well he did find me. I missed my footing and made a noise. He grabbed me." Helena shuddered again at the recollection of it. Mrs Hubbard was momentarily at a loss for words so Bert took his chance.

"And she told him a cracking yarn, hanging up there like a fly in a web. She got him eating out her hand. I never seen the like of it. I nearly gave myself away I was that far out the hole I'd gone down, listening in." The children crowded round, wide-eyed and silent as the tale unfolded. Mrs Hubbard was all ears too but when he finished she clapped her hands at the children.

"Stop pushin at her like that," she shouted. "Get off to bed the lot of you. Light's out in ten minutes and no arguin." The children trotted off behind the curtain leaving the three of them alone among the tables.

"We'd best be off now," Bert said.

Mrs Hubbard sniffed. "Aye, and not before time. You don't like what I'm sayin, Hogarth, but I'm right and you know it." She turned to Helena. "You goin to be all right? You goin right back? You'd better. You look all done in, and no wonder."

"I'll be fine," said Helena. "Bert was great, Mrs Hubbard, honestly he was. And no, I'm not going right back. I'll be here tomorrow and we'll see what happens. I'll go after that."

"You tell Spratt he's to come with you," the old woman said. "Tell him what you heard. It aint my boys'll be goin up there. I'm not havin them seein the mess they'll make. Get along with you now. Otter looks half dead."

Chapter 5

The light the next day was quite different from how it had been. The sun was hidden behind layer upon layer of grey cloud and the air was heavy with unspent electricity. Sounds were muffled and dull. Helena went with Bert to feed the mule. Melodie was jerking about restlessly in her stall. Bert said it was probably just the weather but he couldn't be sure. She had a knack for sensing when things weren't right. And indeed, by the time the three of them said goodbye to Mrs Spratt they could feel the tread of giant boots like a constant tremor through the land.

"That's them on the move," said Spratt. "Lots of them by the feel of it." He got down on his knees and put his ear against a rock. "They're still a long way off but they're coming."

All day long the ground around the boot groaned and cracked. Spratt judged it too dangerous to take a look until it fell quiet. They'd know then that the two sides were assembled and that the combat was about to begin. He, Bert and Mrs Hubbard sat in conference at one of the tables while Helena looked on. They were deep in their discussions when the boot shivered with an ear-splitting roar, louder than any sound Helena had ever heard. It was followed by a crash of metal as if two enormous express trains had met head-on at high speed. The children, a few of whom had ventured outside, came rushing in and went straight under the tables.

"That's it," exclaimed Spratt. "That's their battle cries. Next they'll start their stamping! That's how it always is." He was right. As the thumps rippled through the earth the boot began to shake and dance as if it was alive.

"What are we goin to do?" cried Mrs Hubbard.

"Stay right where you are," said Spratt. "Everyone's as safe in here as anywhere. I'll go out and take a look. No," he said as Bert rose as if to go with him, "I'm doing this on my own. One man down would be more than enough. I'll be back very soon. Everyone stay indoors." He picked up his binoculars and strode out through the toe.

The minutes ticked by and he did not reappear. Helena went to the edge of the toe hole. The desert seemed to be cowering below the mountainous clouds. As she watched a chill wind began to blow into the boot and the first drops of rain fell like bullets, sending puffs of dry sand up as they did. The wind rose higher driving twigs and curtains of sand before it. The drops fell faster; the wet patches on the ground merged together. In less than a minute the land was drenched. Lightning ripped across the sky and a towering peal of thunder broke behind it. Bert came and stood beside her.

"Here it comes!" he shouted, leaning out and examining the sky. "This is a big one."

"My goodness!" shouted Helena over the roar. "I've never seen rain like it."

Wave after wave of water was travelling vertically towards them. The noise of the rain on the boot was deafening. Only yards away a torrent of dirty water was foaming over and through the rocks, swirling the sand away from tree roots. They fled back inside to find Mrs Hubbard rushing about with buckets to catch the jets pouring in through holes and cracks in the leather and dripping faster and faster through the thick curtains overhead.

"Get the tubs out quick," she shouted to Bert. "We'll have water to wash the kids and their clothes, and mine too. We aint had rain like this all year."

While Helena and Bert were watching the storm roar in, Spratt had clambered over the rocks to a look-out point behind the boot. He didn't need his binoculars. The sight that met the naked eye was awesome enough. All the benches were packed with seated giants, backs like castle doors, thighs like table tops wrapped in sacking and animal fur, knees as big as the boles of ancient trees. Here and there along the rows, staves poked up like young saplings growing out of the throng. On the left the colours were all red and black. The benches at the far side of the arena directly opposite him were empty, the ones to the right full to bursting with wild-haired giants wearing black and yellow.

"Bogolans over there," muttered Spratt, "and Svalbad there."

The storm wind drifted in and the black banners with the yellow wolf head began to flap and twitch. Spratt could feel the tension in the ranks, building like the storm, until it would have to break and spill. Lightning flashed across the clouds overhead but the sky was strangely quiet. There was no shouting, no cursing, and no stamping either, only a low-level continuous giant murmur which, to a small man like Spratt, sounded like the far-off boom of the ocean on cliffs, rising and falling without end.

A sudden hush among the spectators and two men, one in red livery the other in yellow and black, stepped out from behind the empty benches. They raised their trumpets and blew a single blast. The giants rose en masse. Spratt could see nothing but hairy backs once they were upright. It wasn't until they sat down again that he was able to see who had entered. He recognised Seamus Bogolan immediately. The other, wearing a helmet with a real wolf head grinning from the front of it, was evidently the chief of the Svalbad clan. Spratt clapped his hands over his ears as a roar rang out around the seats. A few large hailstones clattered onto the rocks. He looked up at the sky, reckoning how long they had before the deluge enveloped them and turned the sand to treacherous mud.

The two judges, now occupying the benches under the canopy, appeared indifferent to the threat from the clouds. They called the trumpeters over. The trumpeters jumped to attention, put up their instruments and sounded a note. Each of them in turn shouted some words, inaudible to Spratt under the shouts from the benches. Three young giants stepped forward from either side, wielding clubs and staves. They bowed to the judges and took up their positions facing each other.

"That's what we thought. Small fry first, then the big hitters. If it holds off," he murmured, as a few more hailstones pinged off the rocks. He was standing up by now, confident that not one giant would look back up the hill and catch him spying on them.

There was some sparring and skirmishing at first, then, spurred by the roars of the crowd, one of the Bogolan contestants lashed out hard at the smallest of the Svalbad team, knocking him to his knees. The giant managed to get upright once more but was no sooner on his feet than a second Bogolan combatant dealt him a mighty blow on the chest, sending him sideways. The first Bogolan returned to the attack, swiping the winded giant on the back of the head with his cudgel. Spratt winced. The Svalbad giant fell forward face down in the dust. A thin trickle of blood oozed out of an ear. He lay still. There was a triumphant roar from the Bogolan benches.

Despite the shock of finding themselves so quickly one man down, the other two Svalbad giants still had plenty of fight left in them. One of them ran at the Bogolans. He swung his club in a wide arc, low down, aiming for the lower legs of the giant who had knocked his comrade out. The youngster had bared his chest and was strutting round the arena waving his arms at his supporters as if the fight was already over. The Svalbad's aim was good. Wood met calf muscle with a deadly thud.

"Ouch!" said Spratt. "Serves you right, you puffed-up fool! Basic rule of one-to-one engagement. Never turn your back on your opponent. Makes you wonder what they teach them these days."

The Svalbad benches erupted as the Bogolan giant toppled like a fallen oak to lie, writhing in agony, in the mud. He would have met the same fate as the man he had just dispatched if his companions had not come to his aid. Two murderous blows from either side and the Svalbad attacker joined his unconscious comrade on the sand, blood pouring from his nose and mouth. Both judges rose to their feet. The flags went up. Those warriors who were still upright bowed to them and withdrew from the arena.

"Warming the crowd up," said Spratt, by now totally engrossed in the combat. The unconscious pair were lifted off and stewards began raking the surface and scattering sand over the spilt blood. "Who's next I wonder?"

He did not have long to wait. As the skies deepened to purple, the wind dropped. There was a dense, dark stillness. Both judges stepped beyond their shelter and looked up as if asking the heavens

how long they would forebear to shed their load. They shrugged
their shoulders and nodded to the trumpeters. A second blast pierced
the air. This time only two giants stepped into the ring. Huge they
were, "like sharks after minnows", thought Spratt, marvelling at the
weaponry, the breast-plates, the gold on the helmets, the high boots
and metal-studded shields. They stood to attention in front of the
judges. Seamus Bogolan stepped forward and jerking the red-scarfed
warrior's hand high in the air he shouted, "I give you the great Liam
Bogolan!"

Liam Bogolan bowed to his cheering supporters while the
Svalbad benches booed.

The Svalbad leader then stepped forward. "Glaumar Svalbad, the
one and only!" he shouted to roars of appreciation from his side of
the ring. The flags went down in a blinding flash of lightning. A
peal of thunder ripped the sky.

The two giants circled each other, axes at the ready in their great
hands and swords clanking in their scabbards. Glaumar Svalbad
jerked forward like a snake, slicing at Liam Bogolan's right arm
with his axe. Bogolan swung his shield up and the axe glanced off
the surface with a clang. The benches were almost silent. All Spratt
could hear was the thump of the giants' boots, the hoarse sound of
their breathing.

The storm had waited but it could wait no longer. As the two
great shapes continued their slow dance roundabout each other,
the first proper rain began to fall. Liam Bogolan rushed forward,
pulling his sword out as he went. He lunged at Svalbad but tripped,
or perhaps slid on the wet earth, as he did. The earth shook as he
crashed down. Before he could regain his footing on the slippery
surface, Glaumar Svalbad charged at him, raised a great boot and
brought it down on his opponent's chest. As he did so he unsheathed
his sword and raised it in his left hand. Spratt pulled his jacket over
his head and peered through the rain and mist. A sudden flash of
colour behind the fighters caught his eye. It looked like the flags
had gone up. But either the two giants churning the mud up in the
ring didn't see the signal or one of them at least was determined to

secure victory, to avenge the fallen brothers. Liam Bogolan might have been glad to drop his sword but he was pinned down securely by that monster boot and was in no position to make terms. Flags up or down, it made no odds. The sound of Glaumar Svalbad's broadsword whistling through the air and the howl of agony unleashed by Liam Bogolan was something Spratt knew he would never forget. Spratt's last clear view of the arena was of a torrent of blood spurting out of Liam Bogolan's severed left arm, the shield lying useless at his side.

There was chaos on the benches. Giants were fighting their way off the seats. The stewards were frantically trying to keep the two clans apart as they left. It was almost dark by now and what Helena, standing in the toe hole of the boot, had seen as an approaching curtain of wet was falling in a chilling downpour. Spratt hugged his jacket round his head and set off slipping and sliding back down through the rocks.

"Excellent," he said, as he arrived dripping wet at the boot and seeing Bert and Helena rolling out more barrels to fill. "And the rain has stopped their nonsense for the moment. There's a lot of damage been done up there though. Two young Svalbads down and Liam Bogolan with his arm hanging off. They'll live but not him I doubt. From what I could see, Glaumar Svalbad's sword went right through to the bone. What a mess it made, blood pulsing out like a freshwater spring."

"Was there any of them still out there when you came away?" said Bert.

"I didn't stay to see. It was emptying fast when I left," said Spratt.

"That'd be right,' said Mrs Hubbard. 'Giants hate rain, dirty pigs the lot of them. They'll be back though. Like you say, they'll be back for vengeance, specially if that arm was hacked off after the flag was up." She handed him a towel and he rubbed his bald pate until it shone.

"I'm afraid you're right, ma'am," said Spratt. "There were a lot of very angry giants when I came away. They'll not be satisfied with fighting it out in a ring any more. We should prepare for a change in tactics, a major offensive by one side or the other: heavy artillery, boulders certainly, bows and slings, and they may use their catapults as well. I have it on good intelligence that the Svalbad engineers have devised a long-range catapult on wheels. They haven't used it so far but they will now. It'll let them stay well back if they want to limit their own casualties and still inflict considerable damage. The problem for us here is that their technique for aiming these machines is poor..."

"It's what you said last night," said Helena. "They could hit the boot without even meaning to. We've got to have a plan. We can't sit by and wait for the children and Mrs Hubbard to be smashed to smithereens under a boulder."

"Hold on now," said Spratt. "There are other questions to consider. If this turns into all-out war we need to think who else they may bring in as allies. I do not wish to raise anxieties but we must consider the possibility of witches."

"Why would witches get involved?" said Helena. "What's in it for witches? I've never heard of them being interested in gold."

"It aint gold the witches want," said the old woman, "it's being on the winnin side; it's my kids they're after, and my bats but they can get bats easier than kids. But even more than the kids, witches is always after one thing – power and influence. That's how they spread their poison."

"The problem with the witches," said Spratt, "apart from their foul ways with anything that lives and breathes, is that whoever they ally themselves with has an almost insurmountable advantage. They're airborne and they can hide in the clouds."

"And they don't care what they do to win," said Bert. "I've never seen more than one at a time, whizzing about on a broomstick, but I'll not forget it. It made me sick in my stomach just watching her whipping about the sky. She was all on her own but she still killed a whole herd of good cattle stone dead with one wave of her wand."

"Absolutely," said Spratt. "You scale that kind of damage up and with just half a dozen of the creatures you're looking at a massacre such as we haven't seen in a very long time."

Chapter 6

Helena and Bert were sitting at the dining table in her flat. Bert and she had decided that, since they could do nothing immediate to help, the next best thing was to report what had happened to Mrs Purselain. They hadn't managed to get hold of her though, so Bert had called up Bridie instead. Helena was in her dressing gown. Bert was still in the same clothes, although he'd taken his jacket off and hung it to dry over the back of his chair.

"You know how Spratt said it would change everything if witches get involved?" Helena piled up the supper plates as she spoke. "Why can't we get some extra help ourselves? If the witches are on the side of the giants why can't we ask some of your other contacts over there to come to Mrs Hubbard's aid?"

"Like who for example?" said Bert.

"Some of your knights or some of the heroes, I don't know, out of the ancient myths for instance. They must be somewhere over there. If everything that's ever been imagined is there, then they're there too."

Bert chortled. It was the most cheerful sound Helena had heard in a long while.

"It isn't like that," he said. "They're not somewhere just round the corner, waiting to join in. They're in other places."

"But you get to them when you go sometimes," said Helena, "so they are there."

"Yes but... Have you ever eaten a pomegranate?" said Bert after a moment. "You know when you cut it open there's all those red pips inside."

"What on earth are you talking about?" Helena broke in but Bert went on as if he hadn't heard.

"You know how in between the clumps of pips there's like a layer of skin, white and thick? I'm telling you, that's what it's like. It's like one big fruit with all these compartments in it, so the one set of pips don't touch the others. They can't get at each other even if they're all packed together. Walter Bogolan liked your story because he never heard of the fellow that wrote it. That fellow's story's not in Bogolan's world, if you get me. There's no way you can start mixing people in one set of tales with people in another, unless they've already been mixed before. Mark you, there's some things that do mix, or put it this way, there's things that are in every place. Good and evil like, but they've got different shapes mostly."

The door bell rang.

"I'm not staying long," Bridie said when Helena had taken her coat. "I've got to get back. I've got my sister's twins staying with me this week and there's no-one but me to keep an eye on them."

Bridie said nothing while Bert described what had happened but as soon as he'd finished, she reached for her coat again. Her tone was unsympathetic as she pulled it on.

"There's nothing we can do for now. Both of you would be better getting some sleep. Amelia will be in the shop tomorrow. Best thing is to talk it through with her."

"That wasn't much use," said Helena once she and Bert were on their own again. "She might as well not have bothered coming. You know what, Bert, before I saw how bad the situation is, I was thinking I'd go along to the charity shops and find some new clothes for Mrs Hubbard. It seems so pointless now."

"You did her a nice shawl," said Bert. "She never had anything like that from anyone. Funny how we never thought of taking her clothes, only for the kiddies. But you're right. She needs something else to wear. She'll not be happy in that shawl until she's got something nicer to go with it. Women're like that I reckon." He scratched his head. "If you don't mind me asking, why d'you want to tidy her up? Does it bother you she's like she is?"

"I think it's partly to do with not having any family of my own. My mum and dad have been gone a long time. I've no brothers or sisters, no aunts and uncles. I'm an orphan, like the children she takes care of. I'm not trying to say 'poor little me'," she said, noticing Bert's puzzled look. "I admire what she's doing, however badly she does it and it strikes me she needs a bit of looking after too. Even if she doesn't like the idea," she added, remembering the way the shawl had been received. "Hang on a sec," she said, realising Bert was about to follow Bridie out. "There's something else I need to know before you go. The witches, these horrible women you tell me fly about and do dreadful things to innocent children..."

"They're not women," said Bert. "They look like women, mostly, but underneath they're not anything like men or women. You're thinking of what used to happen over here, in the villages. That's got nothing to do with real witches. Real witches are evil, pure evil. They're in the pay of you know who."

"You know who?" Helena raised an eyebrow.

"The one we don't say," said Bert. "Him with the long tail and the forked hooves and the smell of sulphur."

"You mean Satan?" The word rang out in the quiet room.

"Hush!" said Bert. "It's a bad idea to say the name. Specially now." Helena snorted.

"Did you go to church when you were a kid?" she asked. "I didn't, except at Christmas sometimes. I don't believe any of that mumbo jumbo about the saved and the damned and hell fire and fallen angels and the rest of it. Like I was telling Walter Bogolan, endless torments in the fires of hell with Satan and his devils doing their worst... It's stories, Bert. It's stories to frighten uneducated people."

"You've just been over there," said Bert slowly and deliberately. "You saw it was real when you were there. If folk can dream up a devil, then there's a devil. It's not possible to have some of it and not the rest. It would be like saying there's Ma Hubbard but there's no Bo-Peep. And Bo-Peep's real enough I can tell you, only she's got goats now, not sheep, and she's put bells on them so she doesn't lose them so much."

Helena had no answer for this.

"So," she went on after a pause, "what you're saying is none of my ideas are any good. It's like Bridie says, all we can do is wait and see what Amelia comes up with. It drives me nuts. I'm not used to sitting around waiting for someone else to solve my problems."

"I'm not saying there's nothing good in them, only whatever we do it'll have to be with our own folk and that's a poor state of affairs if the witches come in on it. Anyhow, I'd better be off and let you get some shut-eye."

Helena saw there was nothing more she could do to keep him.

"I'll come to the shop tomorrow. I want to talk to Mrs Purselain anyway, about something else," she called behind him as he shut the door.

Part 3

Chapter 1

The next day was a Sunday. Bert had pushed a note under Helena's front door before she was up telling her not to go to the shop until two o'clock at the earliest. There'd be no-one there to let her in. But Helena had washed up the lunch dishes and put on her coat by a quarter to, so despite the message, she locked the flat door behind her and was outside the shop five minutes later. The 'CLOSED' sign was facing outwards but she could hear voices. She knocked and heard the noise of conversation stop immediately. She knocked again louder, rat-ta-tat-tat!

"Open up! Amelia, it's me, Helena," she called. After a moment footsteps came across the wooden floor and Bridie opened the door. All three of them were there: Amelia sitting on the little steps she used to get up to the high shelves, Bert hunched up by the window. Bridie shut the door behind Helena and sat back down on the empty wool basket she had turned upside down to make a stool.

"Move over," said Helena, and sat down next to Bert. "I'm early," she said pointedly.

"We're all early," said Mrs Purselain. "I've heard about your ordeal, dear. I hope you didn't have too bad a night because of it."

"No, I slept fine. Where have you got to?" said Helena lightly.

"We were talking about what happens if the children stay in the boot and the rocks start falling," said Bridie. "The tables is all they've got to protect them and we don't think they'll be strong enough. So do they get outside and hide in the cracks round about?"

"The tables definitely won't be strong enough," said Bert. "You've seen the size of what giants throw around. The kiddies are better getting out it if the fight comes near. The trouble is the big fellas aren't going to be aiming for the boot, on purpose. It'll be a misfire. So it's not going to be easy to know when the kids should clear out and when not. They're going to end up spending all day outside. Mavis will be off her head with worry, not being able to see what they're up to, and it'll be fierce out there, even under rocks, with the heat."

"So," said Mrs Purselain, "if hiding outside isn't a realistic option – and I think Bert's right, they won't know when to go and when not – what other options are there?"

"If we're looking at them staying there in the middle of it," said Bert, "I've been thinking we'd do better to break through the sole and make a shelter down below the boot, like a sort of cellar. Course Mavis isn't going to like that. A hole in the sole's bad news with the muck it'll make and the wildlife that'll creep in but we could make it solid. The air'd be bad mind. We'd have to dig it wide or we'd have them suffocating instead of being mashed."

"That's a brilliant idea," Helena chimed in, "but it'll be a huge amount of work to dig down deep enough to make it really safe. You'll need pick-axes and shovels. There'll be loads of earth and rocks to take out. You'd need to use all the older boys. The adults on their own'll never manage it."

"We'd get Spratt to organise it. He was in the Engineers," said Bert.

"Of course," said Mrs Purselain, "if Mavis can be persuaded."

"Even if she agrees there's likely to be some children get hit before Spratt gets the hole dug," Bridie said. "It's bandages and stretchers and sewing thread we'll need. Plenty of clean cloths too, and bowls."

"And antiseptics and pills too or medicines that'll take the pain away and bring down high temperatures," Helena butted in again.

"No," said Bert, "we can leave that side of things to Ma Hubbard. She's got more than enough potions and pills and she's got stuff for cleaning cuts. She's never done wiping the blood off one or other of the kiddies, and patching them up."

"I haven't any spare bowls at home," Helena said, "but I do have some old sheets. They're good because they're soft and absorbent. I can tear them up into smaller pieces and take those over."

Mrs Purselain nodded. "We can get hold of bowls if we have to but Mrs Spratt may be able to help out there, and with thread and bandages. So that's another decision taken."

"That's all fine," Helena was getting impatient, "but neither of those decisions deals with the real question."

"So, what's the 'real question', since you're such an expert?" said Bridie, flushing with annoyance.

"I'm not saying I'm an expert. What I meant was where will they go in the long term, to be safe? One or other of those giant families will win the war but the war's just a means to an end. The end is first of all excavating the mine and once that's done, getting the gold out of it. Once they're at that stage, from what Bert said, that's when the children are really at risk. We have to have a proper evacuation plan before the fighting's over."

"What d'you mean 'we have to'?" said Bridie, just as belligerently. "What if we can't? You can't start moving the kids until you know where you're moving them to."

"Nonsense," said Helena, "people move all the time over here without knowing where they're going. They leave somewhere because it's too dangerous to stay."

"Yes, and they die too," said Bridie. "If those kids go wandering across the desert, by the end of the first week Mavis Hubbard'll have half what she started with. It'll be no time at all before there's nothing left of them but a pile of bones picked clean by the birds and the rats."

"In plain English, you mean they've had it," Helena said. "We can perhaps keep them safe underground below the boot while the war goes on but once it's over and the giants come looking for labour, we just throw the towel in, let them come and help themselves – is that it?" She was cross by now, both at how Bridie was speaking to her and at Bert for not backing her up.

"It won't help if we start arguing," said Mrs Purselain interrupting. "The truth is you're both right. We do need a plan but

Bridie's been out in the desert many, many times. She knows what can happen to healthy, full-grown adults when they get dehydrated. It's far worse for small children, especially for children like the ones Mrs Hubbard looks after. They die very quickly."

"Maybe the thing to do is to start by getting some stores stashed away along an exit route?" said Bert. "We'd have to hide them real well, to stop them getting pinched and spoiled, but we could do it."

"That's it!" said Helena. "Lay down stores along the route we're going to take once we do leave. That kills two birds with one stone: we have supplies ready at the staging points and you've checked out the route ahead of the exodus. Brilliant! Now, let's think how we divide up the work... You'd have to do the stores, Bert, because you drive the cart. You'd need one strong boy to go with you – one would be enough wouldn't it? I can help organise the digging teams, make sure they do as Spratt needs them to. Mrs Hubbard'll have to get the stores ready but she'll need you to help, Bridie. We could do with more hands but it's manageable," she paused, looking round. "So, when do we go? I can be ready by tomorrow afternoon."

No-one spoke. Bridie was looking at Mrs Purselain and Bert was examining the floor very intently.

"What is it?" she said. "What's going on?"

Still no-one spoke. Then Mrs Purselain broke the silence.

"Helena dear," she said and Helena cut across her, her enthusiasm of the past few minutes turning to anger.

"Amelia, when you say 'Helena dear' like that, you know what happens? I get warning bells going off in my head louder than any giant throwing stones."

Mrs Purselain put up her hand to stop her.

"Let me finish, Helena," she said. "Bridie, Bert and I have talked it through very thoroughly before you got here. We all agree you can't go again at present. It doesn't matter whether you like the decision or not. The risks are too high."

"I knew it!" Helena exclaimed. "I knew it when I walked through the door." She swung round and pointed her finger straight in Bert's face. "You lied to me. Goddamn it, you lied! You knew you were meeting without me so you could hatch your little plot. You're like kids in the playground, ganging up on one poor child they don't want to play with." She was on her feet by now. "The risks are too high! What rubbish! It wasn't Bert or Bridie who entertained Walter Bogolan and lived to tell the tale."

"It's nothing to do with whether you know what it's like or how useful you can be," said Mrs Purselain. "To be honest, that meeting you had with Walter Bogolan is what decided us. You're known now, Helena. You're a prize they'll want to grab. The safest option is for you to make yourself useful over here."

"Oh so you've got a job for me after all! Do you mind telling me what it is I'm supposed to do while those children are crying their eyes out, terrified, in a hole in the ground? If it's knitting, you can forget it. You can't bring me into this and expect me to sit quietly on the side-lines making little jerseys. It's unfair, it's insulting… you should have thought what it would do to me, showing me all that, before you sent me there."

"I agree with that," said Mrs Purselain in the same calm tone. "If I'd known what we know now I wouldn't have involved you but it's what people call the wisdom of hindsight. It's useless. The least we can do is protect you now. I *am* sorry, you know."

"No Amelia, sorry won't do." Helena barked back at her. "You made this situation. You can't just cut me out. And there was me thinking what a great team we are. What a fool I am. What a complete idiot."

"You're no idiot," said Bert. "I won't have you saying that. You did marvels. I never seen anything like it with that Walter, and I said so to Amelia, but you haven't any idea of what's coming. Witches, if there's witches, aren't any kind of being you can deal with. They're not going to be sitting listening to your stories if they get hold of you. It would be different if they weren't around but the chances are high they will be. You haven't got the skills to get out of their clutches if they get their hands on you, and it'll be one of the first things they do once they spot you. They'll know Amelia will move the earth to rescue you and that will let them get at the kids, magic them to do what they want with them, so they become more and more powerful."

"What you're saying is that I can't go because if I do I'll actually make the children even less safe."

"I'm afraid that's exactly it," said Amelia. "You know the expression 'two wrongs don't make a right'? Well, that's what this is. I ought not to have risked sending you over there but it'll only make things worse if I give in and let you go back."

Helena was near to tears.

"Well, that's it then, isn't it? I'm not standing here being lectured by you lot like a child who's been told off for something he didn't do. I've got the message. You go off and do your heroic deeds and I go back to my house and pretend none of this ever happened." She grabbed her bag.

"Don't go like that, Helena," said Mrs Purselain and she got off the steps and came over. "If things turn out well there'll be other chances to go."

"No there won't," Helena brushed away the tears and stared straight at her, "because I won't let there be. I won't be taken down a road so far another time then told the rest of the way is barred. I'm a quick learner. I won't need another lesson like this." She went over to the door and opened it. "Goodbye. I hope it all works out," and she walked out, letting the door swing shut behind her.

Chapter 2

The weather changed. For days there wasn't a glimmer of sunshine. The clouds hurled themselves across the sky. Cold draughts whistled in through the badly-fitting window panes of Helena's flat. She stuffed tissues in the cracks and pushed cushions against the front door as if to barricade herself against the world outside. Then she set about unravelling the jersey she'd been knitting. It was a silly, small act of defiance and by the time the wool was lying in a heap on the floor she felt ashamed. Phyllis would never do something so childish and petty. None of the knitters would.

With nothing to do and no-one to talk to, she had plenty of time to think about her group of knitters. It didn't take her long to decide that she hadn't distinguished herself with them either. Not that she'd outright rejected their offers of friendship but she'd shown little or no interest in them. They hadn't held that against her. They'd understood what she was giving in return for their labour (very little as it now appeared to her), and they'd made a lively group round about her. It made her think of the first time in the back shop when the wool poured its colours over her feet. She'd stood there and let it happen, as solid and inert as a stone in a pond. The thought made her even sadder. She'd left it all too late. The group would be disbanded. There'd be no more knitting meetings, no chance to make amends or start afresh. She'd have to play the part allotted to her right to the end: unmake what she'd made and try not to make the same mistakes again, like she'd said to Amelia Purselain.

She was dropping her rubbish in the bin at the back door when Mr Frank popped his head out.

"Good morning," he said. He looked at her with a frown. "Oh dear. Is it the weather or have you had some bad news? There's a face on you like a wet Monday, as my old mother used to say."

"Hello Mr Frank. Some news, nothing dramatic – disappointing though. It's got me thinking."

"Too much thinking's not good for anyone. I've just brewed up. Do you want to join me?"

"Yes please," she said, smiling in spite of herself.

"So what's on the to-do list on this nasty, wild morning?" he said, handing her a mug. "No hikes up on the fells, I hope. It isn't the weather for it."

"No, I won't be going out again for a while," she said. "The one I did the other day ended up quite an adventure. I was coming back down and took a short-cut through the fields. I didn't see the sign. There was a bull. Luckily I was near the gate and I got over in time. It was like something out of a movie except it was totally real. My goodness, the noise of those hooves thundering over the grass! I don't think I'll ever forget it."

"You were very lucky," said Mr Frank. "Bulls are dangerous when they're not running with the cows. You may not know that, being a townie."

"I've got a meeting with the knitters later. I'm not looking forward to it."

"I thought you were enjoying your meetings?"

"I was but we've got to stop knitting. That's my bad news. The children are being moved."

"I'm sorry to hear that," he said. "Do you know where to?"

"I've no idea. I don't even know exactly where they are at present. It's all a bit of mystery." Mr Frank held out the pot to her. She shook her head.

"No, I'd better get back upstairs," she said. "I've left everything out in the kitchen. I need to put things straight before I go. We're at Gloria's today."

"Don't you go fretting over this," said Mr Frank and he patted her arm. "I've got a feeling something nice is coming your way before the day's out."

For a second Helena could have sworn it was Mr Spratt not Mr Frank standing there looking up at her. "Yes, yes," he said, "it's not so bad really, is it?" This time she actually laughed.

"You are so right, Mr Frank. Someone was watching over me the day I found you!"

Gloria came to the door with an oven cloth in her hand.

"You're bright and early," she said. "I'm baking cakes and they're just coming out of the oven." Helena followed her through to the kitchen. The oven door was open. The air was warm and sweet with the scent of the hot cakes and Gloria's fringe was plastered on her forehead. "My goodness, Helena," she said wiping her face with the back of a floury hand, "you look dead-beat. Is anything the matter?"

"I slept badly last night, that's all," she said. "The neighbours were making a lot of noise."

"You look like you've had more than one bad night. You're so pale."

Helena went over and peered at herself in the mirror. There were circles under her eyes and her dark hair emphasised the pallor of her face.

"I see what you mean," she said. "I'm thinking I'll take a little holiday, get away from them next door and have a change of scene. I can now. I've just heard, the camp's being dismantled. We're not to knit any more stuff." She waited, expecting a horrified reaction to the news but Gloria kept on thumping the cushions back into shape.

"It doesn't mean we've got to stop." She straightened the throw over the back of the sofa. "If we can't knit for those kids we can knit for others. I've still loads of wool anyway. Here, get busy with this," Gloria held out the corkscrew and a bottle of wine to Helena.

Wendy waited until midway through the evening before bringing out the socks she had knitted with the brown wool.

"I don't think it's worth putting them in the bag," she said. "I don't understand what happened. They kept getting bigger and bigger. Look!" She stretched them out.

"Blimey!" said Sheila, putting her hand in one of them and pulling the leg of it right up to her armpit. She gave a chuckle. "You got any very large men, like giants, in need of socks in that camp, Helena?"

Helena looked up from her knitting with a start.

"Needing socks? You never know. Put them in. I'm sure someone can use them," she said.

The morning after the knitting group meeting Helena woke up feeling a whole lot happier. She lay in bed thinking how easy they'd made it for her, those five women. What she'd thought was the end wasn't an end at all, only a shift in direction. They would go on meeting and they wouldn't even need to depend on The Twisted Yarn for wool. Phyllis had said she could keep them supplied for decades with what came into her shops. In the nicest possible way the group had taken ownership away from Helena. She wasn't 'the boss' or even the instigator any more. It was surprising how good that felt.

There was London too. Sheila had apologised for not bringing Helena in on it but said they'd all assumed she wouldn't be interested. They were going down in early December, to see the Christmas lights. It was a package deal: two nights in a hotel with a show thrown in – a spot of Christmas shopping, a gallery for some 'high culture' as Gloria put it, and one or two nice restaurants.

"Count me in," Helena had said.

"For the hotel as well?" Pat asked. "Have you sold your house?"

"No it's there but it's got a tenant in it and it'll be much more fun staying in a hotel. It'll be a new experience."

There were noises from the sitting room. Helena got out of bed and went through, thinking she must have left the window open by mistake. But the window was tight shut, the tissues she used to stop the draughts still poking out of the cracks. It wasn't street noise she could hear. For the first time ever in daylight hours the desert was making itself heard. Breakfast was eaten to the accompaniment of dogs barking, bats squealing and the occasional shriek of a child. What were they trying to tell her? She'd given up the fight too easily? They were missing her? The latter seemed unlikely, seeing how little she'd been there, but it was a nice thought. There weren't any answers to these questions and after a while, muffled though it was, it stopped being intriguing and was just a nuisance. By eleven o'clock she'd had enough. She put on her coat and picked up her library books.

"Enough's enough," she said to the empty room, "Make as much noise as you like. I'm going out. If I still hear you outside, at least I'll know it's a psychiatrist I need, not a change of scene." She shut the front door firmly behind her and stood for a moment at the top of the stairs listening. Nothing. Not a sound. She hopped down the stairs with a grin on her face.

The books had been returned and Helena was idling her way home when she caught sight of a little figure that looked very like Bridie, fifty yards ahead of her. The person was carrying a brown suitcase and weaving her way in and out of the shoppers.

"Where's she off to?" Helena wondered. "She's going the wrong way for the wool shop." She followed the figure, keeping well back. The woman switched the suitcase from hand to hand as she walked, as if it was heavy. Helena was reminded of her first time in the desert and how she'd followed Bridie with her big, black sack of blankets.

The woman turned right at the crossroads and set off, faster than ever in the direction of the station. "She's going for a train. She must be off to see that sister of hers," thought Helena. "No point trailing after her. I don't want to talk to her after all – her less than anyone out of that three." She turned to retrace her steps.

She was about to cross the road and lose sight of the suitcase carrier when she looked back down the street. The woman was standing facing away from her. The suitcase was on the ground by her side. Was she giving her arms a rest? Could she be looking for a taxi? Curious, Helena walked back a few yards towards the stationary figure. As if this was what she was waiting for, the woman picked up the case and set off once more. "OK," said Helena quietly, "OK, I get it. You want me to follow you." Bridie – by now Helena was certain it was Bridie – didn't look in her direction, not once.

They'd gone another hundred yards along the road, one behind the other and always the same distance apart, when Helena decided to put her theory to the test. She went into a gift shop and let several minutes pass before she stepped back out onto the pavement. Bridie was on the far side of the road, still fifty yards ahead of Helena, still facing away from her and rummaging through her handbag as if she'd lost something. Helena walked slowly in her direction. Immediately Bridie picked up the case and began walking away once more.

"How much longer will she keep this up?" Helena wondered. "Where does she think she's taking me this time?" Bridie speeded up. She was almost running now. They were on another busy street and Helena found herself dodging in and out of the shoppers. A little boy dropped his teddy out of his buggy. Helena picked it up and ran after the buggy. This time when she looked around Bridie had disappeared. Helena went up to a young man selling newspapers.

"Did you see a little woman carrying a suitcase?" she asked. "She came this way a minute or two ago."

The man nodded.

"She went that way," he said, pointing down a narrow street to the left.

"You sure?" she said. "Is that a short cut to the station?"

"I dunno," he said. "You wanna buy a paper?"

She held out a coin and he stuffed the paper in her bag. When she reached the turning into the side street the young man had pointed to, she looked back at him. He gave a jerk of his head as if to say, "That's the one!"

She walked a few steps along the empty street, hearing the echo of her footsteps off the walls as if in a tunnel or an underpass. All the buildings on the left side were boarded up. There was an air of dereliction and decay about the street, with the blind windows and the grass growing up through the cobbles of the pavement. At the far end there looked to be a solid brick wall about fifteen feet high. "This can't be right" she thought, "it's a dead end." A door flew open to her right and a woman with a headscarf tied round her hair stepped out onto the pavement. She had a mat in her hand. She shook it violently and began slamming it against the wall. Dust flew out. Helena crossed the street.

"You looking for Braithwaite's?" said the woman, pausing for a moment. "Round the corner."

"Round the corner?" said Helena. "Can you get round the corner? It looks like a dead end."

"Looks is deceptive sometimes," said the woman, and she gave the mat a final shake. "Braithwaite don't need to advertise himself but he's there all right." Without another word she went back in and shut the door.

Helena walked the last fifty yards to the brick wall. The street did take sharp right and sure enough, there was a shop. A sign, like one of those you might see outside an old inn, hung out from the wall, and on it, in copper-plate handwriting, 'John Braithwaite. Clothing and Household Goods Bought and Sold'.

That explained it. A second-hand shop. Bridie was bringing stuff to sell. Helena pushed open the door. A smell of old clothes and wax polish wafted out at her. Huge pieces of furniture piled high with dusty crockery were stacked down one side, racks and racks of clothes and shoes on the other. The brown case Bridie had been carrying was lying open on the floor and an old man was lifting clothes out of it. He looked up.

"Good afternoon," he said. "Can I help you?"

"Good afternoon," said Helena. "I saw my friend ahead of me, carrying that suitcase. I followed her." She stopped.

"You've missed her," he said. "She's gone again. She went out the other way."

"I wondered..." said Helena. "So there's another way out?"

"There's always another way out, don't you think?" he said and he pulled himself onto his feet. "Do I know you?" he said. "Have you been here before?"

"No, never," said Helena. "I must say this town is full of surprises. I'd never have found you if I hadn't been following Bridie."

"Was it her you were after, or is there something else you want now you're here?" said the man.

"I wasn't after her at all actually," said Helena. "I saw her and I followed her. I'm not sure why." She looked around.

"She was delivering stuff." He pointed to the nearly empty case. "Maybe you've got it round the wrong way. Maybe what matters isn't who you followed but why you've come. Have a look round. It'll most likely come to you what really brought you here." He knelt down again.

Helena wandered over to one of the clothes racks and ran her hands across the coats and suits. An idea was forming in her mind.

"You're right; I do know why I've come," she said after a moment. He gave no sign he'd heard her. He snapped the catches on the case shut and set it beside other cases and bags lined up along one wall. Helena went over to one of the rails and began pulling out one skirt after another. She stopped finally at a long one in navy blue jersey. With this over her arm she moved across to another rail and hooked down a dark red wool jacket with patch pockets. She held them up.

"These are the ones," she said, and there was a note of triumph in her voice.

"Good choice," said the old man. "Much too small for you but then I'm thinking they aren't for you. Am I right?"

"Absolutely," said Helena. "How much do I owe you?"

"A fiver for the skirt and six quid for the jacket. Those are good pockets on that jacket and it's nice wool too. Whoever gets that jacket'll get good wear out of it."

Helena walked back through the town, as happy as a sandboy with her purchases. As things stood there was no way of getting them to Mrs Hubbard, but the way she had been led to the clothes shop, the man's welcome and then finding the right clothes for the old lady – she couldn't have dreamt of a better way to strike back at the injustice that had been done to her.

Chapter 3

For some days there was peace and quiet in the flat. It was a restful at first but when the silence persisted Helena began to feel uneasy. Had she lost the special powers Mrs Purselain had alluded to? Had the desert and its occupants finally turned their backs on her? The answers to those questions came at around three o'clock on a Sunday morning, when the street was empty of cars and not a soul was about in the town. She was jerked out of sleep by a series of dull thuds, like the boom of distant shelling. The thuds grew louder and more frequent. At their peak they were so close, the alarm clock on Helena's bedside table jumped about as if possessed by a wicked sprite. She listened hard for the noise of the children but either their cries were blotted out by the fighting or they were somewhere else and inaudible to her. There was one last crash that she thought would bring the ceiling down on her head and then nothing more. She switched on the light and looked around. The room was unscathed, the pictures all hanging straight on the walls, no dust and rubble on the furniture. She went through to the sitting room and looked down into the street – all calm there too.

The following night was the same: no noise at first but once the hands on her alarm clock had moved past midnight, alarming crashes and thuds which went on intermittently for more than an hour. But still not a whimper or a cry from a child. Were they already dead? Had one of those crashes she'd heard destroyed the boot and everyone inside it? Or had Bert and Spratt achieved the impossible and dug a hole so deep that no sound escaped?

In the thick of the third night's turmoil she came to a decision. Since, through no fault of her own, she couldn't be of the slightest help to either Mrs Hubbard or the children, the only thing left to her was to get right away from the action. She had already told the knitters she was planning a holiday. She would go to the seaside. If the cacophony of the giants' war pursued her there she would buy a plane ticket and get right out of the country. In the morning, heavy-hearted and weary with lack of sleep, she looked out a case and began putting things in it.

The case was already half-full when there was a ring on the bell. She went to answer it, thinking it would be one of the knitters but, to her complete astonishment and dismay, standing there glum-faced and empty-handed was Bert Hogarth.

"Can I come in?" he said.

"What for?" she said and she didn't move.

"I was passing the door and I thought... I was wondering... remember you said you'd some old sheets we could have." He stopped and looked down at his shoes.

"You've got some nerve coming here like this," she said, addressing his bent head. "You think you can have it one way one day and another the next? You were in the shop. You went along with the decision. The charity shops are full of old sheets. If Amelia's sent you, tell her she can get them there." She went to shut the door. He put his toe in it though so she couldn't.

"Amelia doesn't know I'm here," he said, peering at her through the crack. "Let me in. I need to talk."

Helena pulled the door back an inch or two and looked at him again. There was a mulish expression on his face and his foot stayed in the crack of the door. After a moment she pulled the door wide open and walked back into the sitting room. He came through and sat down on the sofa in his usual place.

"You going somewhere?" he said, pointing to the case.

"It's none of your business but yes, I am," she said. "I've had too many broken nights since you kicked me out. First I couldn't sleep for the children crying and now I can't because the giants are tossing rocks around and probably killing more than each other. It's driving me insane. I'm getting out. Why aren't you over there anyway? What are you doing back here? I thought you were going to make a shelter."

"That's all happening," he said. "Spratt's doing wonders and it's going deeper every day. I've been taking stuff along the route like we said. There's been no kiddies hurt yet – well, not while I was there. You're hearing stuff again, even though Amelia's said you're not coming back? That oughtn't to be happening."

"No, I know," she said, "but you can't tell Mrs Purselain, can you? She'll know you've been here to see me and she'll not be pleased."

"Amelia's done it for your own good," he said. "But there's no point trying to convince you. You've made up your mind. Hubbard's as sick as a parrot that you're not coming back. And I wish you were there as well but you're too big a prize, see."

"Look Bert," she said, thinking she was being unreasonable in the circumstances, "it's not Amelia that's going to stop the noise in the night. It's bigger than she is and you know that as well as me. You can tell her you came and collected the sheets. I had them ready to take to the recycling but they're still here as it happens." She went through to the bedroom and came back with two bags. "The sheets are in here," she said, holding one out, "and this one's got a jacket and a skirt for Mrs Hubbard. I got them for her the other day. She may as well have them before she sets off on the road."

Bert looked at her, his mouth agape.

"You're some woman," he said. "I've never met a woman like you. You get all het up about not being allowed back and still you go buying stuff for the old woman. What makes you do it?"

"For goodness sake, Bert," Helena stamped her foot, "I've *told* you. You know what I think about Mrs Hubbard. You know I think she needs all the help she can get. I've been stopped from helping her directly, but that doesn't mean I don't think about her and worry about her. Mrs Purselain can bar me from going but she can't take the thoughts out of my head. I guess that's why I can hear the children. Maybe I'll always hear them until the last one's dead in the sand." She bit her lip hard, determined not to cry this time, and pushed the bags at him. "Take everything and go. There's nothing more you can do here and I need to finish my packing."

He got up and made for the door.

"Amelia's right in another way too," he said. "You'll be back over there. I know it. I don't know how but I do."

"I doubt it," she said. "Amelia only said that to make me feel better."

Bert shut the door gently behind him, leaving Helena uncomfortably aware how close she had been to asking him to call by again. She went over to the case and threw the clothes in a heap on the floor and kicked the lid shut.

"Who do you think you're kidding, Helena Otterley?" she said. "You're not going anywhere." She flopped down in the armchair.

Some time later that day Mr Frank looked up to see his lodger slip out of the side door and walk briskly down the High Street.

"There's a woman on a mission," he said to no-one in particular.

It was Bert's last throwaway remark that had done it. It had sown a seed in Helena's mind that in the space of a few hours had put out a dozen different tendrils, all of them heading in the same direction. After she'd put the case back in the cupboard she'd sat down in the chair by the window with a pad of blank paper and some coloured pens. An hour later and the white page was criss-crossed by a mess of lines and multi-coloured circles radiating out from a stick figure drawn in black at the centre. Every circle was attached to a line like a thread and every circle had at least one word inside it: 'books', 'make-believe', 'the shop', 'the wool', 'colours', 'knitting', 'desert – heat and dust', 'Bert', 'Bridie', 'Mrs Purselain', 'nursery rhymes', 'Mrs Hubbard', 'orphaned children', 'the boot', 'giants', and – in the bottom corner, in a box not a circle and drawn in red ink, the word 'WITCHES' in capitals.

She studied the page and added in some more lines, linking 'books' to 'make-believe' and 'nursery rhymes'.

"Right," she said, "that's enough to be going on with. I know what I've got to do." She put the pad aside and stretched like a cat waking from sleep.

Like many middle-class English children of her generation, Helena had grown up with books like 'A Child's Garden of Verses' and 'Now We are Six'. At the age of sixty-two she could still reel off lines of poetry she'd learnt by heart before she went to school. When Mr Frank saw her scurry past the shop door what she was on her way to look for was a poetry book from her childhood: The Golden Treasury of Children's Poetry. In London she would have tracked one down in no time. But she wasn't in London and she wasn't going to use her old book-dealing networks for this search. She would go first of all to the charity bookshop at the far end of the High Street.

The man on the desk there was well-informed and helpful. He had heard of the anthology but he hadn't ever seen one. She left her name and telephone number and asked him to phone round some of the branches to see if anyone had a copy. Having the rest of the day in front of her with nothing particular to do, she decided she would look on the book shelves of each one of the town's many charity shops. Two fruitless hours went by while she rummaged among piles of old paperbacks and DVDs jumbled together on the shelves. She had one more to do before she was back outside the flat.

There was a van at the door of the shop and a couple of young men were unloading it, in and out like ants. Helena had decided she wouldn't bother going in, seeing the mess of new stock piled up near the entrance, when she heard a crash. A cardboard box of books had overbalanced from the back of the van and was now lying up-turned in the road. Only a foot away from her, face down in the gutter, lay a copy of The Golden Treasury. She bent down and picked it up. Some of the pages were loose but it looked as though there were none missing. What should she do? If the box had been handed in to the shop at the other end of the street where the knowledgeable man was in charge, the anthology would have been priced at its true market value, but the helpers in the shop where the anthology was being delivered were unlikely to be so well informed. Helena knew she could probably have the book for a pound or less, given its poor condition, and the fact that it was a book of poetry as well, but her conscience told her that nothing good would come of such a gross deception.

She went into the shop with it and explained to the two ladies on duty that she wanted this book most urgently and that she knew it was worth more than it looked from its condition. What would they accept for it? The tactic failed. They got flustered at the suggestion that it was 'valuable' although Helena was careful not to use the word itself. One of them took it off her and said it would have to go away to their estimators. They were sorry they couldn't sell it to her that day but if she left them her name and address they would let her know a price as soon as possible.

"Snatching defeat from the jaws of victory! That's me, every time," she muttered as she stumped off home, empty-handed. Two days later there was a voice-mail message from the first shop. The man had tracked down a copy of the anthology. It was in poor condition: the back cover was missing, so they wouldn't be putting it up for general sale. Helena could have it for ten pounds and he'd get it mailed to the shop straightaway if she was interested.

Next she had to buy a book of nursery rhymes. She was waiting to pay for it when she heard a familiar voice at her back.

"Hello," Wendy said. "Fancy bumping into you. That's a lovely book. I gave it to my niece last year. Who's it for?"

"Me." The word was out before Helena could stop it. "No, I mean for some children I know. By the way," she went on quickly, "I'll probably not make it to the next meeting. Can you tell them. I'm going to be away for a week or two."

"Nice," said Wendy. "Where to?"

"Walking. I'm packing one bag, taking my compass and seeing where I get to."

She added the books to what she'd already stowed in her rucksack: a bottle of water, a penknife, a fork and spoon, extra clothes, a large box of matches, sun-cream, plasters, anti-venom tablets, the compass, a pad of paper, pencils and a pen, and – for no other reason than because it felt right – three large balls of Mrs Purselain's knitting wool and a pair of knitting needles. There remained only one thing she had to do: find a way of crossing the divide between the High Street and the desert.

Chapter 4

The days were shortening. From early on ordinary people with a home to go to were in front of their televisions behind closed curtains. On the evening Helena chose the town was deserted. The moon wasn't quite full and it was coming and going behind big clouds as she walked the short distance to the shop. She didn't stop when she reached it – short of flinging a brick at the window, there was no way of gaining entry from the front – but went twenty yards further on to where a cobbled lane led up the side of the greengrocer's. The lane took a sharp turn at the back of the shop yards and ran at right-angles, parallel to the main street. Each yard had its own stout wooden door set into a twelve-foot high stone wall. She worked her way along, trying one door after another – locks and bolts on every one. She stood for a moment pondering her next move. A step-ladder was the only answer. She would have to go home and get hers. It was risky but it was the only way.

It took her another hour before she was once again stationed outside the wool shop yard with the steps in place. She climbed up and looked over. The moon was behind clouds but she could see well enough to know she would never get the ladder standing firm among the mass of scraggy bushes growing close up to the wall, even assuming she managed first to lift it over and drop it down. But all was not lost. It looked as though there was only a rickety fence between that yard and the one behind the butcher's and the butcher's yard had almost no undergrowth by the wall.

"Perfect," she whispered. Not only could she get over but even better, she could leave the steps somewhere well out of sight. She climbed back down and moved the ladder ten yards along and up she went for a final look at where she would land. Satisfied with what she saw, she climbed back down, picked up her rucksack and made the ascent once more. This time she leant over and let the pack drop onto a patch of bare earth. Now it was down there out of reach there was no going back. She swung her leg over, so that she was astride the wall and pulled on the ladder. It came up with a little suck out of the wet earth in the lane. One smooth heave and it was over the wall. She paused for breath before testing her weight on it. It sank a little under her foot but otherwise felt steady enough. She climbed down. There was a shed in the corner of the yard. It was locked but she managed to push the ladder in the gap between it and the wall. You would have to look hard to find it. Having removed as many traces of her passing as she could, she climbed over the fence and tiptoed up to the wool shop window.

At first there was nothing to be seen through the dirty pane but when she wiped her hand over the glass she could make out minuscule pricks of light in the murk, like fireflies in grass. She concentrated all her efforts on them. They grew stronger, merged together and began to take on colours and weave about in the centre of the room. She tapped the window.

"Let me in," she hissed. "Bert said you let Amelia out one time, now let me in." Nothing happened. The colours didn't fade but they came no nearer the window. How long did she have before they disappeared again? She began saying the nursery rhyme out loud.

"...she whipped them all soundly
And sent them to bed."

As she said the last line she pressed her forehead and both hands hard against the glass. There was a sound like the splintering of ice on a pond. The colours were dancing about just the other side of the glass. She began again, louder:

"There was an old woman..." She heard that queer sighing groan she'd heard the very first time and the window buckled like plastic in a fire. She was neither inside nor outside the storeroom. It was pitch-black, and warm, then suddenly cold, oh so cold. Her bag bumped against her back. She felt dizzy, sick. The air smelled different, the scent of sage bushes and juniper filled her nostrils. Wherever she was, it wasn't in the yard on the High Street.

"Wow, I've done it!" she said out loud, dusting the grit off her hands. "Christ, it's freezing."

She swung the bag off her back and sat down for a moment to wait for her breathing to quieten and her head to clear. At first she heard not a sound. Little by little however, as Mrs Spratt had said, she began to catch the rustlings of small animals and sometimes their squeaks.

Now she had got this far she began to think properly about what she planned to do once she got to the boot. If Bridie was there she was bound to try and get Helena sent back straightaway. Could she do that? Maybe she couldn't but Amelia would, if she found out Helena had disobeyed her. And if Amelia whisked her back to the High Street that would be the end of it. There'd be no more chances, not through the shop and that seemed to be the only route.

It was more difficult to work out what Bert might do. He'd come of his own accord to see her at the house but he was unlikely to stand out against the other two. Perhaps it would be safer not to go straight to the boot after all. It might be wiser to seek shelter with Mr and Mrs Spratt and do her negotiating from there. At least that way she wouldn't fall straight into Bridie's clutches. She didn't need to wake the Spratts. She could go round the back and wait out the rest of the night in the shed with Melodie. She got the compass out and took a more southerly direction.

It was all going so much better than she'd hoped. She'd been worried about landing in the desert in the dark without Bert to help her but there was nothing to be frightened of. The desert was fast asleep, like a great, slumbering beast. The air was cold but the walking was keeping her warm. The cold and darkness meant there were no flies, no spiders, scorpions or snakes to worry about. And overhead a million, million stars to keep her company, and the crusty old moon sliding across the sky. Seeing the sky like that she could understand why her father wouldn't come in from his telescope on clear nights. They used to tease him, but really they loved those starry evenings as much as he did: hands round a mug of hot cocoa, out in the mysterious night-time garden and bringing the pock-marked face of the moon sharply into focus.

The part of the desert she was walking through stretched out, as serene as a Japanese garden, smooth, sandy slopes broken here and there by spiny bushes and rocks that were too small to hide a hunting lion. She hitched her bag higher on her back and quickened her pace. Halfway across one of those wide scoops of sand, virginally white and unblemished in the moonlight, her boot caught on a hidden root. She staggered, sending sand spurting up, but she couldn't regain her balance. The ground began sagging like wet mud under her feet. Had she stumbled on one of those dreaded sinkholes she'd been warned about? There was a sighing, hissing sound and nothing to grab hold of. The desert was opening its mouth like a monster to swallow her whole.

"Help! Bert!" she cried and she dropped like a stone, straight down in the dark.

Chapter 5

A tangle of branches and twigs followed her to the bottom of what she quickly realised was not a natural hole. She was scratched and bruised and shaking so hard that at first she couldn't stand up at all. She could see right up to the sky above her head through the mess of broken branches that had been laid across the top by whoever had dug the pit. The hunter wasn't after small animals like rats and mice. Even quite a big rat could have scampered across the opening without danger. It was something heavy like a lion or an antelope they were hoping to catch. She managed to get back on her feet, pushing away the bits of twig and small branches that she'd brought down with her, loosening a shower of sand in the process. The branches were too small to help her get out but maybe if she could pull down some of the bigger ones hanging out of reach above her head, she could devise some means of hauling herself up high enough to get a grip on the edge.

She jumped as best she could again and again but to no avail. She thought of her step-ladder tucked out of sight behind the shed, so near and yet so impossibly far. Both her legs were trembling uncontrollably by now, so she sat down and stretched them out as best she could for a few minutes. But the horror of her predicament was too much and she got back on her feet and fumbled around in her bag for the knife she'd packed. Digging out toe holes in the rock walls and trying to climb out that way was her only hope – that, or waiting meekly for her captor to come and check his trap.

She began to work away at the rock. She'd been digging and scraping for a good while, to little effect, when she felt a kind of shiver in the earth. It wasn't giant footsteps but it did feel like footsteps of some kind and they were passing not far from the hole. She held her breath, listening. Out of the darkness came a voice, a soft female voice. Who could it be? What kind of woman would be out in the desert in the dark of night? Bert's words came flashing

into her mind: "They aren't women. They only look like women."
Fear gripped her and she shrank back into the darkest corner of the
pit.

Whoever it was might have gone on by had there not been
a mess of broken branches sticking up out of the sand. A shape
appeared in the ragged hole over Helena's head. It sniffed loudly. The
sniff was followed by a hoarse chuckle.

"Praise be!" the creature said. "My nose tells me there's something
nice down there. Bless our Seamus and his hunting traps. And aren't
we the lucky ones this time. Come on over here Violet, Lily. See
what the good earth has sent to bless us."

"Whatever is it?" said another female voice. "What you found
this time, Iris?"

"I don't rightly know yet but we'll see in a minute."

The first one said, "Let's take a look shall we? Something tells me
we're going to be eating well."

It took them no time at all to pull back the branches. The
moonlight fell aslant the hole. Although Helena was huddled down
as small as she could get, she knew it was no use. If these creatures
were witches – and what else could they be? – she might just as
well sit out in the bright moonlight. Spratt had told her how they
flew about at night, not only because that left them free to do their
wickedness unchecked, but also because for them the pitchy black
of night was as bright as a sunny day would be to ordinary men and
women. This, as he had been keen to stress, was another compelling
reason for one or other of the warring giant clans to bring the fiends
in as allies. With a witch or two up there in the sky hostilities could
go on long after the sun had disappeared. As the last branch was
pulled back one of the hags let out a shriek that made Helena's blood
run cold.

"For pity's sake it's a human and a woman too. Smell the beauty
of her. Oh my dears, what a prize! What a feast!" She leant over and
poked Helena with one of those branches she had been trying in
vain to reach.

"Bring it out, dear Violet. Make it come out of its little hidey hole.

Let's get a proper look at it."

The third witch came round to the other side.

"Give us that branch, Violet," she said. "I can prise it out from here. Maybe it's hurt. Maybe it needs a little bit of cherishing and nourishing." She let out a horrible laugh and she dug hard on Helena's back with the branch.

"Come on now. Don't be shy,'" said the Iris one, and between them they began to thump and pry with their sticks on all parts of her body until Helena could take it no more and stood up.

"My, I haven't seen a specimen like that since I was an innocent girl in pigtails," said Violet in admiration. "Where has she come from?"

"Never mind where she's from. It's where she's going that matters!" said Iris who evidently felt that the prize was hers since she'd been the first to look in the trap. "Now be a dear, Lily, and fetch the net and the sack. We'll need both to get her back home. Mustn't bruise her any more than she's already bruised. Wait till Eglantine sees."

Helena snatched hold of one of the branches they'd prodded her with and held it in front of her like a weapon. If they were intent on catching her she was going to put up as much of a fight as she could. She heard them muttering together as they spread the net out on the ground and she pressed back as hard as she could against the wall of the hole, thinking that whatever this net was, it would be less likely to trap her if she stopped it surrounding her completely. It happened very fast. They tossed the horrible thing into the hole. Helena kicked and fought it off. They pulled it back up and spread it out again, gabbling curses.

Iris took charge again. "That's enough of the nonsense. Hold her still will you, Lily dear, while I make sure it's over her. She's a little frisky but we'll soon quieten her down."

Helena heard her shout a string of strange syllables and as they rang out she felt a sharp pain shoot along her arms. Her immediate reaction was to rub the pain away but try as she might she couldn't move her limbs. Her arms hung like dead animals, solid and inert.

The net fell heavily right down to her feet. They tightened it so that she fell to the ground and they hauled her, bumping and banging, up to the surface. Three quick tugs between them it took and she fell face forward, scraping her forehead and right cheek in the dust and tasting blood in her mouth.

Now she could see them for the first time. One was fair-haired, the others dark. They were all dressed the same, leather jerkins buttoned all the way up to the throat and below them tight breeches such as soldiers used to wear, and boots with shiny buckles. Their garb was unremarkable enough, since breeches are obviously more suitable wear than skirts if broomsticks are the way you travel. What was unnerving about them was the eerie, yellowish glow they gave off, and the smell that wafted from them as they moved about, a stink of putrefaction. Helena had no time to dwell on these details however, her efforts being concentrated on freeing herself now she was back out of that hole.

"Let me out of here," she said, on her knees and shaking the ropes of the net. "I've done nothing wrong. I'm a stranger here but not an enemy."

"Oh listen to it," said Violet, the fair-haired one. "Listen to it singing like a canary. It's so sweet it makes me cry."

"Stop talking as if I'm not here. I can hear what you're saying," she growled. "Undo this net and let me out."

"Eglantine's not going to like it though," said the one called Iris. "She'll have the tongue off it if it makes a noise like that."

"She'll have the tongue off it anyway," said the third one, Lily. "You know what Eglantine's like about tongue. I'm having the eyes though. I'm thinking lightly grilled, soft and liquid in the middle and crisp on the outside. Oh, just the thought of it makes me hungry."

"Get the sack, dear," said Iris. "We'll not get it back safe in the net." And before Helena knew it they'd pushed her head-first into their sack and drawn the neck of it tight. Now she was in a net inside a sack. The cloth of it was so thick she could hardly breathe. The last thing she had a conscious recollection of was of being lifted up and slung like a carcass on one of the stronger branches from the trap.

When she came to she was lying on the ground. They'd taken her out of both the sack and the net but tied her hands and legs with twine that was cutting into her wrists and ankles. Helena had already been severely bruised from the fall into the trap and the mauling and poking they'd given her but her anxiety was by now so acute that she felt no pain other than the chafing on her wrists and ankles from the twine, and the hardness of the rubble under her ribs. She kicked and wriggled her way round so as to be able to see where they were. They were some distance off, sitting round a fire. The carcass of a smallish animal like a rabbit or a desert hare was sizzling over the flames.

There was a faint scuffling noise further back in the shadow of a rock and she twisted round to see what was making it. It could have been a lion or a hyena and she wouldn't have cared. At that moment she would have been happier to die in the jaws of a healthy animal than in the hands of the three by the fire. There was no animal though. Her eyes made out a wicker cage and crammed inside a small child shivering in the cold. As quietly as she could she shuffled across the sand towards the cage. The child poked a finger out, whimpering.

"Who are you, little one?" she whispered.

"They call me Be-Be," he muttered.

"And how did they catch you, you poor mite?" she asked him.

"I was watching the goats for my aunty. It were blazing hot and I fell asleep and they nabbed me." Two big tears made streaks down his cheeks.

"Don't cry," she said. "We'll get out of this. I'll put my arms close up to the bars. You must undo these knots, then I'll be able to open the cage and let you out." There was a shriek of laughter. She twisted round and looked back at the fire. They were pulling the rabbit off the embers and tearing it apart.

"It won't do no good," he said. "You can't undo the knots. They're magic. Once they've got you no-one gets away." He began to cry more loudly and she shushed him urgently. But it was too late. The fair-haired Violet looked across and saw that she'd moved.

"We've got a naughty one here," she said getting up. "She's off making friends with our tasty morsel. We can't have that." She walked over and kicked Helena several yards away from the cage out into the bright moonlight. The child was slumped head-down against the bars.

"Now then you lovely lump, let's be having a proper look at you," she said, rolling Helena over onto her back. "You hungry, pet? You fancy a bit of that nice rabbit? Best eat when you can, I always say." She gave Helena another kick in the ribs before rejoining her companions.

Violet's exertions had moved Helena much closer to the fire so she could easily hear what they were saying. It seemed that they were waiting for a fourth witch, the one they'd called Eglantine who had a liking for tongue. The fire flickered and sparked. The witches stopped chattering and slumped against one another like sleeping dogs. The minutes ticked by and the cold penetrated deeper and deeper into Helena's bones. She was shivering uncontrollably when, all of a sudden, the one called Lily straightened up and cocked an ear.

"She's coming now," the hag said and the other two got to their feet and stared into the night sky. Helena stared too but she could see nothing except the stars and the moon nearly out of sight on the horizon. Then she heard a sound – a faint whooshing sound – and a shape materialised high in the air coming fast in the direction of the fire. A fourth witch was steering herself expertly down towards the camp. She landed her broomstick in a puff of sand some yards beyond the fire and came over to join them. She was inches taller than her companions and her voice was deep and melodious, not unlike Amelia Purselain's Helena noticed with a start.

"There's a warm and savoury smell from on high," she said. "I trust you've kept food for me."

The three of them gathered round her like children, plucking her jacket, all excited and noisy.

"There's food all ready for you, dearest Eglantine. But wait till you see what else. We've a prize for you that'll make the juices run down your pretty chin."

"A prize? What kind of a prize? If you mean the boy, he's not much of a prize. We'll not get one good meal out of him while he's as thin as he is." The witch plonked herself down by the fire and, seizing the leg of rabbit one of them held out, she ripped it apart and began stuffing it greedily into her mouth, bones and all. Lily hovered near her. Helena watched with revulsion the way her hands clenched and unclenched, as if she was desperate to touch, even stroke, the horrible apparition, but didn't dare to.

"Not the boy, dear, something so much better than that bag of bones. A real live woman with a real wagging tongue and eyes that make you want to poke them out and eat them raw. Brown they are. Lovely brown eyes."

"And she's got skin as soft as silk. I'm having the skin. I'm wrapping it all round me and making myself look like new." The fair-haired Violet hugged herself rapturously as she spoke and did a little jig for sheer joy. Eglantine belched loudly, spat out a bit of gristle and got up.

"Where is she, this prize specimen?"

"Over there, all tied up like a pretty parcel." Iris pointed towards the bundle that was Helena. Eglantine came over to her.

"Well, well," she said, poking at her with her foot. "Where've you dropped in from I wonder? Where've you come from?" she hissed at her, bending down so Helena smelled her breath, foetid and hot from the rabbit.

"She's blind as a bat wherever she's from," said Iris. "She couldn't see one of Seamus Bogolan's traps back there, and you know they're as plain as a pikestaff for anyone with half a brain. We found her lying at the bottom of it. She's not come easy. We'd to carry her in the sack and she's been rolling around but she's settled now. She tried talking to the boy but we put a stop to that."

"I don't like rollers and I don't like mischief-makers," said Eglantine in that voice of hers. "Have you got her to say anything yet?"

"Let me out, let me go. That kind of thing. Nothing useful though. You want her to talk? We can make her talk, if you want her to."

"No, I don't want her to talk and I don't want you to either. Now sit quiet, the lot of you, and let me think a bit." The three witches sat down dutifully and fell silent. Eglantine was the boss, that was for sure. Helena waited in dread. There was nothing to hope for, judging from how she'd torn away the flesh of that rabbit and crunched up the bones, the stink of her breath, the arrogance of her, the curt way she spoke to her fellow witches.

Eglantine said nothing for a long, long time. The embers began to die in the fire. Finally she stood up and spoke.

"I know you've probably been planning how to share her out. Well, maybe you'll have to wait a while to get your tidbits. This is how I see it. She's fallen in Bogolan's trap. The law says she's his, not ours, even if it was us that found her. We can take no notice of it, I grant you that. But things are haywire at present and I think we can do better than just slice her up and make a good meal out of her. We'll be better taking her over to Bogolan and doing a bit of bargaining there. You've not seen what I've seen. I've been out watching. Bogolans will beat the other lot if they go on the way they did today. We need them as allies and we're not going to have them if we up and steal the best catch anyone's seen in years. So, put the brake on your broomsticks my ladies, and tighten your belts. This lovely specimen's going with us over to his place, and so's the boy. We can throw him in as an extra. Bogolan will like that."

The three listening said nothing. From the set of their shoulders and the expressions of sullen discontent that crept over their faces it was obvious to Helena that they didn't agree with their boss. But presumably previous experience had taught them that when Eglantine spoke, it was better to fall in with instructions than flout them. All she could feel was relief in the moment. As things stood any delay was a blessing. One of them tossed sand on the dying fire. The other two came and stood over her. Lily gave her a half-hearted kick in the ribs and said in Eglantine's direction, "Well if we've got to lug her all the way there, mind and make sure we get the bits we like. Seamus Bogolan's partial to liver but he isn't keen on eyes."

"And he's no use for the skin," said Violet bending down over her so Helena could see too how horribly pitted and scarred the witch's cheeks were underneath a thick layer of paint. In her excitement the witch began panting like a dog and dribbling gobs of spit from shrivelled lips onto Helena's scarf and chest. She stretched out a clawlike hand and stroked Helena's face in a dreamy kind of way, again and again. The touch of it was loathsome but no matter how hard Helena shook her head, wriggled and squirmed to get away, the hag went on doing this for some moments, as if she loved her.

"Feel that Lily," she beckoned the other witch over. "She's old for a human but she's got cheeks as soft as thistledown."

"I'm deadly poisonous to witches though. You try wrapping my skin round your body and you'll die of strangulation in seconds. Ask Walter Bogolan what he knows about me and my powers." Helena spat the words out.

Eglantine marched across to them. "You got her talking? Well, don't. Put something in her mouth. Shove her back in the sack and string her up. I'm not for going all that way with a gabble of noise at my side."

"She's saying she knows young Walter Bogolan. She's a strange one and no mistake," said Lily and she tied a disgusting bit of rag round their captive's mouth so there was nothing further she could say.

Chapter 6

Helena's journey from that camp to the giants' headquarters was a confusion of nausea, pain and terror: the choking gag on her mouth, the stench of the sack, a searing ache in her bent back, agonising cramp in her feet that curled her toes and grabbed her calves in a vice.

It was almost light by the time they stopped. They pulled her out of the sack and propped her up. She had no means of supporting herself because her hands were tied fast so she kept slipping sideways. Every time she did one of them, but mostly Lily, kicked her back upright like a stuffed doll. On instructions from Eglantine, Violet poured water into her mouth, so fast she couldn't swallow it and it dribbled down and made a wet patch on her front and in her crotch. Once the drinking ordeal was over she collapsed flat out on the sand, taking deep breaths of cold, clean air into her lungs.

The witches had arrived at the foot of what looked like a sheer mountain. In front of them was a heavily barricaded wooden gate, roughly the height of a two-storey building. It appeared to open directly into the rock face behind it. She watched Eglantine go up and bang on a small door set into the big one. It opened immediately and the witch went inside. That left Helena, the boy in the cage and the junior witches. Her bag was there too, she noticed.

At first she was so thankful to be flat on the ground with all the weight off her shoulders and arms that she wanted to do nothing except lie still and watch the light seeping back into the sky. She could see the hags better in the dawn. The yellowish glow they gave off had faded. They were all quite small, about Bridie or Amelia's height she reckoned, and as the light rose they looked as if they could be blown off like dandelion seeds, wraithlike, almost transparent. Eglantine reappeared. Helena heard her say that none of the giants were about yet but she'd left a message for Seamus Bogolan and she'd handle him on her own. The three hags vanished at that, as if taken off in a sudden gust of wind.

For a while there was no noise at all, only the gradual brightness of the rising sun sweeping across the land, sketching out humps and hollows. Helena lay there in the dust thinking wistfully of her last visit, the desert storm and how the very next day as she'd left again, the harsh landscape had begun its brief blooming: millions of tiny shoots poking up to the light and softening the grey and brown. There wasn't a shoot or a leaf to be seen where she was now lying but, close up to her eyes, an exquisite, miniature universe of crystals of pinks and ochres and greys.

She might well have fallen asleep from exhaustion and shock but she saw Eglantine get to her feet. Instantly, like a prisoner in a torture chamber, Helena readied herself once more. The witch didn't come towards her though. She went and got Helena's bag, opened it up and began pulling things out, the clothes, the first-aid kit, and the knitting wool and needles. She stopped and Helena heard her give a snort. She walked over with the needles in her hand and looked down at her. Helena shrank away, expecting to be poked, or worse. Nothing of the sort however. Eglantine tipped Helena's head back with one bony hand and stared at her. Helena saw a pair of dreadful dark eyes fringed by long lashes, a small, straight nose and a cruel mouth. The smell of her was overpowering.

"As I thought," the witch said, letting her hand drop. "You're one of Purselain's. It could only be a Purselain spy who'd be daft enough to bring her knitting with her. What are you making?"

A question – a perfectly sensible question! Violet had taken the gag off Helena's mouth to let her drink and hadn't bothered to put it back on, so she could easily have answered but she didn't trust herself to speak normally to the flesh-eating creature looming over her. Eglantine leant down again.

"You lost your tongue? I asked you a question. Now, I'll try again, one more time," and she spaced out the words, as one might if speaking to a foreigner. "What – are – you – making?"

"A jersey, for the child," Helena forced herself to answer. "He's freezing cold in that dreadful pen you've got him locked in. He needs food and clothes and comfort, not being caged up like a wild beast."

"He's not feeling anything for now," Eglantine said, looking across at the cage. "He's fast asleep. Sun'll warm him up soon enough and we aren't starving him. You don't starve a goose you're fattening for the kill. It doesn't make sense to do that, does it?"

"I was knitting jackets for hens before," Helena said, deciding this last remark was deliberate provocation and best ignored. "That's how I met Mrs Purselain."

"I believe you," the hag said and to Helena's amazement she squatted down on her haunches as if for a proper chat. "I believe you because I know Amelia Purselain well enough to know it's exactly the kind of fool she'd take under her wing."

"You mean you know her personally?" There was no answer to this from the witch. "If you don't mind me saying," Helena said, thinking she should try and keep the creature talking, "you sound a bit like Mrs Purselain. You've got the same kind of voice. I remember the first time I met her I was surprised by her voice, very melodious and strong. Yours is like that too."

"It's not as strange as you think." The hag's face stretched in the hint of a smile as she said this. "We come from the same line."

"That I don't believe," Helena retorted. "I asked Mrs Purselain if she was a witch and she was furious. I don't believe she was lying."

Eglantine sniggered. "No she wasn't lying. Amelia's no witch but she's got powers. You know she's got powers. How else would you be here? And she got them from her ancestors. She doesn't like to be reminded who they were but she knows. There's none of the witch in her, in the way you mean though. She can't stand the sight of meat. She's a rabbit that one but a clever one." At that she got up and went back to the bag and repacked it with everything she'd taken out. Having done this she walked over to the cage and pushed it round so that it was facing away from the sun, and from Helena. There was no sound from the child. Then she sat down on her rock again, eyes closed, and remained like that without speaking for twenty minutes or more.

Had Helena not been so riven with anxiety and pain, she would certainly have been thinking hard about what the witch had said about Amelia Purselain and their common ancestry. But the sun was getting hotter and hotter every minute. The flies were buzzing round her face, settling there and crawling about however much she tried to flick them away. Sweat was forming under her armpits and trickling down between her breasts. There was dirt in her hair, under her nails, even up her nostrils. The ties were biting into her wrists and her hands were beginning to swell badly. Something had to be done, and quickly, if she wasn't to pass out again. No more fainting away, she told herself firmly. Fainting was not an option. There was no knowing what might become of her if she did. She must try and get Eglantine's attention. She tried a quiet cough – it had absolutely no effect.

She pushed herself up on one elbow and said a little louder, "Excuse me." Still nothing. Did witches sleep sitting up? "Will you loosen these ties before my hands drop off!" This time she'd shouted as loud as she could.

Eglantine jerked round with a start and looked across at her.

"Did you say something?" she said.

"Yes I did. I asked you to undo these ties round my wrists. They're making my hands swell up. I can't go anywhere so I don't see why you have to keep me tied up like a pig for market. I'm dying of the heat. I need to get into the shade."

For a moment Helena thought the witch was going to stay sitting right where she was, enjoying the spectacle of her misery. But she came across and pushed her over so she could see the blue-red welts round Helena's wrists and the way her hands had puffed up like blown-up paper bags. She unsheathed a knife she had in her belt and with one expert gesture she sliced through the ties. Then before Helena could ask her to free her ankles as well, she leant over and cut through the cords round them. Helena pulled herself onto to her knees and forced her stiff old legs back into service.

"There's water in that jug," the witch said, pointing to the shady side of a rock. "Drink if you want but keep away from that cage. You go anywhere near it and it'll be the last thing you do. You'll be rat or lizard before you can blink. I'm warning you."

Helena nodded. She helped herself to water, squatted behind a rock to relieve her bursting bladder and found a place out of the sun. The witch took no interest in any of this but went back to the door and banged on it again. This time a face appeared at a hatch high up. She shouted up at it. "I'm not waiting much longer. If Seamus Bogolan doesn't want to see me I'll take my prizes elsewhere."

The face disappeared again and shortly after there was a scraping sound. Someone was pulling the door wide open.

"Get up," Eglantine barked. "We're going in."

"What about the child?" Helena asked. "Isn't he coming too? Can't he come out of the cage? He won't run away either."

"Leave the boy out of it," she snapped. "He's none of your business. Now get a move on or you'll be back in the sack like before and I'll be dragging you over the stones – and pick up that bag. You can take your rubbish with you."

So it was that, reunited with her possessions, Helena limped into the headquarters of the Bogolans on her own two feet.

Chapter 7

The entry hall was as big as an aircraft hangar, echoing and empty. As they went deeper the walls began to glisten with moisture. Down at Helena's height it was all gloom and shadow but high overhead she could make out straggling clumps of moss, stains of damp growth round the candle sconces that were spaced at intervals along the way. There was a smell of earth and wet rock and the air was pleasantly cool after the heat of the sun.

They left the first hall and passed through one craggy passageway after another, some piled high with dry brushwood, others with blocks of stone stacked neatly all along their length. Helena hobbled over the worn slabs, trying to ignore the pain in her legs, and keeping as close as she could behind Eglantine and the giant who had opened up the main door. He'd picked up an enormous brand when he let them in. It was giving off clouds of smoke and, every now and then, showers of sparks and lumps of burning fibre which she had to dodge as she went. Its light cast his shadow back over them, jigging and swaying in time to his steps. He'd said nothing since he let them in and Eglantine didn't seem bothered to talk to him either. Hadn't one of the witches mentioned how she liked peace and quiet? Judging by the easy way the witch was following the giant it looked as though this wasn't the first time they'd brought Seamus Bogolan and his brothers something to bargain with.

Helena was beginning to think the trek through those barren spaces would never end when she saw, some twenty yards ahead, down a straight stretch of corridor, another huge door, barred like the outer one. The giant nodded at Eglantine.

"They're through there," he said. "Do you want the tiddler in with you or do I put her in the pond till you're ready?"

Helena held her breath, waiting for Eglantine's decision.

"Put her with the boy," the witch said after a moment. "Give her a stool to sit on, if you can find one small enough. She's old for a human and she's got aches and pains."

"I'll see what I can find," he said and he reached over behind Eglantine and plucked Helena off the ground. This time she didn't shout and wriggle as she had done with Walter Bogolan. Protest was pointless as things stood. He tucked her and her back-pack under his arm, like a mother might carry a naughty child, and the last thing Helena saw and heard, before he turned down a passage that led away from that central alley, was Eglantine banging on the door.

The passageway they were now in was much lower than the one leading from the outer door. From time to time he swung to one side or bent his head to avoid the rocks that jutted down or poked up from the floor but he didn't alter his pace as he did so and walked briskly as if these obstacles were familiar to him. All the while he hummed softly to himself. Helena was lulled into a doze by the rhythm of his steps and the vibrations in his chest from his humming but she came wide awake with a jerk when he stopped. He propped his smoking brand up against the wall. She felt him push open a door. He stepped inside. The door immediately swung back hard behind him. The giant dropped Helena and her bag down in the dark.

Aghast at being tossed aside like this, Helena grabbed hold of the cloth of his trousers and clung to them. The ordeal of the witches and the journey to the giants' castle was as nothing compared to this: trapped in the belly of a mountain, the wrong side of a door so heavy that none but a giant could move it, and surrounded by air as black and solid as rock. Panic had its icy fingers round her throat again. She clutched the trousers with one hand and raised the other in front of her face. She knew she'd moved that hand – she'd felt herself do it – but in the absolute dark of that space it was if it had ceased to exist.

"Don't leave me." Her voice came out like the bleat of a frightened lamb. "Please bring a light." She felt him try to brush her hand off him but desperation made her grip him even harder and cling like a toddler to his leggings, looking up in the inky blackness to where his face must surely be.

"Leave me the light if you're going, or prop the door open. I give you my word I won't go anywhere. Don't leave me in this darkness."

Right at that moment the door swung open and another man – much, much smaller than the fellow who had carried her in – was framed in the dim light of the passageway. He was pushing a big barrow on which was balanced the cage with the boy in it. And, the relief of it! Helena saw there was a light, a proper oil lamp sitting precariously on top of the cage. The door closed again as he stepped inside but he brought with him that weak but blessed pool of light from the lamp.

The giant had dumped her down in the centre of an expanse of flat, smooth rock. Behind them the floor sloped upwards into a jumble of rocks and blackness. On the opposite side was a sheer wall which appeared to stretch limitlessly into the darkness overhead. At end of that wall and barely discernible in the light of the oil lamp, there was what looked like a huge, lidded barrel. The distance between the door and the barrel was fifty feet at least. The air felt different from the passageways, intensely cold and damp. The man set the cage down and bowed to the giant.

"Get a seat for this woman to sit on," said the giant bending down to him. "And bring another lamp. She's scared of the dark." He gave a chuckle. "Oh, and a cover while you're about it. She can't go far so you can put something against the door to hold it open." Helena breathed a sigh of relief. For one moment she had thought the barrel was the pond he'd mentioned to Eglantine. Apparently not, however. She was even to be allowed to sit down.

The man bowed again without speaking. He wheeled the barrow out but brought it back almost straightaway, this time with an enormous stone in it which he tipped out and wedged against the door. As soon as he'd done that he and his barrow disappeared once more into the depths of the corridor. Outside the door the smoke from the smouldering brand curled round and spread about in a lazy, indecisive way and, seeing this, Helena judged there was no airway to the outer world anywhere nearby.

"I'm off," said the giant once the door was wide open. "I'll be back to collect you when they're ready for you. Sim will keep an eye on you meantime."

"Is that the name of the man with the barrow?" she asked.

"That's him," he said.

All this time there had been no sound from the little boy. Helena waited until she was sure the giant was out of sight and she went over to the cage. He was inside but curled up so tight in one corner it was hard to believe he was a living child at all. She tapped gently on the roof.

"Be-Be, it's me, Helena, the woman the witches caught in the trap. I'm going to try and open the door and let you out." He didn't move. She lifted the lamp down so that the light shone directly into the cage itself and began to fiddle with the fastenings on the door. She was so intent on this that it was some minutes before she realised that Sim had come back and was watching her from the doorway.

"You're wasting your time," he said. "You'll not be opening that any time soon. Spell-bound he is. He's only coming out if she wants him out."

"Don't you believe it," she said, although her heart sank hearing this. "I've spells of my own at least as powerful as any of hers."

"Oh sure. That'd be why you've come all the way without a fight, eh?" he said sarcastically.

Helena ignored this and went back to the knots as if she knew what she was doing. He gave a 'huh' of contempt and threw down a log, which he evidently thought would do duty as a stool, then he went back out and dragged in an enormous woven carpet which he dumped in a heap at the door, all this without another word. Helena hauled it over to the cage and the oil lamp. When she looked round he had disappeared. She was busy rearranging the heavy carpet to make a cave of warmth she could slide down into when the passage lightened again, first shadows jumping and jigging on the stones and then the man himself, carrying a second oil lamp which he placed beside the log.

"That's your lot," he said. "Don't be thinking you can find your way out. You start climbing up those rocks and you'll end up dry bones and dust."

"How do I call you if I need you?" she asked. "That giant, whatever his name is, said you were to keep an eye on me so you'd better not go too far away or he'll not be pleased."

"You mind your own business," he said. "I know what I'm doing. I'm Lurgan Bogolan's right-hand man. I don't take orders from rubbish like you."

It was almost comical the way he puffed out his chest as he said this. He was right about breaking open the cage though. After ten or more minutes, during which the child barely stirred, she was no further forward than when she began. As fast as she managed to undo one complicated knot she found another just the same underneath it. She sat back in frustration. What else could she try? Should she take the glass off the lamp and try and set the thongs alight with the bare flame? It seemed improbable but it looked like the only other resource to hand. Sick at heart, her fingers aching from fiddling with the knots and her cuts and bruises throbbing, she stared blankly into the gloom.

"This won't do at all," she said, giving herself a shake. Her voice was lost in the surrounding emptiness. "There has to be a solution. I have to get you out, Be-Be. I know it." She looked more intently at the great barrel over in the far corner. It was so far off from her, so near that towering rock-face. "I don't want to go over there, Be-Be," she said, "but something tells me I have to. Wait here. It's stupid saying that," she added, glancing at the child curled up tight like a little hedgehog.

She picked up one of the oil lamps, stepped off the carpet and walked towards the wall. The light from the lamp made the drops of water along its fissures gleam and wink like diamonds. As she came right up to it she saw there were rusty shackles dangling at different heights all along it. She shuddered and looked back at the pool of light in the middle of the carpet. It wasn't so far off yet it felt quite out of reach, as if she'd crossed an abyss. The air smelled different on this side of the dungeon too, something more than the smell of damp and darkness.

"Can a smell be sinister?" she wondered. "I've never heard of such a thing." She grabbed hold of one of the shackles but immediately let it drop again with a cry. Blood oozed out of a cut in the palm of her hand and she felt sick.

"I pity you," she said loudly, "but whatever you are, you won't stop me." She wiped her hand down her trousers and held the oil lamp up higher so that it shone on the barrel. There was something hanging from a chain on one side – a cup of course, water for the guards or the poor souls who were chained to the walls. She felt the air thicken with the despair of those who had wasted away in that pit and she stamped her foot on the rock, an infinitely small sound in the blackness.

"I pity you, with all my heart. I pity you but I can't help you. I've come too late. I can help the child though, and I will. Please let me pass. I must see what's in that barrel." She shuffled across the rocks to the barrel, the lamp held out in front of her. She didn't want to let go of it but she could see that she would need both hands so she set it down carefully on the ground beside her and seized hold of the lid. The wood was unexpectedly warm and smooth under her hands. Standing on the very tips of her toes and peering beneath the lid she saw why. What looked like steam was rising gently off the surface.

Her arms were aching so much, she was on the point of letting the lid slam back down when all of a sudden the water began to tremble, like a kettle coming to the boil. Tiny, iridescent bubbles rose up and burst like stars. A whirlpool began to form at the centre. Out of it came a ribbon of crimson light which seemed to hover above the swirling water.

"It's like the wool in the back shop," she thought and she let go of the lid with her hands and leant further in so that it was resting on her head and shoulders. She dipped her fingers in the water, trying in vain to catch the ribbon of colour. It rippled across the surface then curled back round on itself to form a ring like an oval picture frame, and at the centre Mrs Purselain's face appeared, blurred as an image through a wet window-pane.

"Use the books and the wool, the books and the wool. Hurry now." The words were indistinct, like the hiss of water on a hot surface but Helena heard them. As fast as it had come the image wobbled and melted and the water went dark. She let the lid fall, picked up the lamp and turned back to face the carpet. It looked far away and very small. Despair gathered round her again, tight as the cloths round a mummy. She began to gasp for air. The flame in the lamp guttered and died. "Whatever it is intends to keep me here forever," she thought and she fell to her knees and crept along the floor, pushing the unlit lamp in front of her as she went. It took her several minutes before she finally reached the pool of light from the second lamp and felt the rough texture of the carpet under her hands. The cut on her palm was still bleeding but she could breathe more easily. She wrapped her hanky round her hand and pulled out the matches. A scratch, a flare of brightness and the quenched lamp was alight once more. She took the nursery rhyme book out of the rucksack and flicked rapidly through the pages. "Let me know when to stop," she whispered. "Show me the page. Please."

There it was, of course!

'One, two
Buckle my shoe
Three four,
Knock at the door,
Five, six,
Pick up sticks,
Seven, eight,
Lay them straight,
Nine, ten,
A big fat hen...'

But Mrs Purselain had said use the books *and* the wool? She felt in the bag and broke a length of yarn off one of the balls. She tied this through the bars keeping it in one hand and pressing the page flat with the other.

"This has got to do it. Listen," she said to the little heap of silence in the back of the cage and she began again, but this time with her own version:

> 'One, two,
> Little Boy Blue.
> Three, four
> Turn to the door.
> Five, six,
> Show me your tricks.
> Seven, eight
> Open the gate.
> Nine, ten,
> Come out of the pen.'

She gave a sharp tug on the wool as she came to the end of the rhyme. Two of the knots gave way with a dry crack. *"One two..."* she began again. This time before she reached the end of the rhyme there was a stirring in the back of the cage. The child rolled over as one does when asleep, and pushed on the door from inside. There was another sharp crack and it fell forward flat onto the ground. He crawled across it, bleary-eyed and bewildered.

"Boy Blue's my real name," he said, "but my aunty never calls me it. She says it's a daft name. She calls me Be-Be but I think that's just as daft."

"You'd rather I called you Boy Blue?" said Helena. The child nodded.

"I'm cold," he said.

Helena pulled one corner of the giant cover round his shoulders.

"Boy Blue's much better," he said and snuggled up against her. "It's nice being out of that cage," he added, like an after-thought. She tucked the carpet tighter round his shoulders and over her knees.

"We've got Mrs Purselain to thank for that," she said. "I would never have worked it out on my own. Now you're out, we stick together. We don't let them bully us or separate us. Agreed?"

He didn't answer and Helena saw his eyes were shut. Watching him she felt her own eyelids beginning to get heavy. She turned down the wicks on the lamps. The cavern shrank to a small pool of weak light at the carpet. She shifted the child gently to one side and made a nest for herself and her little companion inside the carpet. She would try to sleep like him. Perhaps an escape plan would come to her in her dreams.

It was the cold and damp that woke her once more, penetrating through the cover and into her bones. Boy Blue was a little warm bundle beside her, out of sight under the carpet and so small you'd have to know he was there to make out his shape. She rolled over, careful not to wake him, and lay facing the doorway. One oil lamp had burnt out but the other was still sitting in its pool of yellow light.

It seemed at first as though all was as quiet and dark as before but then the doorway began to show up more sharply. Someone was coming and whoever it was had a light with him or her. She pulled the cover up over her nose and feigned sleep. It was so dark they'd have to shine any light right on her face before they'd be able to tell whether she was awake or not. Through half-closed eye-lids she saw it was Sim in front but followed close behind by someone else about the same height. They clumped into the room and Sim put the light down on the floor by the door.

"You get the kid in the cage," he said, "I'll bring the woman."

The other man walked past her and stopped at the cage which was behind her back. She heard him shift it on the floor.

"It's empty. There's no-one in there," he said, as if he expected this to be the case.

"It can't be." Helena heard the alarm in Sim's voice and felt him tread hard on the bottom of the blanket as he came over to the cage. "Lurgan told me Mistress Eglantine – honoured is her name," he added fervently, "had spell-bound the kid out at the gate. Spells don't wear out that quick, not hers anyway."

"Look for yourself," said the second one. "He's not in there, not unless he's shrunk or his name's Tom Thumb."

From the next noise it seemed as though Sim must have tipped the cage on its back and looked down inside.

"By the powers!" he breathed. "It is too. It's her. She's done it. She said she could and I didn't believe her. Why would I? I never seen anyone break one of Mistress Eglantine's spells before." He was saying all this as if to himself. Whoever the other man was he was evidently following his own train of thought.

"Where's he gone anyway, the lad I mean? It won't matter if he's out the box as long as we bring him to them. But there'll be trouble if we can't find him."

"You stoopid or what?" said Sim. "You got any idea what this means? If this woman here can undo spells? The boy's not what matters, it's her."

The other man didn't answer and judging she'd be best to 'wake up' while Sim was still awestruck at her powers, Helena began a lot of exaggerated stretching and yawning and sat up slowly, making sure she kept Boy Blue well out of sight under the cover.

"What's going on?" she asked.

"What's going on is me and Norrie here is taking you along to the hall. You and the kid. So where've you hidden him? Where's he gone? If he's scarpered he's done for. I warned you about that."

Sim's chin was jutting out as if he planned to catch something on it. Attack was his best hope, he'd evidently decided, and who could blame him? He'd be lucky to end up no worse than a rat or lizard if 'Mistress' Eglantine found he'd lost half the booty she'd brought.

Helena sat very upright to look as impressive as possible and pulled the cover over her shoulders for greater effect. She hadn't put a comb through her hair or wiped the grime from her face since she fell in the trap. She was well aware she probably looked more like a mad old crone than the authoritative figure she wanted to appear. No matter. The important thing was to be as awesome and dictatorial as possible.

"I told you I would be taking him out of the cage," she began in her haughtiest tone. "Never doubt a woman's powers, Mr Sim, especially when a child is in danger. Next time, if there ever is a next time, remember you'll be safer assuming I'll do what I say than that I won't."

There was enough light for her to see that she was having the effect she hoped for. Both men were listening hard, so she continued, "The child is here beside me. I will wake him up but he stays with me outside his cage from now on. You will on no account try to lock him up again, do I make myself clear?" She waited. Sim nodded like a marionette. "When we go to meet Seamus Bogolan," she went on, "you will tell him that you returned to find I had released the child. If you don't I will. It will be obvious that something unusual has happened anyway because you certainly don't possess the powers to set him free. Do you understand?" He nodded again. "Right," she said and she shook Boy Blue gently and whispered in his ear, "Little Boy Blue, time to wake up."

The child opened his eyes and pulled the blanket back. Helena glanced up and saw, written on Sim's face, such an expression of relief that she knew, as if he'd said the words out loud, what he was thinking: perhaps after all he wasn't destined for a horrid end in Eglantine's stewpot.

Chapter 8

After the darkness of the dungeon Helena was nearly blinded when the door to the giant's hall was flung open to admit them. The light bounced off the walls festooned with shields and swords, the tables laden with brass goblets and silverware, and the giants themselves, many of whom were wearing gold necklaces like ships' anchor chains round their huge necks.

Wooden tables and benches stretched away, a hundred yards or more, to a raised platform at the far end. Sim and Norrie stood waiting for a signal to move forward into the open space. Three giants were seated on the platform, behind a very high table. On the right-hand side of the largest giant sat Eglantine.

The glare was hard on the eyes but the noise was worse, like the boom and shriek of a winter storm magnified a thousand times. Helena remembered Bert telling her that the expression 'raising the roof' was first used of a famous family of giants and how they meant it quite literally at the time. No roof could be raised in the Bogolan hall, seeing as there were several thousand tonnes of rock and earth above it, but because the noise couldn't escape, it ricocheted off the walls and shields, roaring and crashing about the small gathering at the entrance like a cornered beast.

No-one took any notice of them at first, all eyes being turned towards the high table. Eglantine had climbed up among the dirty dishes. She had her back to the hall and was showing off her party tricks. She engulfed her companions in what looked like a snow shower. The flakes turned into feathers which went from white to pink and finally to all the colours of the rainbow before they melted away. Helena was surprised at how pleasing it was, not at all the kind of thing she expected from the creature she'd watched bite into that rabbit leg.

Since they were apparently not to be called to account for themselves straightaway she began listening in on the conversations of the giants closest by. One of them, a morose-looking fellow with a beard like a rat's tail, was grumbling about how it was fine to celebrate a good day's fighting but it wouldn't put Brother Liam's arm back on, and if that witch was good for anything she'd be better bringing him round than shaking a pillow of coloured fluff all over the room. There were murmurs of agreement from one or two of the others. Helena recognised the name of the injured giant as the one who had been downed by the Svalbad warrior the evening of the great storm. There was no time to learn more however. At a signal from one of the serving men, Sim gave her a shove and they set off down the middle of the hall to the platform. Eglantine was now standing on her chair watching them.

"Who let the boy out of the cage?" she shouted as they came up.

"Saving your honour, Mistress Eglantine," Sim was down on one knee as he addressed her and Helena couldn't help feeling sorry for the man, "the woman you left us to guard used her powers to free him. We couldn't stop her."

"What do you mean you couldn't stop her? Stupid man! You left an axe so she hacked the bars apart? You're meat in my bowl if you did."

"Nay, Madame," said Sim, and Helena was relieved for him that he'd had the wit to bring the cage along too. He lifted it up so that the whole assembly could see that not a single bar was broken. "She opened the door."

The hall fell silent. For once Eglantine was at a loss.

"Well, well, Mistress Eglantine," said the largest of the giants whom Helena guessed was Seamus Bogolan, "A human that can undo one of your spells? I've not seen one of those before. Bring her up."

A giant seated below the platform lifted her bodily – an experience she was getting used to by now – and set her down in front of him.

"Someone find a chair for her to stand on," the senior Bogolan said. "She can't see anything from where she is and I can't see her either." It was true. The most Helena could see was the underneath of their table and the legs and boots of the three giants. A chair was found and she was again hoisted onto it so that she was now standing looking directly at the buckle on Seamus's belt and, above it, the plate-sized gold medallion on the chain draped over his chest.

"Good evening," she said, thinking it would do no harm to take the initiative, as she had done with Sim. "I hope you have all dined well. I have not eaten as yet but I'm sure the legendary hospitality of giants will remedy that soon. The boy also needs some food. Children need regular meals and bedtimes – I'm sure you agree."

He made a noise that sounded like distant thunder but which she took to be a chuckle and she knew that she was dealing with a giant who'd dined well and drunk a healthy measure of strong beer.

"Well, well." he said again, as if to gain time. "You've a talent or two more than most humans I've met and a tongue to match. Who are you? Where've you come from and what are you doing here?"

"My name is Helena Otterley. I've come from the same place as all humans come from and I'll be going back there again in due course, once I've restored the child to his aunt and made sure she has what she needs to look after him."

This was less pleasing to Seamus. He frowned.

"Who says you're taking the boy anywhere? He's mine. Mistress Eglantine's just given him to me."

"I think you'll find that's not the case. I mean, Mistress Eglantine," and the way Helena said 'mistress' could leave no doubt in a listener's mind as to what she thought of the title, "is mistaken. She can't 'give him to you' as you put it because he doesn't belong to her. If he belongs to anyone it's to his aunty. He has to go with me when I leave."

"When you leave, eh? And what makes you think you'll be leaving here any time soon?" He was growling now and Helena saw that she had stupidly overplayed her hand. She would have struggled to find a convincing answer on the spur of the moment but, whatever protective spirits had kept her and Boy Blue safe thus far, came to her rescue again. Further down the hall she heard a voice ring out.

"Brother Seamus, that's her. That's the cheeky one I was telling you about, the one I had in my paws that afternoon," and Walter Bogolan strode up the hall and came and stood below the platform. Helena held out both hands to him. He grasped them so hard she gasped.

"Walter Bogolan!" she said. "How nice to see you again. The circumstances are still not as I'd wish them to be but I'm glad you're here and I hope you will show the same magnanimity to me as a guest in your home as you did that afternoon we first met." She withdrew her hands and bowed to him.

"See what I mean?" said Walter, turning to Seamus. "She's never short of an answer this one."

Eglantine had remained silent throughout all this but now she spoke: "I'm not having it."

"What you not having this time, Mistress?" said Seamus, ignoring his brother for the moment.

"I'm not having her upsetting everything. She's better in pieces than making mischief like she's doing."

"What's the mischief, sister?" he said. "Undoing your spell? Likely that was a lucky chance. Stay your hand and hold your tongue. Let me hear more from the little lady with the big voice," and he waved at her to sit down again. Walter took his chance.

"She tells a mighty fine yarn, my brother. We're ready for a yarn aren't we? Let's hear her story before we decide what we're doing with her. She's a prize this one. It'd be a pity to squander such a treasure."

A yarn! Of course! She should have known. Bert had warned her. Why oh why hadn't she anticipated something like this?

Seamus was watching her closely. "You got a good yarn for us? You say you're hungry. Well, here's your chance, missus. Sing for your supper, if you don't want to end up in the pie."

"I am here under duress," she began, still hoping she might appeal to his better feelings. "I fell into your trap out there in the darkness and three very unpleasant witches took me captive. They carried me here, bound and gagged like a common criminal. Your men put me in a dungeon on a hard, cold floor. I haven't eaten or slept since I left my home. I am no enemy of the giants. I'm sorry, but I can't tell you a story in my present state. What I can do is read you a poem from my book and later, once I am rested and have eaten, I can entertain you properly."

He looked at her sceptically.

"All right," he said with a nod, "read to us."

"Boy Blue," she called, holding out a shaking hand. "Hand me up my bag. I need my books."

She took the book of nursery rhymes out, horribly aware as she did that there was nothing inside it that was going to satisfy her host, no matter how well he'd dined.

"This time I really am on my own," she thought, catching sight of Boy Blue's anxious face below her. She opened the book at random and held it out flat like a choirboy his score. "Here we are," she said and the tables fell silent. She glanced up at Walter who was watching her intently. He nodded as if to say, "I'm with you" and it came to her with a shock that she wasn't completely on her own at all. Down below, in the well of the hall, little Boy Blue was urging her on with every fibre of his being and looming over her like a kindly bear, was the curious Walter Bogolan.

"You can do this," she muttered under her breath and turned back to face Seamus. Holding the book out proudly, without a downward glance, she began her recitation.

A Sorry Tale of Three Witches

Three witches flew out
One wild, stormy night.
The moon was all hidden,
There wasn't a light.
They flew like the wind,
As fast as they could,
Hoping to get to the dark
Of the wood.

But the lightning flashed out
With a terrible crack.
Witch One hit the ground
With a mighty great thwack.
Witch Two looked backward
To see what she'd heard
And saw close behind her
A hideous bird.
She screamed in the claws
Of that swooping-low owl
And then she was gone
With an ear-splitting howl.
The third witch flew on
as fast as she could,
Still hoping to get
To the dark of the wood.
But the broom was all wet
It slipped from her hand.
She fell like a stone
On hard rocky land.
And that was the end
of those terrible witches.
They were out to do harm
But they finished in ditches.

Seamus Bogolan looked at her for a moment as if he expected her to go on.

"That's it?" he said, but his tone was mellow. "That's a good one. I like it. You hear that, Mistress? She doesn't like witches any more than I do, saving yourself of course, and she's got a rhyme to prove it. She's lively, this one. 'Finished in ditches' – that's neat!" And he brought his great hands together and began to clap. The rest of the company took their cue and the hall erupted in a storm of applause that threatened to bring the shields on the walls crashing to the ground.

Eglantine was not giving up though. There was no applause from her, just a look which made Helena quail inside.

"Look at her,'" the hag snarled. "What is she? A lump of old mutton, like string unless you boil her for hours. She's mine. I brought her here and I'll take her away the same."

Seamus bristled at this but before he could even open his mouth Walter jumped in.

"No-one's taking anyone out of here without we say they can. She's under our roof. She fell in Brother Seamus's trap. It seems to me if she's anyone's she's his."

"Just what I was about to say," said Seamus, pleased to be supplied with such a ready retort by his young brother.

"I'll turn her into sausages before I let her go," hissed the witch.

"Don't you be trying any funny stuff in here," said Seamus. "Our old da set rules about magic and I've never seen any reason to change them. Entertainment's one thing, mucky magic's another. Giants like their meat caught and killed the proper way. You touch one hair of her head and you'll not be sitting at my table again. Take her away and give her some food," he said motioning to one of the attendants. "See she's got a bed and a light." He pointed a very large, stubby finger in Helena's face. "I'll hear your proper story later and it'd better be a good one."

Walter reached out to lift her off the chair.

"Wait a minute, Walter," she said. "Thank you, Seamus Bogolan, for your fairness. I will do my best to entertain you well. There is one other thing before I leave you though. I must take the child with me. He needs food more than I do."

"I told you!" cried Eglantine, bouncing up again. "She's trouble. You give her one thing and she'll want the rest."

"Hold your tongue, you pesky creature," said Bogolan, clearly out of patience with his ally. "The boy's no use to us."

"If that's so, let me have him back," said Eglantine. "Give him to me and I'll leave you now."

"No, I don't think I will," said Bogolan. "I think we'll do just as the woman asks. Take the pair of them away."

Walter didn't need telling twice. He snatched Helena off the chair and slung her high on his shoulders, grabbed Boy Blue and the bag and marched down the hall to cheers from the giants.

This time they went in a different direction and there were proper carpets on the floors and throne-like chairs placed here and there. Walter said nothing until he set them down in a huge room lit by chandeliers. There were two sofas at one end and a table in the middle.

"They'll bring you food and covers," he said. "You can climb up on those sofas and rest. You better not sleep too long though. Brother Seamus'll want a yarn as good as you gave me. If he doesn't get it he's like enough to go with Eglantine. Moody my brother is. Unpredictable."

"I understand," Helena said, walking over to the sofas and trying unsuccessfully to hitch herself up onto the seat. Walter came over and lifted her up. She looked at him.

"My stories aren't going to satisfy him, Walter. I think you know that as well as me. I know what was going on in there. Your brother doesn't like Eglantine but he doesn't need to like her. He just needs what she and her like can do: fly through the air, see at night. I know you've lost one of your best men – your brother I think. Seamus will be under pressure to win the war without more injuries like his."

"How d'you know about Liam?" asked Walter.

"I have my ways," she said. "Walter, I need your help. I meant what I said when I told you that afternoon. I have no quarrel with giants, but I must get this child back to his aunty. You've got to help us get away."

"You've taken leave of your senses, woman," Walter said.

"Really I haven't," she answered, and there was no mistaking the pleading in her voice.

"I can't help you with anything that goes against Seamus," he said grumpily. "Do as you're told. Find a good yarn and you'll maybe stand a better chance of bringing the boy out alive." He went as if to touch her cheek, then drew his hand back. "Helena, eh? Pretty name that."

Helena and Boy Blue were alone again. Food was brought but neither of them could manage more than a mouthful. Helena kept looking at the little figure perched beside her on the sofa. How could she hope to save him? The only stories that she could think of all had terrible endings for giants. She was sunk in misery when all of a sudden the door swung open again and Walter reappeared. He was carrying a great flagon of beer which he took a swig of, before setting it down on the table.

"You still here?" he said lurching slightly, so she realised this was one flagon of many that he'd drunk while she'd been racking her brains and finding nothing. "You've no sense after all. There isn't a thing we can do if you take yourself off, back to where you come from. Eglantine can't get at you in here, so what's stopping you?"

"It's not Eglantine that's stopping me," she said, kneeling up on the sofa. "How can I go back when I can't take the boy? He can't come with me back there, so I can't go."

Walter looked at her, evidently baffled by the logic.

"He isn't yours though," he said at last. "You can leave him here fine. He's not your business."

"He is my business, Walter. It's like you helped me in there. He's in the same mess as me. You know I can't just look out for myself. If you were in my shoes you'd do exactly the same."

"Are you married?" he said.

"No, I'm not as a matter of fact," she replied, wondering what was behind this sudden change of subject. "I don't have to worry about a husband, only about the child."

"That's fine, so we could get married," he said thoughtfully, running his fingers through the black curls of his beard. "I could make you my wife." He nodded his head as if he'd found the answer. "How old are you anyway, Helena Otterley?"

"I'm sixty-three at my next birthday," she said, hoping her face didn't show what she thought of the idea of being wedded and bedded by Walter Bogolan. "I'm an old woman."

"You sure?" He took a lock of her dark hair between his fingers and studied it closely for a moment. "Old humans are supposed to have grey hair, aren't they? There's none there that I can see. I reckon you're not being straight with me. It wouldn't matter anyway. Giants are in their first youth if they're sixty, or seventy. I'm a hundred and twenty and I'm good for a long time yet. Seamus is near enough two hundred."

"Yes, but I'm not a giant. Humans don't live that long. I'd be no use to you as a wife. And I am telling the truth about my age. It's genetic why my hair hasn't gone grey. Some humans go grey at twenty and some never go grey."

"Genetic, eh? See, that's what I mean. You know things. You're clever. You could teach me, and you tell good stories. You'd keep me entertained. I've a soft feather bed and a fine pile of gold all my own. There's plenty would like to share a bed with me."

She laughed in spite of herself. Walter looked upset at that. "You've no cause to mock. You're in a tricky situation. You'd be better with me than in a pie."

"I'd be better with you, whether there's a pie or not," she said quickly. "I wasn't laughing at you Walter. I laughed because I wasn't expecting you to say that. I am really touched by your offer but there are all sorts of difficulties. I'm not big enough for a start. I'd get lost in your bed and you'd get cross at me for disturbing you. It would be like sharing your bed with a large mouse and I know giants don't care for mice. I tell you what, give me a little time. Let me think about your proposal. Come back in five minutes and I'll give you my answer. Will you do that?"

"Five minutes. That's all you've got," he said. He lurched to his feet and left the room.

When he returned she was ready. This time she stood up on the sofa.

"Here's what I've decided," she said. "I'm driving a bargain with you, Walter, but it's a fair one. You save me from having to entertain your brother, get me and the boy out of here safely and I'll marry you, not straightaway but as soon as I've done what I have to do." He looked at her in disbelief.

"You still going on about that? I can't get you out and that's an end of it."

"You can, Walter. Really, you can and it needn't bring you any trouble to do it. You've seen I have special powers. You can tell Seamus that when you looked in the room it was empty. You can say you went looking for us before you raised the alarm."

He scratched his beard thoughtfully again. "And if I do that, you'll marry me?"

"If you do I'll marry you, but only after I've taken the child to safety."

"How do I know you'll keep your promise?"

"Because I'll give you my word. That's what we do where I come from."

"Where's your word?" he said.

"In my book of course," she answered and opened the nursery rhyme book. He took the book from her and held it awkwardly. "That's it there?" he asked, pointing at the print.

"That's it, right there," she answered. "Shall I give it to you?"

"Yes please," he said and passed the book back to her. She tore the page out, folded it and handed it to him.

"That's a bond between us Walter, but it won't hold if you play me false."

He took her hand in his great paw and knelt down so they were almost face to face.

"I like you Helena Otterley," he said. "I liked you when I first met you and I like you more meeting you again. I haven't got fine words but I mean to do right by you."

"So, hide me in your knapsack, put the child in your pocket and let's be gone before our plans come to nothing, dear Walter," she said. He went as if to pick her up but she stepped back. "I trust you Walter but I must see you put Boy Blue in. The child first, then me." He nodded, picked up the boy and slid him into the breast pocket of his waistcoat. Next he lifted her off the sofa and right up to his face. He looked her hard in the eye but she held his gaze without blinking.

"I like you, and I trust you, Helena Otterley," he said and thrust her down in the depths of the pouch at his waist.

Chapter 9

Hidden in Walter's pockets, Helena and Boy Blue were transported back along the corridors and out to the gate. They heard him speaking to the guard and the screech of the door across the rock. They registered the change in the air and the sounds that reached them through the cloth. Now they were back in the desert the steady thud of his steps across the land told them both that Walter was carrying them far away from his mountain fortress. At last he stopped. He pulled Helena out of his pocket, like a schoolboy might a pet mouse.

"This is where you want to be, isn't it?" he said. Helena looked about her and spotted the dark shape of the Spratts' house in the distance. There was no light at the window but the sight of it was enough to make her want to laugh and cry at the same time.

"Oh yes. This is it! Wonderful! Put me down please, Walter," she said because she was still high in the air in the palm of his hand. "And get the child out too."

He pulled Boy Blue out of his waistcoat and placed him gently on the ground but he held onto her.

"I'm not wanting to let you go," he said. "I've an idea I'll not find you again. I don't want that."

"Walter, don't doubt me now," she said. "You have my word. Let me do what I have to do and the rest will follow." He sat down heavily on the sand, crushing small bushes like tufts of grass. Helena was now standing up, balanced on the slope of his thigh and still held fast by in his hand.

"Don't be sad," she said looking up at the expression in those dark brown eyes. "You've been so kind to us."

"Give me something of yours – something else as well as your word," he said. Helena didn't hesitate. She undid her scarf and tied it carefully round the wrist of his left arm.

"There," she said, "keep that. That'll remind you of me. It's what we call a 'keepsake' in my world. It's different from when someone gives their word but it's a good thing for one person to give to another, if they like each other."

"Do you like me?" he said.

"Like you? Of course I like you," she answered, meaning it with all her heart. "You've done something good and kind. Every human loves a man who is good and kind – why would we not love a good, kind giant too?"

"Liking's good enough," he said. "Giants aren't much use at love. We're a rough lot, you'll have seen that, but we aren't all bad. It's not me that eats humans," he added quickly, as if she'd accused him.

"No, I know it isn't, Walter," she said. "You wouldn't have saved us from ending up in your brother's pie if you ate humans. You have kept your side of the bargain. Now you must go back before they miss you. Tell them you've been out looking for me because you found I'd vanished. And I must get on my way too. You will hear from me before long. I promise."

"I ought to give you something too," said Walter. "A keepsake like you call it."

"I suppose so but it doesn't matter if you can't. It'd probably be too big for me to carry anyway."

"No, I can," he said. "I've got the very thing and it'll fit in your bag too. Here, take this." He pulled out a length of string as thick as her finger from inside his shirt. Tied to it was a wide-necked glass bottle about eight inches high with a stopper in the top. It was full of what looked like brown dust. He shook it and Helena saw glints of brightness swirling round among the brown. "It's grains of gold from where we're going to dig. I've been keeping it safe but you can have it."

"Are you sure you want to part with something so precious?" Walter thrust the bottle at her so she took it from him and put it in the outer pocket of her back-pack. "Thank you Walter. I'll keep it safe for you. Now go, quickly."

"How do we say goodbye?" he said, and she heard again the sadness in his voice.

"We often give a person we like a hug when we leave them," she replied. "I would like a hug, Walter, but it will have to be a gentle one or I'll be going on my way with broken bones."

He picked her up in both hands, tossed her in the air and caught her again, and rubbed her face gently against the surprisingly soft, black curls on his face.

"Go safely, Helena Otterley. I'll be waiting for you." She reached out and stroked his face. "Dear Walter Bogolan, you are truly a king among giants," she said at last.

He shook his great head. "I'm not a king and I've no wish to be one. I'll be your husband though, if you keep your promise." And with that he set her down.

He was out of sight in three bounding strides and there was nothing for them to do but get themselves into the safety of the Spratts' house. The night was half over; there would be light in the sky within a couple of hours. If they hid at the Spratts' house until daybreak they'd easily reach the boot in daylight. Not that getting to the boot would be the end of the ordeal but once they were with the children and Mrs Hubbard they'd be safer than out in the open desert.

There was a simple reason why the house was in darkness: there was no-one to open the door when she knocked. The stable was clean and empty of all food and bedding. Melodie had evidently not been there for some time. Helena tried the door but it was locked.

"They've gone away. We're going to have to break in," she said, picking up a stone.

"No, miss," Boy Blue said. "There's no need. See." He pointed to one of the upstairs windows which was open a crack at the bottom. Quick as a flash he pulled himself up onto the downstairs window ledge and onto the porch roof. He paused for a moment before leaping sideways to catch hold of the ledge outside the window. In two ticks he had the window up high enough to squeeze through and he disappeared. Moments later Helena heard him behind the door.

"Come round the back, miss," he said. "They've locked this one and there's no key but the back's just got a bolt on it."

They slept a little, from sheer exhaustion, but were both awake again when the sun began to send its first pale rays across the land. As soon as it was properly bright outside Helena shouldered her bag and went out of the back door, leaving Boy Blue to bolt it behind her and exit the same way he'd first entered. Satisfied that they'd left no evidence of their stay, for ordinary eyes at least, they set off towards the boot.

The weather was perfect – a sky flecked with clouds and a light wind to keep the temperature down and disperse the flies. Ordinarily Helena would have loved the walk but she was deep in thought, thankful that Boy Blue was running on ahead and that she had no need to talk to him. It wasn't only Spratt's stable that was bare of food and bedding. The kitchen cupboards were empty, the beds were unmade. It looked as though Mr and Mrs Spratt did not expect to be back for some time. The possibility had to be faced therefore, that she and Boy Blue would find a similar state of affairs once they got to the boot. She had been so focused on getting away from the fortress she hadn't once considered what they might do if there was no-one left at the boot. And it might be worse than that. All those crashes and thuds that had come through to her in the High Street could mean dead bodies, carcasses of children half-eaten by rats and hyenas. She stopped suddenly. If that was the case, she couldn't risk letting him see such a sight. She must take Boy Blue to safety first.

"What you stopping for, miss?" he shouted, looking back.

"I'm wondering if we're doing this the wrong way round. I'm thinking we should go and find your aunty first."

"But we're nearly there. Besides I don't want to go to my aunty's."

"What do you mean you don't want to go to your aunty's? That's where you belong. She'll be worried sick about you."

"She's probably got another boy already," he said dismissively. "And she isn't my real aunty. You don't need to worry about me, miss." He clambered up a rock a few yards off, and looked down at her from his vantage point. "I'm guessing you're thinking the same as me," he said from up there. "You're thinking they've gone already, like Spratt." She shaded her eyes and looked up at him.

"Something like that," she said.

"So there's only one thing to do." He jumped down lightly and beckoned to her. "Let's go and find out."

The boot loomed up ahead of them. They crept into it on tiptoe and both of them stood aghast at the scene of destruction that met their eyes. From the direction they'd come in it had been impossible to see what had happened. The boulder that had landed on it had staved it in at the heel. It had smashed on impact and chunks of rock were lying among the broken tables and benches. The curtain through to the back had been ripped down and the kitchen area was open to the sky. The floor was strewn with rubble, and the broken tables were covered with a thick coating of gritty dust. There were no dead bodies, no bats – no evidence of life at all.

The entry to the tunnel leading to the underground shelter was clearly visible because the inside was now as bright as day. Helena felt ill at the idea of folding herself down into that dark hole – it reminded her horribly of Seamus's animal trap – but she was determined Boy Blue wasn't doing it instead of her. There was no knowing what he might find.

"You stay here and keep watch," she said. "You'll hear better than me if anyone's coming."

She took her box of matches out of the bag and slid awkwardly into the gap. Spratt's team had cut steps and once she was past the opening she felt her way down each one in the dark. The tunnel was narrow and descended steeply. The walls felt cool and firm under her bare hands. Once at the bottom she struck a match. In the flare of it she made out a low-ceilinged space about twice as long as it was wide. There was no-one there and Spratt's team of child labourers had left nothing behind, not a shred of cloth, a spade or an empty box. The only occupants of the space were the stout branches, erect as sentinels along the length of it, holding back the weight of the earth overhead. A third match spurted briefly and she took in the marks of spades and pickaxes on the walls, the lumps of bedrock jutting up out of the earth here and there. "My goodness," she breathed, "what a labour, what a feat of engineering!" She climbed back up.

"We're too late, they've gone," she said as she emerged from the hole. "I really think the best would be for us to go and find your aunty. That's what I told Walter I was going to do."

"You mean you'd stay with me at my aunty's?" Boy Blue looked hopeful.

"For a bit. Then I'll have to go on."

"Go on where?" he said.

"To try and find Mrs Hubbard and the children. That's what I came for."

"You'll never manage it on your own," he said. "You don't know about the desert. You'll fall in another trap and the next time I won't be there to get you out."

Helena laughed at that. "You didn't get me out, Boy Blue. The witches got me out and I'm wise to them now."

"You're being silly," he said stamping his foot, "and we're wasting time. There's no point taking me to my aunty's. I won't stay. I'll run away. And when I do I'll find the children much quicker than you ever will. You need me," he said. "I'm much better than you at tracks. I know what to look for."

"I haven't the energy for a fight," said Helena. "I'm sure you're right that you know more about the desert but you've only just got out of a very bad situation and whatever comes next could be even more dangerous."

"I know," he said, "but if I'm in danger so are those other children. I know them a lot better than you do, miss. I play with them. They're the only friends I've got. I'm coming with you so there's no need to go looking for my aunty. What we have to do is make sure they haven't left anything we should take with us and then we can go."

Helena gave a sigh and squatted down so she could look Boy Blue in the eye. "You're very persistent," she said. "I give in. I just hope I'm doing the right thing."

He grinned.

They began to look under the broken furniture and in what remained of the kitchen to see if there was anything at all they should take with them. It seemed that, even if the boot-dwellers had left in a hurry, they'd done a thorough job of clearing the cupboards and packing up the clothes and blankets. It was Boy Blue who found the only treasure, although at the time Helena didn't see it in that light: a pointy black hat, very crumpled and dirty, the sort of hat that a child might wear for Hallowe'en.

"Where d'you get that?" she asked. She was sitting down by now, feeling worn out and old.

"It was in Ma Hubbard's cupboard, through the back. I know what it is too," he said proudly. "It's Belle's hat. She didn't have it on when she fell in the well. That's why she drowned. It was a good thing she did too – she was a nasty one."

"Belle's hat? Who is Belle, for goodness sake?"

"Like I said. She isn't any more. She's dead and drowned."

"But *who* was she?"

"Ding-Dong Belle was a bad, bad witch. I never saw her but I heard about her, from my aunty. She used to tell me Belle would get me if I wasn't good. I never knew she was lying until Ma Hubbard told me. We've got to take it with us. It maybe doesn't have any magic left but I don't see why Ma Hubbard would keep it if it was just any old hat."

Helena straightened the point of it and looked inside. "It looks perfectly ordinary to me," she said. "What kind of magic might it have?"

"It might stop them seeing us if we get under it. It might show us things we couldn't see without it... I don't know but there's no point leaving it here."

She had to agree and there was certainly nothing else useful that they could take away from the desolation of the boot. She had folded it into the bag and they were about to leave when Boy Blue put up his hand. His sharp ears had detected something.

"Someone's coming," he whispered. He pointed at the opening to the underground chamber and the two of them half-fell, one behind the other, down the steps. Helena could hardly breathe, so terrified was she that yet again they were about to be trapped by witches. What use was an old hat if Eglantine was roaming around out there? But from the thump of the footsteps it sounded more like heavy-footed men, possibly soldiers looking for booty. There was the crash of a bench being kicked over. Someone swore loudly. The footsteps went off towards the kitchen area. There was silence for a minute or two, then the crash of feet over the tables again and a man spoke, only a few feet above their heads at the underground entrance. Helena nudged Boy Blue hard in the ribs. Both of them knew that voice. It was Sim, Lurgan Bogolan's 'right-hand man', who'd brought them the cover and light in the dungeon.

"Nothing there. They've got it wrong. She's took it after all."

"What about down there?" the second man's voice – Norrie's of course. Boy Blue tensed at her side. If they came down the steps they were caught like lobsters in a pot. Sim spoke and, in the darkness of the bunker, Helena reached out and squeezed Boy Blue's hand.

"Down there? That isn't the kitchen. Instructions was to look in the kitchen."

"I know but she might have moved it."

"And how d'you propose we search down there in the dark? You a cat or you got a light in your pocket by chance?"

Helena could picture the sneer on Sim's face. There was silence from Norrie and after a moment Sim went on, "We've done what we came for, what we was told to do. We've looked and it's gone, if it was ever here. We tell them we did a thorough check of the premises. If they ask us, we say we did up above and down below. You follow me? We looked ev – ree – where."

"Yessir, ev – ree – where." Norrie repeated the words.

"Right, that's it. Job done." Sim sounded well satisfied. "Let's get moving." There was more scraping and banging but it was clear the two men were working their way out towards the toe hole.

Helena and Boy Blue let another hour pass before they risked climbing back up to the daylight. They inched their way out of the boot, Helena starting at every little noise. She felt brutally exposed and hopeless about which direction to go in but Boy Blue ran off straightaway behind some boulders beyond the boot. He came jogging back after a few minutes.

"I know which way they went," he said triumphantly.

"Sim and his friend?"

"No, no. The kids. Come on miss, we'll find them if you keep up with me. I'll show you." He pulled on Helena's arm. "They've took a wagon," he said, kneeling down in the dust, "but it's not the kids pulling it – look!" He waved a long, coarse hair at her. "That was on a twig over there," he pointed. "It's off an animal, something like a horse or a donkey."

"Melodie, of course," she said. "Bert's loaded Melodie up and taken her."

"Lucky for us," he commented. "We'll get on fine if we follow her."

"Boy Blue," she said, because she was so puzzled by this child by now. "How old are you? Do you know?"

"Of course I know," he said. "I'm six but it's like I'm an old six. I've been six since I don't know when."

"So why didn't you behave like an old six when you were locked up in the giants' fortress? I don't understand."

"I didn't have a choice," he replied. "I can do tracks and things out in the desert but I can't do witches. No-one can, unless they've got the powers. I haven't got the powers. That's why we make a good team. You've got one kind of power and I've got another."

Helena held out her hand. He looked at it for a moment as if he didn't understand. Then he took it and, side by side in companionable silence, they began following the marks in the sand.

Part 4

Chapter 1

While Helena was getting ready to defy Mrs Purselain and return to the desert, back at the boot the giants' war was bringing other problems besides the threats of falling boulders and airborne witches. Each night Mrs Hubbard had to send a group of older boys to keep watch on the cave where she kept her precious stores of grain and flour.

"Those giants are the least of it," as she never tired of telling Bert and Bridie. "They're not thieves like the scum we've got now, all the riff-raff what goes about with an army. Like rats in a barn they are, scavengin and thievin and leavin their germs and nastiness for others to clean up."

Bert saw what she meant. Camps were springing up all over the place. Nothing was safe. Every night you saw more fires flaring up in the distance and heard shouts – drunken shouts more often than not – and the clash of weapons as the night wore on. He registered this worrying change but, being a man not much given to rumination about things he couldn't control, he didn't stop to consider it deeply. Besides which, as he said whenever Ma Hubbard started up with her worries, he was far too busy to sit about thinking.

Each morning, once the boys were settled in their duties, digging or carrying out the soil and rocks from the underground shelter, he brought the cart round to the toe-hole and loaded it up. He was working his way in a westerly direction, towards a range of mountains, faint as a pencil-line on the horizon. Every new expedition meant estimating as best he could the length of a day's march for a group of small, under-fed children.

The last two journeys he'd had to sleep out under the stars, he was so far from the boot by the time the light went. He began taking one of the lads for company. It wasn't that he was scared to head off into the unknown. The further out he went, the fewer rascals he met on the way, but there was always the possibility of a broken axle or some other mishap that he would be hard put to manage on his own. He and Archy, since it was mostly Archy that Mrs Hubbard was prepared to send with him, got themselves into a routine and, had it not been for the underlying worry about attacks at the boot, Bert would have been content to go on indefinitely searching out clever hiding places and secret water holes, checking that the supplies already hidden away had not been tampered with and sitting high up on his cart while Melodie steered them over the rough ground.

Archy was a willing learner, easy with Melodie and quicker even than Bert to spot good places for their stores. Once they were out of sight of the boot they both agreed it was hard to believe there was a war going on at all. The sky stretched a limitless blue canopy over their heads and the only noises were the creak of the cart or the occasional hrrumping snort from Melodie shaking the flies off her eyes.

There had been no more rain after the great storm. The trickles and drips they found in the rock crevices couldn't possibly meet the whole cavalcade's needs, so they carried dozens of goatskin bags of water that had to be hidden away in as dark and cool a spot as could be found. They were aiming for that hazy range of mountains but not because they knew what they'd find once they got there. What drove them was the wish to put as much distance as possible between the children and the giants, once the time came to abandon the boot. This was something that Bert and the boy began to talk about after a while.

"It just goes on and on, doesn't it?" was how Archy began.

"It won't go on forever though," said Bert. "It isn't desert right to the end of the world even if it feels like it sitting here."

"I never said it was, but we'll be at the mountains before we get out of it. It's going to be hard on the little ones, walking like, in this heat, with no let up." Archy said this last bit almost in a whisper. Bert looked sideways at him and saw the tightness in that young face. He ruffled Archy's hair.

"We'll manage. We've done a good job with hiding our stuff so far."

The boy was only putting into words what Bert was thinking often enough. He'd even said it out loud to the others the evening before, measuring the distance he and Archy were covering every time they set out and knowing full well the miles between each of the precious refuelling places, as Spratt called them. Bert's pleasure at having safely stashed away yet another consignment of precious cargo was always dampened by these kinds of conversations.

The days passed. There were no further fights on the arena the other side of the hill. Spratt reported that the Svalbad had been seen hauling enormous lumps of wood and metal towards the boot, maybe to build digging equipment or some kind of weapon, like a canon. Anyway, they were a long way off. There was still time.

Bridie and Mrs Hubbard were busy from dawn till dusk, sewing other bags from pieces of sacking to hold food and clothes. It had taken Mrs Hubbard several days before she could bring herself to try on the skirt and jacket Helena had bought for her but once she did she kept them on. She never asked about Helena however, and Bert didn't offer anything. He tried not to think about Helena himself. It was like a sore spot, remembering how he'd not stood up for her in the shop, even though he knew Amelia was right.

The giant's war began to spread its poison into every nook and cranny, opening up old wounds that had nothing to do with gold, and rubbing small neighbourly disputes into full-blown hostilities. The desert groaned and heaved like a sick man, and crackled with fire. The tension was not only out there in the wilderness, it came right inside the boot and lodged itself like an unwelcome guest at the table where Bridie and Mrs Hubbard were sewing and packing and shouting at the children from early morning until the light went. Despite Spratt's best efforts to focus their minds on departure, neither woman was prepared to discuss it before the last sack had left on the cart. Bridie was adamant: if there was going to be a pitched battle somewhere near at hand while they were still getting ready to go, they'd have to go down in the shelter. What was the point of making it if they were never going to use it?

The thuds and bangs that woke Helena in her bedroom marked the first major outbreak of hostilities. The battle was waged five miles from the abandoned arena. There was no damage to the boot but the ground shuddered all night long. The next morning Spratt went out alone to the site of the battle, led to it by the vultures wheeling overhead, and the whiff of blood and rotting flesh.

There was no more fighting close by for the next three days and Spratt resumed his reconnaissance sorties with the boys. They were on their way back from one of these missions when they heard a new sound: in the far distance the rise and fall of a marching song. Spratt told the boys to get back and let Bridie and Mrs Hubbard know he was taking another look and he made off towards the singing.

The chorus got louder and clearer with every yard he covered, deep bass notes like drums punctuating a high-pitched, rhythmic chanting, not unlike the chirr of millions of cicadas.

"That's giants," he muttered. "But who's making that shrieky noise?"

By the time he got to the top of the hill he was ready, or so he thought, for anything. Nevertheless he couldn't help rubbing his eyes in amazement at what he saw. No more than half a mile off, towering up over the plain like a copse of giant redwoods were ten Svalbad warriors. They were leaning on their shields and chatting together, apparently quite indifferent to what was going on round about them. Pouring onto the plain from the north, gathering in drifts at their feet, was what looked to the naked eye like a plague of insects, a vast swarm of little purple beetles with white wings settling on every available patch of flat ground. He put his binoculars up and took a closer look. Dwarves! Thousands upon thousands of them, making a fine old racket as they marched.

"Well, bless my soul," he muttered, stroking his bald pate. "What a stroke of genius – an alliance of the very large with the very small, and both sides after the same darn thing!"

He studied the scene more carefully. What he had mistaken for wings were minuscule white banners each with a black crest, a crossed pick and shovel, at the centre. He trained the binoculars on the giants, bringing them sharply into focus. As he did so he saw a movement in the ranks of small men nearby. A passage was being made; the dwarf soldiers lining it were standing to attention. A golden chariot appeared from behind a rock. It was drawn by three very large mice each with a liveried dwarf at its head. There was only one person in the chariot, a dwarf with a flowing white beard wearing a gleaming helmet, a purple cape tossed back over his shoulders and an unsheathed sword lying across his lap. Spratt let go the binoculars in amazement.

"It can't be?" He looked again. "Yes it is. It's got to be. Grando, Dwarf of Yurtz!" he exclaimed. "Still alive, after all these years. Well, bless my soul. Wait till Mrs Spratt hears this."

The chariot drawn by the three grey mice made its way into the middle of the circle the giants had formed. The dwarf got out using his sword like a walking stick to help him, and unhooked his helmet, which he handed to one of the soldiers in his retinue. He waved an arm imperiously. Immediately the soldiers round about began pushing back, creating an enormous open space. Once the dwarf commander was satisfied he took a megaphone out from under his cloak and shouted something up at the giants. Spratt watched as the dwarf soldiers scattered and the giants lowered themselves to the ground to sit cross-legged round about this forceful little creature. The dwarf raised his microphone again and launched into a speech, not one word of which was audible to Spratt from where he was hiding. Several minutes passed while the little figure continued to harangue the giants. Spratt glanced skywards, at the angle of the sun. How many more hours of daylight? Not enough for him to worm his way down and listen in. Time to get back and report on developments. He began scrambling back down the rocks the way he'd come.

Chapter 2

"Where on earth have you been?" Bridie was at the boot hole as Spratt jogged the last few yards. She grabbed his arm. "We've been worried sick."

"I'll make a full report as soon as the children are in bed," said Spratt. Gruel was made and fed to the children who were sent down into the underground bunker still dressed in their daytime clothes. Spratt positioned himself at his favourite 'debriefing' place at the table end.

"Ready?" he said.

"We've been ready since you got back," said Mrs Hubbard with a trace of irritation. "What you seen that kept you all this time?"

"The reason we've not been hearing anything is that the Svalbad giants have been away getting reinforcements. A whole army as a matter of fact," he said, enjoying the expectant looks, the way the three of them were hanging on his words. He could hold an audience's attention just as well as that white-bearded old soldier out on the plain.

"More giants?" said Mrs Hubbard. "Where've they got more giants from?"

"Not giants," said Spratt, "the exact opposite in fact. I've been watching an impressive demonstration of the power of the very small. Can you guess who?"

The two women looked at him without speaking.

"You give in?" he asked, unable to contain his secret any longer. "I've just seen Grando Dwarf of Yurtz."

"You never!" said Mrs Hubbard, "It aint possible. Grando's dead. He's not been seen about for eons."

"Maybe," said Spratt, "but he's not dead. In fact he's very much alive and he and his army are setting up to do the Bogolans a deal of damage any time now."

"You sure it was really Grando? It could have been someone

dressed up like him." Mrs Hubbard still looked sceptical.

"Three reasons I'm sure," said Spratt. "First what he was wearing, second the way he took charge of those Svalbad giants. They sat down like a bunch of school kids when he told them to. But if that's not enough for you – his chariot. What do you think was pulling it?"

"Dogs? Rabbits?" said Bridie helpfully.

"No, not dogs or rabbits, or lizards for that matter," said Spratt.

"What then?" said Bridie.

"Was it mice by any chance? Three big mice?" said Mrs Hubbard. Spratt nodded. "Well I never. D'you get a look at their tails?"

"Put it this way, I would have if there'd been any to look at. And I'll tell you what else – every one of those mice was being led by a dwarf," said Spratt.

"That's it," Mrs Hubbard got up. "If it aint Grando himself it's his son, or his grandson more like. There isn't anyone else I know what drives around in a wagon with three blind mice and no tails in the harness. And what happened next?"

"I left while he was giving a pep talk to the giants. I couldn't hear what he was saying because I was too far away but I can tell you he means business. He's no more than six miles distant, with an army of ten thousand well-armed soldiers all about the same size as him but like a swarm of purple locusts spread across the plain."

"It's as well you went for a second look," said Mrs Hubbard. "We need to get movin."

"We can't go till Bert gets back," said Bridie who was having difficulty following all this. "He needs to take the rest of what we've got here and we won't know which way to go unless we follow him. How does this dwarf army change things?"

A question like this was what Spratt loved best. He cleared his throat, gave his jacket a tug and began, ticking each point off on his fingers.

"Point one: over the hill where the Bogolans were digging first is the only spot they know for sure there's gold. Point two: the Svalbad know they've got to get their hands on it. Point three: from what we know, Bogolans have outmanoeuvred them every time so far. Point four: this means they've only one option – get more men, lots more men. Point five: who do they ask? The obvious ally when you think about it – Grando Dwarf of Yurtz whose territory adjoins their own up in the north and who's got enough trained soldiers to be able to stand the losses but, Point six: Grando's an old dwarf and he drives a hard bargain. He's only coming in if they can show him some gold and give him a cast-iron promise of more once the fighting's over. He'll be in a hurry to get on with it. Conclusion: Mavis is right. We're practically out of time. We need to go."

It was late the following day when the boot suffered its first hit, a small projectile that smashed into the right side. It didn't tear the leather but it sent the beam holding up the curtain sliding halfway down to the floor.

"A few more like that," observed Bridie, "and we'd be as well carrying what we've got and meeting Bert on his way back. It might be better, anyway, to go while it's dark."

"We've already agreed to go early, in daylight," said Spratt who had a low opinion of Bridie's grasp of the situation. "A good general doesn't change his plans at the first piece of stray ordnance. There is still no evidence that the boot is a target. We go tomorrow if the action is close by and we sustain further damage."

He had just finished speaking when a heavy object bounced against the boot again. Bridie gave a shriek.

"Control yourself, woman," barked Spratt.

"Don't speak to me like that," snapped Bridie. "The children are terrified down there and you're going on about stray ordnance or whatever it is, like it's a game of Cowboys and Indians."

"It most certainly is not a game," said Spratt. "Now please, both of you, go and join the children while I take a last look round outside."

Spratt woke at about midnight and lay in the dark listening intently. The air was as thick as stew in the bunker. The children were sprawled around under their covers, all of them sleeping peacefully. But Spratt could feel the tension. Bert had better get back on time.

It was coming now, like that storm, racing across the land carrying all before it. He stepped carefully over the children and climbed up to the surface. It was sharp outside compared to the warm fug underground but he hardly noticed it as he headed out of the toe hole. The first impression was of complete peace, the desert barely visible in the darkness, a soul-shrinking emptiness. He stood there waiting for his eyes to get used to the dark and felt, rather than saw, a little figure come to join him – young Billy.

"There's little creatures!" whispered the boy. "I saw one of them earlier. They've got their eye on us. See, over there!" He stuck out a finger. Spratt peered into the darkness. There was a rustling in the bushes not more than fifty yards away. It could have been a big bird settling on a branch but the boy was probably right. His eyes would be keener than his. Billy nudged him again and pointed further over.

"See, over there now. That's him again, or a different one. Mum says giants don't go out at night mostly. They like their kip too much, but it doesn't stop them sending others out for them. They're everywhere," he murmured. "We're leaving tomorrow, aren't we?"

"I think so," said Spratt, who was finding it was unexpectedly comforting to have this keen-eyed lad for company. "We'll need to wait for Bert though. One last load to go and us with it. Come on," he put an arm round Billy's shoulders, "time to get back down. A good soldier rests when he can. There'll be nothing hitting us tonight."

Daylight came with no further alarms. The hours dragged by. Bridie kept sending one of the children outside to see if they could see Bert so there was a constant dither and turmoil in the boot. The children squabbled and fought. Every five minutes one or other of them was in tears. Spratt said nothing, although privately he thought the chief culprit was Bridie who was fussing and fretting enough to try the patience of a saint. He decided he'd be better getting out and having a look around. It couldn't be worse than staying in the chaos of inside. He made his way towards where the missiles had been coming from. This time he didn't have to go nearly as far. He heard shouts and, mingled with the shouts, the squeak and groan of machinery, the patter of many tiny feet. There were more shouts, angrier now, and curses. He crept closer.

"That's it!" he heard. "Steady now! Tighten that rope! Bring her on ... easy lads."

There was the sound of heavy objects being dragged across the ground, the crunch of equipment being manoeuvred into place. Someone broke into a song not far from where he was hiding.

'Grando Dwarf of Yurtz,
He had ten thousand men
He sent them down to the bottom of the mine
And he brought them out again.
And when they were in they were hot
And when they were out they were cold.
But he never cared if they died like flies
As long as he got his gold.'

"You sing that when you're back at base," Spratt heard a gruff voice say over the other side of his hiding place, "and you'll be hanging five feet off the ground with a noose round your neck."

"It's true though," said the singer. "They don't give a monkey's if we get rubbed out. You heard what happened yesterday?"

"Depends," said the gruff voice. "Lots of things happened yesterday. Grando did a walk-about. Some of the lads got gold coins."

"Sez you."

"No, it's right. I had one in my hand. I bit it too. It was gold, all the way through."

"Hey lads, stop arguing and give us a hand," called a third voice from further away. There was a thud after a moment and the same voice shouted, "Stop pissing about and lift the bleeding thing up. One, two, three!"

There was a loud creaking noise, a lot of fierce hammering and someone gave a yell of triumph. The dwarf who had been singing earlier came right back to Spratt's rock again, humming the same tune.

"What d'you think you're doing sitting down?" Spratt heard the gruff voice say.

"I'm having myself a well-earned smoke. Here's us working like bleeding bandits for the big boys and what do we get for our pains? A handful of gold coins – for the lucky ones – and squashed like bluebottles for the rest of us. You didn't see what I saw."

"What did you see Mister Know-all?" said another voice.

"The mess on the seat of Aegir Svalbad's trousers when he got up. Seven of the guys in number eight platoon copped it. He never looked before he sat down and they didn't move fast enough."

"I don't believe it," said the same voice.

"OK," said the singer. "Ask them yourself. See if they've got the same number of men they had yesterday morning and if they haven't ask them why not."

"It's collateral damage," said the gruff voice. "It always happens in war."

"Collateral damage, my eye and aunt fanny," said the singer. "It's making pals with the wrong side, that's what it is. The Bogolans'll win this one or I'm a tin soldier."

"That's enough of that. You put a sock in it right now or you're on report. Now get moving, at the double!" The older dwarf had evidently had enough. There was the scutter of little feet as they moved off. After a minute or two Spratt put his head over the rock to see what they'd been doing. What met his eyes set him off at a run to the boot.

"Emergency meeting now, in the kitchen," he barked as he ran in. "All children downstairs. At the ready. March!" The children poured down the hole as fast as grain down a funnel.

"The dwarves are changing the terms of the engagement," he said as soon as they'd all gone below ground.

"Meanin?" said Mrs Hubbard.

"Meaning that one of the catapults has been stationed in close proximity to the boot and trained directly at it. I didn't stay to examine it in detail. It didn't appear to be primed and ready for use but it will be, in a matter of hours rather than days."

Mrs Hubbard sent up a wail. Bridie leant over and patted her on the back.

"There, there, Mavis. It's going to be all right. We can go as soon as we get the children in line." She turned and pointed an accusing finger at Spratt, "Didn't I tell you we ought to have gone last night? We'll be pulp in the sand before Bert gets back and it'll not matter a whit whether there's supplies along the way or not."

"No! We aint takin the children out of here in the heat of the day," said Mrs Hubbard fiercely. "I aint havin it. The little uns 'll not last half an hour out there." She turned to Spratt. "You say the machine's not ready yet?"

He nodded.

"Well then, we go as soon as Bert's back when the sun's lower. It aint as good as goin at first light but it's better than fryin like meat in a pan and usin up precious water straight off."

Mrs Hubbard pulled herself up to her full five feet. "Get them kids back upstairs. I'm needin to speak to them proper. And I need them in teams, Spratt – new teams not like the diggin ones – every team with a big boy and a big girl in it, and everyone with their own bundle to carry, even the little uns."

She climbed up on her high chair and waited until the whole assembly was ranged in front of her, seventy pairs of eyes all fixed on Mum.

Her instructions were short and to the point: the big boys and girls were in charge. Each of the little ones had to carry a pack with their cover and a cup for water. Spratt and Bridie sorted the children out, giving each group a name to know themselves by – Partridges, Eagles, Hawks, Pigeons and Owls. This done, the leaders were told to report back as soon as they were ready. No more than an hour passed before the children were lined up and waiting at the toe hole and the cart was spotted in the distance by the keen-eyed Billy.

Bert had passed the killing machine, as he called it, on his way in, so wasn't surprised that the signal had been given for departure. He unharnessed Melodie though. Despite Bridie's protests he couldn't be moved on this.

"She's been out in the scorching heat for days. She needs a feed, a rest and a good drink and she goes nowhere till she's had them."

The first missile came whistling in at around four o'clock. It overshot the boot and landed fifty yards beyond the heel. That time the boot bounced and dust and debris rattled on the leather like hailstones. The children clung to one another, some of them crying, some of them screaming.

"A practice shot," said Spratt when the women had quietened them down. "If we're lucky there'll be a few more like that before they get the range right, but we're going to have to move fast once we're out, to get out of range."

He turned to Bert. "Your horse rested yet? If not we're setting off anyway. There's only three hours of light left." There was a second menacing crash and a rock, or something like it, landed even closer. Bert ran outside and backed a jittery Melodie into the shafts and within minutes pronounced himself ready. The children were put into pairs and the teams, each with a leader at the front and one at the back, exited quietly from the toe hole.

"You coming or what?" said Bert, seeing Mrs Hubbard hanging back.

"Yes, I'm comin. I need five minutes here on my own. Give me five minutes," she said. "I aint comin back I know that, and I've been here a long time."

"Suit yourself," said Bert, "but don't be long about it. We need you. You're no use a pile of broken bones now things is happening for real."

The line began to move off at a brisk pace, the two old dogs, Rover and Bonny, trotting behind in the shadow of the cart. Mrs Hubbard went back inside. She sat down for a moment and looked round.

"Aint much worth missin when you look at it," she said aloud, "but home's home when all's said and done and I seen all kinds here, sadness and silliness, and happiness too."

She stroked the shawl under her jacket and hitched herself to her feet. She made her way through to the kitchen and surveyed the empty shelves.

"We've done a good job of clearin the place," she said with satisfaction. "The rascals aint goin to find much." She opened her own cupboard to take one last look. Standing on tip-toe she could just see the very top shelf, and there, tucked away at the back in a corner, was the witch's hat she'd lent to Bridie.

"My, just as well I looked," she muttered. "Belle's hat. We don't want them getting their paws on that." She climbed on a stool and lifted it down. She was about to push it into her bag when she stopped. "Who knows?" she said. "Mebbe it was meant... Mebbe she'll be back... she could use it..." She shook her head as if annoyed at herself but after hesitating for a moment put it back in the cupboard and shut the door. "No point hidin it. If she's meant to get it it'll be as safe there as anywhere." She picked up her bag and stick and walked out.

She was still within sight of the boot when the boulder landed. She'd heard the scream of its flight so had crouched behind a rock to see what was coming. It was like some giant meteorite arcing out of the sky, tearing the air apart before crashing to earth. This time the Svalbad giants and their tiny allies had judged the distance exactly right: the boot was split from top to bottom.

Chapter 3

"Little Jeanie and Mercy aren't doing too well." Bridie had done her rounds of the children on the evening of day three. "Mercy's leg's swelling up where you took that thorn out. And Jeanie's got the runs. She's needing extra water. As fast as she takes it in at one end she's squirting it out at the other."

This was how it was every evening, a long roll-call of injuries, an anxious discussion about food and water, a sense, all the time, of impending catastrophe.

Once the children were bedded down nights were a relief of a sort. Bert and the bigger children lit the fires in a circle. The children slept under their blankets inside the light and the warmth and anyone old enough took a turn at standing guard through the dark hours. Spratt thought it odd that they hadn't been followed but decided the intention must have been to force them out and clear the area round the boot.

There were other hazards in the daytime: snakes and biting insects, quicksands and dangerous spiny plants. At night big animals came sniffing around, staying beyond the fires but leaving fat prints in the sand. The night-time shadows terrified the boys keeping watch but it was the injuries to legs and feet that were the most to be feared.

"Remember your feet are your most precious possession. Watch where you put them," was how Spratt ended each morning rally. But bad things happened all the same, like Mercy's thorn and Peter's twisted ankle and Benjamin's hornet's sting and always, above their heads and under their feet, the burning, exhausting heat of the sun.

Every day they managed a little less walking than the day before. Every day the grown-ups had another child to worry over. By day five the infection from Mercy's thorn had spread visibly up her leg and into her groin. That evening Bridie made up a bed for the child on the cart and she and Mrs Hubbard took turns bathing her with cool water to try and bring her fever down. She tossed and turned, her hair plastered to her skull, and her breath coming in shallow gasps. At about one o'clock she fell into a deeper sleep and everyone except Mrs Hubbard lay down to get some rest. The night was very still. Somewhere a bird called hoarsely, once, twice, three times, each time coming nearer. Mrs Hubbard tensed. Mercy opened her eyes and looked up at her.

"It's better now, Mum. It don't hurt at all any more," she whispered.

"That's good," said Mrs Hubbard, swallowing hard. "That's my girl. You have a nice sleep. I'm right here beside you." She bent over and stroked her hair back and kissed her on her forehead. Mercy sighed and shut her eyes. There was the sound of wings. The crow landed on the top of a rock beside the cart. It perched there for a moment, black wings neatly folded, its bright eye fixed on the child. Then as suddenly as it had come, it lifted itself on clumsy wings and flew off into the dark. Mrs Hubbard put her hand over Mercy's heart and gave a little dry sob.

They buried Mercy at daybreak before they got the children up and they marked the spot with a circle of stones. The children must have seen the mound but they said nothing. Billy who was leading the Eagles, Mercy's team, took the hand of Sammy who had been her partner and walked the children off ahead of the rest of the group. No-one spoke at the morning break.

So Mercy was their first loss, felt as keenly as any first loss, but others followed in quick succession, first Leonard the little boy with the club foot who had struggled so valiantly to keep up and to carry his bundle. After Leonard they lost Polly, a child who had not long come to the boot before they left. Polly was one of those five-year-olds that look more like a two-year-old than their real years. Mrs Hubbard hadn't had her long enough to feed her up so no-one was very surprised when Bert went to wake her on day seven only to find she too had slipped away to where there are no more hungry dawns, no terror and tiredness.

They were getting used to cracking open the rock and laying

the small corpses in the sand. After they buried Polly they no longer tried to hide what they were doing from the children. They gathered together round the hole, let the children shower the still shape of their comrade with sand and helped them make the stone circle. There were some tears but mostly the children were silent and subdued. Mrs Hubbard had a distant, hard look in her eye. She watched her brood like a hawk, noting every slip, the ones that kept falling back, that had to be waited for, all the time and for longer and longer. Every day they struggled on a little further, came to rest in another place in that hellish land, scratched around for fuel and carefully shared out the day's meagre rations.

After Leonard and Polly they had three days with no further deaths or injuries. They were beginning to think that perhaps their luck had turned, when another even more terrifying disaster befell them. When the count was done in the early morning there was no sign of Tom, a healthy ten year-old. Ebony, the leader of his team remembered waking up and seeing him walk off to the edge of the circle. She hadn't gone after him because she supposed he was just going to have a pee like all the children did. Perhaps, half-asleep, he hadn't known where he was and he'd wandered off in the wrong direction?

They sent a party out but they came back with nothing, not a sign. The possibility had to be faced, as Spratt said to Bert out of earshot of Mrs Hubbard and Bridie, that they were being followed after all, and that the intention of whoever or whatever it was that was on their trail was to steal the best of the group, little by little when their guard was down. It would almost have been a comfort to think it was an animal but the fact of the victim being a fit, older child... Once they were on the road again Mrs Hubbard pulled Spratt to one side and confronted him.

"Spratt, this has got to stop. We've got to get somewhere soon where we can stay put, somewhere we can build a wall against pirates and thieves. If we go on wanderin like this we'll lose the lot of them."

"I know," he said. "Bert knows too. I've told him to get ahead of us and find just such a place. It won't be tonight I fear, but soon, very soon. I promise you."

Chapter 4

Because Helena and Boy Blue had stayed so long in the bunker before they dared come out they only set off as it was beginning to get dark and they didn't go far before they pitched their camp. They found shelter in a rocky dip where there was almost no vegetation to burn so it wasn't long before their fire died back to ashes. There was no moon, nothing but a canopy of stars glittering in the icy blackness. They sat shivering under their covers, backed up against a shelf of rock, Helena thinking regretfully of the scarf she'd given Walter.

"Hey," she said, suddenly rummaging in her back-pack. "What about this?" She held up the crumpled black hat. "Let's see if we can make it work some magic for us." She thrust her hand back in the bag and pulled out the balls of wool. "I've got an idea. It's completely mad but I'm going to try it anyway." She turned the hat upside down and dropped the balls inside. She shook it for a moment while the child watched her, his teeth chattering. She reached inside and pulled out the balls again. "Damn," she said. "It's not doing anything."

"What's it supposed to do?" Boy Blue asked.

"I don't know. You said it'd still have some magic. We need things to keep us warm. I thought it'd make a scarf for you."

"Mebbe you have to say something," he offered helpfully. "Mebbe you need to speak to it."

"You're probably right," Helena said. "I've needed a rhyme of some kind most times I've been in a mess."

"Or it could be it needs you to say a spell," said Boy Blue.

"I don't think I can do spells," she said, "and I can't think of any nursery rhymes about knitting. There's 'Three Little Kittens' of course..."

"Three Little Kittens?" said Boy Blue.

The three little kittens

They lost their mittens
And they began to cry
Oh mother dear, see here, see here...' She came to a stop. "I can't remember the rest." She shivered and pulled the blanket up higher. "It's mittens *and* hats we need."

She pushed the balls back in and shook the hat once more.
'Dear hat, please help we are so cold,
Show us the powers you had of old.
Knit up the wool – make a scarf or a hat –' she stopped.

"What rhymes with hat?" she said. "I can tell this isn't right..." She said the line again.

'Knit up the wool – make a scarf or a hat –
You surely can do something like that.'

"That won't have worked," she said. "It didn't come to me like the other times." She tipped the hat upside down. The balls tumbled out again. "I'm sorry Boy Blue. Either I've not got the right words or it's not got any magic left."

She began stuffing the balls back in her bag. "Ouch," she said. "Of course! Silly me!" She pulled the knitting needles out of the bag and waved them at Boy Blue. "It can't knit hats if it hasn't got needles."

She dropped the needles in alongside the wool and this time the rhyme came to her easily,
'Please knit one, then purl one
And, hey fiddledy-dee!
Make a hat for Boy Blue
And another for me.'

The hat bulged out then began to twitch and heave as if a small animal like a kitten or a ferret was trapped inside. "Look! It's doing something," she squealed, nearly dropping it in her excitement. "Think hard about a hat, Boy Blue, really hard." Boy Blue was on his feet now, jumping up and down.

"I am, miss! It's like a tea-cosy, miss, like what my aunty's got."

The twitching stopped. The hat had a big round bulge in it. Helena thrust her hand inside and brought out two perfectly finished hats, like old-fashioned tea-cosies.

"Wow!" said Boy Blue and pulled his on, right down to his eyebrows.

"There's something else," said Helena, taking out the needles and looking down inside. "Hey! Look at these!" She pulled out two pairs of lumpy gloves and waved them at him. "A pair each. It's made gloves and we didn't even ask it to. Clever, clever hat, and clever you, Boy Blue!"

"Clever both of us, miss. You thought of the needles."

Although small for his age Boy Blue was possessed of a wiry energy. He darted off from time to time, looking for signs of the children's passage, most of which Helena would never have noticed on her own. One of those times he came back with a handful of fleshy leaves. He stuffed a few of them in his mouth, chewed hard, and spat them out again.

"Here," he said. "They don't taste nice but they're good for stopping you getting dry, but don't swallow them. You'll get sick if you do."

At the long break that he insisted they took while the sun was at its zenith, he took to running off with a pointed stick he'd cut using Helena's knife. He never stayed away long and he never failed to bring back roots or leaves they could eat raw or, the more leathery ones, cooked in the billy on the fire. When Helena asked him how he knew all this stuff his answer was simple: the goats.

"I watched what they eat and I tried it myself. Sometimes I got belly-ache but not often. I can eat most of what they eat."

Every day she learnt some new bit of desert lore and as darkness fell, they lit the fire and pulled on their warm hats and gloves.

Chapter 5

When Walter got back to the fortress, he did as Helena had asked. He opened up the room Helena and Boy Blue had been kept in, raised the alarm and sent a servant to inform Eglantine that her captives were nowhere to be found. She was in the great hall, expecting to seal the pact with Seamus and already in a bad mood when the servant arrived. On hearing the news she was gripped by a rage so intense she kept losing the shape she normally took. She spun round and round and melted into a black cloud that gave off a stench of blocked sewers and rotting corpses. Out of that cloud came a screech of pain that made the servant's hair stand on end.

At first Seamus barely gave the news of Helena's escape a second thought. It was all of a piece with the woman. He had bigger things to worry about. However, it wasn't long before he began to see that this loss put his strategising in serious disarray. If there was no obvious benefit to her in staying with the Bogolans, Eglantine wouldn't hesitate to go over to the other side. A terrifying prospect. In Seamus's slow mind someone had to be punished for the loss of this hostage. The obvious candidate was his younger brother who had whisked her out of the hall. Punishing Walter wouldn't bring the woman back but it would show Eglantine he meant business.

Seamus took no pleasure in reaching this conclusion. It would be overstating it to say he 'loved' his younger brother but he certainly preferred him to the rest of them. Once the idea was fixed in his head however, nothing would budge him. Brotherly love counted for nothing when his own reputation and the family's future were at stake. Seamus thought he had worked out exactly what he was going to do but the following evening when he saw Walter saunter in for supper, with such an expression of glowing contentment on his face, a doubt entered his mind. Why on earth was he looking so happy? Seamus helped himself liberally to roast goat and pondered the question. It took him until the servant was passing round the pudding before it dawned on him. Walter must have struck gold somewhere out there in the desert. Seamus's slow mind took off at a lumbering gallop. Supposing the woman had told him where to look, something like, "I'll tell you where to dig if you stop your ears while I say my spell"? Walter was the most upright of the brothers but he would never be able to resist such an offer.

Seamus finished his pudding, gave a satisfied belch and got up from the table, showering goat bones and bits of pastry on the floor. It was a good thing, he reflected, that he'd decided to eat before speaking to Walter. He'd have handed out some routine punishment, like tunnelling. But making Walter haul out rocks and repair walls for a week wouldn't give Seamus the result he needed. He had to go about things more cunningly. He would meet with him on the pretext of discussing the campaign. Walter was clever but no-one could beat Seamus Bogolan for cunning.

"Start off with something easy and work your way round to it. He'll jump right in, like that silly woman did. Straight in my trap." He called one of the servants. "Send brother Walter to me," he said. "Tell him I need to speak with him in the war room now."

He was poring over a map spread out on the table when Walter walked in. "You sent for me, brother," he said cheerfully, "and here I am."

"As I see." Seamus didn't look up.

"I looked in on our brother Liam," said Walter. "He's not long for this world, you know. Ma's wailing like a banshee in there as well."

"I know," said Seamus. "Everyone knows it's just a matter of time."

"We'll wipe them out, every last one of them, won't we? I told Ma we'd cut them to ribbons, feed them to the pigs, stick their dumb heads up on pikes in the desert, let the crows have their eyes."

"You're one for the words, aren't you?" said Seamus, sitting down and examining his brother at the far end of the table. "It isn't words that'll fix this lot. It's having your wits about you, cunning. The Wolves have got the fancy machinery but what's machinery if you've no cunning?"

"Nothing at all, brother," said Walter judging it was better to wait until Seamus invited him to sit down.

"I'm in a bit of bother with that witch though," said Seamus. "Now we've lost her prizes."

"How's that?" said Walter. "They weren't hers – the boy maybe was but not the woman. Like I said, she was in your trap."

"It doesn't matter. That witch thinks we haven't treated her with respect. We should have kept the woman safe, whether we needed her or not. Now she's gone we're like to lose Eglantine with her. And I need Eglantine. I need control of the air. What are we going to do if she goes over to the Wolves? Then we'll have nowt but cunning to play with. Sit down, will you."

Walter obliged. "So what are you thinking of doing, brother?" he said.

"That's why you're here. I thought maybe you could put your mind to it. Two heads better than one, eh? When I saw you at dinner time I says to myself, I'll get that young brother of mine to put his thinking cap on. He looks like he's been made over new. What's with the cheery grin, eh? You found gold out there?"

Walter looked down at his wrist. "Aye I have. Not gold exactly but something like it."

Seamus leant forward. "If you've found more gold you gotta say. You know the house rules. It's share and share alike."

"I haven't forgotten. You seen the hag since we found the woman had scarpered?" Walter said, wanting to get the conversation back onto safer ground.

"No, but I have to soon. You know how it is with witches, they don't like waiting. What I'm thinking is, we need a hook to hold her on. She wants that woman and I don't give a damn if she gets her. I want the fighting done with. If we have her and her pals on our side we've got control of the night and the air. I heard Grando's come in with the Wolves. He's got lots of men but we can squash them like bed bugs. They're not much use to the Wolves till they start digging."

This was a long speech for Seamus and he flopped back on his chair as if it had exhausted him.

"There's no way we can get the woman back," said Walter abruptly. "She did it with magic and she'll be back at her place by now. Unless the boy's kept her this side," he said as an after-thought.

"We don't know, do we?" said Seamus eyeing him hard. "But we can tell the witch she's still here, and we can offer to help her find her and tell her she can skin her alive, poke out her eyes. Whatever she wants. That Eglantine was telling me how when she was outside waiting at the gate she was wanting to get on and gobble the woman up, clothes and all. So the way I'm seeing it, your cheeky story-teller could be more use to us now than when she was locked in that room."

"Not if we can't find her," said Walter who didn't like the direction the conversation was going in.

"That's where you come in."

"Me?"

"Yes you. You're going to use your wits and find the woman. Wherever she is, if she's hiding she's more like to show herself if it's you that's looking for her. She thinks you're her protector." Seamus spat the word out and looked at his brother.

"Are you accusing me of something?" said Walter who was beginning to wonder if Eglantine had seen inside his pouch.

"Why would I do that?" said Seamus.

"Maybe because you already know what I'm going to say," said Walter quietly.

"I'm not interested in what you're going to say – you say too bleeding much," said Seamus whose temper was rising with each passing moment. "This is a war. I'm commander in chief. I say what's happening. If I say it's you that's helping Eglantine find the woman that's what's happening."

"Wrong again, brother," said Walter, by now on his feet. "The witch can search for herself. She's got plenty of her own kind that'll be happy to help her. She doesn't need any help from us. But if she does go looking for her, I'm telling you now, I'll do my best to make sure she doesn't get a hold of Helena Otterley."

Seamus sprang to his feet, spluttering with rage and banged his fist on the table. "Where is it? What's she told you?"

"Where's what?" said Walter, genuinely surprised by the question.

"The gold, the treasure she's found. You know what I'm talking about. I know what's happened. You didn't watch her properly in that room because she's told you she'll take you to the gold."

Walter laughed. "Is that what you think?" he said. "Helena Otterley wouldn't know what a seam of gold looked like if you pointed her straight at it. It's her that's the gold, brother, not any old rocks in the ground."

Seamus looked blankly at his young brother. "What do you mean, she's the gold?"

"I love her," said Walter, "and as soon as I can, as soon as I find her again, I'm going to marry her."

For a moment Seamus looked completely dumbfounded. But as Walter's words sank in, he bared his great teeth like a cornered bear and let out a sound somewhere between a laugh and a bark.

"And there was me thinking out of all my brothers you were the one with the most sense," he growled and he pushed his chair back and got heavily to his feet. The blood flooded to his face and the veins on his forehead stood out like ropes against his skull. He strode right up to Walter at the other end of the table.

"You won't be marrying anyone, least of all the Otterley woman," he snarled, poking him in the chest with each word. "You'll be married when Ma and me decide and when you do it'll be one of our kind not that pipsqueak of a jumped-up, spell-busting hooman."

"It's not Ma or you that's going to decide," said Walter knocking his hand away. "It's me and Helena between us. She's given me her word. That's good enough for me."

Whether it was the way Walter brushed his hand off him or what he said, the effect on Seamus was like an electric shock. He took a step back and swung his fist. There was a great crack as it smashed into Walter's jaw. Walter staggered, blood dripping from his open mouth. Seamus raised his fist again.

"That good enough for you too? You're lucky I've not got my axe about me. If it was you that let the woman go it's not just a sore face you'll have. And if you stand in the way of me finding her I'll run you out the country." Before Walter could say a word, the head of the Bogolan clan slammed out of the room.

Seamus's heart was thumping so hard it felt as if it would burst out of his chest. His plodding brain was trying to make sense of what he'd heard. Brother Walter a traitor! The only one of the family Seamus thought he could rely on absolutely. The woman had magicked him, that was obvious. All the more reason to get hold of her. He'd tear the liver out of her when Eglantine started chopping her up. But they had to find her first. If Walter couldn't be trusted there was only one other brother he could turn to. Lurgan was the one to handle it. He didn't need to know anything about Walter. Best keep that secret for now until the woman was caught. Seamus stood still for a moment, his hand over his pounding heart.

"Easy does it," he thought. "Now's no time to get agitated. A cool head. That's what we need. I've run the family right ever since da died. Never once had to lift my hand against any of them. Never thought it would be Walter that would push me over the edge. I was right to do it though. Gotta show him who's boss. Can't have him speaking back like he did. He'll come to his senses, once the magic's off him. I lurv her! Whoever heard such rubbish!"

Seamus sniggered. He began to breathe more easily and his mind slowed to a more normal pace. It was going to be all right. After all he'd got what he was after – a confession. It wasn't the confession he'd wanted or expected but it was better out than in, as Ma would say.

He called a passing servant and told him to find Lurgan and bring him to a room close by the great hall. Their meeting was brief and businesslike. Eglantine's shrieks kept echoing through the wall and the stink of her disintegration seeped under the door and lay thick and choking on the air. Even without those factors neither brother would have looked to prolong it. There was no warmth between them, Lurgan being the second oldest of the family and much less in awe of his elder brother than the rest of them. Once the meeting was over Seamus removed himself to another part of the fortress where he couldn't smell Eglantine or hear his mother's wailing.

Lurgan was a willing helper: Helena had made a fool of him and his man Sim. That was reason enough to go after her. Not knowing much about witches and how their minds work, he went to meet Eglantine assuming she'd demand a squad of men to track the pair down. But Eglantine's mind was temporarily fixed on a completely different matter. The woman herself could wait. She'd get her soon enough and when she did there'd be none of that stupid chattering. What she needed first and foremost was to 'rescue' Belle's hat. A human who could break spells, fly out unaided from the depths of a mountain – it was unthinkable what might happen if the hat fell into her hands.

When Eglantine told Lurgan task number one was to find the hat and bring it to her, he simply bowed and said he would instruct his men. His private view was that it was a stupid quest but he told himself it was 'her fight not his' and fewer men would be put to trouble if that was all she wanted. Having made sure that the Svalbad giants and their allies had not set up camp near the boot, Lurgan told Sim and Norrie what they were looking for and sent them on their way.

Later that same day Seamus and Eglantine met once more and reached agreement on the matter of air-support and night-flying: the three junior witches would be put to work, leaving Eglantine free to go after Helena. Both parties were satisfied with the deal.

Chapter 6

The witches knew that Mrs Hubbard had Belle's hat but Eglantine's magical powers were not strong enough to show her exactly where it was hidden in the boot. All she had to go on were the vibrations it gave off, similar to the ones from her own hat but much fainter. She directed the men to look in the kitchen and especially in Mrs Hubbard's cupboard but by the time the two men marched in through the toe hole, Boy Blue had found the said hat, and given it to Helena who had stuffed it in her bag and taken it down into the bunker. Sim had lost much of his awe of Eglantine since discovering Helena could undo her spells and since he had no means of sensing the hat by its vibrations and no intention of crawling down a tunnel for 'that crazy witch', the mission was fruitless.

Lurgan was in the workshop putting the finishing touches to a new shield when the searchers returned. They gave him their story.

"You looked everywhere?" he asked fixing them with a stern eye.

"Ever-ree-where," said the pair of them in unison. Sim went on quickly, before more questions could be asked, "There's nothing there, nothing but the rock that hit it and some broken bits of furniture. Hubbard and her crew cleared the place, or the Wolves did."

Lurgan began polishing his shield again. "You'd better go and tell her. See what she wants next."

"Us?" said Sim, turning pale and remembering Eglantine's threats in the hall. "Wouldn't she take it better from you, sir?"

"But it wasn't me who did the search was it?" said Lurgan, grinning at the look on the face of his servant. "Finish what you started. And wait for your orders."

Seeing he was being given no choice in the matter, Sim yanked on Norrie's sleeve.

"Me as well?" squeaked Norrie.

"You were there too," said Sim, and he kept tight hold of Norrie's sleeve.

"That's right," said Lurgan, "you as well. Now get out of my way. I'm busy."

The two of them shuffled out, following the stench drifting along the passage from the hall.

Eglantine was no longer whirling about when they entered. She seemed to be expecting them and was standing facing the door. She was clad in a hooded robe which concealed her face completely. It fell in folds to the floor and rippled round about her feet when she moved, like a smooth-skinned reptile. The two men stood jittering with fear at the door.

"Well?" she said. "Where is it?"

Sim held out his empty hands.

"Please my lady, your graciousness, there was no hat. We couldn't find it anywhere."

There was a screech of exasperation and a jet of green bile spurted from the mouth hidden within the hood.

"You useless fools! You didn't look properly. I know it was there. I felt it!"

"Begging your pardon, ma'am," said Sim. "I assure you we did a thorough search. The boot is very damaged but we looked everywhere. There was no hat."

The witch took no notice of these excuses. She began pacing round the hall, dragging the glinting folds of the gown behind her. Sim and Norrie waited, not daring to speak again. From under the hood they could hear mutterings. Suddenly the witch's voice rose to a shriek. Norrie grabbed Sim's hand in terror.

"It's that interfering Purselain again, I know it. And that bat-bashing old cow, Hubbard. I should have finished her and her scabby brood off a long time ago." The witch seized her broomstick and swung her leg over it. She pulled her hood back, showing a face so rotting and decayed that both men nearly fainted with horror. "Get out of my sight. Go on, be off with you! Tell your master I don't need his rubbish. I can do better myself. He'll hear from me later."

Sim and Norrie fled on trembling legs as Eglantine shrugged off the robe and shot off at break-neck speed through the open door of the hall.

It was high noon when she got out of the fortress. She would have much preferred to travel at night but darkness was too far off and she'd waited long enough. She shrank herself as small as she could and set off on her broom. At the immense speeds a witch can travel the sun had still not set by the time she was hovering like some huge wasp over the wrecked boot. She flew lower, looking as Boy Blue had done, for signs that would tell her which way the children had gone. But she was thwarted in her search. Boy Blue had made sure the marks of the cart were scuffed out as they went and had ordered Helena to walk on the rocks not the sand so that they left no footprints. She twisted and turned for several minutes and ended by flying off towards one of the many campfires that were beginning to prick out in the gathering dark. All that night she hopped from one hearth to another, and the men who'd been happily drinking and brawling felt the cold wind of her passing and shivered, drawing closer to each other.

By morning she was no nearer finding her quarry and she had to come to earth and rest. The next night had nearly ended and she'd had no more luck than on the first one when she caught a whiff of charred wood on the wind. She looked around but there was no fire burning so, following her nose, she flew closer to investigate. Boy Blue and Helena had done a good job of covering the ashes of the children's campfires when they came upon them but others that they had not yet reached were lying open to the skies, easy clues for the sharp nose of a witch. She gave a gleeful cackle. She was finally going in the right direction.

She travelled on as soon as darkness fell the following day and in less than five hours she had found the children asleep inside their ring of fire. Hovering there in the light of the early dawn, she examined the situation and made her next plan. There was no sign of the woman, but no matter. She would take a child instead and she'd make sure she got one they'd want to keep; a healthy, big boy would be best. She might not have found Belle's hat but a child was almost as good – a juicy bait to catch the woman with. She'd seen for herself how Helena had defended Boy Blue.

She waited out the glare of the following day before setting off once more. This time she was ready and she didn't have to wait long. She saw a boy pull off his cover and make his way to the outside of the circle. She flew closer, watching him swaying sleepily as he peed into the sand. Quick as a cat after a mouse, she pounced and swept off skywards with her prey dangling from her hand.

The air was so thin above the desert that Tom would have died there and then if she hadn't suddenly spiralled back down and landed her broom. She laid it down and began to wind him up, in yard after yard of sticky thread that she spun from her mouth. She made sure he could still breathe as she went, reasoning that she'd never catch the woman with a dead mouse. Now all she had to do was find the two of them. She hooked the bundle over the broomstick and turned back the way she'd come.

There was no cave for Helena and Boy Blue the night Eglantine found them.

She spotted their fire far below and flew in closer. It would have been easy enough to catch them once they were asleep. She could wrap them up just as she had the boy, but that would mean denying herself the exquisite pleasure of playing that impertinent Otterley woman like a pike on a line. She had another plan.

At midnight when the fire was low and the two were curled together asleep under their covers, she crept up noiselessly and, making a sound like a cat vomiting up strings of grass, she began to draw from her mouth not threads this time but a length of rope. On and on it came, until the coils lay deep and glistening in the moonlight. She left it lying there, only feet from the sleepers, and slipped back into the darkness.

"Hey, look at this," said Helena shivering and pulling herself to her feet as the dawn broke. "Where's it come from? Whatever is it made of?" She bent down to pick up the end of it.

"Don't touch it, miss!" shouted Boy Blue. "I know what that is. It's what they call a witch's windings. It'll tie itself all about you if you touch it and you'll not get it off."

Helena jumped back in horror.

"A witch's windings? You know what that means? She's found us," she said. "She's after us, Boy Blue. We're in real trouble now." She looked around as if she expected to see Eglantine appear from behind a rock. There was no sound but the whisper of the morning breeze over the sand. She pulled Belle's hat out of the bag.

"We need to get moving. I can feel her, through the hat, Boy Blue. She's ever so close and getting closer. Come on."

They gathered up their possessions, kicked sand onto the ashes of the fire and set off at a trot. But the heat was rising fast. It wasn't long before she called to Boy Blue to walk more slowly and they resumed their usual pace, she slightly to the rear, both of them looking back and upwards all the time, imagining witch shapes in every bush and bird. They went on like that until evening with no sightings of the witch, nor of the caravan of children either. At last they had to stop.

"Tonight's the night, Boy Blue. I can feel it." she said as she brushed aside pebbles to make a smooth seat for them both. "It's coming and I've nothing in the world to fight it with, except Belle's hat and my books."

Boy Blue was blowing on the flame beneath the twigs. He twisted round and sat cross-legged with his back to the fire.

"You see that bottle thing the giant gave you. Why don't you try putting that in the hat."

"Walter's gold?" she said, surprised. "I'd forgotten all about that. What do you think it would do?"

"I don't rightly know, miss," he replied, "but I was thinking like you, we haven't got much on our side, against her tricks you know. I thought maybe the gold would go into something more useful."

"Something more useful than gold?" Helena couldn't help a wry smile. "It's just as well Walter isn't around to hear you say that. He'd have trouble believing there's anything more useful than gold." She took the bottle out and gave it a shake. "OK. It can't hurt to try it."

She dropped the bottle in the hat, shut her eyes and after a moment, began to speak,

'Dear hat take the gold as a present from me
Please make it work to set us free.
Without your aid we will be caught
All our endeavours come to naught.
Walter's gold is all we can give.
Use it please and help us live!'

She tipped the bottle out and gave it a shake. "No. It looks exactly the same. Nothing's happened this time, Boy Blue."

"Open it up, miss," said Boy Blue in what Helena called his 'wise old-man's voice'. "You can't tell unless you do."

She unscrewed the stopper, sniffed and held it out at arm's length, looking at it in wonderment. The air above the neck of the bottle shone with a soft golden light.

"Oh my goodness, clever boy! How extraordinary!" she exclaimed. "The smell! It reminds me of the garden back home... fresh rose petals, lime blossom. Wallflowers and vetch... honeysuckle, mint, thyme... Oh, I could sniff this forever! Can you smell it, Boy Blue? It's lovely, green and damp."

Boy Blue was smiling from ear to ear, his nose twitching like a rabbit's.

Their delight was cut short however. Both of them heard it at the same moment and recognised it for what it was: a rush of air such as is made by the beating wings of a very large bird, or a broomstick. A moment later there was a solid thump and Eglantine appeared over the brow of the rock, her broomstick in her right hand and under her left arm a cumbersome bundle of what looked at first like dirty grey rags. The coil of 'rope' that Boy Blue had stopped Helena handling in the early morning was wrapped neatly round and round her waist. From where they were standing below her on the flat ground she looked in silhouette like a sagging balloon on legs.

"How very unpleasant to see you again," said Helena, quickly pocketing the bottle and wafting the scent away with her hand, "although we have been expecting you. What foul thing have you brought with you this time?"

The witch cackled.

"Here they are, my chicken pie and the old hunk of gristle and bone that goes with him. What's that you say? What have I got here? Dinner, that's what. All wrapped up, nice and cosy. Not like that little bag of disobedience by your side. No, this one's warm in here, done up like a tasty fly in a spider's web." The witch gave a hoot of demonic laughter.

She put the bundle down by her side, making sure Helena and Boy Blue could see there were two eyes staring up at them from within the mesh – Tom's eyes, blank and wild. Helena felt her throat rise with nausea, but, remembering the way Boy Blue had shouted at her about the rope at the start of the day, she didn't risk trying to touch the boy or the web he was bound in.

Now Eglantine was close up, Helena and Boy Blue could see by the light of their fire that she was a dreadful sight, unrecognisable as the 'woman' Helena had talked to outside the giant's fortress. The repeated transformations she'd suffered in the giants' great hall had left her with one eye much smaller than the other, no bigger than a large pea. The eye had slipped down her face and was now lodged below her cheekbone. Her mouth was disfigured by two pustular sores at either corner and both cheeks had clumps of brownish, matted fur growing out of them. The face was grotesque enough but it was the hands Helena's eyes kept coming back to: three clawlike fingers and a twisted thumb all ending in very long, hooked nails. The backs of the hands themselves, down to where the jerkin cuff met the wrist, were pocked with hairy warts and weeping scabs like those at her mouth. This festering, stinking shape was moving round the bundle on the ground, pawing it every so often, just as a cat paws a mouse that refuses to dance for it.

"This time I reckon I've got you either way, you lump of old gristle with the noisy tongue. That won't be waggling much longer. I'm hungry for it but I'll have the boys first. Once I've spat the bones of them out, I'll have you, slowly and in little pieces. I'll keep you alive while I'm cutting the bits off you, but first I'll skin you and Violet shall have that, every last bit of it. Lily will have the liver."

"You are the essence of evil," said Helena, holding tight to Boy Blue's hand with one hand and shielding her nose and mouth from the witch's stench with the other.

"I am too," said Eglantine, "I am indeed and I'm going to show you just how evil I can be. Now get out of my way. I need to get a heat up in that fire of yours. I've roasting to do and no time to waste. It's taken me longer than I expected to catch up with you."

"You're roasting nothing on our fire," said Helena and kicked at the burning branches.

"Oh yes I am," replied the witch. "I'm roasting the boy here, the one in the web first. You can stay and watch if you want or, if it makes you queasy, you can take yourself off, and the whipper-snapper with you. You'll not get far mind, now I've found you, but you can have a little wander while I'm busy. It'll take some time to cook him nice. I like them done slowly. It hurts them a bit more but a good cook doesn't cut corners, does she? Makes them extra tender when they're done like that."

"You can stop that now," said Helena. "If I'm supposed to be scared by your talk it's not working. You're even more loathsome than I'd thought possible, and far more stupid as well. You're a disappointment, Eglantine. Did your father, or whatever monstrous being sired you, ever tell you that? A real disappointment. I thought for a little while back there that there was more to you than pure, undiluted evil."

The witch smiled and flicked out a forked tongue to catch the pus collecting at the corners of her mouth.

"That's us all right. Eglantine, Violet, Iris and Lily. E V I L. The E V I L crew!" She gave another hideous cackle and began tossing the sticks Helena and Boy Blue had gathered onto the flames. Boy Blue pulled on Helena's hand. She looked down at him. He was jerking his head towards the rocks, as if to say, 'Follow me, over there'. She raised an eyebrow and he pulled at her again. They began to tiptoe away from the fire.

"You taking a walk? Giving up the fly in the web just like that. There was me thinking she cared about children. Poor little sod, she's no use to you, is she?" The witch bent over Tom and spat a thick gob of spit into his open eyes.

At that moment, if Boy Blue hadn't held onto her, Helena would certainly have lashed out at the witch, no matter what the consequences. But Boy Blue grabbed her and held her in a grip so tight she wondered afterwards if she was with the child or Walter Bogolan. He held her like that until they were standing out of earshot of the witch. Only then did he let go of her.

"That hurt," said Helena, rubbing her arm.

"Sorry," said Boy Blue, "I had to. She nearly got you. You touch her and we're done for. The windings'll get you or she'll make a parcel of you with thread like what's round him."

"So why isn't she coming over to us and touching us herself? We couldn't stop her if she did. That's the easy way for her to get us."

"It doesn't work like that," said Boy Blue. "I don't know much about it except what my aunty's told me but I do know that there's things they can't do against good people. If they catch you asleep or fainted, they can do it. She's talking big because she knows you'll fall asleep some time. She isn't in a hurry. She's planning on eating him," Boy Blue swallowed hard, "and when you fall asleep that's when she'll catch you again. Same with me. They caught me napping so they could have eaten me any time. Only reason they didn't is cos they're greedy. They wanted me fatter than I am."

"Like Hansel in Hansel and Gretel?" said Helena.

"I don't know about them," he answered, "but I know she's making that fire and I know that boy's going to be screaming inside in no time at all."

"Gretel pushed the witch into the oven," said Helena more to herself than to the child. "Is that what I have to do?"

Boy Blue was only half-understanding this but the word 'push' was enough. He stamped his foot.

"You're not listening. I said no touching. Touch her and it's over."

"OK, no touching. So what can I do instead? Wait a moment! I think I know," she said, feeling the shape of the bottle in her pocket. "But in case I'm wrong, if I fail and she wins, here's what you have to do. You whisper over and over 'care of Mrs Purselain, The Twisted Yarn, 134 the High Street, BB6 8QF'. Will you remember that? Say it after me."

"Care of Mrs Purselain, The Twisted Yarn, 134 the High Street, BB6 8QF."

"Keep saying it. I don't know if it'll work but she's your only hope. Now stay where you are, right here," and with that she seized Belle's hat, jammed it hard on her head and walked back out of the shadow of the rock. Eglantine was down on her knees, blowing up a good blaze.

"You back already?" said the witch, not bothering to look round for the moment. "You going to give me a nice little shove in the back and make me tumble in the coals or has he been saying not to do that? He's a clever one. I might keep him and train him up. It's a while since I had a monkey to do tricks for me." She turned round and saw the hat. "I might have known," she said. "I was looking for that. I'll be glad to get it back."

"It's too late, Eglantine. You've left it too late."

The witch glanced up, puzzled, at the woman's tone. Helena seemed different. There was something about her she hadn't seen before, some quality in her voice and the way she was standing so upright and still in the firelight. Helena stepped closer. "There's not much time left," she said.

"No I know there's not," grunted the witch. "There's no time at all left for this tasty morsel." She pushed Tom a little closer to the blaze. Strands of the sticky wrapping sizzled like hair in the heat of the fire.

"There's all the time in the world for the boy," said Helena. "I mean for you. There's not much time left for you. Have you ever heard the word 'nemesis', Eglantine? You're looking at your nemesis right now, me wearing Belle's hat."

Eglantine gave a snort and turned back to the fire.

"What rubbish you humans talk. Yabber, yabber, yabber. It's high time that tongue stopped wagging." She poked at the fire. Helena drew the bottle out of her pocket and very quietly pulled out the stopper. The sweetness of it wafted out.

"Yuck! What's that disgusting smell?" said Eglantine. She scrabbled round on her knees to face Helena. A trickle of green bile slid from her open mouth at the sight of the glowing bottle. She hissed and lunged forward, trying to grab it out of Helena's hand. Helena swung her arm back out of reach.

"No, Eglantine. You can't have it but you can have what's in it, every single grain." She tipped a little of the dust into her hand where it lay shimmering like a patch of sunlight. The witch pushed herself onto her feet, seizing a burning stick from the fire as she did so. She bent over it and muttered some words under her breath. The stick jerked like a snake, straightened up and began to give off a sooty-brown glow. Helena saw what was happening. Quick as a flash, before the wand could begin its work, she tossed the dust at the witch. Eglantine gave a screech and leapt high in the air, right over the fire. A spark flashed from the point of the hat, found its mark on the witch's hand and the wand disappeared in a puff of smoke. The gold dust missed her, all except a few grains that landed on her boots. Where each one settled a pinprick hole appeared, the points merging rapidly into one big hole as the witch flew through the air. With no boots or feet to support her, she fell to earth with a terrible crack, crumpled up and cursing. Helena poured more of the dust into the palm of her hand, ran round the fire and scattered it over the witch's bent back. Instantly she could see the fire flickering and blazing through the holes the dust had made.

"Goodbye Eglantine. Good riddance," she said as she showered a thin stream of dust onto the witch's outstretched arms, over her hair and breeches. The bottle was three-quarters empty by now and all that was left of Eglantine was her face, one ear and a few strands of hair, the whole apparition floating three feet above the ground on a scraggy bit of neck. The mouth was trying to say something but since it was no longer connected to anything, no sound could be heard. Helena turned and flung a pinch at the broomstick. With the remainder cupped in her hand, she looked one last time into the witch's distorted face.

"You're nearly gone, Eglantine, so here's the last rhyme you'll ever hear:
Now *I* spit in *your* eye,
Shrivel and die, shrivel and die."

Very carefully she blew every last grain into the witch's eyes. The face vanished and as it did the stink of corruption was replaced by the fragrance of a summer garden after rain. Not daring to trust her eyes, or her nose, Helena walked backwards and forwards across the space where Eglantine had been, her arms outstretched, ploughing through the cold air as if she was swimming. Nothing, there really was nothing there.

She felt a rush of joy and triumph and then felt it fade as fast as it came: there was a new smell, not the sweet scent of the gold dust which had evaporated already, a foul rubbery smell that hung in the air like a miasma. Helena put her hand over her mouth and retched violently. One look at the bundle lying at her feet and she knew what was making it. The sticky stuff round Tom was beginning to char and smoke. There was not a moment to lose, and maybe it was already too late. There was only one thing to do. She knelt down and thrust her hands underneath the bundle, her fingers sinking into what felt like hot, gritty syrup. Would she be able to pull them out again? She tugged. The gluey substance made a sucking noise but slowly released its hold. Certain now that the web had lost its power to snare whoever touched it, she plunged her hands back in and pushed the bundle with all her weight. It didn't move, not an inch.

"Boy Blue, Boy Blue," she shouted. "Come here. Quick!"

There was a scratching noise from the other side of the rocks and Boy Blue sprang into view, looking around as if he expected to find her wound up in the witch's toils. He slid down the rock and ran over.

"You've done it. She's gone!" he said.

"She's gone but this poor child's still as stuck as ever," she said, kneeling down again by Tom. "The stuff he's in seems to have lost its power but it makes him incredibly heavy. It's like trying to move a rock and he's beginning to burn up. He'll die if we don't move him."

Boy Blue leant over the stinking, smoking bundle. "I know who that is, miss. It's Tom Piper." He got down beside her and they pushed again. The bundle moved an inch or so. The melting web was all over their hands and clothes and the campfire felt as if it was licking at their backs.

"We're not doing it right," she said. "We could kick the fire out but we'd have no heat and we need that. Let's try and do it by thinking."

"How?"

"We've got to think him away from the fire. You did it with the knitting in the hat, remember? You thought your tea-cosy hat out of Belle's hat."

"That wasn't me. It was Belle's hat did that," said Boy Blue uncertainly.

"Belle's hat and us," said Helena. "The hat couldn't have done it without our help. Anyway we need to try. We're running out of time. He's getting hotter and hotter."

"Do we need a rhyme maybe?" said Boy Blue.

"Not this time. This time's it's up to us. Come on. Concentrate. Like with the hats, see him move. Ready – one, two three."

Boy Blue shut his eyes. His forehead was creased in a frown.

"Push!" said Helena, and they did. The bundle moved, but not much. "Again," said Helena. "See him move, in your head. Now, p u u ush!" The bundle scrunched a bit further across the sand and the pushing felt easier. "One more go," said Helena. "One, two, three, pu u u u ush!" This time Tom shot forward so fast they both fell flat, arms outstretched and Belle's hat fell off her head. They got up, giggling and picking sticky lumps of the web off themselves.

"Well done, to us!" said Helena and she caught Boy Blue up, spun him round and set him back on his feet.

"Are you sure that witch's really gone?"

"I think so. I saw it disappear. There wasn't much left by the end." Helena laid more branches on the fire now Tom was at a safe distance. She retrieved Belle's hat from where it had fallen, and, almost absentmindedly, dropped it into the flames.

"I wish I could've seen her shrinking away." Boy Blue was pacing round the campsite as he spoke. "If I'd've seen her myself, it would've been better. What's happened to her stick? Where'd it go?"

"I put dust on the broomstick as well," said Helena. "And I'm not sure it would've been good for you to see it go – it's an 'it' not a 'her'. It looked like a woman but like my friend Bert says, witches aren't women, they're fiends. It was horrible. The gold dust made holes in it, like moths make holes in woollen jumpers. It was more witch than holes at first, then more holes than witch and by the end there was just a free-floating bit of face. Revolting, but successful. And it wasn't me that did it either, it was both of us, and that." She pointed at the hat curling and browning in the ashes.

"Why are you burning it?" said Boy Blue. "It's saved us from freezing once and now from being eaten. Why do you want to burn it?"

"I don't know," said Helena, "I can't explain. I threw it in the fire without thinking. No, don't try and pull it out!" she said as Boy Blue picked up a stick and tried to hook it up. "Really Boy Blue, it's time to let it go. We've had as much from it as we're supposed to get."

"But it still had powers," said Boy Blue. "Now we'll not have anything to help us."

"You're right but I'm right too," said Helena. "Magic's no different from anything else, like food or money or special treats. It doesn't do to get greedy. We'll find other ways to manage if we have to."

She knelt down at the fire again and addressed the smouldering hat directly,

"Thank you dear hat for all you have done
For our warm hats and gloves
And this battle we've won."

A sputtering noise went up from the fire and the hat, fully ablaze by now, shot up into the night sky. It pirouetted once over their heads like a dancer taking a final bow before the curtain, and soared up into the darkness until it was no more than a tiny pinpoint among the stars. "There you are, you see," she said. "It wanted to go."

Boy Blue crouched down beside Tom who was lying on his back, staring unblinking at the sky.

"How're we going to get this stuff off?"

"I'm not sure," she said. "If the web's stuck to his skin – that's what it looks like – we can't just pull it off like wrapping paper." She began gently pushing the fibres away from his eyes. As she did so two tears trickled down from those orbits and the strands of sticky stuff coating his cheeks began to dissolve. Another smell, this time like rancid milk, rose on the air. The web began to dissolve before their eyes, bubbling like yeast and breaking into patches on his neck and shoulders. Tom made no sound as he cried but the tears kept welling up, as if someone had turned a tap on inside him. The effect of this on Helena was dramatic. She too burst into tears but not silently like Tom. She began to bawl like a lost child, bent over the mummy-shape, so her snot and dribble mixed with the wetness pouring down Tom's face. Seeing this, Boy Blue marched across to the other side of their campsite and put his fingers in his ears.

"You make a terrible noise when you cry," he said when at last she dried her eyes.

"I've never cried like that before," Helena said, blowing her nose. "It kind of cleaned me out. I feel heaps better. And look what it's done. Tom's nearly free."

Boy Blue went across to Tom. He was still lying with his arms tight by his side but the tears had stopped. All that was left of the web were a few grey rags and damp patches where it had soaked away into the sand.

Chapter 7

There was no obvious sign of physical injury to Tom from his flights through the air or from being ravelled up in Eglantine's web, only they were quite unable to get him to speak. He sat dummy-like by the fire; he lay down when they lay down and the following morning he ate a few spoonfuls of gruel from the communal bowl but throughout all this not a word passed his lips.

"She's magicked him and now Belle's hat's burnt up we can't undo it. Maybe he'll never talk again," said Boy Blue, looking fearfully at Tom who was as still as a post and staring straight ahead with those awful blank eyes.

"Give him time," said Helena. "He's had a terrible shock. He's not come back properly yet. He'll speak when the horror fades and he begins to realise he's safe. Come on. Probably if we find the rest of them that's what will help him most."

She went over to the older boy and took his arm gently. "Tom," she said, "are you ready? Boy Blue and I usually walk until midday, then we rest and walk some more when it's not so hot."

He looked at her blankly but when she motioned him to go in front of her he did so docilely, like a well-trained dog.

On and on they went hour after hour, Helena dabbing away the sweat that brought the flies buzzing round. At the midday resting point Boy Blue went off to hunt for something that would fill their bellies better as he said. Helena was half-asleep when he got back and thrust his woolly hat under her nose. It was heaving with inch-long, wriggling white larvae.

"Ugh," she said drawing back, "they're disgusting. You know what they remind me of?"

"What?" said Boy Blue picking one out of his bonnet and letting it crawl along his finger in the sun.

"They look like tiny versions of Tom, when he was all wrapped up in that stuff. Don't think I'm going to eat them. I can't. Not after what we've just been through."

"That's silly," said Boy Blue. "It's nothing to do with Tom or witches or anything bad. People have been eating these forever. They're full of goodness. Nice to taste too. Wait till they're cooked, you'll see."

Tom was dozing in the shade. He got up and silently took a rag out of his pocket and held it out to Boy Blue.

"See, miss," said Boy Blue, "Tom's not bothered and if he's not why should you be? He knows what they are. You do, don't you?" he said, but the other boy gave no sign he'd understood. He went back to where he'd been sitting and closed his eyes once more. Boy Blue tipped the larvae into the cloth and tied a knot.

The larvae were still wriggling, but less much less vigorously, by the time the fire was burning that evening. Boy Blue heated a flat stone in the fire then tipped the worms out onto it. They arched and flicked for a moment then fell still and began to turn from greyish white to brown. Helena watched from a distance, reliving the encounter with Eglantine, remembering the smell of the web as it turned brown and hot round Tom, knowing how close they'd been to losing him for good. Tom took no part in the making of the fire or the cooking but when Boy Blue pulled the stone off and left it to cool, he came and sat nearer, waiting, as it seemed, for his share of the treat. There were fifteen unappetising-looking, curled, brown caterpillars each. Helena sat with her hands in her lap, staring down at her share. Seeing the boys set to with such an appetite however, she finally picked out the smallest one and nibbled it, eyes closed. The texture wasn't unpleasant, not unlike a prawn except less chewy.

"It's quite tasty," she said and took another one. This time she looked at it closely before popping the whole thing in her mouth.

"I told you," said Boy Blue. "People go for miles looking for these. You can eat them hot or cold. They keep for days and they don't weigh nothing once they're cooked. My uncle always takes some when he goes out. He keeps them up inside his hat where there isn't anything can get at them. He goes for days with them and a pipkin of water." He scraped what was left of his share together and dropped them back in the handkerchief. Tom held out his cupped hands and did the same. Helena, who was surprised at how full she felt after only eating three, copied the boys.

Most other nights they'd lain down to rest as soon as the eating was done but this time Helena reached over and took the nursery rhyme book out, thinking that perhaps it would comfort both boys to hear one or two simple rhymes before they slept. She found the one she was looking for and began reading out loud.

> 'Little Boy Blue,
> Come blow up your horn,
> The sheep's in the meadow,
> The cow's in the corn;
> Where is the boy
> Who looks after the sheep?
> He's under a haystack
> Fast asleep.
> Will you wake him?
> Oh no, not I,
> For if I do
> He will surely cry.'

"Tst! That's not about me, except the sleeping bit, but not under that haystack thing," said Boy Blue dismissively. "I haven't ever seen one of them. I never had a cow either. Goats is what I know, smelly beasts but you can use every bit of them. My uncle says that's what counts. Read it again."

Helena did so. He looked even more dissatisfied.

"I thought I'd maybe not heard it right," he explained, "but it's not about me what's written in there. You know how you do rhymes? Can you make up one that fits, like with goats instead of sheep, and my aunty and how she gets mad at me if there's not as many when I get back as there was when I left?"

Helena shut the book. Tom was curled in a ball by the fire and seemed to be sleeping. Boy Blue sat watching her. She shut her eyes and waited for inspiration.

"Here we go," she said at last. "This is the best I can do."

'Little Boy Blue
Why look you so glum?
The sun's in the west
and the goats are all gone.
While you were sleeping
They wandered away.
They're lost in the hills
At the close of the day.
Your uncle will beat you,
Your aunty will too.
Is that why they call you
Little Boy Blue?'

Boy Blue clapped his hands with pleasure.

"That's better, much better," he said, "isn't it Tom?" There was no answer from the other boy. "See in the book," he said after a moment, "has it got a rhyme about Tom?" Helena saw that once again he had that special look, when the old man inside him was speaking through the six year-old boy.

"Hmm," she said. "A rhyme about Tom? You're right, there ought to be. Let's have a look." She opened the nursery rhyme book at the index and ran her finger down it. "Of course. Here we are:

'Tom, Tom the Piper's son,
Learnt to play when he was young,
But all the tune that he could play
Was over the hills and faraway...'

There was a little snuffly sound. She looked up and stopped. Big wet tears were rolling down Tom's cheeks.

"Oh Tom," she said, inwardly exulting at the unforeseen effect of the rhyme. "It's upsetting you."

She put the book down, went over to the boy and knelt down in front of him.

"It's because of the music, miss," said Boy Blue. "His dad taught him to play the pipes but then he went wandering off and Tom hasn't ever seen him again. That's right isn't it, Tom?"

Tom nodded. Helena patted the boy's tears away with her hanky, watching him carefully. Something about him was changing. She still couldn't get him to look at her but the awful blankness was gone. She was deliberating whether to try and get him to speak when Boy Blue gave an 'excuse me' kind of cough on the far side of the fire. She looked across at him. He shook his head and put his finger to his lips. She put the books in the bag, marvelling in passing at how completely she trusted Boy Blue's judgement in these matters.

"Dear Tom, don't you worry," she said. "We'll find your dad. I expect he's missing you as much as you've been missing him. That's enough books for tonight. Time for sleep. We've got another big walk ahead of us and – who knows? – tomorrow could be our big reunion."

Chapter 8

Helena had no means of knowing the true state of affairs among the other children. The cull of the weaker ones had gone on relentlessly. Six more graves had been filled with little bodies of Dan, Oswald, Susie, Caitlin, Felicity and Patrick. Everyone knew how fast that death toll would grow if they didn't find a better resting place soon. The children had to be fed something more substantial than gruel and leaves and the flat pancakes that Mrs Hubbard and Bridie baked in the ashes for breakfast. They struggled on, still miles ahead of Helena and the two boys, aiming for a cave further along the valley that Bert and Billy had seen on their final expedition out of the boot.

As the shadows lengthened Bert and Spratt took the dogs Bonny and Rover, and went on ahead to gauge whether it was possible for the rest of the company to reach the cave before dark. The children sank down wherever they were. Some of them fell asleep immediately. A slight wind sighed through the tufts of wiry grass and little showers of pebbles clinked down into the crannies of the rocks under feet and legs. The big children stood uneasily on the outside of the circle. The temperature began to drop. Small teeth were chattering; there were little whimpers now and then. Mrs Hubbard and Bridie peered through the gathering dark. At last they heard the huffing breath of the dogs. Bert and Spratt were close behind.

"It seems all right, as far as we can tell." Spratt was crouching down to give his report. "The dogs were wary at first. There are some very old bones at the entrance but they didn't seem to scent anything further back. We should camp at the front tonight and have a proper look in the daylight. It's possible it is being used and whatever it is is out hunting. It's a risk but since we can't stay here, Bert and I think we should go for it."

Mrs Hubbard got to her feet.

"This'd better be it," she said, and her voice was choked. "Look at em. They're not fit to walk another step. Get em up, Bridie. Give em a biscuit and let's get going."

Bridie handed out the biscuits and the caravan straggled off once more.

They woke with the first light, and the cave looked even better by daylight than it had in the dark of the night. Bert and Spratt squeezed over the huge rocks that were piled up behind the opening and came back to say that there was a big flat area twenty yards in. Best of all, they'd heard the drip of water even further back. Mrs Hubbard let the older children go in with Spratt. The little ones were sent outside to play with Bridie which they did with whoops of joy.

"Bless them," she said. "Poor little scraps aint had a decent meal in days and they can still play leapfrog."

Among the adults the delight was short-lived. The cave was a boon but it was a respite, not a final stopping place. They would use the halt to restock their supplies. Some of the cuts and bruises would have a day or two to mend and fade, but they'd have to go on. For how long? How far? How much more of this could any of them take? Mrs Hubbard left Marigold, one of the older girls, in charge of the little ones and scrambled up the low rocks leading back into the cave. One look was enough.

"It aint happenin for me," she said coming back out to the entrance where Bridie was pounding roots into flour.

Bridie stopped.

"What isn't happening for you?"

"The back of the cave, up there where they're getting the water from. There aint any chance at all I'm gettin up there. I don't mean won't. I mean can't. You think you can? Here give us that." She held her hand out for the pestle. "You better take a look."

Bridie being as small as Mrs Hubbard but a great deal more flexible, did manage to squeeze her way through to the other side. She came back to report success and it was decided that all the children except the night guards should be allowed to sleep up there. It was a satisfactory end to the day. Even the fact that Mrs Hubbard couldn't get up there and see it for herself was turned into a 'good thing' – one of the adults had to stay at the entrance. They bedded down in the dark.

Late on in the night, Mrs Hubbard was awakened by something but she couldn't say what. The dogs were sound asleep beside her. Neither stirred when she got to her feet. She crept outside. It was so still it felt as though the desert was holding its breath. Gerard, one of the boys on guard, came over to her.

"You seen owt unusual?" she asked. "There's sommat goin on and I can't see what."

"No. It's as quiet as the grave," said the boy.

"That's it exactly. Like a grave. Something good's goin on."

She pulled the shawl from under her jacket and felt it. "It aint far off either, by the feel of it. Here, feel this," she said, holding it out to him. "See what I mean?"

Gerard touched it. He felt more than heard a strange vibration, something like a cat purring, coming out of the wool. He snatched his hand away and she chuckled. "There aint nothing to be scared of. It's just sendin a message. She's up to something and she's winnin, whatever it is."

She was about to turn back inside when the sky was spilt asunder by a single reddish flash.

"Yikes! What was that?" said the boy, ducking as if he expected to be hit.

"Lightning but not any normal lightning," she said. "That's evil burnin up. I seen it before. Something nasty's done for. No wonder this here shawl's hummin like it is. Well, well. Wonders never cease."

She nodded to the boy to go to his post and went back to lie down by her dogs.

Four days later, it was getting dark when suddenly Rover's hackles went up and he gave a low growl. Old Bonny cocked an ear and gave a single bark, as if she wasn't quite sure what was bothering him.

"What is it, Rover boy?" Mrs Hubbard was on her feet with her stick in her hand. "Something to worry about?" She went outside to join the guards who were standing in a little knot. And then she saw it herself, a faint light like a will o' the wisp, bobbing along on the same track they'd followed days before.

"Looks like a fairy light to me," one of them said.

"It's scary anyhow," said another.

"It aint scary and it aint a fairy light either," said Mrs Hubbard. "It's a burnin branch or sommat like that, and I know who's carryin it."

"Who?" Gerard asked.

"The Otter. It's the Otter's what's comin. I said she would and here she is. Off you go and see if she needs a hand, though if she's gotten this far I doubt she does." She stumped back into the cave, a proper big smile on her face, and shouted up the back, "Bridie, Bert, we've got a visitor."

A grumpy face appeared over the rock.

"Bert isn't here. He's off at the traps with Spratt. Mary's just been sick all over her blanket. What d'you mean we've got a visitor? Who is it anyway?"

"It's the Otter. She's got here at last."

"Helena Otterley? You're joking! What was Amelia thinking of. She's just one more mouth to feed and there's isn't enough to go round as it is. I'm not coming down. There's Mary's mess to deal with and no-one but me to do it," and the face disappeared again.

"Silly woman, actin like a jealous kid," Mrs Hubbard muttered. "You stay right where you are if you're feelin like that."

She stepped out into the night, expecting to see Helena in the middle of a crowd of her boys but to her complete astonishment the first person she clapped eyes on was Tom Piper, the boy they believed was snatched by brigands or wild beasts. He was well ahead of the main posse and running like the wind the last few yards. He threw himself so hard into her arms that the pair of them would have been a heap on the ground if there hadn't been a rock that stopped them.

"Tom Piper, well I never! Where've you sprung from?" Mrs

Hubbard picked herself up and held him out at arm's length, studying him as best she could in the half-light. "I'm thinkin it weren't wild beasts what took you after all. What was it? No, let me guess – you don't rightly know, is that it?"

Tom nodded and burst into tears.

"I was all wrapped up like a caterpillar," he sobbed, "but that big lady got me out. And she read me a poem about me and she says we'll find my dad..." He stopped because Helena was now only yards away, hand in hand with Boy Blue, and all the big boys and girls trooping after her.

"Dear Mrs Hubbard! We've made it!" called Helena, dropping Boy Blue's hand and running to give her a hug. This was almost more than Mrs Hubbard could cope with but she covered her confusion in her usual way.

"About time too. I was givin you up for lost. You went by the boot?"

"I did once I was able to but I had to get away first," said Helena.

"What from?"

"The witches and the giants. I've dealt with Eglantine though. She'll not be troubling us again, though I don't know about the others."

"You done it with the hat?"

"Belle's hat? Yes, we found it. It was all thanks to Boy Blue. I haven't got it now though. I burnt it."

"Why did you do that? It was a good hat. It still had magic in it."

"I know. I'm sorry if you wanted it," said Helena. "I just felt I had to. It saved us before and we wouldn't be here if we hadn't had it. But..." She fell silent, suddenly close to tears.

Seeing this Mrs Hubbard took command.

"Well, you'd better come in. Aint no point standin about when we could be sittin down."

Some miles away Bert and Spratt were completing their trap-setting, hoping for richer rewards than the night before: two small bush rats and a ground squirrel, enough to flavour the stew but not to give anyone a taste of real meat.

"Things is bad," said Bert as they turned away from the last one and set off back. "How long do you think we ought to hang around here? You thinking weeks or days?"

"Another week at the most," replied Spratt.

"The trouble is," said Bert after a while, "we don't know where we're going. We haven't got a destination, have we?"

"The mountains," said Spratt. "We get to the mountains and we stop properly. We build the old lady a good homestead and we get everyone settled – somewhere with running water, not that brackish stuff we're using here, maybe with trees so the kids can climb and play again."

"Right enough, it was never much of a life in that boot," Bert continued. "It was hand to mouth the whole time and never enough food or water, but it was home. The mountains mayn't be so easy either. Supposing there's other folk there already. They're not going to like a pile of kiddies coming out of nowhere and messing things up."

"You want my opinion?" asked Spratt.

"What's your opinion?"

"If we could just make sure of our supplies I'd say leaving it was a blessing in disguise."

"The boot? How's that?"

"Those kids need more than running around half naked in the hot sun. They need schooling and training and all the rest of it. There's good brains among them and all going to waste."

"Right enough," said Bert again. "That's what I said to Helena. She could teach them. I told her that. But we aint got Helena here since old Amelia panicked and stopped her. It isn't Bridie or me that can do the learning for them. And not your good wife either, if she was here."

"She could teach them to cook," said Spratt a little defensively. "She's a good cook, my wife. She'd make something good out of the rubbish we've got here." He gave the bag with the dead animals in it a shake. They walked the remainder of the way in silence, concentrating on where they put their feet as the darkness gathered.

"Hey up," said Bert as they rounded the last corner and saw there were still children playing outside, "something's happened. Those kids should be inside by now."

"You'll never guess who's here," shouted Alice, seeing the two men. "It's that lady, the one Mum calls the Otter. She's just come and you know who she's brought with her? Tom! Tom! He's alive. The beasts didn't get him. And that boy who looks after the goats, he's there too." She went skipping back to the cave before they could say anything.

"Well if that don't beat all," said Bert, grinning from ear to ear, "and I just mentioned her too. Talk of the devil. I said she'd be back and now she is. What a woman. They broke the mould when they made that one."

Helena had composed herself by the time they'd walked the last few yards and she came out of the cave entrance with her arms outstretched to greet them.

"Hello Bert. Good evening Mr Spratt," she called. "The bad penny's turned up again! It's good to see you both." And then, remembering the dark and empty house she'd broken into, "Where's Mrs Spratt?"

Spratt shook his head regretfully.

"She's gone to stay with her mother. It wasn't safe for her to stay on her own and she wouldn't have managed this journey on foot."

"I've brought Tom Piper back with me," said Helena as they went into the cave. "Boy Blue and I rescued him from Eglantine."

"You mean Eglantine, the big witch? She got Tom Piper?" said Bert in amazement. "You've been messing with her? You're lucky to be alive."

"I know," said Helena, "I nearly wasn't. But the tables got turned and she's the one that's dead, not me or the boys."

"She can't be. Witches don't die."

"No you're right, she didn't die exactly. She just vanished into thin air, but not because she did it herself. Walter's gold did it."

Bert scratched his head. "You'd better go back to the beginning and tell it proper. I can't make out a word of what you're saying."

Chapter 9

The tale was told. The men went up to join the children and Bridie, leaving Mrs Hubbard and Helena alone in the bright moonlight. Neither of them was inclined to lie down, so they sat quietly, enjoying the peace of an unusually warm night.

"What's next?" said Helena after a while, voicing the thought in both their minds.

"More walkin soon enough, more of them fallin down and not gettin up again."

"How many have we lost?" said Helena quietly. "I saw one grave early on. Well, I thought it must be a grave." Her voice tailed off.

"That was **Mercy**. She went first. She got a thorn and it went bad. But there's been others since, too many. Leonard and Polly – you never saw her – and Dan and Caitlin and Felicity and Patrick."

Helena sucked in her breath in dismay.

"And how many of the rest of them do you think are really too weak to go on?"

"We've got two of them on the cart but one's on the mend so he can mebbe walk again once we go but there's plenty more need a ride and that horse aint getting much to do all the cartin. Bert isn't sayin owt but I can read him like a book and I know he's worrit."

"What about Bert's supply chain? How many more of these stops before we get past the last one?"

"Bert's plannin on getting on ahead again, with some of the boys. The further out we get less Spratt worries about them followin us, so he says Bert can take three of them, but they aint got much to take. We're collectin eatables every day, as we go but we're eatin it all when we stop. There's another problem too," she said after a silence "I wasn't sayin nowt in there while you was talkin but this business with Eglantine, that's like to give us more problems."

"How?" It hadn't crossed Helena's mind that something bad could come out of Eglantine's disappearance.

"Once the rest of em hear about it, the squad she flies about with, but maybe not just them. They'll be after you, or us."

"Wherever we go?"

"Mostly. Not if we cross a river, mind. They can't get over water so that would stop them but where's the river hereabouts?"

"Maybe it's at the mountains? Mountains usually have streams."

"You reckon? Mountains like those?" Mrs Hubbard waved her hand at the dark horizon.

"I don't see why not," said Helena stoutly. "As long it doesn't have to be a huge great river, just a stream."

"A stream does fine. Runnin water, that's what keeps them back. Lakes and ponds is no good."

"So we have a plan." Helena was determined to end the conversation on a cheerful note. "We have to go slowly on towards the mountains, letting Bert and the boys go ahead and take any provisions we don't need straightaway. We know we have to cross a river, so as soon as we get a bit closer, Bert and the boys go looking for a river, or more likely, a stream. And we join them as soon as they find one. We cross it and the first place with shade, and vegetation for Melodie, we stop."

"And if the fiends come on us before we cross the water, what then?"

"Straight off I don't know but I'll think of something. Something'll come to me or us. Or maybe we've already got something that we haven't realised? That's happened to me a lot lately."

"You mean with the wool and the books and that?"

"Yes, but other things, not things exactly. Finding myself reciting poems and rhymes as if someone else had taken over my tongue and my brain, and talking back to Seamus and making Boy Blue get out of the cage. All sorts of things. The deal I made with Walter. I didn't mention in there but..." she paused, unsure of how to continue. "I did something crazy," she went on in a rush, "I said I'd marry him. It was the only way to escape. I was desperate. So, strictly speaking, I'm engaged to be married to a giant, Mrs Hubbard." She looked over at the old woman, trying to gauge her reaction to this revelation but Mrs Hubbard was looking steadily into the embers of the fire and her face was lost in the shadows.

"I wonder why?" Helena went on.

"Why what?"

"Why all this has happened to me? I've never had much imagination. I've always been a practical, down-to-earth sort of person. We did loads of nice things when I was a child but it was all very regular, very predictable, if you see what I mean. We went on holiday to the same seaside town year after year. Even when I was grown-up and earning good money and I could've taken my mum and dad off to all sorts of exotic places, we mostly went back to the same old haunts. It was as if we couldn't think where else to go but I don't think it was that, not exactly."

Mrs Hubbard broke in impatiently. "Aint things like keepin goin back to the same place that stop you bein adventurous. Too much change aint good for nobody, not kids nor old folks. You put a plant in the ground and leave it and it'll grow and give you a good crop. You keep movin it about and it aint never goin to get the chance to grow. Growin's a long, slow business."

"Yes, I know, but ....?"

"But what?"

"But what does that mean about me now? It doesn't explain why someone so ordinary has these amazing adventures. And staying in one place – I've not stopped moving since I last saw you."

"You're muddlin me up now. You was sayin about how it was when you were a nipper and I was sayin it was a good way to start, like feedin a plant so as it can grow proper and make a crop." Mrs Hubbard paused as though she too was sorting out her thoughts. "I know it wasn't much of a life for my brood in that boot but it was reliable and reliable's important for kids, even if there's no feather beds and roast meat. But a woman like you, well you can get out of tight corners because you've got resauces – natrel resauces like they say! But kids aint, well, some of them have but not many, and they soon run through them. See my Billy, now there's a clever boy but if

I don't watch him, he'll use all his cleverness up in one go and spend the rest of his life wishin it back."

There was another long silence.

"The fact is your mum and dad set you in good soil, fertile. So you went ahead and growed all sorts of good things, inside you. The only reason you didn't know they was there was because you weren't needin to know – things like standin up to Eglantine and speakin your mind and makin the spells come off. Anyway," she said, "We've done enough talkin for one night. Talkin's fine but it don't change much. There's walkin still to do and it's long past my bedtime."

Helena held out her hand and helped the old woman to her feet.

"Thank you," said Mrs Hubbard. "Thank you for comin back, Otter." She unfolded her cover and lay down on it. "I never had a daughter of my own. If I'd had a daughter, I'd have liked her to be like you." She pulled the cover up over her face.

The next day things took a turn for the worse again. Hector fell while climbing and fractured his arm and they discovered ants had got into one of their remaining sacks of grain. They tipped the grain out in piles onto a cover and the children were put to picking the ants out, so there were ant stings as well. But Helena couldn't help feeling happy in spite of these troubles. She made plans in her head as she sat helping de-ant the grain. She'd start a group of the older children on writing. They had no paper or pencils but they could make the letters in the sand or with stones on the rock surfaces. The little ones could begin with their counting, and all of them could do more to help Bridie. She announced this to the adults in the evening when the children were tucked away in the back, Bert nodding and grinning like a proud father showing off a gifted child. Spratt looked approving too but Bridie wasn't to be won round with the promise of more help.

"Once we're on the way again there's not going to be time to do lessons," she objected. "It's as much as the children can do to keep up. There's no point forcing them to do learning as well."

"I wouldn't force them. We can turn it into a game," said Helena, surprised, and thinking of the books and pens Bridie had brought once long before. "I've never done this kind of thing before but I guess I can work something out. I can use my books anyway. They've got counting rhymes in them."

They moved on to discuss the possibility of the witches' reprisals and it was decided that the children should no longer keep watch at night, night being when a raid was most likely to happen. The adults would go out in turn instead.

"Maybe nothing'll happen if Seamus keeps them busy enough," said Helena hopefully.

Mrs Hubbard shook her head.

"It won't matter even if he does. If they get it into their heads they've got to avenge Eglantine they'll find a way."

Chapter 10

Violet, Iris and Lily were indeed out and about on Seamus's business but, as Mrs Hubbard had warned, not so busy that they didn't have time to plot their revenge. Of the three of them Violet was the most incensed at Helena's escape and it was she who kept nagging at Iris and Lily about the skin and the eyes and the rest of what they'd lost. Their nightly swoops across the desert brought them no success while the tribe was in the cave but once it set off again and was back out in the open, finding them was child's play to the witches. It was Mrs Hubbard's sharp eyes that picked them out, like three tiny dots on the blank page of the night.

"They're up there now," she whispered to Helena and Bridie. "Can you see them? You have to watch hard – they're so fast, like bats."

For the anxious watchers down below, that night seemed to last forever. Finally the light began to flood back into the sky and they all got up to move on as fast as possible.

The weather had changed and the sky was a little like it had been the day of the great storm all those weeks earlier: clouds massing in towering heaps, a gritty heaviness in the air. Their route took them through a steep canyon and the sheer walls on either side channelled the wind. Clouds of dust spiralled upwards like genies out of a bottle, blotting out the sun, and bits of twig bowled along, scratching legs and ankles. Before long they had to stop and wrap cloths round the children's faces.

"If we haven't got enough to face, there's a storm brewing," grumbled Bridie. "We might as well go back where we came from and sit in the cave and wait for our end. At least we'll die dry if we go back there."

"There aint no-one turnin back and sittin in no cave," said Mrs Hubbard. "Witches aint stoppin us from goin on. We haven't got this far to sit down and die, wet or dry. You'll see, Bert'll find us shelter."

They stopped earlier than usual because Bert did find them a rock with a big overhang, not a cave as such but a place where they would be protected from the rain when it came, because the rain was bound to come. Once they got out of the mouth of the canyon the lightning was clearly visible, flashing through the clouds. Helena helped settle the children and decided she would take a look round. She had only been gone a minute or so when Bert heard her running back, shouting as she came, "Spratt, Bert, get the spades off the cart. We've got to dig like mad."

Bert jumped to his feet.

"What have you found?"

"It's not me," she said, "it's you Bert. You found this place. We're right by a dried-up river bed. It's going to fill up if the storm comes."

"Are you planning on making a swimming pool for the children?" said Bridie sarcastically.

"Not a swimming pool," said Helena, who had decided by now that it must be because she'd disobeyed Mrs Purselain that Bridie was so hostile. "We need to deepen the channel so that we have a proper river flowing when the witches arrive." Bert looked at her in admiration.

"You know about that too?" he said.

"Only because Mrs Hubbard told me the night I got here. Come on. We don't have to move rocks, only dig out where we can see the water's gone before."

There was a sudden rush of hailstones as they stopped for a rest, and then a hush. They looked out into the darkness, waiting. Then they heard it, coming like a drumming and a roar over the land. They ran back to the rock, heads down against the howling wind and stood watching. Had they done enough? How quickly would there be a river that would thwart the witches once and for all?

The witches were within a mile of their quarry when the storm broke but it didn't stop their flight. They tightened their grip on their sticks and flew on through the clouds. They were flying high in the air so the ground was invisible below the mass of roiling black beneath them. The broomsticks bucked and spun in the howling wind but they drove them on, one thought only in mind.

"I'll be as good as new with that skin," shrieked Violet and did a double somersault for joy.

"And the eyes, remember the eyes!" Iris shouted, swooping in close and nearly unseating her sister.

"Cut the good bits out first then roast the rest I say," cried Lily. They swung their brooms earthwards. The clouds thinned and parted. Below them the landscape was unrecognisable. The rain was thundering down and the rocks were shining black in the wet. But it wasn't the sight of the rocks that brought them to a juddering halt in mid-air. In front of the overhang, where with their night vision they could see the huddle of children and grown-ups, there was a fast-flowing river, deep and wide and getting wider by the minute. For a moment they hung there motionless but witches are no different from other flying creatures, they have to keep moving or they drop like a stone. They circled round and round, screaming their frustration and Mrs Hubbard saw them.

"They're up there now and they can't come on," she said, pointing. "Listen, you hear them? Squawkin like parrots they is."

The watchers on the ground could hardly make them out through the pelting rain but they could hear a hoarse cawing from way up in the sky.

"Is running water really enough to keep them back?" said Helena who was shaking, not so much from the cold and wet as from fear and had stationed herself among the children as far to the back of the overhang as she possibly could.

"It ought to. It always worked before," said Mrs Hubbard, who was keeping a sharp eye on the three shapes all the same.

"So why aren't they going? Why aren't they giving up?"

"They will but not straight off. They'll try and find a passage. I doubt they can though. Not now you've done that diggin. And if they can't get over tonight they'll not be back."

"Not even if the stream dries up again by morning?" Helena hadn't dared voice this question before.

"No, not even. See, that's the difference between this place and the cave. If we were in the cave, it wouldn't matter how deep we went inside, they'd get us anyway. Here, it's like we're the other side of the water even when it goes again."

Dozens of pairs of eyes stared out anxiously through the rain while the three witches squawked and shrieked, up and down the river. Sometimes their cries sounded so close and loud that Helena was convinced they'd found a way over and everything was lost. But at last the noise of their screeching faded away, leaving nothing but the rush of water yards from the shelter. By that time the storm was already exhausting itself, the sky was beginning to clear and the first few stars could be seen. The torrent in front of the overhang thinned out to a trickle and finally melted away altogether, leaving sharp channels, broken branches and damp silt as its only trace.

Helena's delight at the vanquishing of the witches was marred by how she was feeling about Bridie. The jibe about the swimming pool was still rankling, although there had been worse in the days before that. It crossed her mind that she should mention it to Mrs Hubbard but when they set off the following day she had other things to worry about. Zac, one of the youngest ones in her group, kept falling down. Every time he did little Benjamin lay down in the dust beside him. She had her work cut out cajoling them back onto their feet, carrying one or other from time to time, feeding them little sips of water and letting them rest.

In the rest of the caravan the mood was buoyant. The downpour had washed the dust out of the air and the light was bright and clear. Breathing was easier and, although Helena kept falling behind with the two boys, everyone else walked more briskly than they had for days. It was decreed that there would be a special supper to celebrate the witches' defeat, so once the fires were lit a thicker gruel was made with a few spoons of Mrs Hubbard's precious honey to top it off. Helena found it hard to join in the good cheer. Her back ached from carrying Benjamin and, if she allowed herself to think about it, she realised the sweetened gruel had only made her long for something tasty like a spicy sauce or a piece of strong cheese.

She finished seeing her brood under their covers and returned to the fire. Mrs Hubbard came and sat down beside her. Here was the opportunity Helena had been waiting for but she couldn't summon up the energy. Why waste time trying to get to the bottom of a few unkind remarks. People said things like that when they were tired.

Mrs Hubbard tossed a handful of sticks on the fire and looked across at her companion. "When you goin to start the lessons?" she said.

Helena was surprised by the question.

"I don't know. Soon I hope but Bridie's not keen, I don't think."

"What makes you think that? Sullivan brought the books and the pens. She's been wantin them learnin for longer than I can remember."

"I think it's not that she doesn't want them to, it's me she doesn't want doing it. She seems to be mad at me all the time. Have you noticed?"

"Be hard to miss it," said Mrs Hubbard. "She aint pleased you're here, and it's obvious why."

"Because of Amelia? How I disobeyed her? That's the only reason I can think."

Mrs Hubbard chortled. "What are you laughing at?" said Helena indignantly.

"You, thinkin it's to do with Amelia. It aint got nothing to do with Amelia. It's Bert who's the problem."

"Bert? What's the matter with Bert?"

"Aint nowt the matter with him, unless bein in love's a matter."

"Being in love? Bert? Who with for goodness sake," said Helena as a suspicion began at last to form in her mind. "You're not meaning with me?" It came out a like a squeak.

"Well it aint with me. It don't look like it's with Sullivan and it definitely aint with Spratt, so who's left?"

"For goodness sake, Bert isn't interested in me. We're friends, nothing more."

"That's as may be but Sullivan don't see it like that, and there's your answer." Mrs Hubbard sat back and eyed the discomfited

Helena. "You've got some good ways of telling some things but it seems to me you aint much use at spottin the men that's got hankerins for you." Since Helena seemed to have been struck dumb she went on, "See how you never said about marryin Walter Bogolan, when you were tellin all what happened that evening, why d'you think you didn't, eh?"

"I don't know. Well, I do but it had nothing to do with Bert. I thought you'd all laugh. The idea of me promising to marry a giant..."

"Are you sure it wasn't a tiny bit because you knew Bert's got a fancy for you and you didn't want to bust his fancy wide open?"

"No, absolutely not!" said Helena, more indignantly than ever.

"Well it wouldn't matter anyhow. A man don't stop lovin just because he's got a rival, even if he is bigger than him. But, like you said, strictly speaking, you belong to Walter. You goin to marry him?"

"No, of course I'm not marrying Walter. He knows that. I'm sure he does."

"Excuse me sayin so but you don't know nothin about giants either. Walter'll be expectin you back. He's not goin to like it if you run away."

"I'm not running away! I can't marry Walter that's all. I had to say I would. It was the only way to get him to help us."

Mrs Hubbard poked the fire. The flames rose again. In the light Helena could see the disapproval in the old lady's face.

"He's a good giant that Walter. He'd make a good husband." The tone of voice matched the look.

"Yes but for a giantess or whatever they call them, not for a human. I'd be like his mascot. He'd keep me in a pocket and get me out at dinner time and make me do tricks for his brothers. Walter's maybe a good giant but I'm a human and an old one at that. An old woman can't be kept like a pet mouse. I said that to him."

"And what did he say?"

"Nothing really, not about that anyhow. He kept on about me not being old at all and about him being young too, as if he could really see it happening."

"Like I told you!" said Mrs Hubbard, triumphantly again.

"Oh stop it!" Helena was both alarmed and exasperated now. "We've just got the witches out of our hair and you go raising another horrible problem about Walter, and suggesting Bridie's jealous of me. So, you mean Bridie fancies Bert? It never crossed my mind."

"No, I see that. Like I said, it aint your strong point. I seen that before with humans. You know all sorts but you aint much use at seein inside folk."

"Loads of humans are very good at seeing inside folk as you put it. It's just me who isn't – no husband, no kids of my own. I've been thinking about that, being with Boy Blue and Tom. I never realised before how nice it is having kids around."

"It aint ever too late. Walter'd make a good dad, so would Bert for that matter."

"Oh, come on! I'm nearly sixty-three! I'm not going to start raising a family at my age, even if I could, which I can't. This desert may be as real as the world I come from but you still can't magic babies out of thin air!"

"I wouldn't be so sure about that, but I can see you been givin it some thought," said Mrs Hubbard. "Well, if you aint for havin any of your own, maybe Walter and you could adopt. There's plenty here'd like to live in a giant's castle and eat red meat every day and go out with their daddy huntin and fightin."

"I can't believe you're talking as if it's a real possibility. I am not marrying Walter and I'm not setting up house with Bert. If Bridie wants Bert she can have him with all my good wishes for their future. I am not in the marriage market full stop. Anyway, if I was marrying anyone it'd definitely be Walter, not Bert." She stopped short.

"See! It's like I said. You're good at knowin stuff but you don't know what's goin on inside your own head, or your heart more like."

"You mean I don't know I like him. But I do! I wouldn't have said I'd marry him if I hadn't, not even to get away. He's a lovely man – I mean 'man' too. I know he's a giant but what's nice about Walter is he seems like a man, a very young man but a fine one. If he was a tenth the size he'd be perfect."

"So what are you goin to do?"

"Oh Lord, I don't know. If I were at home I'd write to whoever it was but Walter can't read. If I wrote a letter someone would have to read it to him and I don't like the idea of that. But you're right, he has to be told, somehow, before I go."

"You plannin on goin back soon?"

"I'll have to, not right away but eventually. I can't stay here forever. I know you think I'm wrong about what's real and what's not and I know the ground we're sitting on is as hard and solid as the ground back there, but I belong there, not here. Amelia was right when she said to me that I can only ever be a visitor here, but I can come back and I will."

"I'm not so sure of that. You make your bed and you lie on it. You choose there instead of here and it aint clear to me that there'll be an openin back over again, not to us like, though mebbe somewhere else. So mebbe if that's what you want you're better with Bert than Walter. In the old days before things went bad here he was off visitin all sorts of places. He used to come and tell us all about it."

"If Bert can come and go like that I don't see why I shouldn't. What's different about him?'

"There's nothin much except he isn't goin back every time, leavin someone pinin who's been made a promise that aint been kept."

"So Walter would be why I couldn't come back? But what about Bert with Bridie?"

"They're both from your side. It aint the same. And there's no promises been made neither."

Helena's good cheer had seeped away like the rain in the sand by the time Mrs Hubbard was snoring beside her. Sleep wasn't coming for her though. She got up and went to sit out on a rock in the darkness. Mrs Hubbard was right. She ought not to have made that promise to Walter if she didn't mean it. It was a terrible betrayal of trust. She'd never have treated a friend at home that way. It was all because deep down she still didn't believe what she was in the middle of was real. So Walter could be fobbed off with a kindly lie because 'not being real' his feelings weren't real either. And yet, she'd seen for herself how he looked when they parted, the sadness in those big brown eyes. She'd felt the warmth of his cheek on hers when he lifted her up for that last embrace. That was all real enough. How could she be so blind and so selfish! And there was Bert to consider as well, although she felt less to blame for him. But it was a problem all the same, how to tell Bridie she wasn't a rival, how to let Bert know about Walter, about just 'being friends' and keeping it like that. But that was nothing compared to Walter. She needed to talk to Mrs Hubbard again but the old woman was snoring louder than ever.

The next day the path they took climbed gently all day long; they were finally at the edge of the foothills. The mountains loomed up, sharp shadows marking the crevasses, lumps of crystalline rock winking in the sun, fierce as diamonds. They saw a pair of eagles wheeling far away and at the midday stop, three buzzards circling up on the air currents, calling back and forth with their mewing cry. Helena was helping Zac and Benjamin most of the day but her thoughts were still on Walter and her betrayal of him. She was miserable. The droop of her shoulders and the absent-minded way she was speaking to the children told Mrs Hubbard exactly what was going on. Not that Mrs Hubbard felt bad about having spoken as she did. No point pretending. It was pretending that had got Helena into the pickle she was in. Once they were alone in the dusk again, she lost no time in returning to the questions.

"I'm so tired tonight," Helena began. "I've not felt this tired since I arrived."

"You didn't sleep much I doubt, and you aint had a good day either. You're worriting about Walter. I can see that."

"I am. I've been so thoughtless and selfish but I can't see how I can make it right. I'm scared too. If I go and find him he could take me prisoner. He could kill me if I don't do as he wants."

"Walter Bogolan wouldn't do that," said Mrs Hubbard with a

snort. "You see how it is," she went on, realising she'd have to take this clever woman through the whole question one step at a time, like a child. "See when you're thinkin of your own safety, then you've no problem feelin it's real. Like bein killed or roasted on a spit. But you aint been givin Walter the same consideration." She emphasised the word. "It can't just be your feelins that count."

"No I see that," said Helena. "It's what I've been telling myself all day. It's what makes me feel the worst."

"Well, that's a start. If Walter knows you're carin about hurtin him he can't be hurt as much. He'll be hurt, but not so as he feels he's no better than a bug in your hair. There aint no chance he'll kill you either. A giant like Walter doesn't kill what he loves. Giants treasure their gold, they don't throw it away."

"So you think if I talk to him, he'll understand?"

"He'll not like it that's for sure. Mebbe he'll understand, mebbe he won't. You won't know till he says. What you gotta look at next is what's goin to happen to you. There aint just Walter in this. There's you."

"How d'you mean?"

"You're goin to suffer for it. You're goin to have to live with the regret of it, after, and that'll be hard, mark my words. You aint got any idea how hard." Helena sat silent. "There aint no hurry anyhow," said Mrs Hubbard. "Walter can wait. You need to get some sleep tonight or it'll be you that's ridin in the cart tomorrow. Here I'll give you sommat that'll get you off. That way you aint goin to be sittin out there worritin again." She tipped a single small pill, black and shiny as a peony seed, out of a bottle in her bag. "Swallow that, it's good for dreamin problems away."

Helena looked at it doubtfully but did as she was told.

She fell asleep as soon as she lay down, and her sleep was full of strange dreams: colours at first, like in the back shop, writhing and looping across her closed eyes, and hordes of children running past her. Were they trying to get away from something? She began to run after them across an open stretch of sand, her feet getting heavier and heavier as if she was sinking. She caught hold of a

branch and held it. The sand turned to water and out of the water
came bubbles. There was music and the children came towards
her in a column, one behind the other. They began splashing in
the water. Helena turned in her sleep. The cover slipped from her
back but she slept on. The children had vanished. She was filled
with such a desolation she began to cry. Mrs Hubbard was beside
her, holding out Bridie's handkerchief. "No need for tears," she said,
"you aint really alone." The scene changed. She was riding along on
Melodie but it wasn't Bert holding the bridle. It was Walter, walking
at the mule's pace and singing as he went. She leant forward and
touched his arm, "Walter what's that over there? It looks like a lake
but is it a mirage?" He didn't answer. "Mirage," she thought, "he
doesn't know what a mirage is."

"No it's real," he said, as if she'd said the words out loud. "It's real
like I'm real."

A flock of white birds flew up.

"It'd be nice to live by a real lake with birds like that," she said.

"We can too, if you stay with me."

She knew he'd said the words but she couldn't see him. She was
alone again, walking along a narrow path that ran along a cliff face.
The path stretched away and she pressed to the rock face, taking
each step as if it was her last. Suddenly there was nothing in front
of her but space. A scream ripped the emptiness. Eglantine swooped
down on her broomstick. Helena was miles in the air, gasping for
breath and clinging onto Eglantine's jacket. Eglantine jerked the
broomstick and Helena felt herself falling headlong to earth. She
was deep in something soft. A feather bed! Walter was there again
and he was patting the covers with his enormous hands and saying,
"Where are you, my dark-haired missus? Come up here beside me
and tell me a story." At that, darkness came round her eyes and she
slept on, deeper and quieter at last.

"You slept well? You look like you did," said Mrs Hubbard
the next morning, with a sly smile. Helena shook her head in
wonderment.

"Lord knows what you gave me but it worked. I dreamt the whole night long, about everything. I can remember a lot of it too, which I normally never do. You put that pill on the market back where I live and you'd never have to worry again about not having clean water out of a tap and meat on the table! People would pay you a fortune to know what's in it. The children kept appearing and disappearing. You were in it too. I was crying and you lent me a hanky. I heard some music as well – there were bubbles. It was like they were making the music."

"Hm, you heard music? What kind of music?"

"Very simple, like a reed pipe."

Mrs Hubbard said nothing, just nodded her head.

Part 5

Chapter 1

The going was harder as they left the plain behind. Melodie had to pick her way carefully over flinty stones which rapidly gave way to a mass of sliding scree. Several times the wheels of the cart stuck completely and they had to dig them out as if they were in a snowdrift. After three hours of this Bert pulled Melodie to a halt.

"The cart's stopping here," he said and he began unharnessing the mule.

"How are we going to carry the food and water?" said Bridie.

"The mule'll take some of it. The rest goes on our backs," said Bert. "Spratt and me'll go up the hill a way and see how far this stuff goes."

The pair of them set off, leaving Melodie tethered and the children in huddles on the flat rocks that poked up like islands out of a stone sea.

Two hours later the men reappeared, rattling down the slope. "It's a tough call this one," said Spratt. "Near enough another mile of this stuff before we're off it. Beyond it's bushes and grass, but thick and tough so it'll be hard for the ones with short legs. Snake territory as well."

"You seen any streams or water holes?" This was Bridie who was in charge of the water. There was a cooling breeze on these slopes but the children were thirsty with the climb and clamouring for more than she could safely give them.

"No streams but way over that direction," Spratt pointed to the right, "there's a big clump of trees and bushes."

"How big?" said Bridie.

"Bigger than a copse but smaller than a wood and we reckon

there must be water not too deep down for them to be as high as they are."

"We aimin to get right there by nightfall?" Mrs Hubbard asked doubtfully. "Looks too far, for the little uns."

"Probably not tonight but definitely tomorrow, and maybe we can set up camp for a day or two."

That evening when they made camp at the far side of the scree slope they had something other than sand and stone to lie on. Boy Blue and Billy took the scythes to the clumps of grass and cut piles of it for bedding. There was an undeniable feeling of 'getting near' but to what it wasn't yet clear. The clump of trees seemed an unlikely final destination. The following morning, as Helena was rolling up her cover, Boy Blue came sidling up.

"You ready yet, miss?"'

"Nearly," she said, "but there's no hurry. We've not got so far to walk today."

"No but Tom and me, we've got something to show you, before the rest of them find it."

He led the way over the tussocks of grass. The slope was gentle enough and she was thinking that they'd do the day's march easily if it went like this all the way to the wood. But suddenly, like in her dream, she had to stop. There was no way forward. Boy Blue had led her right to the lip of a deep basin about fifty feet in diameter and about half that length from the top to the very bottom. The sides of it were steeply curved, although not impossible for an agile climber to scale. There had been landslides too, great shoots and fans of ancient slurry stretching from the upper edge to the bottom like frozen rivers, and in between them the bedrock strata looping and folding up and down in clear lines of grey and brown and dirty yellow. The floor of the basin itself was beautifully clean of all debris, almost as if it had been swept. Tom was down there, in the middle and leaning up against what looked like a tree trunk or a post of some kind.

"Goodness, isn't it amazing how you can't tell this is here until you're right at it," she exclaimed. "It's like the crater of an old volcano or where a meteorite fell or something. How did Tom get down there?"

"It's easier than you think. Over there – see that fall of mud, right beside it, there's steps." He pointed and Helena could see quite distinctly what looked like man-made steps cut into the clayey bank.

"Stranger and stranger," she said and found herself looking round to see if there were other signs of human activity.

"There's nothing to be scared of I reckon," said Boy Blue, noticing this. "Tom and me think this is a good place."

"You're right," she said, "it does feel good. It feels peaceful. What's that in the middle?"

"We don't know but it's all carved. It's been done on purpose."

"I'll have to take your word for it. I'm not going to try to get down those steps without a good stick. Let's go back and tell Bert and Mr Spratt and see what they think." She waved to Tom to come up.

"Aren't you coming down?" he said. Helena gasped –

"Did you hear that – how his voice carried? That's a remarkable acoustic. You could put plays and concerts on down there, if there was anyone to watch them." They waited while Tom came back up the steps.

"Could you hear me?" he said. "You've got to come down, miss. It's incredible when you're down there in the middle. I think it's a sacred place. I think it's the spirits that have carved that trunk and left it there."

The waiting adults reacted in their different ways to the news of what Helena called the amphitheatre. Bridie was cross at having to wait for them to get back, "with it getting hotter and hotter all the time". Still now they knew it was there, everyone wanted a look at it, even if it was slightly out of their way. So instead of taking all their belongings and beginning the march proper, they set off in single file behind Tom and Boy Blue, leaving Melodie and the two dogs tied up by the sacks and covers.

Tom led them round the top of the hollow to the steps. It was then that they heard for the first time the pipe music Helena had heard in her dreams, faint on the morning air but unmistakeable. Mrs Hubbard had contrived to get behind Helena and now she poked her hard with her stick. Helena looked back.

"He's here," she hissed. "He's collectin us up for a dance."

"What do you mean? Who's here?" whispered Helena.

"You'll see soon enough. If it's who I think." The words were hardly out of her mouth when a figure appeared on the far side of the basin. He was dressed in a patchwork suit of red and yellow and blue and on his head was a flat black hat with a feather poking up like a pennant. Music streamed from the pipe in his hands. He leapt surefootedly down the side and strode out into the middle of the arena.

"Welcome!" he said, arms outspread. "Welcome to Hillbilly Hollow. Here's where the real magic begins!" He turned with a flourish of his arm. Six other figures appeared at the lip of the basin, three men and three women, all in motley too, and each carrying an instrument, the women fiddles, two of the men drums and the other, bagpipes. All of a sudden at the front of the line of children there was a yell.

"Dad, Dad, it's me!" and Tom went tumbling down the steps and hurtled across the flat ground until he fell into the arms of the pipe-player. There was an almighty rush of children behind him, not stopping until they were gathered in a circle round the strange figure. The five adults stood alone at the top.

"Tom, my boy!" The man held Tom back at arm's length and looked hard at him. "After all this time..." He wrapped his arms round the boy's head and held him close. "I went back looking for you but the house was empty. You'd gone, your mother had gone. I heard about the pig. I knew it wasn't you that stole it."

"It was that Horner," said Tom. "He hid it in his cart. Everyone knew it was him, Dad. But no-one dared say cos of who he was. It was big healthy pig and he made it into chops and sausages." Tom started to cry, big, heaving sobs. "I got a leathering. They put me in the stocks, for a whole day. I was looking and looking for you, everywhere, for years."

"Me too." The man hugged Tom tight and wiped his own eyes with the back of his hand. "So let's celebrate, shall we?" he said to his son with a grin. "Come on down!" he shouted up at Helena and the others high up on the edge of the crater. "What's keeping you?"

"We're comin," said Mrs Hubbard, "but we aint as quick as them." She sat down and began to shuffle down the steps on her bottom.

The man laughed.

"Hello there, another familiar face! Get up on your feet, Mavis Muffet. You were a fine dancer when I last saw you."

She huffed. "That was a long time ago, Piper. I aint been Mavis Muffet for many a long year. I was marrit after I was dancin. It was the dancin what did it. That's where I met Hubbard." She stood up though and climbed down the rest of the steps and walked across to him.

"Where've you been all this time? You left your boy all alone. He's been lookin for you, pinin for you."

Because of that extraordinary acoustic, all this was perfectly audible to the remaining four up on the edge. Now each of them in turn made their way down to the bottom. The six musicians followed and began playing as soon as they were down on the flat. Backwards and forwards went the notes. Feet began to tap and hips to sway. The musicians made a line and began to hop and skip round the arena. One by one the children followed on, stamping and skipping and hopping. Bert joined the end of the line as it weaved about and, on his way past, grabbed Helena who grabbed Spratt who grabbed Bridie who grabbed Mrs Hubbard. On and on they went, raising clouds of dust. At last the instruments fell silent. Everyone clapped and cheered.

Mrs Hubbard pulled out a hanky and wiped her face. "I aint been jiggin like that for centuries I reckon," she said.

"Does the heart good, eh Mavis Hubbard?" The piper laughed. "Now tell me – What good fortune brings you here?"

"Good fortune isn't what I'd call it," said Bridie. "One disaster after another is more like it."

"Aha! A lady who doesn't see the silver lining, only the cloud that hides it. Pray what is your name, good woman?"

"Bridget Sullivan's my full name," she said with something like a curtsey, "but they mostly call me Bridie."

"Let us leave Bridie in the kitchen with her cousins, Cornish Pasty and Apple Turnover," he said with a bow. "From now on, it shall be Bridget, by decree." Bridie blushed with pleasure.

Helena stepped forward. "If you don't mind me asking, who are *you* and what brings *you* here? This is a lonely spot for a bunch of music-makers and thespians to make their home."

The man bowed to her. "Whom do I have the pleasure of speaking to?" he asked. "I like to know my interlocutors by name."

Helena laughed at that.

"This interlocutor's called Helena Otterley, your others... well, Mrs Hubbard you already know, Bridie, Bridget if you prefer, has introduced herself and our two gallant men are Mr Jack Spratt, sadly without his lovely wife, and Mr Bert Hogarth, sometimes known as Cornelius." She gave a sweeping bow and it was his turn to laugh.

"Excellent, Mistress Otterley. David Piper, at your service. I hereby nominate you Mistress of Ceremonies!" He took off his feathered hat and placed it on her head.

"I don't know about mistress of ceremonies," said Helena, settling the hat more firmly on her head, "but spokesperson I can certainly do. Here's how it is, Mr Piper. We've walked for miles and miles from Mrs Hubbard's boot. We've lost some of our dearly loved children on the way. We've been beset by witches, wild animals, insects, thorns and always, hunger and thirst. We are trying to find a resting place, to build a proper home for these children so that they can learn and grow and take their place in life. Right now we've left a mule, two dogs and a pile of bags and stores further back down the hill. We have to go back and collect those because we must get to the copse over there," she pointed to the trees, "before the end of the day."

"You will be most welcome," said the Piper. "Our own encampment is there. We have all that you need, tucked away in those very woods. Collect your belongings and we shall escort you there without further delay." He turned to his musicians and nodded. The band started up a jig and set off across the arena with the children and the grown-ups behind them. Led by the musicians the whole company sprang up those steps as lightly and easily as a herd of mountain goats.

Chapter 2

Hidden in the heart of the copse were a dozen round huts made of woven twigs and branches and covered with skins and cloths. There were no doors and no windows to these dwelling places but the floors were swept clean and there were raised wooden pallets for sleeping and sitting on. The huts had been built in a circle round an open space and in the centre of that space was a fire pit. An enormous blackened stew-pot hung from a trivet balanced on stones over the flames.

It had been easy to find the way. There were strange man-made objects to guide them, shrubs twisted into animal shapes, stones piled on rocks to look like men standing guard, hollows filled with shining pebbles laid out like snail-shells. As they came nearer, colours flashed in the trees and bushes: flags and pennants fluttering in the breeze. Melodie at the head of the file, was moving forward faster than ever, ears twitching. She swayed her head from side to side, a sure sign as Bert said, that she approved of what was happening.

Three days passed. How they slept and ate, how the children romped and jumped and climbed!

"Today," said David Piper, standing up at breakfast time, "now you are rested, we shall have a festival."

"What kind of a festival?" asked Marigold.

"A festival of make-believe and music – how does that sound?"

There was a cheer from the children. Bridie had a worried frown on her face.

"Aha! Mistress Bridget, the very woman!" cried the Piper, holding out his hand. "Come."

Bridie made her way forward.

"The children must put themselves into groups. Six groups and one of my fine musicians in every group. You who know these children better than anyone here" – there was loud huh! from Mrs

Hubbard at this which the Piper ignored – "can help them do that."

"They were in groups when we were walking," said Bridie. "They could be in those again."

The Piper looked at her. "As you wish," he said lightly. "But think why they were in those groups, Mistress, and whether it might now be time for a new mix. More fizz perhaps?"

Bridie looked mystified but Marigold got up. "I'll help. I see what the Piper means," she said.

"Me too," said Alice.

"Good girls," said the Piper. He turned to Helena and Mrs Hubbard. "We shall need a good meal to round the celebration off. Please see to it. That leaves our friends, Mr Spratt and Mr Hogarth. We shall make a group of our own, and Mistress Bridget will join us as soon as she has finished with her other duties."

The company assembled as the moths and bats were beginning to flutter among the branches. It was a wonder to behold all that had been done and learnt in the space of a few hours. The children did their turns like old hands and the singing was judged the best anyone had ever heard. At last it was time for the Piper's team, Bert and the Piper, Spratt and Bridie. There would be no singing in this act, so the Piper announced, and no music except the drums which Bert was going to beat quietly in the background.

"This is how it works," he said, looking down at the rows of children cross-legged in front of him. "We shall act a play for you. But this is a play with a difference, a play with only one word. The word is 'rubarbara'. Can you say that?"

"Rubarbara!" shouted the children.

"Excellent. Let us see if one word can tell a story." He bowed to his audience and turned to Bridie and Spratt who were lined up beside him, the one looking as ill at ease as the other. He motioned to them to begin.

Spratt and Bridie mimed their farewells. Bridie sat down and appeared to be rocking a cradle.

"Rubarbara, rubarbara," she cooed. She got up after a moment and tiptoed over to the other side of the open space and began to prepare food on an imaginary stove. The Piper crept in, slyly, slowly, sneakily. A few of the children gave a shout but Bridie took no notice and kept on stirring her pot over the flame and pretending to taste what was in it. The Piper crept further in and got down on his hands and knees, crawling across to where Bridie had been rocking the cot. Bert beat the drums a little harder. The Piper leant in and lifted the baby out of the cot, looked around like a dog that's stolen the Sunday roast and started to back out. The drums rose to a crescendo.

"Rubarbara!" shrieked the children, to no avail. The Piper leapt beyond the circle. Bridie turned back from her stove to discover the loss of her baby. She began to wail, "Rubarbara!" Spratt came onto the stage and added some more questioning rubarbaras to hers. Real tears were pouring down Bridie's face and Spratt had his arms round her and was stroking her hair. They walked out of the circle. The Piper reappeared, holding an imaginary bundle in his arms which he set down on the floor.

"Rubarbara," he said in a greasy, greedy voice and rubbed his stomach. The children hissed and booed. He began to light a fire.

"He's gonna roast that babe," shouted Marigold from the back. "We gotta stop him. We gotta shout for the babe, so as its mammy and daddy hear where it is!" She pushed her way through the ranks of children, stepping on ankles and legs as the adults watched in awe. "Ready?" she said. "Right – now!" And such a rubarbara went up that the trees shook with the sound of it and the nesting birds flew up in dismay.

Spratt and Bridie appeared on the edge of the circle. The children gave another great shout and the couple burst in upon the kneeling Piper who jumped to his feet. Bridie rushed to pick up her baby. Spratt seized hold of the Piper and held him fast. He hung his head as Spratt reeled out one rubarbara after another in a torrent of condemnation and when he ran out of breath, he led the guilty man off the stage to the cheers of the children. The actors returned for a bow. But Marigold hadn't sat down.

"What punishment are you going to give him?" she said,

addressing her question to Spratt. He was momentarily at a loss but collected himself quickly, "It's not for me to determine the punishment," he said. "That is a matter for you all to decide. You must make sure the punishment fits the crime." Without waiting to be told, the children got into little huddles. Soon there was a buzz of chatter rising in the darkness. Helena had been watching them in increasing admiration. Mrs Hubbard leant over and tapped her on the knee.

"They're enjoyin theirselves aint they? Piper's good at this sort of thing. You goin to read us sommat out your book next, seein how you aint had time to learn a song?"

"Anything in a book is going to be tame after what we've seen tonight."

"To you mebbe but not to us. We aint in the way of readin."

Helena went into the hut and brought back the anthology.

"I do have a poem I'd like to read but it's very long. Maybe I'll read some of it tonight and more tomorrow."

"We aint rushin them off to bed," said Mrs Hubbard. "This here's a festival. Festivals is supposed to go on and on, or they did was I was young."

Helena looked through the pages until she found 'The Pied Piper of Hamelin'.

"It's here, I thought it would be. It's about another Piper, a magical one."

"That'd be Piper's great-grandpa," said Mrs Hubbard. "He was the magic one."

All this time the children were busy, taking their duties as sentencers very seriously. Finally Marigold and Billy stood up and came into the centre.

"There's two opinions," she said. "Billy's going to tell you about one opinion and I'm telling about the other and everybody's to choose which one we go with. Billy's first, then me." She sat down, leaving Billy to make his case to his audience.

"We think Piper ought to be put to work with Bert. Bert's good with building things. Piper's got to make the stocks he's going to be put in. And then he's got to sit in them all day for a week with only water to drink and a bit of bread to eat, so as he learns his lesson."

There was clapping from some of the children. The others looked anxiously at Marigold. How could she match that? She stood up.

"We thought about doing something like that but we didn't see how it was going to change Piper's mind about eating babes. And another thing: Piper's good at lots of things so we don't want him running off when he's been punished. When Tom was put in the stocks for the pig he never stole, that's what he did when he got out, didn't you, Tom?"

Tom nodded.

"So we've got to find a punishment that sort of lasts. What we've decided is Piper's got to be with Mum. He's got to help her and Bridie with the little ones. Not on his own though. He's got to watch how they do it and learn. And we think he'll not like doing that, not at first anyhow, so he'll feel he is being punished. But later when he gets used to it, he'll see it's fun being with babes and the little ones and he'll not want to eat them any more. So that's our punishment. Now which one are we having?"

Spratt stepped into the ring. "You've done a grand job," he said. "Now we need a final vote. Can I have hands in the air for Billy's proposal." Fifteen small hands went shooting up. "And hands in the air for Marigold's." Three times as many rose in the air. "That seems to be the decision then," he said. "By a majority vote, Mr Piper is sentenced to be taught how to look after children."

There was another great round of applause. The Piper stepped into the ring and bowed to Mrs Hubbard.

"I will report for my first lesson tomorrow, ma'am, if that is acceptable to the company."

"That'll be fine," said Marigold, who was still standing out at the front. "We'll be checking with Mum to make sure you're doing it right."

"Now let's have a bit of quiet," said Mrs Hubbard. "Otter's goin to tell us a poem out of one of her books. I want you sittin nice for her."

Helena opened her book and waited while the children shuffled and settled. Then she began.

"This is a poem about a magical Piper. He was the great-grandfather of our own Mr Piper. The story happened a long time ago in a town in another country far away from here. They had a problem in that town, as you will hear." She began to read:

"Rats!
They fought the dogs, and killed the cats,
And bit the babies in the cradles,
And ate the cheeses out of the vats,
And licked the soup from the cook's own ladles,
Split open the kegs of salted sprats,
Made nests inside men's Sunday hats...

"They didn't know what to do about those rats. But then along came this strange man, wearing funny clothes," she said. "Who do you think it was?"

"I know! Piper's great grandpa," shouted Gerard.

"Exactly," she said, "and what does he do? He tells all the important people in the town, like the mayor and the councillors, that he can take the rats away but he wants to be paid for his services."

"He should be too," said Bert. "Dirty creatures, rats."

"The mayor's at his wits' end with the rats. They're eating everything so he says he'll pay the Pied Piper one thousand guilders if he can do it. That's a lot of money. The Piper thinks this is a fair bargain so he agrees to help. Listen to what happens next:

"Into the street the Piper stepped,
Smiling first a little smile,
As if he knew what magic slept
In his quiet pipe the while;
Then, like a musical adept,
To blow the pipe his lips he wrinkled,
... And ere three shrill notes the pipe uttered,

You heard as if an army muttered;
And the muttering grew to a grumbling;
And the grumbling grew to a mighty rumbling;
And out of the houses the rats came tumbling.
Great rats, small rats, lean rats, brawny rats,
Brown rats, black rats, grey rats, tawny rats,
Grave old plodders, gay young friskers,
Fathers, mothers, uncles, cousins,
Cocking tails and pricking whiskers,
Families by tens and dozens,
Brothers, sisters, husbands, wives—
Followed the Piper for their lives.
From street to street he piped advancing,
And step for step they followed dancing,
Until they came to the river Weser,
Wherein all plunged and perished!"

"'Perished' means they died," she said, seeing some of the little ones at the front looking puzzled. The children clapped with delight, and the Piper standing back in the shadows smiled a quiet smile. "So what d'you think happened next?" she said.

"The rats aren't really dead. Rats can swim. I've seen them. They get back out and come after him," shouted Hector.

"In the story they were really dead this time," said Helena, "Shall I tell you what happened?" Nods from the children. "Remember the Pied Piper had driven a bargain with the mayor. The townsfolk had to pay him one thousand guilders. But he looked a funny sort of fellow, like a gypsy or a hobo, and once the mayor saw there were no more rats he decided he wasn't going to pay the Pied Piper after all. This is what the mayor's thinking:

"To pay this sum to a wandering fellow
With a gypsy coat of red and yellow!
"Beside," quoth the Mayor with a knowing wink,
"Our business was done at the river's brink;

We saw with our eyes the vermin sink,
And what's dead can't come to life, I think.
So, friend, we're not the folks to shrink
From the duty of giving you something for drink,
And a matter of money to put in your poke;
But, as for the guilders, what we spoke
Of them, as you very well know, was in joke.
Beside, our losses have made us thrifty.
A thousand guilders! Come, take fifty!"

"That's bad," said Alice. "That's him breaking his promise. Piper won't be pleased at that."

"He didn't change his clothes from when that man said he'd give him all the money," piped up Samuel from the front row.

"No, you're right. The Piper was wearing the same clothes. He had kept his promise to the townsfolk, to the letter. He wasn't pleased at all," said Helena. "But he had another trick up his sleeve. The Mayor and his friends had forgotten about the magic in his pipe."

"I know, I know," said little Dominic, putting his hand up. "He's going to lead the mayor into the river and drown him and his friends, like the rats."

"Well he might have. He didn't like the mayor but, like how you want to teach our own Piper a lesson about looking after little ones, the Piper in my story wanted to teach the mayor and his friends a lesson they wouldn't forget. So he came up with a different idea:

"Once more he stepped into the street;
And to his lips again
Laid his long pipe of smooth straight cane;
And ere he blew three notes
There was a rustling, that seemed like a bustling

…

Small feet were pattering, wooden shoes clattering,
Little hands clapping and little tongues chattering,

And, like fowls in a farmyard when barley is scattering,
Out came the children running.
All the little boys and girls,
With rosy cheeks and flaxen curls,
And sparkling eyes and teeth like pearls,
Tripping and skipping, ran merrily after
The wonderful music with shouting and laughter."

"He's pinchin the kids!" shouted Billy.

"He isn't pinching them," said Marigold fiercely. "He's rescuing them. They like the music. He's going to take them somewhere better than what that mayor's got."

"Exactly!" said Helena. "In this story all the children want to go with the Piper. He must have done his lessons with Mrs Hubbard really well because this Piper loves children.

"After him the children pressed;
And, lo, as they reached the mountain's side,
A wondrous portal opened wide,
As if a cavern was suddenly hollowed;
And the Piper advanced and the children followed,
And when all were in to the very last,
The door in the mountain-side shut fast."'

She stopped speaking and laid the book aside. There was a hush in the children. At last a little voice spoke from the back, "That poem's about us, except we did most of it without the Piper."

Chapter 3

What she had seen at the festival convinced Helena she had to get the children started with proper lessons. Songs and plays were all very well, as she said to Mrs Hubbard, but they needed some basic grounding too: their numbers and their letters. There was nothing for it. Ignorant though she was about teaching small children, she must open a school. She would start by teaching them how to spell their names and how to write the numbers for their ages. This time the proposal met with universal approval, Bridie even offering to help with the littlest ones. Helena began her preparations and, since there were almost no resources and she had never taught before, very quickly decided she was as ready as she was ever going to be.

The morning the new school opened for lessons a small group of children assembled outside Helena's hut. She sat the children down, welcomed them and told them that they were going to learn about all sorts of things. They would not be sitting inside all day. They would explore the countryside and learn about its plants and rocks and history. Before any of that could begin though, they must start by learning how to write their names, their first name and their surname.

"Does everyone know what a 'surname' is?" she asked, seeing a number of blank faces staring at her. There was a lot of head-shaking and no-one spoke.

"It's your second name, the one that all your family has. You have a name that is only yours, like David or Marigold or Tom, but you have another one as well, that you share with your mother and father and your brothers and sisters, if you have any. That's your surname."

"What if you don't have a mother or a father?" said Boy Blue, who had insisted on being allowed to be in the first class. "There's lots of us don't have a mother or a father."

"But you must have had a mother and father once," Helena said, feeling she was in danger of losing control already.

"Course," said Angela scornfully, "everyone knows you can't exist without a mum or a dad made you, but that doesn't mean you know who they were. I don't know who my dad was. I sort of know who my mum was but I don't know what her name was."

"I could take my aunty's name," said Boy Blue. "She's Mrs Weaver. But she's not my real aunty and I don't like her, nor my uncle either. I don't see the point of being named after someone you don't like."

Helena was so deep in this unexpected dilemma that she didn't notice the Piper had stationed himself at the door and was listening in. He coughed a little cough. She looked round, and coloured with embarrassment at the idea of someone seeing how badly the whole thing was going. He came right into the hut without waiting to be asked.

"Mistress Otterley, you have started in quite the right place," he said.

Helena looked at him. Was he mocking her? That was too much if so. Someone else could take over if she was to be inspected at her first lesson. But there wasn't a hint of mockery in his eyes.

"As you know, we Hillbillies think our names are one of our most precious possessions. My name is something that cannot be taken away from me. It's important that I like it and that it fits me, the 'me' I think I am. Let us seize this wonderful opportunity therefore. The children who haven't got a second name – a surname, as your teacher quite correctly calls it – can call themselves whatever they want. You may all be 'Hubbard' if you wish. Those of you who have one already may keep it if you like it or, if you think it no longer matches who you are, you may change it to something that suits you better."

The idea took root instantly. The camp was abuzz with words. Everyone began trying out new names. Bert proved to be particularly clever at finding names to fit and Helena thought of her conversation with Mrs Purselain again, so long ago, and smiled to herself. Gradually as the week went by, more and more children had fastened on a first name and a second that he or she was happy to own.

Helena noted the names down as the children made their choices. Once the list was complete she tore a blank page out of the back of the anthology and carefully wrote out the whole list in alphabetical order. A meeting was arranged to formally welcome all the new names.

This was the list of names:

Abby Heartsease *aged 7*
Aisha Hasty *aged 5*
Alphonse Sprightly *aged 8*
Alice Moonshine *aged 9*
Angela Golightly *aged 9*
Anemone Sweeting *aged 12*
Archy Bowman a*ged 12*
Benjamin Goodswimmer *aged 5*
Billy Broker *aged 11*
Boy Blue *aged 6*
Briony Mullen *aged 8*
Bobby Shaftoe *aged 10*
Catriona Shining *aged 7*
Charly Hubbard *aged 5*
Claire Dainty *aged 4*
Courtney Polloni *aged 7*
Deirdre Sullivan *aged 8*
Dominic Hubbard *aged 6*
Dunya Swanally *aged 8*
Donald O'Leary *aged 11*
Ebony Flinders *aged 11*
Edwin Foster *aged 7*
Fred Happy *aged 7*
Gerard Swordsman *aged 12*
Gillyflower Blossom *aged 4*
Godwin Blanchet *aged 7*
Hector Paris *aged 10*

Harry Goodboy *aged 4*
Hope Singer *aged 9*
Ivan Wheeler *aged 8*
Jack Foster *aged 7*
James Quicksilver *aged 10*
John Mountjoy *aged 4*
Jeanie Swift *aged 7*
Keith Pieman *aged 9*
Luke Hubbard *aged 10*
Lily Pikestaff *aged 12*
Malcolm Greatly *aged 8*
Marigold Makepeace *aged 11*
Mary Lamb *aged 9*
Maudant Frobisher *aged 8*
Nadya Lightly *aged 7*
Nerissa Segal *aged 6*
Obe Attila *aged 10*
Octavia Tiptree *aged 6*
Olga Sullivan *aged 9*
Osman Watcher *aged 5*
Pedro Horseman *aged 9*
Pietor Liebermann *aged 11*
Rebecca Applecheeks *aged 8*
Rosalie Gently *aged 9*
Rueben Stone *aged 7*
Samira Goldilocks *aged 4*
Samuel Rasin *aged 5*
Sheila Clearwater *aged 11*
Sonya Hugget *aged 7*
Tessa Hubbard *aged 6*
Tom Piper *aged 10*
Vincent Winner *aged 10*
William Whaler *aged 8*
Zac Superman *aged 6*
Zuma Hubbard *aged 5*

Chapter 4

The days passed in lessons and chores and play. The sun shone as hard and hot as ever but the trees and shrubs protected the company from the full force of its rays. There was water in the well and simple food on the table. In the morning Helena and Bridie took the children through their multiplication tables and their reading and writing and in the afternoon they went off collecting berries and roots, cutting the tough grass for Melodie and the two goats the Hillbillies kept, or helping Bert who was building a bigger hut so all the little ones were under one roof. The Piper and his troupe were often away up the hill behind the huts, practising hard for their next foreign adventure. Tom had been promised he could go with his father this time. It seemed that nothing could come to disturb the peace of their lives. Mrs Hubbard had never looked so relaxed and Bert was full of building plans – a school room, a kitchen shelter. Helena listened politely but found it harder and harder to enter into the discussions. She decided to go to the amphitheatre on her own one late afternoon, to walk her discontent out of her system.

"It's as if I don't feel I'm really alive unless something remarkable or awful is happening. And I'm ducking the one thing that I have to do. I have to go but I can't. And, if I'm honest with myself, it's because I don't know what to do about Walter." She said this out loud and looked around, as if expecting the spirit of the rocks to counsel her. But the desert gave her nothing back except the noise of her footsteps on the dry earth.

She kicked a loose stone and watched it bounce down into the amphitheatre then turned and began to walk slowly back. As she came to the last stretch she saw Jack Spratt striding out towards her. He waved and came on rapidly.

"I'm glad to see you're on your way home," he said. "Mrs Hubbard said I ought to round you up! It makes you sound like a stray sheep but that's what she said."

"She knows what she's saying," said Helena. "I definitely need a shepherd to lead me home, or show me the way."

"I can lead you as far as the huts but beyond that I'm afraid I can't help you," he said, a little stiffly. "I've got to go looking for my own lost sheep pretty soon, my wife you know. I must get back to her."

"You're going to leave?" said Helena, realising she'd been so immersed in her own situation she'd not given a thought to how Spratt might be missing his wife.

"Yes, I'm going soon. There's nothing more for me to do here now we're out of the danger zone. If they move on they will have the Piper to help and if they don't, well, I hear there's a township the far side of the mountain. The older boys and girls may get work there, or training."

"So this is the end," said Helena wonderingly. "Once you go everything changes."

"It's not the end of anything," said Spratt. "I'm a small cog in the machine. I won't be missed."

"Oh but you will!" cried Helena. "You're part of what we've lived through. When you go part of our history goes with you."

"Now, now," said Spratt, alarmed at the intensity of this. "You mustn't get carried away."

"I'm not being carried away," said Helena. "Any one of us leaving will change things for all the others. And it's not just you. I have to go as well, so it won't be one small cog in the machine, it'll be two. And if two go, will the machine still run? That's the question."

"The machine will work fine, even if Bridie and Bert go too. Mrs Hubbard has managed those children on her own for generations. She has never had as much support and help as she has now. Bert's not planning on leaving for the moment, nor Bridie. They will, eventually of course, when the time's right. We have to do the honest thing, each of us. If the honest course is to stay, one stays. If it is to go, one goes. It's quite straightforward. You have to be clear and detached about your objectives. Don't get sidetracked onto non-essentials. It's what they teach you in the army – useful advice when one is faced with a multiplicity of competing priorities."

"Faced with a multiplicity of competing priorities," Helena repeated the words. "It's easy to say it, Mr Spratt; putting it into practice is another matter".

"You're not a child, Helena Otterley," he said, and Helena heard the reproof in his voice. "You know what you have to do." He bowed to her and walked off.

Helena, Bert and Bridie were sitting round the fire. Mrs Hubbard had already retired to bed and Spratt was nowhere to be seen.

"I was talking with Spratt this afternoon," Helena began. "He's leaving soon, to find his wife."

"So I believe," said Bert. "We'll miss him."

"I've got to go as well," said Helena who was still smarting from Spratt's last remark.

"Why's that?" asked Bridie. "What's the hurry?"

"No hurry, but I need to find my friends back there again and pick up my own life."

"Are you going to see Walter Bogolan before you go?" Bert spoke out of the shadows.

"Why do you ask that?"

"Mrs Hubbard said you'd made a promise to him. That was how you got away." It was Bridie who spoke this time and in the light of the fire Helena could see her bright eyes watching.

"Mrs Hubbard's right. I did make him a promise and I ought to see him again to tell him I can't keep it but I don't see how I can. We're miles away from the Bogolan castle and I've no way of getting in touch with him."

Bridie broke in: "You can't take yourself off as if it doesn't matter what you said, whatever it was."

"I promised I'd marry him," said Helena since that seemed to be what they were waiting for her to say. "Did Mrs Hubbard tell you that too?"

"No she didn't but we thought it must be something big like that. And now you say you can't?"

"No, and I never could."

"But you love him, eh, even so?" Bert's voice was soft in the dark.

"I don't know if that's the right word. It's true that I do love everything here, everyone. Every child, all of you." Helena felt her two companions shuffle slightly either side of her. "Another thing Mrs Hubbard said to me… she said I'd better get ready for the sadness of losing people. We were talking about Walter when she said it but it goes much further than him. I'd like to see Billy in a trade and Gerard learning how to be a blacksmith and Marigold making speeches and changing the world, and I won't see any of it."

"You would if you stayed," reasoned Bert.

"Yes but sooner or later I'd have to go. Spratt said you'd both go in time. We're all the same. We don't belong here. We maybe don't belong anywhere, because we're caught between here and there. I wouldn't mind that if I was sure I'd get back here again and see how things have changed but I've no idea whether that could ever happen so I have to tell myself that when I go it's 'for good'."

"Amelia said you weren't to come back and you did. If you do things right you'll be back. Maybe not right here, some place different but magical all the same."

"It's not magic I want," said Helena, "it's belonging. I've felt more at home here than I have ever since I was a small child. The truth as I can see it now is that's what brought me back. I told myself it was 'to help' but the real reason is I wanted more of this, more of the children and you, more of Mrs Hubbard's special kind of magic."

There was a cry from one of the huts and Bridie got up to see what was wrong.

"D'you think Mrs Hubbard knows I'm going?" Helena asked Bert, not wanting a silence to come between them.

"She knows and she's ready for it. She's seen more than you come and go over the years. Mind you, she doesn't usually get so close to passers-by, like she has with you."

"Is that what I am, a passer-by?"

"It doesn't mean you haven't been a wonder. A comet passes by and no-one says it isn't a marvel. You're a marvel, Helena Otterley, and don't let anyone say you different."

"Oh Bert," said Helena with a lump in her throat. "A marvel is the last thing I am. I've had a lot of luck and a few wacky ideas that worked out right. Either that or Amelia's been keeping an eye on me, keeping me safe. Mostly it's been you four, until the lessons, but they don't count."

Bert stood up and stretched.

"I'm not going to argue with you. I'm not wanting to cut this short neither but if Bridie's not coming back I'm off for my kip. Good night," he said abruptly. He walked a few steps off, then seemed to hesitate and came back to where Helena was still sitting by the fire. "I'll do whatever you want," he said. "If you need help to go or stay or find Walter Bogolan, whatever it is. I'll help you. If you want."

Not trusting herself to speak or meet his eye, Helena held up her hand. He took it in both of his and held it tightly for a moment and, just as suddenly as he'd come back, he slipped away into the shadows.

Chapter 5

Helena was tidying up after lessons, the shouts of the children coming faintly to her from outside. I'm not so essential, she thought, life will go on the same, or better, whether I'm here or not. A shadow moved across the door of the hut. She looked up. Boy Blue was leaning against the door jamb.

"Hey, you gave me a shock," she said. "I thought you'd gone to play with the others."

"I was waiting for you, miss," he said.

"For what?"

"For talking. Before you go."

"Who said I'm going?"

"No-one said but I know. You're going to find that giant, aren't you – the one that helped us?"

"Is that what you think I ought to do?"

He nodded.

"Maybe I will, maybe I won't. It'll be dangerous for me if I do." Helena came and joined him at the door and they both sat down outside with their backs against the wall.

"Because of the witches, I know," said Boy Blue. "Because you'll be over the river again and they'll come after you."

"I don't need to go back there, if I don't look for Walter. I can stay quite safe by leaving from here," said Helena.

"Not really," said Boy Blue. "Safe on the outside but not on the inside. That giant – he must be waiting for you somewhere." He drew a circle in the dust with a stick. "It must be for him like it was for me. You think the whole world's forgotten about you. You know you're going to die and your bones are going to crumble to dust and not one person will care or know."

She looked at him.

"You felt like that but that can't be how it is for Walter," she said. "He's a big strong giant. No-one's going to lock him in a cage or kill him."

"They don't need to," said Boy Blue with a faraway look in his eye. "You can hurt bad enough without being locked in a cage."

"I wish you could come with me," she said. "We've been so happy. We've had so many adventures."

"That's right. You won't have nothing to help you when you go," said Boy Blue. "We used all Walter's gold. You burnt the hat. I said you shouldn't have. Mum said that too."

"It's not Belle's hat that would save me. It wouldn't work twice over. If I go looking for Walter I'm going to have to rely on me and me alone."

"I could come with you."

"I wish that too, more than anything in the world. You know I don't have any children in my world. You – and Tom, but Tom's found his dad again so he doesn't count. You are all I have, Boy Blue."

"What'll I do while I wait for you to come back? Will you come back?"

"Of course I'll come back, if I do things right. What you have to do is get on with your learning. Read your books. Write your stories. Draw your pictures. Go on adventures again – better ones, not so dangerous."

The leaving was set for the following week. Spratt would have liked to go sooner but Helena insisted she had final work to do on the children's lessons. Each of those days she woke with a twisting pain in her stomach. At the last fireside gathering there was none of the usual talk. Bert and Bridie left Helena and Mrs Hubbard alone once the children were all settled. Helena was sick at heart but not so Mrs Hubbard.

"I'm goin to miss you," she said in remarkably cheerful tones. "But you done good by us. You set the children learnin and they're going to keep it up after you're gone. I'll see to that. You'll see the change in them when you come back."

"Will I get back?"

Mrs Hubbard rubbed her bony old chin.

"It's like I said before. You won't be comin back if you leave sommat big undone. You know that. You don't need me to say it twice. I'm not flubberin about you goin. I says to myself 'she needs to go'. Mebbe it's the end for you and me. I don't know, no more does anyone. But it aint the end. If you can sort out Walter as well as you done the rest there aint no need for you to worry. But you've got to care or it won't work."

"I'm scared," Helena said. "It's not just the witches. It's Walter himself, the other giants and the war. And that's just what I know about. What about all the rest? I never thought I'd fall in a trap, and look what happened because of that. Will it be dragons or trolls, or what, this time?"

"It won't be dragons, that's for sure. They're quiet beasts and there's none about that I know of and there aint any trolls in the desert. The witches is a risk I grant you, but if you're off the road and well hidden by nightfall they're not goin to find you. I aint got no crystal ball but sommat tells me it'll work out fine. Walter'll be lookin for you. It's not like you're doin this on your own. And the way I see it, if both of you're lookin you'll meet up somehow. I'm not sayin it's goin to be easy but you'll be doin right and that's a big protection."

They fell silent.

"I'm givin you sommat tonight," said Mrs Hubbard after a moment.

"Another dreaming pill?" said Helena. "I don't think I'd better. I've got to be all present and correct for Mr Spratt tomorrow. You know what he's like about being on time."

"No it aint a dreamin pill. It aint a pill at all but it is in a bottle." Mrs Hubbard pulled out a small phial full of dark liquid.

"Whatever is it?" Helena reached out but Mrs Hubbard held it back.

"I've been makin it for you. The fancy name's 'desert essence' but we don't call it that. We call it liquid gold. It's liquid and it's made with desert sand and rocks and roots. It looks black in the bottle but when you pour it out, it's like a deep golden colour. You put a drop or two on a cloth and you take a little sniff now and then and you get right back here, not like you are now but it feels like it. It don't work for me because I'm always here but they say it's that real you have to pinch yourself to make sure you're not dreamin. You must use it sparin mind. You do it too often and it won't work so well."

Helena laughed at that.

"So I'm to be a recreational drug-user in my old age. Well, I suppose it's never too late to begin."

Mrs Hubbard looked upset.

"It aint a bad thing. You make it sound like I'm givin you sommat bad."

"No I didn't mean that at all," said Helena, and the tears welled in her eyes. "I was laughing at myself, for wanting to go back to my boring, ordinary life in that other world."

Chapter 6

As Old Mother Hubbard said when they finally got up from the ashes of the fire that evening, there was no easy way to leave, but leave Helena and Spratt did, the next morning at first light, with the children assembled to wave goodbye and the adults standing in a mournful huddle to watch the pair of them march down the track and out of sight. Tom came with Boy Blue for the first half mile, looking back over his shoulder, as if scared to lose sight of the village. Finally he stopped altogether. He gave Helena a hug and started back on his own up the track.

"He gets nervous about leaving his dad," said Boy Blue.

"I know," said Helena, and took his hand in hers. "You'll have to go back quite soon too. See the rock ahead? We'll go to that and then we say goodbye."

Spratt was a hundred yards in front, marching briskly, not looking back.

"It's all right for him," said Helena, pointing. "He knows where he's going. He's got the scent of home in his nostrils."

Boy Blue didn't answer. He just kept walking, holding tight to her hand. The rock loomed up, closer and closer. Her legs felt like lead. Boy Blue stopped. They looked at each other, her eyes blurred with unshed tears.

"I love you, Boy Blue," she said. She put her arms round him and kissed him on his tufty hair, his forehead.

"I love you too, miss, lots and lots." He reached under his jersey and held out a neatly-folded piece of paper. "You said about writing stories and drawing. I drew you a picture."

She took it from him, blinking away the tears.

A square house with four windows, a door and a chimney, a path at the front, and flowers in the garden. A little stick figure was walking up the path with a bag in its hand. There was a smiling face in one of the downstairs windows.

"See, that's me." He pointed at the window. "I'm looking out of the window of our house and you're coming home from an adventure. I've made us some porridge – you can't see it in the picture but it's there."

Helena was crying again.

"It's real what I'm saying," he said, and he looked so solemn that Helena began to laugh through her tears. "That's better," he said. "You need to go, miss. Mr Spratt's waiting." Quick as a flash, before she could catch him in her arms again, he ran off up the path.

"Tell that giant I was asking for him," he shouted. "Goodbye, miss. Come back soon!"

Spratt had disappeared round the rock. She looked back one last time. Boy Blue, the only child she would ever have, was already out of sight. There was nothing to do except put one foot in front of the other over and over again.

Helena walked that stage of her journey like an automaton, barely registering her surroundings, as numb and emptied out as Tom had been after they rescued him from the web. Spratt was a solicitous companion, leaving her to herself for the most part. They were together while they traversed the scree and came out through the foothills. Once that part of the journey was done Spratt had to turn off towards another range of hills to the east, to find his wife and her family but Helena would keep as close as possible to the route the caravan of children had taken on the outward journey.

On the morning they had to part they were up before the sun had hitched itself above the horizon. It was bitterly cold but neither of them thought to blow a blaze up out of the ashes of the fire. Spratt fastened his jacket and tugged his bag over his shoulders.

"You got your compass safe? You know how to use it?"

Helena patted her pocket and nodded.

"You take good care of yourself," he said.

"And you do the same," said Helena. "Thanks for keeping me company. I hope you find Mrs Spratt well when you get back. She'll be pleased to see you." They shook hands.

"I'll be off now," he said.

"Me too." Helena turned southwards and set off once more.

The walking was easy. With no Spratt out in front to lead the way she had to look up, take in her surroundings and she felt better for it. In the first couple of days while they were making their way down the mountainside onto the plain, they had noticed how around midday a breeze would announce itself. At first there'd be no more than an occasional puff, a sigh, a flutter. Sometimes it would lose heart, evaporate back into stillness and heat. Most often however it gathered strength as the day wore on, so once they stopped they had first to shake out their clothes and wipe the dust from their faces.

On the fourth day, when she got out of the hole she'd bunked in that night, the wind was already up and blowing steadily. The sky was yellowish grey and the landscape that should have been sparkling and sharp in the morning light was opaque, glaucous. Not far ahead, enormous clouds of dust and sand were being sucked up and whirled about. She stepped out to face it but had gone no more than a hundred yards when the full force of it hit her, slapping her about like a dead leaf in its turbulence. Tiny grains of grit peppered her bare skin as sharp as wasp stings. She wrapped her scarf round her face like a camel-driver, leaving only a token slit to look out of but even that wouldn't do – the sand was being driven into every fold and gap. She had to scurry like a rat, right under a rock. The sandstorm raged for hours before she was at last able to clamber out of the hole and go slowly and carefully on her way again.

The following evening she reached the overhang where the witches had been driven back by the river of storm water. She slipped her bag off her back and walked along the twisting lines of the dry river bed, picking up bits of firewood as she went. This camp marked another kind of end. The next day she would step across the divide onto unprotected ground. Beyond the river bed there were still more days of travel to be done.

By the time her fire was burning the moon was high in the sky, casting the same eerie white light across the land as it had the night she first arrived when she'd fallen into Seamus's trap. The silence was so deep and solid she could hear her blood murmuring through her veins, her heart beating, the crunch of the sand as she shifted. She built up the fire until it was giving out a steady heat and curled up beside it with her cover round her. She drifted off into a light sleep.

At first it was as if those she'd left behind in the mountains were tumbling over one another pell-mell to reach her. Hands stretched out. She pushed the cover back and tried to grasp them but they vanished like smoke. Beyond the glowing ashes of her fire was a rocky outcrop, bright where the moonlight touched it but dark and smooth on the side facing her. In the middle of that surface, some four feet above the surrounding ground, a small door had appeared, like a cupboard door. Helena stood up, swaying drunkenly in her sleep and walked across to it. The door had no handle but she pushed it gently and it swung inwards into the rock. Sitting there as large as life was Amelia Purselain in an armchair upholstered in shabby brocade that Helena recognised straightaway. She was half-turned towards the door and smiling.

"You can't come in, dear," she said, "but we can talk a little if you like."

Helena leant in at the doorway, resting her elbows on the shelf.

"How did you know where I was?" she asked.

"I've been following you. Not all the time of course."

"I never knew," said Helena. "I'm sorry I disobeyed you. Are you mad at me?"

"No, I'm not angry." She sighed. "Some call it stealing fire from the gods, others eating of the apple. Same story, different characters. Obedience is the safe option, isn't it? There's a price to be paid though. You know that, don't you?"

"You mean the witches?"

"In your case, yes. Witches, ogres, giants, fallen angels, demons. They all have parts to play, depending on the story. I can't stay long but I can give you one or two pieces of advice, if you want them."

"I do, I do. Amelia, I am so afraid of what will happen to me when I cross the river bed tomorrow. I have nothing left to fight them with."

There was a chuckle from the chair.

"Helena, how little faith you have! You have everything you need to fight them."

"What have I got?" Helena was indignant.

"You, yourself. What your life has taught you, what you've found out while you've been with the children and Mrs Hubbard. Witches can't deal with any of that. But you have to work it out yourself. I can't tell you how. It will be hard, Helena, harder than anything you've done so far but you can do it. Remember what matters most is honesty."

"Will you be there? Will I feel you somewhere near to help me?"

Mrs Purselain shook her head. "There are rules in the game though, and the witches must follow them."

"What use is knowing that if I don't know what the rules are?" said Helena desperately.

"You'll find out soon enough." She stood up beside the chair, a faint image in the darkness, and getting fainter as she spoke. 'I hope we meet again some day. Good luck, Helena. You have done well so far. You have more than fulfilled my expectations."

Chapter 7

It was midnight the following evening when Helena heard the drone of their brooms and spotted them coming fast towards her, three hunched shapes in the sky. They landed one after the other and came over to where she was sitting, dragging their sticks behind them.

"Don't try to run away! You're done for. We're going to chop you into little pieces, you slippery worm." It was all Helena needed to hear to know instantly that Iris had stepped into Eglantine's empty shoes.

"I'm not scared of you and I'm not running anywhere. I knew you'd find me once I crossed the river."

Violet was hopping about full of a childish excitement. Despite the dark Helena could see her face was fissured and pustulent like Eglantine's had been on the night she evaporated into thin air.

"Keep still, dear!" Iris said. Helena heard the irritation in her voice. "The woman is ours. I've told you I don't know how many times, you'll have the skin once the rituals are complete."

Helena pricked her ears up, remembering her dream. Rituals? What rituals? Violet hung her head like a naughty child. Lily shuffled forward out of the shadows.

"Are you sure we can't tie her up, dear? It seems a little risky to have her standing around loose. She's been such a problem every time we've had our hands on her."

Iris shook her head and frowned.

"The regulations say the best effects are obtained when the victim is not bound. Our sister's recovery will be more complete and speedier if the woman is left free. She won't escape this time. I have it on the highest authority that she has nothing to help her, no bottles or spells, or stolen hats either. Stand up nice and straight now and let me begin."

Lily and Violet stood to attention. Iris struck a pose, one hand on her hip, the other extended forward as if to address a multitude.

"The woman here before us, Helena Otterley by name, is responsible for the vanishment of our fair sister, Eglantine. We hereby declare our intention to punish this heinous crime. We shall carry out the execution according to the rituals. The woman will die so that our sister can live again!" Iris dropped her hand and turned to the other two. "Remember, this is Eglantine's only chance. We have to do things exactly right or it won't work. Eglantine will stay vanished and it'll be all the worse for us." Iris turned to Helena. "You've heard what I said. We follow the Golden Rule of Three – you know what that is I suppose?"

"No I don't," replied Helena.

"It's very simple. The rules say you must be given three chances to outwit your captors."

"What do you mean 'three chances'?"

"Questions, wishes, tasks we have to answer or do. I grant you it's a silly exercise. All it does is delay your end, but I've checked and we must do it. There must be no cutting of corners. Once you've had your three chances we'll finish you off. Oh, there's another thing I nearly forgot. Hold up the water bag, Lily."

Lily held up a bulging goatskin bag that gurgled as she lifted it.

"Show her the bucket, Violet,' said Iris.

Violet held up a metal bucket.

"That's what we go by. You've got the time it takes for all the water in the bag to drip into the bucket. Then the game's up for you, you nasty murdering creature."

Lily hooked the water pouch on the branch of a nearby shrub. Violet put the bucket underneath. The first drips plinked onto the metal. Helena saw she had no time to lose. The three witches were now lined up in front of her.

"Let's get going," Helena said. Quick as a flash she took out her box of matches. "You know what children's sparklers are like, straight metal wires with stuff bound round the wire that burns with a bright white light and sparks when they're lit?"

"I know, I know," said Iris. "Why are you wasting time talking about them?"

"It's because of the horrible smell you give off," said Helena.

"Oh, the common rudeness of her!" Violet exclaimed.

"You stink," said Helena. "Like rotten eggs, if you want to know. Like the sulphurous smell of a lit sparkler, only a thousand times more horrible. I don't suppose you can you turn yourselves into sparklers?"

"Of course we can. It's child's play," said Iris.

Lily gave a tut of scorn. "You're a silly woman if you think you can get rid of us that way. It won't work. We'll..."

"Shh, dear," Iris interrupted her before she could go on. "We do as the crazy creature asks. We don't give her clues to help her, do we?" Helena heard the drips falling in the bucket.

"It's child's play is it? OK. As my friend the Piper says, let's have some fun."

"Right," said Iris, "you have to shut your eyes while we change shape. Count to ten, then open them."

Helena shut her eyes and began counting out loud. When she opened them, there in front of her were three large sparklers, stuck upright in the soft ground. She struck a match and held it against the tip of the middle one. It began to throw a rain of sparks onto the ground, the light pricking down the stem at a terrific rate. Quick as a flash she pulled it out of the ground and pressed the nearly spent rod onto the sparkler on the left. Would it catch? Could she hold it steady while the chemicals caught fire? Suddenly the second sparkler fizzed. The sparks began to bounce to the ground. As it did the first sparkler went out, leaving her with only a black metal wire in her hand. She had no chance of lighting the third one. A white-hot pain shot through the palm of the hand holding the dead sparkler. She threw it to the ground. Iris reappeared where it fell. Right behind her Violet popped up where the unlit third sparkler had been. Of Lily however, there was not a sign. The second sparkler, lit by the fire of the first and not by Helena's match, had burnt to its root and now stood stiff and black in the sand.

"Misery and mortal fear! Now there's two to bring back!" Violet cried, seizing the spent firework and waving it in her sister's face. "This is Lily, sweet-scented Lily. Oh my dear Iris. You should have listened. She said to tie the woman up and she was right. Now she's gone. It was you, not the woman, that did it. You burnt her to a stick. Oh woe is us. Two to bring back, not one."

Iris pushed Violet's hand with the dead sparkler away from her.

"The graunchy grumstick's played a wicked trick on us but tying her up is not the answer. Be calm. She's only got two chances left and the bucket's filling up. Eglantine will bring our sister Lily back." Hearing this, Helena walked over to the branch where the goatskin was suspended. The bucket was now one third full and the drips seemed to be falling faster than ever. She had no time to lose. She came back to where the two witches were waiting.

"You see time's running out. What's next? You'd better hurry," said Iris.

"The drips are falling and the bucket is filling," the witches chanted in unison.

Helena put her fingers in her ears and shut her eyes tight. One witch burnt to cinders by the magic and sparkle of childhood. What was next? Remember, Bert had said. Remember the good and the bad. She must go back... something to do with her skin... shingles, was that it? Feel the pain, the ache in her limbs, her head, the torment of clothes touching her skin. Get them off! Get them off!

The witches watched curiously as she wrenched off her jacket, ran her hands over her arms, picking, prodding, scratching. From the elbow joint to just below the shoulder, her skin began to break out in discoloured blotches, scaly patches. She pulled her tee-shirt and jersey over her head and snapped open the fastening on her bra. Shivering in the freezing night air, she ran her hands over her bare breasts, shoulders, rib cage, belly. Wherever she touched more scales and blisters erupted like hideous flowers on the surface of her skin. Off came her boots, kicked under a rock. Her fingers sought the belt of her trousers, loosened that and let them fall round her feet. Her pants went next, and the socks last of all. Cold feet on the cold earth. No more than ten drips in the bucket and she was as naked as a worm in the moonlight.

"What's she doing?" asked Violet and stepped closer to Helena. She gave a shriek. "She's ruining my skin. She's making a spotty, scabby shell grow all over her. Stop her dearest, before there's nothing left for me to wrap round me."

"You can't stop it now it's started," said Helena. She bent over and scratched a kneecap, shedding flakes of dead skin onto the ground. "It itches too, enough to drive you mad at times."

Violet let out another piercing shriek.

"Make her stop! Magic a cure, dear sister, quickly, quickly. Oh my poor skin."

"That's for the woman to do," snapped Iris. "The rules say..."

"Oh bother the rules," spluttered Violet. "You promised me the skin and look at it! It's worse than I am and getting scabbier by the minute." And she stamped her foot in impotent rage.

"There's only one way to make my skin smooth again," said Helena, listening with one ear to the change in note of the drips in the bucket. "The witch who most desires it, and that means you Violet, must change herself into a pot of soothing cream. The other witch, which means you Iris, since Lily is no longer with us, must spread it onto any parts I can't reach. It only works if you rub it in thoroughly and all over. As my mother used to say, the best ointment in the world can't work if it stays inside the pot. When you're ready I'll shut my eyes and count to ten again."

Helena waited breathlessly, to see what they would do. Violet fell on her knees in front of Iris, grabbing at her jacket.

"Dear sister. Look at me. See the state of me. I need that skin. For pity's sake let's do as the woman says."

Helena shut her eyes and began slowly, "One, two..."

When she opened them again there was a glass jar of dark brown ointment open on a flat rock in front of her. Of Violet there wasn't a sign. She dug her fingers into the grease and began wiping it on her arms and down her trunk. The effect was immediate and dramatic, as if a live wire was being applied to every spot the ointment touched. No relief from the itch but a pain like toothache travelling up and down her limbs, through her skin into her organs and settling at last somewhere behind her eyes, blurring her vision and muddling her thoughts.

"Mustn't give up," she gasped, gripping the jar with both hands and biting her lip against the pain. "Mustn't smash the jar. Must use it all up." She began the rubbing again. The shooting pains subsided and in their place came a feeling of being wound in a choking web of corruption. At last she held the jar out to Iris. "Rub what's left on my back and over my buttocks."

Iris flashed her a look of hatred mixed with fear.

"You think I don't see what you've done, you wicked, scheming woman," she snarled. "You've tricked our tender Violet and wiped her out. I'll have her back though, and Lily and dearest Eglantine. Before I do I'll tear you limb from limb, string your guts over the thorn bushes like bindweed."

"Oh shut up and get on with it," croaked Helena weakly. "There was nothing tender about Violet. She's round me like a loathsome, filthy blanket. You can kill me if you like but you'll be killing her too."

Iris snatched the jar and began slapping the ointment on the middle of Helena's bent back in silence. It felt as if someone was scrubbing her with stinging nettles. She swore under her breath. The witch stepped back and threw the empty jar on the ground and kicked Helena's trousers towards her.

"It's done. Cover your shame you horrible creature," she said.

"No. Not yet," said Helena, pulling herself upright with some difficulty and stepping away from her clothes. The grease on her body made her shine like an unlit candle in the dark. "This is it, Iris, our last battle. Just you and me, a fight to the finish."

She picked up a stone and flung it at the witch. Iris didn't move. She simply waved her hand and the stone bounced like a rubber ball at her feet.

"You're stupid," she said.

"No I'm not," retorted Helena who, having seen what happened to her stone, was now sure about the terms of the engagement. "The bucket is still not full and the rules say I have one chance left. It's not stones we're throwing at each other, Iris. We're going to fight it out with words. Words are our weapons."

"As you wish!" said Iris and quick as a flash she shot a barrage in Helena's direction. "Lies! Deceit! Filth! Corruption!"

Helena ducked and they skimmed past her and fell with a clatter against the rock.

"Honour! Justice! Loyalty!" she shouted back and watched in dismay as the words flew high in the air and landed yards away from the witch.

"You won't last long if that's the best you can do," the witch said and without a pause she hissed, "Greed, envy, hatred, betrayal." This time the words sped like arrows straight at Helena. She hopped this way and that. Envy and betrayal missed their mark but greed caught her a glancing blow on her thigh and hatred, flying low, buried its point deep in her left ankle.

"Arrgh!" she gasped, pressing on the dark hole it left and hopping around with the pain. Before she could rally, "tyranny and slavery" ran out of Iris's mouth like ropes and wrapped themselves round Helena's legs. She fell down, kicking violently to free herself.

"Fortitude, honesty, loyalty, patience, tolerance," she cried and got to her feet again. This time she had more success. Iris gave a grunt and bent double under the weight of them. But only for a moment.

"Pulling out of fingernails, cutting out of tongues, torture, blinding, crushing, boiling," she shrieked and it was Helena who felt herself stagger under the blows. Blood spurted from the scabs on her arms and dripped onto the sand.

"Compassion and truth. Help for the sick and injured. Food for the hungry. Protection for the innocent," she gabbled. There was sand in her cuts, sand in her eyes and a noise like the buzzing of wasps in her ears. But she had hit Iris hard. The witch fell and lay curled up, whining like a cur. For a moment the desert fell silent then Iris heaved herself onto all fours, and spat another volley at Helena.

"War! Famine! Pestilence! Gluttony! Licentious abominations!"

Pestilence landed like a thick gob of phlegm in the middle of Helena's forehead. It trickled down into her eyes. The witch's outline turned foggy and dim as the poisons seeped in through her eyeballs. Her head filled with the shrieking and lamentations of the dying. She shook it but the wails grew louder all the time, drowning her thinking. A confusion of images rose up in her mind.

"Free-range hens, grass-fed cattle," she stuttered, "clean oceans, wild salmon swimming free, summer picnics, poetry, music, happiness, friendship, loyalty." She swayed like a drunkard. The witch was dragging herself off to hide behind a rock but she was too slow. The words broke over her in waves. They sucked her up and swirled her round like a piece of seaweed. She landed with a thump on the ground and lay still.

Helena ran her hands over the deep gashes scoring her body. Muzzily she registered that there was hardly a splash to be heard at the bucket. The goatskin bag was hanging like a spent udder on the tree.

Light-headed with loss of blood and half-blind from the pestilence, she could still just make out the tattered, misshapen figure of the witch lying on the sand. She looked tiny, less than half the size she'd been at the start of their battle. There was no movement from that small heap. Helena crept closer until she was standing right beside it. The still shape sprang to life. Iris shot her head round and aimed straight at Helena's bare breasts and belly.

"Destruction! Lust! Tyranny!" Helena flung her arms over her breasts but she was not quick enough and the witch was too close. Every word splattered on her bare body, like gouts of boiling oil. She went down in a heap.

"You're done!" shouted Iris. "I win!" and she fell on her prey, teeth bared as if to tear Helena limb from limb right where she lay. Her hands tightened round Helena's neck.

"Love," whispered Helena, struggling to loosen the witch's grip. "I love the children. I love life. I love goodness and mercy and faith and hope." She scrabbled with her fingers, prying the claws off her neck. "I am love. I am friendship. I am joy and tolerance and compassion and care and peace and serenity," she croaked. "You are trying to squeeze the life out of love, batter goodness into the ground, bury honesty under lies. You can't. The game's over, Iris. The last words are mine. Boy Blue! My dear Boy Blue, we've done it!" Helena fell back on the ground.

Chapter 8

The sun rose smoothly into the sky. A lizard came out of a crack in the rock and sat warming in the morning light. A small brown bird fluttered down onto the branch where the goatskin hung. He eyed the brimming bucket, then hopped down onto the rim and dipped his beak in the water. Only yards away a naked body lay inert on the sand, a bloodied shape patched all over with grit and sand. The bird flew down beside it. It didn't stir. He fluffed out his wings in the dust, hopped onto a hand and gave a chirrup. The hand beneath his claws twitched. He flew back up to the branch and began to sing in earnest. Little by little the torn and bruised body began to move as if to free itself of a burden. The bird rose into the air, higher and higher like a skylark, singing all the time.

The woman, for it was a woman although barely recognisable as such, opened her eyes and reached behind her to feel the weight on her back. She found nothing at first but suddenly her fingers felt something small and pointed like a splinter of wood jammed high up between her shoulder blades. She seized it and pulled as hard as she could. The thing came away with a hideous shriek. She rolled over and flung it towards the tree. It landed with a hiss in the bucket.

She lay still again. The sun warmed her body. Slowly she uncurled herself and sat up. Her cuts were throbbing in the heat. Pus was leaking from her eyes and nose. She wiped it away but more and more poured out of every orifice until she was squatting in a spreading pool of her own filth. She began to heave and retch. She leant to one side. A stream of foul-smelling, grey-green muck and worms poured from her mouth. The frothing mess sank into the sand and the worms squirmed their death throes in the scum and the heat.

"Pestilence," she whispered. "I'm sicking up pestilence," and she gave a sob, whether of despair or relief it was impossible to tell. She pushed herself over onto a clean patch of ground, waiting. Envy came next, like knives on her tongue, and straight after, hatred as hot as hell and burning the skin of her lips; next gluttony, hard, stinking cakes of human shit that stuck in her throat and coated her mouth.

She pulled herself over to the tree, put her mouth to the bucket and slurped at the water. She looked down into the bucket, remembering a time earlier on when she'd pulled something off her back and thrown it away. There was a hissing noise when it fell. She reached an arm into the bucket. The water slopped out and splashed onto her thigh. The coolth of it sank into her and she stretched the leg out and looked at it, her hand still deep in the water. She lifted her hand out and wiped it over the muck on her face again and again, rubbing her eyes with her wet hands and clearing her vision. Now she could see what had made the hiss, a fragment of tooth or bone, sharp as a razor under her hand. She lifted it out and looked at it.

"Is that you, Iris?" she said. "Is this all that's left of you?" She dropped it back in the bucket. This time there was no hiss.

Helena lay in the shade of the tree all day, indifferent to the patter of insect feet across her skin, the buzz of flies round her head. Only once she came more awake when a small grey snake slithered past her face, stopping for a moment to fix two yellow eyes on her before sliding away.

It wasn't until the rocks were beginning to gather shadows about themselves that she propped herself up and took a fresh drink from the bucket. This time she stayed sitting up. She saw that there was no more than an hour of daylight left. She would turn to stone in the cold night air if she didn't move. The mess and blood had to be washed off and she must find her clothes. A painfully slow crawl on all fours brought her to where she had spotted a crumpled pile of white and blue, her teeshirt and her jersey. The teeshirt would have to be sacrificed. She dipped it in the bucket, wrung it out and began wiping the dried blood off her wounds and scrubbing her skin clean of grit and ointment. The crusts and blisters on her skin were already flatter and paler and the deeper wounds seemed to be closing over.

It was dark by the time she finished cleaning herself. She pulled her pants and trousers on but, try as she might, she couldn't find her boots or socks. There was a spare pair of socks in her bag but there would be no more walking until she found her boots. Perhaps, she reflected, this was a good thing. Her legs felt like cottonwool. Hunger gnawed at her guts. She was in no state to walk anywhere, especially not in the thick of night. She padded gingerly across to the tree, took another drink from the bucket and lay down in her cover.

She woke late the following day. The sun was streaming through the thin branches over her head. Her belly was empty and she felt sick but it was a sickness of hunger and she knew it would pass once she ate. She got to her feet unsteadily and took a step or two out into the full sun. There was still water in the bottom of the bucket. She tipped it carefully into her bottle and went searching for her boots. They were lying where she'd kicked them off and she put them on, wondering how she'd not seen them the night before. Despite the pangs in her gut she decided she must set off. She shouldered her bag and limped off over the sand. Only half a mile further on she had to sit down, knowing she must eat or die. There was oatmeal in her bag. She pulled it out, mixed a little in with water from the bottle and very slowly she ate the cold porridge. Then she pulled the cover over her head and slept again, in the full glare of the sun.

The next two days followed the same pattern. She walked as far as her legs would carry her, found a place to rest, ate her cold porridge and tended her wounds. At last, on the fourth morning after her ordeal, she got up feeling stronger. The final battle with the witches had wiped all thoughts of Walter and her search off the surface of her mind but she'd woken with a vivid picture of him in her head and she set off with renewed determination.

The boot, or what remained of it, could be no more than two days' walk away but she had never believed it was her final destination. She had chosen it as her goal only because it gave her a general direction of travel and ought to bring her somewhere close to the site of the battles where she might hear news of Walter.

She reminded herself of what Mrs Hubbard had said: she wasn't doing this search on her own. Walter would be looking for her as much as she was looking for him. If that was the case they were bound to find each other eventually.

She was picking her way across a patch of soft sand, testing each step with a stick before she put a foot down, when she heard it first, a sound like the grumble of thunder. The air was hot but not with the heat of a storm and the sound was low down and too regular to be thunder. It seemed to be coming from a ridge of hills lying in a milky haze a long way off. She set off towards it. The closer she got the louder and more insistent the noise became. By now she could detect a rhythm in the vast, angry booming that thudded through the air.

She was still a good half-mile away when she stopped and tied her scarf over her ears, wedging her spare socks in either side. Never mind how peculiar it made her look, the crash of metal against rock was dangerously loud for the unprotected eardrum. She had reached the foot of the last hill when she caught sight of the head of the hammer as it swung up in an arc and the metal gleamed in the sun's rays. As she puffed her way further up the rise she could see the fist that grasped a handle the size of a gate-post, and part of a huge hairy arm above it. A pause in the hammering and whoever it was brought his left hand up to rest on the rock face. There it was – a shred of fabric that she recognised at once. There was no need to hide from the holder of the hammer. The search for Walter was over.

Chapter 9

She came to the edge of the quarry and looked across at him, waiting to see if he would sense she was there. The quarry was about the same depth as Hillbilly Hollow but its walls were sheer rock except for a narrow gap over to the far side. If Walter had been upright, he and Helena would have been able to look each other in the eye without him having to bend double or she to be lifted up so he could look at her close up with those bad eyes of his. But he was down on his knees, looking intently at a huge lump of rock he'd knocked out. She could watch him in peace for a moment and get used again to the massiveness of him. His red bandana was tied round his head like it had been the day she first met him. It was dark and wet-looking at the edges. He got to his feet and picked up his hammer and began tapping, little blows along a seam of the rock. Helena bent down quietly and picked up a pebble and tossed it towards him. It felt well short but he heard the rattle of it and he looked up in her direction.

What did she expect? A smile perhaps. But there was no smile on that face, rather a look of puzzlement and strain. She saw he had aged since they'd parted and she felt sorrow flow through her like a rushing tide.

"Walter," she called, fighting back tears, "it's me, Helena. I've come back."

He dropped the hammer and turned to face her properly. There was still no smile.

"I see you there," he said. "How you doing, Helena Otterley? You on your way home?"

"Not yet," she answered and she sat down hard, having suddenly no more strength in her legs. "I've left the children though. I've been looking for you."

"I wasn't expecting to see you again," he said and he turned and picked up the hammer as if to start his assault on the rock again.

"So you weren't looking for me at all?" Remembering Mrs Hubbard's words, she felt a stab of hurt.

"I reckoned you'd be back there with your own kind by now. You said as much then. I know more than I did when I last saw you." He stopped and peered at her suddenly. "Has someone been hurting you? Is that a bandage you got round your head? Tell me who it was and I'll deal with them."

Helena pulled the scarf off, feeling a great surge of happiness. He hadn't abandoned her! He was still her saviour and protector. She flapped the scarf and socks at him.

"They were the best I could do for ear muffs. You make a fearsome din when you use that thing. Would you mind very much not hammering for a bit. Can you stop and talk to me. I've been wanting so badly to see you and talk to you."

"What about?" he said. "What is there to talk about between you and me? It's all been said and it isn't worth the paper it's written on." His brow beneath the bandana was creased in great furrows but there was no anger in what he said, just a resigned sadness. "You were the clever one weren't you? But you weren't too clever for Walter Bogolan even so. You were right I can't read but there's people I know that can. I know what you gave me. It was a stupid rhyme. It wasn't your word. You said you were giving me your word and what did you do? You gave me a kid's rhyme about a cat and a mouse. I'm not a cat and I don't like mice." So saying, he raised his hammer and brought it crashing down hard on the rock he'd been looking at. There was a crack like thunder and the rock split right through the middle. Helena gave a cry of pain as the sound reverberated round the quarry. Then they both gasped. In the heart of the broken rock there was an egg-shaped hollow and the sides of the hollow were encrusted with crystals that gleamed green and gold in the sunlight.

"Well, save my soul," Walter murmured, bending over. "Helena Otterley comes back and straightway I find emeralds."

"Is that what they are?" she whispered, awestruck at the beauty of the crystals.

"Looks like it," and he carefully tapped a sparkling lump off one side and came right over to her with it in his hand. They were at last face to face and close up.

"Lift me down, please Walter. Let me look at what you've found."

He pushed the rock into his pocket and picked her up with both hands, so tenderly, as if she was a bird with a broken wing. She stretched out her hand and stroked his face, all streaked with dust and dirt.

"I've missed you, dear Walter. I'm so sorry about the rhyme. It was wrong of me. I've suffered for it too though. I can't make it right I know. I can't take away your disappointment and your hurt but I have come looking for you."

"I'm grateful for that," he said solemnly. "You're not staying though. There's nothing I've got will keep you here. Not these," he gestured back at the glittering hollow in the rock, "not me, not anything." He sat down heavily and placed her on his great thigh, just as he had the night of their parting. She shuffled up closer to his hip and leant against him. His hand enclosed her like the arms of a chair.

"I want to stay. I really want nothing more but I can't. I don't belong here. I did try and tell you but you didn't want to hear me. I admit I did trick you but it was for a good reason. I had to get away from that place and see Boy Blue safe. All that was true. And I do love you. That was – is – true too. But ... I can't make my life with you. It wouldn't work. I have to settle for loving the memory of you, the idea of you." She wiped away a tear trickling down her cheek.

He looked touched by this but his tone was unrelenting.

"Not the real me, eh? I don't really exist, do I? You sitting here all comfy with my hands about you only works because you're inside the story. It's like when a candle's lit, you can see your shadow in the room but you blow it out and there's no more shadow, just darkness all about. I'm as real as real and you know it, but only as long as you keep the candle lit. I know what's coming. When you get back home you'll put me in a story book or write a rhyme about me so you can read it to your grandchildren. It's like a kid catching a butterfly and killing it and pinning it in on a board."

She thumped her fist down on his thigh.

"That's not true! For a start I haven't got any grandchildren to read a rhyme to. I told you that," she said. "The only children I'll ever have are here, right here in this desert. I'm not planning to pin you down or imprison you in a book. And it's not just you I've got to leave, Walter. It's all of them. It's Boy Blue and Tom Piper, Alice and Marigold, little Zac and Benjamin and the others you never met."

He didn't say anything to this, only picked her hand up and turned it over and scrutinised it as if he was looking for some sign in the lines of her palm that might tell him their future.

"You ever coming back? Did she say you could?"

"You mean Mrs Hubbard? She said I might, if I found you and if we parted on good terms. If I said sorry."

"So that's why you came looking for me. It wasn't because you were missing me. It's because you want to go roaming about this side and you reckon you need my say-so to do it. Well, you don't and I'm not giving it. I'm not responsible for you, Helena Otterley. I could have been but I'm not."

"Now you're not telling the truth," she said hotly. "You said just now you'd deal with anyone who attacked me."

"I would too. Like I'd deal with anyone who's being molested. You've got the wrong idea about me. You think I'm like the rest of them. You haven't asked me what I'm doing here when I should be back there, fighting alongside my brothers."

"What *are* you doing here?"

"I'm having nothing to do with it, or them. I'm going my own way."

Her voice was weak when she next spoke.

"You are so good and kind, Walter and I'm just a foolish old woman. I wouldn't be here at all if it wasn't for you. I used up all your gold, you know. It saved me from Eglantine. Your desert is a barren place for all its beauty but there's nothing much waiting for me when I get home. I won't be able to settle, I know that already. I'll have to try and come back. My heart is here, with you and with the children. I'm not asking you to let me come back or to be around if I do. But I am asking you to believe that I really did come to find you because of you."

They looked at each other and he gave a deep sigh.

"I'm never going to find another you," he said after a while. "If you come back, come and find me. I'll be waiting."

"Dear, dear Walter, of course I will," she said. "There's something else I've been wanting to tell you. Mrs Hubbard gave me a dreaming pill one time. It gave me such a strange dream. You took me to a lake. There were white birds and I thought it was a mirage when I saw it so faint ahead of us but you said it was real – and it was."

"The lake? Of course it's real. You want to go there now and see for yourself?"

She looked at him astonished.

"You mean there actually is a lake like the one I dreamt about?"

"There is and it's not more than twenty miles from here." She nodded. He put her down on the ground and got up. First he stuffed his hammer in his pouch and then he lifted her up again, this time right onto his shoulder. "Let's go," he said. Helena twisted round so that she was sitting astride that broad beam, and seized hold of a lock of his hair.

"Are you ready?"

"I'm as ready as I'm going to be," she replied. "Don't go jumping the boulders though or I'll slip off."

"I won't let you fall," said Walter. He reached up his hand and she grasped a finger. He strode out through the gap in the quarry wall in two giant strides. Helena couldn't help but laugh for the sheer joy of it, for the excitement of being with him again, and the exhilaration of being perched high up on his shoulder, swaying and rocking along like a pet monkey or a parrot. Her joy communicated itself to Walter and his step was light and buoyant. There was no need to talk at all. To feel the jolt of each firm tread, to look around at the land spread before her, to smell the scents from the bushes he crushed as he went, she felt more alive than she had ever felt.

Helena and Walter spent one night together at the lake. There were no white birds but there was a desert sunset that set the land alight in pools of red and gold and, as that died away, the aromatic smoke of their fire to keep the flies at bay. And when the sun sank below the distant hills and Walter's glorious bonfire settled into embers, they had each other. And the darkness wrapped around them.

In the morning Helena woke to find she was alone. The shape of Walter's torso had made deep hollows in the soft ground but of him there was no sign. She rolled over and looked around, knowing there was no point expecting him to come back. He'd deliberately left her while she was still asleep. He would be miles away by now, his hammer clunking in his pocket and the dust billowing up from those great boots. As if for final confirmation of this fact, there, winking and glowing on top of her bag, was the lump of emerald-encrusted rock he'd put in his pocket. She got up and wrapped it in her scarf and tucked it down alongside Mrs Hubbard's precious bottle and Boy Blue's picture.

The lake was gleaming violet and blue. In an hour or two the light on it would be too bright to bear but for now it flickered and danced enticingly. She put on her boots and wandered down to the shoreline to freshen up before she... before she left. She forced herself to say the words in her head.

She squatted down with her feet just at the lapping edge and bent over to splash water on her face. The water was clear but choppy and her reflection was broken and distorted by the wavelets. Still she could see well enough to realise there was something funny about the image looking up at her. Her hair seemed to be much longer on one side than the other. She felt the right-hand side of her head with her fingers. Definitely the hair on that side was much shorter and the ends were bristly like a dry paintbrush. Squatting there at the water's edge, she raised her face to the soft blue sky and closed her eyes. There was her answer. Before he'd left her Walter had taken out his knife and very gently sliced off a lock of her hair. At this very moment a little bit of her was travelling with him, probably tucked down against the curly hairs of that barrel chest she'd nestled up against in the dark of night.

She sat back against a rock and she saw how beautiful and fresh the world was in the early light. There would be rain and birdsong in the gardens at home and the soft tints of autumn. Here there were no trees to shed their leaves and no sounds but the whisper of the wind and the rustle of the rushes at the water's edge.

"Both are real," she said out loud. "This is as real as that and I shall come back."

Epilogue

An envelope had been slipped under the front door. Inside there was a single piece of paper.

'Knitters Anonymous
Next meeting Wendy's house
7.30 pm. Tuesday 7th November'

She screwed it up, then on reflection, smoothed it out and laid it on the table. There was a knock on the door.

"It's only me," a familiar voice said. "I've got your mail."

She opened the door. Mr Frank held out a small pile of letters.

"Hello," he said. "I heard you moving about. Good trip?"

"It was great. I didn't want to come home."

"You were away longer than I expected. Come down for coffee tomorrow if it suits."

"Thanks," said Helena, "I will."

The High Street was as busy as ever. Nothing was different. Nothing could ever be different over here. She walked along the road to the butcher's.

"Should I call in on Mrs Purselain?" she wondered. It would feel very strange to see her face to face like any normal person after their last meeting. There was a queue stretching out from the butcher's shop.

"I'll walk on down to the post office," she thought. "I can stop off at the butcher's on my way back."

As she stepped out onto the road to get round the queue she saw the sign on the door of The Twisted Yarn, 'Closed until further notice'. A blind was drawn down over the glass pane in the door. "Where's she gone? Is she over there?" she thought. "I had to come back but she can go whenever she pleases."

She bought stamps at the post office and was on her way back to the butcher's when she thought she saw a familiar figure at the bus stop on the other side of the road.

"Bert," she called, "Bert, is it you?" She ran across the road, dodging in and out of the traffic. "Bert," she called. "You're back already?"

"I'm sorry, miss," he said. "I think you've got me mixed up with someone else. The name's not Bert, it's William." He raised a hand, a pale, long-fingered hand, and settled the bag on his shoulder more securely.

"You're William now?" she said. "All right, I understand. Where are you off to on the bus?"

The man was studying her. His expression was curious but not unfriendly.

"I'm going where I usually go on a Monday," he said, "to the riding school at the end of the line. It's riding for the disabled on Mondays, always has been. I help muck out the stables, tack up the horses, keep the kiddies from falling off. Make myself useful." He stepped out into the road to hail the approaching bus.

"Come and see me," she said. "You know where I live. Don't forget an old friend."

"If you say so." He jumped on the bus. "Where is it you live again?" he said as the driver pulled out and door began to close.

"You know. The flat above Frank's, the newsagent's," she called. He gave her the thumbs-up sign as he sat down by the window.

She waved.

She sat outside in the garden with Mr Frank. Their robin was pecking about, only yards from their feet.

"It's funny," she said, "when I was away I was very ill for a little while. I remember a brown bird, like our robin. It was on a branch and it sang to me. I thought it was what made me better. It seemed like that."

"There's magic in birds," said Mr Frank. "There's magic everywhere if you open your eyes. I've got something for you." He got up and went inside. "Here," he said, holding out a hardback book.

"The Witches of Pendle Hill," she read. "What's this about, Mr Frank?"

"I thought it would give you ideas about places to go, when you've got friends staying. You don't need to go travelling off to places half a world away to have adventures, you know. There's plenty right here in your own backyard."

She stroked the cover of the book.

"I know that well enough. Anyway, it wasn't half a world away where I went. Thank you for this though. Let me show you what I brought back with me." She ran upstairs and came back straightaway. "Look," she said and held out a child's picture drawn on a grubby piece of paper.

Mr Frank took it. "That's nice. Is that you coming up the path with your shopping? I see someone's waiting for you." He took off his glasses and brought the page right up to his eyes. "It looks like a boy. Am I right?"

"Yes, you're right. It is a boy."

"A little friend, eh?"

"More than one," she said, "but he's the best. Now, what about this? Smell it!" She held out a glass bottle. He took the stopper off and sniffed.

"My, that's wonderful. What's in it to make it smell like that?"

"It's a kind of distillation of rocks and earth. The old lady who gave it to me calls it 'liquid gold'."

"She made it for you, eh?" he said and he cocked his head on one side, bright-eyed and watchful like the robin.

"She did."

"Use it sparingly," he said. "It's very special."

"I know," she said. "So's this." She unwrapped the stone and held it out on the flat of her hand.

"In the name of heaven, that's beautiful!" exclaimed Mr Frank.

"They're raw emeralds," she said. "Another very special person gave them to me, just as I was leaving to come back." She wrapped the stone in the cloth again and let it lie in her lap. The breeze stirred the leaves on the apple tree. The clothes flapped lazily on the washing line.

Appendix

Pattern for hens' jackets

Glossary

St stitch
K knit
P purl
yf yarn forward, ie bring the wool to the front of the needle
dec decrease
p 2 tog purl 2 together
gst garter stitch, ie knit, no purl

- Double knitting yarn (100g makes approximately 3 jumpers)
- 2 buttons or 10cm Velcro
- 1 pair of number 8 (4mm) knitting needles
- 4mm crochet hook
- Knitted in stocking stitch (knit a row/purl a row) with garter stitch borders
- Garter stitch = knit rows, no purl

Cast on 41 sts,
Work 4 rows K
Increase for tabs:
Cast on 10 sts at beginning of next row, k14, p to last 4 sts, k4.
Cast on 10 sts at beginning of next row, k14, p to last 14sts, k14.
Work buttonholes: (work these 2 rows straight if using Velcro).
(K2, yf k2tog) 3 times, work to end keeping edges in garter st.
Repeat this row for buttonholes on the other tab.

Cast off 10 sts at beginning of next row.
Next row – cast off 10 sts, k4, p2 tog, p to last 6 sts, p2tog, k4.
Dec 1 st at each end on every fol 6th row until 25 sts remain.
Divide for neck:
Work 11 sts, cast off 3, work to end – complete this half first.

1) k4, p to end
2) cast off 2, k to end
3) k4, p to end
4) k2tog, k to end
5) k4, p2tog, p to end
Work 4 rows straight
10) K to last 5 sts, inc in next st, k4.
11) K4, p to last st, inc in next st.
12) Cast on 2 sts, k to end (11sts)
13) K4, p to end
14) K

Break yarn and rejoin to the other side of neck.
Work to match, reversing shapings and ending at winghole edge.
Next row – k, cast on 3, k across sts from other side of neck.
Next row, k4 inc in next st, p to last 5 sts, inc in next st, k4.
Inc 1 st at each end of every fol 6th row until there are 41 sts on the needle.
Work 6 rows straight.
Change to gst and knit 4 rows.
Cast off.
Sew on buttons or Velcro as desired.
Work double crochet around neck (optional)

Lightning Source UK Ltd.
Milton Keynes UK
UKOW04f2340310114

225693UK00001B/182/P